The Natchez Treasure

by Christopher Lewis

The Natchez Treasure

by Christopher Lewis

Anaphora Press
3110 San Juan Ave.
Port Townsend, WA 98368
anaphorapress.com
info@anaphorapress.com

ISBN-13: 978-1-944628-00-0
ISBN-10: 1-944628-00-2

The Natchez Treasure

The Natchez Treasure

Natchez, in April!

From the river plantations, crepe myrtles – the trees my mother loved – with gray twisted trunks come down to the road to hang their crumpled linens of lavender in the warm breeze.

Creeks rush out of the dark woods, insane with stolen treasure of golden pollen and petals of the mystical dogwood, and shaded by the silent magnolias that fill their blossoms from the sky with fragrance of the world's most tragic dreams:

(Somewhere, sunlight on a back porch, in the hanging sheets and in her glowing petticoats. Smells of wash, of roses in the yard, and of her neck as she knelt to embrace me. The smile in her eyes, like sunlight – the rest of her face I can't remember. I'm amazed to remember even that. I can't have been four when she died.)

In the steaming distance, thunderstorms blossom, blue and white.

Lightning pollinates the horizon, where oaks explode in ecstasy.

In my trembling horse I can feel the power of the river just out of sight over the bluffs as I ride into town...

The oaks! How great they've grown! Mansions of the river merchants – weathered. Rose hedges climb the steep bluffs that end suddenly against the sky – were the lawns always so small? I hadn't remembered it quite like this – like I were looking for my own heart –

(As I search the fading outline of a dream for the yellowed photograph of another young woman standing there, on the bluff, looking down on the river. I wonder if I would recognize her now.)

Then the thunder came.

The massive Mississippi River bluff moved violently in red dust and fell off in the empty sky. My screaming horse climbed the thunder, while my own wild eyes saw, far below, brown godlike arms of water immense as the horizon, which they threatened with erosion.

1

Chapter One

In Gerald's store, above the river landing, I announced myself:

"I've seen the power of the ocean, taking rocks from under mountains at the edge of the continent. It would never think of taking the whole country like this river wants to!"

Gerald, as though he were used to a little more flowery speech by now, or else had forgotten my style, took no notice. "Spring flood," was all his answer.

"A piece of the bluff just fell!" I said.

"Yeah?" he replied. "My house isn't there."

I had a good laugh at that. He looked at me strangely.

"Used to be a part of town under that bluff," I said.

Gerald: "Hasn't been, ten years."

"What a part of town it was!" I said.

"A den of thieves, in its time," he said, out of patience. "Help you find something?"

"I need an ointment."

"Got a prescription?"

"No, it's just a small wound," I said. "A bite."

"A bite!" he said, alarmed. "What kind of animal?"

"A woman," I said, opening the shirt around my chest.

"James Thompson!" he shouted. "How long have you had that beard?"

"Twenty years," I said.

"When you left it was nothing," he said; "a hint of red on your chin."

"There was a time when we had no beards?"

"James Thompson! Home from California!"

"It's not such news," I said.

"How long are you here?" he demanded. "The Natchez paper got a contract to serialize your novel. Now they sell papers in Vicksburg even, and all the way to Jackson."

"I didn't know," I said. "You read it?"

"Jean Lafitte!" he said proudly.

"That went out of print twelve years ago!" I said.

"If you don't give a lecture, you'll be lynched!" he said. "You think he was that complex of a man, Lafitte? A leader in the revolutions of Europe, or just a pirate?"

"Or maybe it was fiction," I offered.

"You know how many strange men sail to Natchez," he said, "to look for the treasure he buried under the bluff? I tell them: the Mississippi River took it – scattered it on the bottom of the Gulf!"

"Do they even consider what was in the coffin?" I laughed. "Bones, or precious stones? Maybe a skeleton, buried in heavy jewels? And they'd die to find out – like he did?"

Gerald whistled. "What a story! Some of the men who come have maps. I'd like to know how much they paid for them! They show which warehouse – where to tear out the floor! And I tell them – yeah, I remember that place! It disappeared in the flood. I never say that I used to know the man who wrote the book – the story that made the world go mad for Lafitte's lost treasure! That, they'd never believe.

"My boy!" he turned to yell with a sudden sternness.

The boy crawled out of the window, where candies were invitingly piled; his face was smeared to the guiltiest freckle with peppermint.

Gerald was going to shout at him; but I said, with a tenderness that surprised even me: "This is your son?"

Gerald stared at his boy, and said to him: "Go tell them at the news office and the train station – James Thompson!" He grabbed his hat. "I'll go to the town hall myself..."

"No, wait!" I said to Gerald. "Give me a moment with you."

"Why?"

"I've needed to talk with you," I answered.

"Are you in trouble?" To the boy, he said, "Go on, go tell them!"

Like a fox released from a trap, the boy was gone in a red blur. Gerald laughed.

Then he looked at me and said, "What?" He looked in my eyes, like he used to.

"It's been so long," I said. "I've thought... what friends we were."

"Why should you care about me?" he said. "I'm nothing. I could have disappeared, like the docks down the bluff. Even my wife wouldn't care, after a month – I'd be like everything else that's just gone. Like Denise. No one thinks to remember her now."

I stared at him in disbelief: "Denise..."

"She's gone," he said. "You didn't know?" He reached under the counter for his spectacles and balance sheets.

After a painful silence I managed to say, "You're angry at me?"

"Life's hard, that's all – no paradise like California," he muttered over his ledgers. "You strike a little gold, live your dream, get rich writing novels. Everyone knows your name. What a life! You really know Mark Twain?"

"As well as anyone, I guess. He's a stranger, even to himself."

He stared at me, over his silver-rimmed glasses: "What's it like to talk with him? You have to be careful what you say, I bet!"

"One afternoon, we were talking of our youth. I told him about you," I said.

"I don't believe it!"

"He understood it all – swimming in the summer creek, the girls we wished we had, the thousand things we didn't know how to say – and how expressive our silence was! He looked off in the distance. 'And now,' he said, 'do you know what you would have spoken, and do you wish you had?'"

"You're getting philosophical," said Gerald. "You always did..."

"I've dreamed of you," I interrupted with fervor; "of your store on the Natchez bluff where roads end, where the world trusts its most precious winnings to the river's tremendous moods; where stories end, change shape, and begin again!"

"Yeah?" he said into his ledgers. "That's not what you said to me when my father gave me the business. You said it was a hell of a place to stay, when life was for getting out on the river's current, finding the limits of the known world!"

"I said that?"

"Those were your words. I never talk like that."

"I must have been jealous," I answered weakly.

"I can't believe you don't even remember what you said." It was Gerald's turn to be fervent. "I never forgot one word."

"I don't even remember why I left," I said. "Hundreds were going: the river to the Gulf. We thought it would be easy – not like the wagon trail through unlimited desert and mountains of unthinkable winter. But there never was a more dangerous crossing, through the Panama jungle to the gold fields. Men died, having no idea..."

Gerald shook his head, the way he always did while reflecting on things past. "We were pretty surprised, when your writings came back around Cape Horn, to realize you'd made it."

"You've done better than I dreamed," I said.

"It's harder than you think. In every difficult success," he said, "I've never escaped the curse of your words when you left."

"I never considered how something I could say would make you feel! But could you understand? Leaving you and everything of home, I left my heart – is it possible to imagine what that is? I was angry – at someone else, not you! Not angry... hurting."

"The wound has not healed?" he asked me gently.

"That night... under that high moon... her face, hair, arms a white bloom, planted by the moon herself on the bank; voice of the illumined Mississippi filling the whole dark universe!"

"You shouldn't have forced yourself on her," he said.

"Did she say that?" I answered with alarm.

He shrugged, returning his attention to his balance sheets. "What is one to assume, from the evidence of that injury? Her family never talked about what happened. But everyone could see that something terrible had happened."

"As though it was their business to know!"

"You both were the only child of local preachers, and you never thought about what people might say?"

"Why would I take the time to think about that?" I replied.

"It would have made things much easier for her if you had. But you ran off; she went to Memphis. In a few months she was back to marry the Wilkins boy; but she didn't go through with it. It was clear she wasn't happy. One night she ran away, they think."

"How could I have known," I groaned, "the crisis that night was brewing? It began with an embrace – one of which I had dreamed, the one that will haunt me forever! And – she confessed love for me! I could not believe it..."

"Why not?" Gerald interrupted. "You were always a favorite with the girls! They loved to talk about your strange, daring speech; even your clumsiness with them was a source of delight to them. They seemed to sense that they were some great mystery to you, and they fed on it. Then – you would kiss them. You knew how to do that! I saw it often enough. Surprise exploded in their eyes, and they would stare back at you with such wild astonishment! Then, most often, you would never speak to them again. How should it have been different with Denise, except that she took it harder? Why are you

5

staring at me like that?"

"I forgot all that," I said quietly.

"That's nothing new, either. You had talent for forgetting such things."

"Perhaps you're right. Maybe that's how it happened... but love has never been so astounded as when she looked at me that night. I didn't know what to do. I was all desperation and desire. I could not speak; and she became frustrated, I think, at my sudden loss of words. She assailed me, she cooed me; she terrified me, she fought with me."

"This did not make it clear that she cared?"

"I didn't understand anything! How could she love me and then become so angry? I'd never seen a woman's anger before."

"Well," said Gerald, "I hope you have gained a little more wisdom since that time."

"I was convinced I had made a fatal mistake. I was sure that she would never again have anything to do with me! Yet every word she spoke in anger remained in my heart, like bruised flowers, pressed in place. I studied them; many nights of many years, until they became like jewels from a box that I would take out and examine; until I learned to recognize their mysterious language."

Gerald was staring at me, studying me as though he had never really looked at me before. "Really?" was all he said.

"I never really wanted anyone but her," I answered in a low voice. It was a prophecy that surprised even me.

"You were a fool not to propose after that night," Gerald pronounced.

"I don't know why that never occurred to me," I confessed.

"Why? Because you were made for misery, inflicting it on the innocent."

I replied:

"Every exalted thought - all philosophy,

the summit of existence

when she stood on the bluff

under the sun, with her umbrella

and silently gazed on the river..."

Gerald sighed and nodded. "Translated from the French – a symbolist poem, quoted by Lafitte? I suspected, when I read that, that you wrote those lines while thinking of Denise!"

I answered further, leaning into a sweeping gesture, "The countryside around Natchez in bloom, is only a memory of that year she grew into womanhood."

"Yep," said Gerald," It's James Thompson all right! You're staying for a while?"

"Yes. I'm to be employed as tutor of grammar and philosophy, at the Wells Plantation."

Gerald stood straight up so suddenly he nearly fell. "You're going into her service? You've got to be joking! I guess it makes sense. They'll come from Nashville and New

Orleans to get a look at you, and test your intelligence. I hope I see you again!"

"Why not?" I said.

"You go into that house," he said, "it's like you're in another universe! The upper class of Natchez society! When we were growing up, we never even knew of their existence – even when we saw their homes, like a closed book of fairy tales. She never even comes into town, except to the larger houses. Only the servants come into the store. She's built the Episcopal Church at the edge of town; but the membership there is limited to wealth."

I smiled. "But I'll be giving lectures at the town hall."

"If you're staying with her, you'd better make it clear what you meant in your story of Lafitte," he said.

"Yes, I will!"

"Like a talk on fiction and imagination," he insisted: "How the character's experience and thought are not really those of the author's. Some people might not know the difference."

"I've written a character you disagree with?"

"Well, yes," he said, "Lafitte! You made him too likeable. He falls in love with a saloon girl and lets her destroy him."

"She destroys his past understanding. His heart and conscience are awakened."

"Yeah," he said, "you don't want people around here to think..."

"I've got it!" I said; "I'll give a lecture on the modern courtesan: how rare is the man who resists her inviting embrace, then pays heavily in disease and broken conscience."

"Then I'm a rare man," he said with firmness.

"But he can't pay more heavily than with the understanding of how she was compelled into that profession. The sadness of her story will be revealed, and the heavy debt of guilt will be paid by all of us. That will get some attention in the press!"

"Curious, scandalous," he admitted, frowning, "and certain to put you into permanent exile from plantation society."

"Count on it!" I said, inspired. "A lecture! I'll spell it out in detail: men of good society make them rich; but a reasonable man would be broken, just to see what society has done to these pretty girls."

"Just like Lafitte was broken!" said Gerald. "Amazing! If you wish to climb the ladder of society yourself, like he did, through the fame of his notoriety, you'd better go back to California."

"You're right." That calmed me down. "But I wish you could understand how much more important than any of that is my return; my desire to begin again, here, where I began..."

"Well," he said after a moment; "we're certainly curious what you've been doing out there in California. I don't know that any of us should be expected to understand the way you think!"

"How I wanted to see her!" I stammered: "Denise! Her face, as it might be interpreted by the years... and the thoughts in her eyes she never dared to whisper – into what would they mature?"

Gerald: "I forgot you could really talk like that! When I read your book, it was like you were standing next to me, talking – I don't know to whom – enraptured in your own strange sayings... I was always fascinated by your thoughts. But they're your thoughts, not mine."

"If I believed in God," I went on, "I'd beg him to allow me to look under the curtains of this world, under the hillside of broken gravestones, at the ruined youth of our ancestors, if he could unveil my heart for me!"

"Help you, miss?" Gerald interrupted suddenly, to someone else...

ଔ

I was not expecting the most beautiful woman I would ever see.

The brown fire in her eyes frightened me, if it's possible to be terrified of beauty.

She held her youth with a noble bearing, a tall and womanly profile that must have made the angels weep with confusion as they rushed to ignite her soaring thoughts, but had to stand a little farther off from the promise of love that filled the satin folds draping her youthful form.

Light-colored, wavy hair fell in an impossible mass in which every hair was perfectly placed, framing soft, thick eyebrows where thoughtfulness ruled over eyes which swam in their own light.

It was not Denise, not by any means – though she could have been about the age as Denise when I first began to notice her. She was not petite and moderately plump; her hair was not black and thick, her eyes were not wide and soft and dark with magnetic dreaminess.

I was not expecting to recognize one who could replace another who had been foremost in my mind so long – indeed, just the moment before! How could it be possible? Outside the door behind her, an apple tree had burst in flame of blossom, its branches weighted with the fragrance of paradise.

Gerald was the first to notice no one spoke. "Do you know who this is? James Thompson, home from California!"

An astonished recognition in her eyes caused such an explosion of beauty in them that I was lost in the mystery of who or what she might be.

With her was a woman of age – my age – who was not used to exalted silence, and realized she had plenty to say.

"You don't say! James Thompson, hidden in that red beard? It's a fine beard, don't get me wrong! Don't tell me I'm that hard to recognize! You haven't forgotten that summer at the creek, I know!" Here she winked at Gerald, who went red. "And now – a famous author! Why did you write that the treasure was under the bluff?"

"I was just telling him, Sarah," Gerald replied, "I was just making that point, that people don't really know what fiction is."

"Grandpa laughed when he read it", she went on. "He said that if it ever was there, it wasn't for long. He mentioned a single gravestone under an old oak. He saw the place once. It still had a piece of the rope hanging down from the branch, with the hangman's knot in shreds. The rope was covered in wisteria that bloomed all summer. That's what he said. Well? He should know. The only ones who knew about it were too afraid to dig. He never said what he was afraid of, but the way he said it scared me. But what I want to know is – is this just made up, what you wrote? I mean, I know that's what everyone

8

always thought – that it was hidden under the bluff – but why did you write it that way? It made a good story – sold a lot of books –"

"It's just to draw people off the trail," I said, winking at Gerald, who gave me a strange look; "and to get rumors going about treasure, and find out what people might know..."

"I see," she replied; "you're really good with these fictions, aren't you? Living in your dreams, like you were still young. But do you think you might know where that oak could be? I've looked around. Did you ever see Denise? Some of us thought maybe she went to California, looking for you. Will you give a lecture while you're here? Are you going down to Port Gibson, to visit your father? He's done well, built a new church with the largest congregation..."

With such a list of questions to respond to, I chose the last: "I would go see my father, if a sermon were what I wanted to hear."

"And he'd love to listen to his clever son as well; but three thousand miles couldn't keep such enemies apart," she said. Even I couldn't believe she said that. But she went on, "Girl!" to the silent vision of beauty who was with her, "don't stare like that! When your tutor comes, he'll have to teach you some manners I guess."

Gerald, with a grin, said, "This is the tutor, if you can believe what he told me."

"No, I doubt that," Sarah laughed. "You don't want to learn his manners!"

"You are my new student, then!" I said. "How exciting..."

"Is it?" the young lady answered immediately. "You've not even begun to appraise my intelligence, and already you've given me a passing grade?"

Speechless, I stared at her.

"Are you this lax in your examinations as well," she went on, "or can you see into the secrets of men? But tell me, sir, what am I to learn?"

"History and philosophy, poetry, and the understanding of the ages: the knowledge of every century." The words were coming out of me from a trance. "These are the gifts of the Muses, which I've been summoned to give to you."

Her eyes softened. "This must be the answer to my prayers."

"If I may accompany you to the house," I said eagerly, "we could discuss..."

"Oh, no," she said merrily, "I could never be seen walking with a strange man!"

"Indeed!" Sarah replied, "What would your fiancé think of that?"

"He will be attending classes with me, don't you think?" said the girl to her.

"My dear," said Sarah, "the details of your education are not discussed with me. If they were, I might mention some things this tutor of yours taught me. Have you read the part of Jean Lafitte that describes his swagger on the streets of New Orleans? And when the women stared at him, how he would grab them, perfect strangers, into the wildest kiss?"

The girl blushed. I may have, as well. She saw this in a glance, and laughed. "Where are your books?"

"They will arrive by steamboat when this passionate river is tamed by the summer winds."

"Now that was beautifully spoken, wasn't it, Catherine?" said Sarah. "Let's make our purchase and go. Someone should warn your aunt that the rogue she's summoned has arrived. I can't believe she's in her right mind, but God himself couldn't change it, I'm sure."

I stared out the door some minutes after she'd gone.

"You haven't lost your touch with the women, have you?" said Gerald.

"She's a child."

"She's the heir."

"Will you go with me to the tavern?"

"That's where you wrote your first story."

"They published it in California. Here, they wouldn't even look at it."

"We never saw that one – it's probably better that way. You go. I have to close the store."

"I'll wait."

"There'll be a crowd waiting for you! No thanks. I haven't been in that tavern since you left."

Chapter Two

There aren't many families like that in America!

The largest house in Natchez – and not only the largest plantation on the Mississippi River, but also the oldest still standing.

In the extensive library in the upper gables of the house, I was waiting for the lady of the plantation. Books were neatly shelved all the way up to the open rafters, ending only in an open space at each window where one could stand and survey the estate. To the east, one could see acres in cotton crowding the horizon, like clouds growing out of the fields. Beyond this, the actual holdings in land and assets, if I dared to tell it – because no one really knew – might be comparable to a colonial empire.

And Catherine was the heir.

The estate was first established as a colonial venture in the Carolinas by the most ancient family in England, to expand its influence and that of the monarchy. Everyone along the river knew this – it was a family that had been allied to the Jacobean kings of England, deeply involved in their reactionary controversies, who fled to the new estate in America from the revolutions that plagued the monarchy after James II was exiled (though not beheaded like his grandmother, Mary Queen of Scots). But the revolution came to the New World, and so the family moved its estate to the western frontier, to the best lands along the Mississippi River.

This family was not just aristocratic, in the way that only a few of the colonial plantation owners had been, such as the first three Presidents, Washington, Jefferson, and Adams. This house itself was a manor of the old world, a transplanted castle from the cliffs of Cornwall to a bluff overlooking the Mississippi River. This legend I'd heard since childhood, and always half believed it; but the books and documents I found in that library not only substantiated the claim, but even established it in a glory beyond any common man's imagination.

The family was not just Tory, loyal to the king throughout the American Revolution; it was the monarchy itself, in secret exile. It was a more ancient dynasty than any that had ruled in England for a thousand years. And though it no longer had any direct influence in the court, its voice in the House of Lords was formidable, and it was an economic power greater than that of the kings.

The ancestral name – what's in a name? Well, this:

The family name held a baronial title since William the Conqueror brought the Norman lords from the northern coasts of early medieval France, from castles on towers of rock by the storming Channel, where the Arthurian legends were written down first. Among these highly learned peoples which William brought from Normandy, there came also from nearby Brittany, whose loyalty the Normans had won, the exiled rulers of Celtic Britain since before the Romans.

The purity of their royal bloodline was set down in pedigrees by the poets of many centuries, in manuscripts which were only in that library. The only other copies had

11

been in Glastonbury, lost in the fire that destroyed that abbey. These were the books that spread the light of truth over the European continent in the dark ages. Old books. Very old. I didn't know they existed at first. Only after nights of study in the huge shadows of that library, I found it in a strange rhymed manuscript, sixth century, from the court of a Welsh king, delineating the exiled kingdoms of Brittany in glorious illuminations and faded ink. And there were other things I found in brightly painted parchments, where I learned that history is, as poets of former ages said, a sacred Muse.

That first afternoon, though, they sat mute on their shelves while I stared at the titles. I paused at another window, the western window with its flawless drapery pulled back. Oaks in a perfect lawn held up the blue sky. Their branches, like another drapery opened to the bluff, revealed, on the other side of the river, the lowlands of Louisiana draining the exuberant waters of spring flood. Cascading miles of whitewater tore off the branches of leaning pines.

And between the house and the river, black rows of slaves drenched the earth with shadows, where only the sky could hear the stark and desperate beauty of their song.

Larger shelves in the shade of that window held the thickly bound illuminated manuscripts. Here were medieval legends, poetry, spells that went back to the dawn of time, when light first spread over the green hills of Europe and England, when even the shadows glowed. Hagiography, and liturgics of the ancient British church. Then, the earliest printed books from Germany, Venice, and the presses of Caxton and Pynson in England, pages of amazing beauty, yellowed only around the edges. What was not there? Had she read them all?

In the dark northern corner of the huge room were closed shelves, but the locks were unfastened. The shelf fronts pulled down, making a wider shelf. Here were the books of her late husband.

A starved archeologist who found the one moveable stone behind a mountain of sand, gasping at the treasures of an Egyptian king, would not have stared with more astonishment.

The Rosicrucian Manifesto! The alchemical engravings of Fludd and Maier! Kabalistic texts, Neoplatonic philosophers, writings of all the greatest heretics, with learned exegeses! My fingers worked quickly through the pages, searching for his own notes.

"How do you like my library?"

The heavy book, like my heart, landed on its dusty shelf. She was already in the middle of the carpet, advancing silently in a cloud of satin crowned by her pile of silver hair.

I introduced myself by saying, "And you want me for a tutor to your niece?"

"That is correct. My husband's papers are over there." She said, pointing to another closed shelf. "You are free to use my library as you wish. However, you must educate yourself in what you are to teach, and this is to be under my supervision. Is this agreed?"

"What will you want me to teach?" I said, looking around in amazement.

"I expect you to complement your learning," she said, directing me to the upholstered chairs, "with more expertise in the classics, and with the conservative philosophy of Edmund Burke and certain thinkers – ideas with which your own writings show no familiarity. You find this distasteful, do you not?"

12

I sat, saying nothing. She gathered her dress into a chair, sat very erect, stared fiercely as a great horned owl out of its nest of feathers in the eave, and with a voice of chilling frankness, spoke:

"I know you have lost your fortune, living foolishly in adventure, dissipation, and ruin."

The silence of her library answered for me.

"It is not necessary for anyone else here to know about this. Your reputation has been purged with the miles. I want you to take residence here, to continue your writings, and to tutor my niece and her companions. I do not have time for it myself. You will have to mend, of course, your moral character. The stinging hatred of social hypocrisy which all your fictional characters preach, you will have to turn against yourself. This will be a bitter discipline for you. But you will learn to love it, you will learn things of which you never dreamed. You will be well rewarded in payment as well."

I sat without moving, but could feel the cold blood drain from my face. Her sharp eyes followed the progress of my shock, and she smiled. "You will learn that literature is part of a tradition, and that purity in manners is genuine only as a reflection of a pure conscience. You shall see that there is an eternity in the affairs of this house. Culture, in this house, is pure. In town, and everywhere else, it exists in corrupt form. What you will learn will make you a rare kind of man.

"And now I want to ask you some questions about my late husband."

"When you call him your husband - well." Hot blood was rushing back into my brain. "I knew his wife in California."

"Yes. You owed her quite a bit of money."

"If you've been in correspondence with her, why ask me about him?"

"You were with him when he died, weren't you? It's believed you received his will, though there are others more interested in that than I. I wish to know only his final state of mind."

"Why did you marry him?"

"Oh, sir, indeed, you're a devil," she said, surprising me with laughter! "He was nearly the ruin of my entire inheritance, the scoundrel! Thank God he decided to leave! Why did I marry him? Because I was in love! Foolishly, passionately - and I knew some things about him that you don't know, things that made me believe, and hope. I dearly wish to know his final resolve. I failed with him. I may fail with you also."

"Surely I can't compare to George Fisher."

"Your influence as a writer may lead others to follow him," she answered gently. "You've met his children from the wife in Texas? And his children from the wife in California?"

"I have."

"Do they ask about their father?"

"Of course. Wouldn't you?"

"What do you tell them?"

"The truth," I said coldly.

"You know the truth about George Fisher?"

"I understand the dream that kept pushing him West, pursuing the dream of the

American Revolution, the dream that made him such a key figure in the revolution of Mexico from Spain, and the revolutions of Texas and California from Mexico!"

"Yes, a true revolutionary, just like your Lafitte!" She sighed. "A daring, uncaring individual, he seems. But there is a deeper mystery that drives him, some veiled dream, some undisguised glory even he does not understand. I have a theory. Your story of Lafitte is a description of the kind of man you saw in George Fisher."

I stood and walked the aisles of her library, staring at titles in the high stacks. "Lafitte - his treasure - I still don't know what it was! Sometimes I wonder if it were nothing other than his own lost conscience. He dreamed of acquiring great material riches, and he obtained that dream through violence. Then he realized it was something else he wanted, and he began to search. He became acquainted with men of great ideas, ideas of revolution."

"Exactly," she said quickly. "George believed in a dream; but what it was, he wasn't sure. It was a dream of men free and independent; but what that was, he didn't know. But he pursued it ruthlessly. No home, no wife could tie him down - no country, either. Didn't he die free?"

"Lonely and broken, like Lafitte."

She settled back into her chair. "I was his treasure, when he came to America as a pauper, an exile from the revolution in Austria. I was his treasure: young, beautiful as any woman is for a few brief years, rich, and passionate! Spoiled, too, knowing I'd get whatever man I desired. And look, my choice - what a powerful and pitifully frail thing is a young woman's heart! Yet it was that very vulnerability of my heart that had power over him, a power that was complete, until my beauty dulled. Then he desired other things: Texas, independence and liberty, new women; and then California. This maker of history, this very complex man, George Fisher!

"At heart, though, he was as simple as any man. Like any orphan boy, he was bewildered by the fact of his own existence."

"I didn't know he was an orphan!" I said to the closed shelf of his own writings.

"All his years of suffering, looking for the image of his mother and never realizing it!" Sadly, she went on: "Running away from his stepfather, angry at his father for the lack of guidance. And, like any orphan, he could not accept the belief of his fathers. He never understood that revolution is against one's own soul. The turning away of this age is a deeper thing than you can imagine."

"Why?" I demanded, turning out of my shadows. "These books belong to earlier centuries, don't you think? Not to this, the nineteenth century, the age of the freedom of thought!"

"You call it the Age of Reason, the Age of Enlightenment, when the timeless traditions of all cultures are overthrown? George Fisher, you know, was brought up in the palace of the Archbishop of Austria, who regarded him as his own son."

"Archbishop!" This returned me to my chair. "I had no idea!"

"His earliest years were spent in the study of the sacred scriptures, with the very finest explanations of their contents by the intelligent and holy Church Fathers of antiquity. He learned to read Latin, Greek and Slavic theologians."

"I never knew anything about this."

"I have obtained all the texts he told me about, over there. You, too, shall read them.

"At the age of twelve, the boy was enrolled in the theological academy, at a time when the faculty began to lean toward liberal ideas. The aged archbishop saw no great harm in that; however, he did not know that his young ward's teacher was a Mason."

"George Fisher was a Freemason?"

"Come, sir, that part you know very well. He had no need to hide it from me. We discussed it openly."

"Discussed things like that with a woman?"

"Now by that remark, sir, you reveal more than you wish. Do you think I can't tell what you are?

"One day the boy brought a book home, innocently enough. It gave many new interpretations of the Old Testament, and of the New as well. The archbishop found it, and read it carefully. The he did something unexpected. George described it vividly. He flew into a rage - stormed through the Episcopal palace, shouting in a fevered pitch against all the heresies of the ages.

"The next morning, he summoned his priests and bishops and marched with them into the academy, even before the hour of prayer was finished, and threw the book down at the feet of the offending teacher. None of his own clergy knew what to think. He quoted some passages. At this, the priests began to shake their heads in amazement. You've no idea, sir, how strange these things sound to someone with an orthodox education!

"Unfortunately, the boy rose to the defense of his teacher. He really did not understand the issues, but thought quite simply that he was being taught the inner truths of scripture. The archbishop roared at him, insane with anger that his own boy had been so led astray. It was quite a shock. George Fisher never recovered from it.

"The boy ran off with his teacher and began a new and very exciting life, involved in daring revolutionary plans. At sixteen he was arrested, and soon had to flee for his life.

"That's how he came to America.

"In the beginning, he discussed everything with me. I was so excited by this bold young man and his ambitions! When he became quieter, I didn't know if he'd forgotten his wild young dreams, or simply took less interest in me. He spent more time locked in this room. He didn't know I had another key. That's how I discovered his correspondence with men all over the world, when he organized the trouble against Imperial Spain."

"All over the world!" I said in repressed awe, looking at the expanse of the library.

"Revolutionaries," she replied simply.

"Here, in the South?"

She laughed dryly. "You seem to think that Lafitte was one, and that he was here not so long ago."

"At all costs, I'd avoid any possibility of interpreting my fiction as concealed Masonic secrets!"

"Why? The public would love it!"

"And the Masons would murder me."

"Is it that bad?"

15

"It happened in New York."

"Yes, that fellow was never seen again. All the accused conspirators were tried, and found to be not guilty – but everyone knew how many Masons sat on that jury. It caused such an uproar that the Brotherhood was forced underground for some decades."

"Why did George Fisher abandon the search for the Natchez treasure and go West?" As soon as I asked, I knew I had said too much.

She, however, seemed prepared for that question. "You assume many things. First, that there is anything at all real in that legend; and there's really no reason that there should not be. Second, that he was interested in it. If he were, he pretended not to be. What could it have been of such great value that it could compare with my inheritance?"

I knew I was on the right track, and I played along. "There are the rumors of Napoleon's apprehension on the high seas, and that Lafitte took part in his capture. These say that the pretended emperor was brought to justice, but that the tremendous wealth with which he tried to escape mysteriously vanished."

"George Fisher was at least as rich as Napoleon, but he renounced this estate because there were revolutions to be started in the West. Why? I've read your novel, sir, and I understand the basic conflict of its theme. The question is this, is it not: what is the shimmering mirage of the treasure of the New World? If it were only great material wealth and no more, the Spanish conquistadors would have been satisfied. What were they searching for? Cities of gold, or the fountain of youth? For the greatest treasures of this world, or for the secrets of eternity? And once they found only a little of the former, did they entirely forget the latter? These legends are far older, sir, than the tales of St. Brendan the Voyager who came to the islands of paradise. Neither your Lafitte nor my George Fisher had the understanding to cope with the truth of that. What I will conjecture is this: perhaps there was something that Lafitte discovered which George knew about, but which bothered him so greatly that he ran from the Mississippi River like he had run from his own homeland. If so, I should like to know what it is.

"The tone of his last letters indicate it. In the end, he began to feel the importance of whatever it was that he was running from. But his understanding was feeble from exhaustion in intrigues and from age. In his letters to me, he imagines me as I was when he first saw me. He never seemed to realize that I, too, had grown old; he certainly never realized that I had grown wiser! But he knew I was the only one who ever understood him."

"Is this the reason you've called me here, then?" I demanded flatly.

"No, sir; you are to tutor my niece, as I've told you."

"I don't see why you want me for that job!"

She sighed. "My niece is in need of a kind of influence which I cannot provide. Do not misunderstand me. I have given her things which have formed her basic character well: a good home, well-examined conservative values, a real sense of faith and purpose in destiny. In spite of this, Catherine remains inexhaustibly curious about art and liberal ideas.

"Everyone who knows her has noticed the unique turn of her mind. It shows itself in curiosity, intellectual quickness, intense romanticism, and an innocent daring of conception in art, music and opinion.

"Besides that, she is at an age where she is fascinated with the undiscovered territory in other people's souls. I did not entirely understand this about her until she read your book. She asked so many unexpected questions that I, too, was forced to read it. She has come to believe that she knows both you and Lafitte from its pages. Her insight will surprise you, I think; it may even frighten you. She is an unusually bright girl, and could use a tutor such as yourself.

"In this country, there are too few talented and imaginative souls with a capacity for true intelligence. Of these, even less are qualified by the degree of professional training that would satisfy me, and there is not one who would submit to my discipline. You have been chosen simply because you have nothing more to lose, and everything to gain.

"I must warn you; you will be carefully watched!"

వ్యవ్యవ్యవ్య

The full moon was rising, hours after she had left me alone in the massive shadows of her library with its pale illumination among the stacked volumes. The moonlight seemed to find a path in the wilderness of unanswered questions.

How much did she know? Could I find out? By reading all these books? Did she know their contents that thoroughly?

How much did she know about me? And why was I here, really? To hear her analyze me in the character of her own late husband's psychology? Angry at his father, searching for his mother to the end of his life, and never even conscious of it! I slammed my fist deep into the upholstery and stood.

And the orphaned sons that can't accept the religion of their fathers, and the turning away of this age, the Enlightenment, when the spirit of man is darkened, a thing too deep for thought. Had she really said all that? Or had I only inferred it from the unspoken meaning of her careful words, or had I only imagined half the conversation? I stared at the staring moon, like a lunatic in the asylum.

Did she know the mind of her husband? Why was she in correspondence with his other wives, the one in Texas and the one in California? What might their communication have to do with me? Did they think I had the information that would lead to the treasure? Which of us had his final instructions, or had he willfully misled us all?

The old witch! The personification of matriarchal wisdom, the unquestioned ruler of Southern society, whatever one might think. In the highest orders of the secret Masonic Brotherhood, we dress the hierophant, enthrone him and gaze at him in wonder. We listen with awe to his speeches in the rituals, when the terrifying secrets of great antiquity are disclosed! Women are not allowed, not even in the lowest orders; yet our knowledge can't compare to such a woman's. We are like boys at play.

What I've been searching for in the eyes of every woman since childhood – invoking the ghost of my own young mother when the world was new – and the things she said to me – I couldn't hear them quite –

Moonlight, spread on the fields like a blanket of cotton.

Chapter Three

And I felt like a new man, dressed like that! Black satin waistcoat and white starched shirt, its fresh linen collar to my trimmed red whiskers, beard to a narrow point, hair combed back and parted. A full ten years younger – and sober besides – I stood at the base of the stairs like a young man who had suddenly come into a fortune, and gazed at the dreamlike colors glowing in flawless plaster that hinted at immeasurable riches.

Light cream-color floated in the immense walls of the entry foyer, with the palest ivory in the heavily scrolled crown mold and in the interior columns in the archways that led to the blue sitting room. Beyond, indescribable yellows of the music room with brilliant curtains. The colors from room to room did not conflict, but opened like unforeknown realms. Inspired mirrors of these hues in the polished furniture everywhere made easy the kind of walking that servants in such a house must learn. One steps as though moved by divine whispers he must not reveal.

The clear voice of the bell called from the door, and I moved in that direction. At this hour, it was among my duties to answer it, when the crown of her Natchez society was likely to call. I was to entertain visitors in the parlor with my intelligent questions until the ladies were ready to come down.

At the head of the stairs, a sudden quickness of steps on the carpet behind a door, oiled sound of the door's catch releasing and, like light spilling into the silence, the rustling of wide skirts. And there was a glimpse of one, like a summer cloud overhead. Her young brown eyes, polished deep with wonder, appeared over the balcony for me to comprehend in less than a second, then disappeared. Another door opens, and all sweet sound drains into it and dissolves.

What went on upstairs, I had no desire to know. Men were rarely allowed up there, men-servants never. But an entire lower wing belonged to me, with study and parlor for the students, a private room with writing table, a huge wardrobe with a four-posted bed, and a narrow stair to the library in the attic. I wanted to go there now, with the redemptive halo of her glance settling into my thoughts, and write volumes for the sake of her morning's questions. We had studied globe and maps, and she had asked eagerly: what's beyond the river? What's Louisiana? What's Texas, and what is California? And what is the terrible forsaken nothingness between, called desert? And what is death? I wanted the bleeding ink to purify my soul and redeem every thought I'd ever had!

ଔ

The strong affinity of thought and sympathy of feeling between young Catherine and myself in that first week of lessons had been sudden, almost meteoric. Meteoric: a flash of light, and a long burning trail following deep into the heart where it disappeared, unknown and mysterious as its origin. What was this recognition? Everything spoken and unspoken seemed not only to affirm, but even to surpass the expectations of an intuition of some strange foreknowledge.

18

She, of course, had the advantage of having already read my thoughts in the form of a romantic novel. She had read my pages deeply; and, as her aunt had warned, she had divined the feelings buried behind them. As a result, my teachings excited her with the promise of new conclusions upon the nature of art and the world of thought. But she seemed to expect something more from me, something that inspired not just intelligence, but the kind of heroic personal virtue that, really, I had never known. My suggestions of topics for intelligent investigation ignited questions of surprising depth, questions that showed she had thought about these things already – thought about them long and deeply, and had been tortured by not knowing the answers.

What was it, on the other hand, that I recognized in her? Those brown eyes invited me to know what it was; but I didn't. If it was not my own thoughts I saw there, it was a clear response to the unanswered questions of my heart! The answers were there in her eyes. The questions within me to which they were responding, though – I was at a loss to say what they could be.

Why was I so surprised by every word she spoke? How did she seem to know what I was thinking before I said it, and what were the feelings excited in her? I could see those feelings plainly displayed; I could her them ringing in her voice. But were I to try to reach out and touch them, which she would not forbid, I would find myself bewildered by the intimacy of something I should know and expect, but which was foreign to my understanding.

It was, after all, only a geography lesson that we had discussed that morning. How had the folding magnitudes of the western mountains, ending against the Pacific Ocean, become a map of my own history in her gaze? And then she said:

"When my nurse Sarah saw me reading your book, she told me that the author had grown up here in Natchez. I didn't believe it."

Continental geography was forgotten.

"That was when she told me how you would hide by the creek," she laughed, "waiting for the girls; and the way you would speak to them from hiding."

"She remembered your words. She said they came out of the thicket like the poetry of a lark blended with the scolding of a jay."

"And then I knew that these could have been the words of no other than same person who had written that book. And I had her show me those places in the woods along the creek. Then, when I read you descriptions of California rivers and forests, I knew you had spoken those words already, and expressed all the same philosophical questions of your themes, in places where I had walked!"

And with unselfconscious innocence she would stare at me, as though to say: don't you understand how it was myself who summoned you here? I am the one who was always be destined to be your student, your disciple, your... what?

Every time, it was the same. I would find myself staring at that face, wondering what it was I read in a face that seems to have emerged fresh from my own dreams. I would forget to speak. She does not. Looking at me confidently as though I should understand, she confronts my intelligence by sounding the depth of my heart, the deep music of her voice that moving me beyond thought again.

If this were love, and it could plainly be nothing else, it was a kind I had never heard of. I wanted to bury my pen in the paper, digging through scribbled pages to discover what this was, until heart and pen were dried up.

ॐ

But I was a doorman. If the bell rang a second time, I'd have to face another stern interview in the library.

I opened the door upon a tall woman, nearly forty, in a black funeral dress which her matronly figure, like ripe eggplant, filled perfectly. Thick ember-colored braids, not quite hooded by dark, elegant lace, smoldered like the veiled immortality of Athena when she stood before Odysseus, so I thought. Her eyes were pale blue of stunning power.

With her were three young men: one by her side, as tall and with identical eyes but dark-haired; and behind him two others not as tall nor so young.

"Don't you remember me?" she sang.

That moment, I did. My eyes took twenty years out of her features. It must have been my expression that made her laugh.

"Emily!" I gasped.

"So you do remember that walk by the creek?"

"That was you?"

"Don't you remember?"

"I do, but I thought..."

"You thought you were talking to Denise? You were so infatuated with her you never had eyes for anyone else."

"What happened to her?"

"No one knows," she answered softly.

"Her parents must!"

"Probably; but her mother died some years back, and her father doesn't talk."

"I'll have to ask him."

"If you can find him. This is my son William," she said of the tall youth. "I married Henry Stuart."

"Really?" I said, leading them into the parlor. "On which of his plantations do you live?"

"We prefer the house in town," she answered, sitting. "But Henry died last year."

"I'm sorry," I said, taking her hand spontaneously and kissing it like I did when we were children. Red began to run in the wrinkles of her eyes, like sunset spreading over the hills.

"My son is devoted to literature and philosophy," she said while her eyes swept the carpet.

"I read Jean Lafitte!" he said with a passion that forced a smile from me.

"These are his cousins," said Emily of the other two. "All are to be in your academy."

"I didn't know the enrollment was expanding this soon!"

"I'm sure you were told that Catherine's fiancé would be joining you," she replied.

"What are you going to teach us," said William; and the other two leaned forward with attentive expectation.

ഇൟഇൟൟൟ

My education had never been complete. There were few universities in the Deep South before the war, and none along the river. The Catholic seminary in New Orleans was for the training of priests. Even the great Louisiana State University was no more than a small military academy on the Red River in Pineville. This latter was beginning to flourish, ironically, under William T. Sherman himself, before he warned the South that its cause was desperate, went north to join the Union army and came back to burn our cities and plantations in his terrible march to the sea. I wanted neither religious nor military training, and so had been self-taught. I was now surprised at the hunger with which I devoured the readings which Lady Wells required of me – books I would not have chosen to study.

The first thing every morning, and the last thing in the evening, we rehearsed scenes from the great playwrights. Meanwhile, she gave me the assignment of writing a play of my own. This, if it met with her approval, was to be performed in the mansion at midsummer before all the high aristocracy of the River states. Her goal in this was to attract students of the best breeding and to build a school of the highest stature. Meanwhile, the publication of my writings was assured; and my salary, which was beyond anything I could have expected, was to grow with my responsibilities.

Chapter Four

Again, I walked through the towering rows of flowers, as Catherine gave their names. Sunlight fell through the fully blossomed apple and cherry branches, where petals were already falling, sailing the still, fragrant air, floating to safety in obscurity. One by one, they unfolded in the light and fell like the opening of every page in the books of paradise.

Hydrangeas, hollyhocks, azaleas. Wisteria arches led into an inner garden of roses, as though revealing the mystical garden at the center of the ordered universe; where, if one found the place, there would be an altar.

I was trying to explain the morning's lesson, and the many layers of meaning in literature. "Emile Zola, the realist," I said. "The purpose of his art is opposite to that of Dante, who was entirely non-literal. You've been my student, now, how long?"

"Tell me again," she replied too quickly: "what is it like in California?"

I laughed. "Do you want me to take you there?"

"That would be splendid!" she said with fire in her eyes. "But there's a better chance of finding gold in Natchez. The treasure is here, somewhere, isn't it?"

"It's a legend."

"I think absolutely it's not, and so do you! Don't try to confuse me with allegories and realities."

"My student is wiser than her teacher," I said.

"My nurse's grandfather saw the place where it's buried!"

"Then you should be asking her, not me."

"I will! And you'll want me to tell you what she says?"

"By all means! We'll dig for it. We won't be deterred by fear of some decayed hanged-man's rope overhead, or what unholy grave we might have to disturb."

"You're making me shudder. Don't you believe in legends? What if it were an allegory, then? I sometimes think it's buried in myself."

"What do you mean?"

"I'm such a mystery to myself," she answered in a quiet voice. "Were you, when you were my age?"

"Most certainly!"

"But now you know yourself, since you've been to California?"

"I've seen a man strike gold, and seen what it does to a man. I found gold myself – a small fortune, enough to be allowed to live by writing and contemplation for a while – and lost it. I've seen the hills of California, gold in the sunset with their promise of the settlers' freedom; and the great sea under the sun, a rich sheet of gold promising passage to the Orient with its undreamed riches, undreamed adventures. I've walked along its cliffs in the gentle showers that fill rivers, and thrust my hand into the rainbow! I searched for an incorruptible treasure. The sun itself has been my companion; and in that light I struck the mother lode of imagination, and a richer wisdom flowed from my pen than people of my generation understand."

"When you went to California," she answered dreamily, "to the house where the rains begin, as I imagine it – to the rivers beyond the deserts, mysterious source of storms in the land of seasonal rivers as you've described them – such a mystic country it seems to me, with waters of a generous sky according to the whims of wet or dry years... don't look at me like you think I'm crazy!"

"Do you write poetry?" I asked simply.

"Me? Why would I do that? I love to read poetry, but I don't know how to write it. Could you teach me?"

"I must write this down, then, exactly as you said it."

"Don't make fun of me! But when you went to California, what were you looking for? If it were gold, you could have stayed here and searched with as much chance of finding it, could you not? Or are you such an impossible adventurer? Like a boy! Why did you abandon the treasure of Natchez, to go looking for the treasure of California?"

"Think of it: what is the treasure of California?" I answered. "Gold in the earth, hidden? Gold – in a lost American civilization! El Dorado – legends more ancient than anyone can know. Cortez searching, and the cities of gold; Spanish gold, ships so burdened with it that they sank. Gold, all that ancient gold, captured by Lafitte! Gold... what's the value of it? I knew a man who found the mother lode; but his own mine caved in on him."

There was a transformation in her face. It melted into her eyes until they flowed large and helpless, exposing her to the soul, and she said, "When I want to know what you were looking for, it's because I want to know what I'm looking for myself. I believe we're alike in mind, you and I, more than either of us understands. I want – I don't know what I want. To look at you, listen to your voice and to your thoughts, to watch your expressive hands shape your ideas into the sunlit understanding of the air! To walk next to you, more than I could have desired anything! Life has never been so strange to me before."

She said no more, but looked directly into my inmost being and illumined it entirely with her smile.

"Do you think you won't be happy with William?" I said, gazing at the cherries crumbling their high blossoms into the waiting roses.

"William – he's so different from me. But he fascinates me like you can't imagine."

"I see. And here he comes."

"Look at him! How can I not love him entirely? Why did you never marry?"

"I didn't know what love was. She knew." By now I had no idea what I was saying.

"Who? Someone here, in Natchez?"

"You've never heard of her."

"Tell me her name!"

"I don't remember."

"I don't believe you. There was no one in California you were in love with?"

"No one."

"Except saloon girls?" with a sly smile.

"Yes. I found them refreshingly honest in their passion."

23

"How could that be, when their passions were all a lie?"

"But their extreme sorrow, their tears for the failure of love, were genuine."

"But you did have one true love?"

"Denise?"

"That was her name?"

"Mysterious and kind," I admitted. "Closer to my soul and more distant than my own existence. But the memory has faded. I know less of her than of my own mother."

"You never knew your mother?"

"At one time, I did. But who I was then I've not been able to recall for almost all my life."

"That's what I would have thought!" she said, staring. "How could I have guessed it? How could we be this much alike?"

"What do you mean?"

"I don't know. I feel lost in this house, but I don't want to leave it. William is calling us to tea. He's as eager as I am for the afternoon lessons!"

❧❧❧❧❧❧

Again, I walked between the towering rows of books, silent and strange in the late moonrise. Faint, unreadable letters on the dark bindings kept their secrets shut from my weak eyes, which flew like dying fireflies between the dim outlines of reality and the fantastic dreams of moonlit insanity, as though searching for some key to a hidden passage and the escape to the garden islands of eternity.

At the same time, I searched my mind for the elements of young womanhood in which are seen the opening of every blossom in paradise. Which is the finest to see, to breathe and to touch? Which is the secret flower? It is not, after all, the ripeness of her form, veiled in a flawless silk of skin, as I always thought before. That could not inspire feelings so profound that one cannot begin to understand them. The perfection of her face? No? Is it not this, then: her eyes, with their promise of the depth of thought as she begins to see into the intricacies of the world, which seem so new and interesting?

Is it the mystery of her heart?

The faded photograph was replaced by a living image.

Denise, it seemed to me, was standing in the shadows like a ghost. She drifted forward from the dark corner shelves away from the window, and her expression was one of anger.

"Did I never tell you, then," I said in my fantasy, "that you were the only one I ever loved? I never did say it, did I? The others meant nothing. I did not have you; they were paper images to conceal your face. They were nothing but wanted posters, in which I kept seeing your own lost face; but you had fled beyond capture."

The wrathful countenance was not appeased.

"Was it I who destroyed you?" I said. "Did I accomplish that so quickly, in the thoughtlessness of one night? But I didn't know what love is. How could I have known? It rose from obscure origins and surprised me in your face, in your speech, and in your silence. Don't go! I came here to look for you...

24

"Yes, there are other reasons, too. There is a treasure that I would uncover – but it is only an allegory for some mystery buried in myself...

"Who is this girl that has such thoughts? My heart cannot help responding – except that it is not the same as it was with you. I have never experienced anything like this. Though strongly romantic, it surpasses mere passion. There is something sacred in this. The fact of her existence challenges me in every way. She knows that I worship her, and she delights in it. She feels this is right – as a child would. She is a child, who needs me to be wiser than I am! And of course I am wiser in the ways of the world, and more learned than any man she has known. But she also needs me to remember what I was when I was younger, better, more idealistic..."

The moon rose past the window, and the crumbling ghost returned to its shadows. It seemed to know that Catherine strangely reminded me of her, and at the same time had clearly replaced her. Denise had always seemed distant. Catherine spoke with the speech of my own heart, freely and without reservation. Her words remained in me like fresh seeds, growing. I re-created her conversation in the moonlight (improving it where I could):

She: "Tell me. Have you ever been in love?"

Myself: "Never!"

"I don't believe you. Think hard. when you were young, like me –"

"How old do you think I am?"

She: "Old enough to understand the world. If you saw things as I do, you would laugh! Can't you remember a time when what existed beyond the horizon was a dream?"

"Of all the things I've seen and dreamed, I've never known a time when what was within my horizons was brighter than any dream!"

"I've never known anyone who responded so seriously to my silly thoughts! Everyone laughs at me, when I speak freely, with feeling. But you and I, we are two birds in paradise, singing our refrains! But do I interpret your meaning rightly? Have you really never been in love? There, a shadow crossed your eyes! Tell me what it was!"

"I could never again bear the feelings of my youth. Was I in love? I can't tell you. The experience was too profound."

"What was her name?"

"Denise."

"She was beautiful, of course."

"I think so. When I was your age, I could not even look at a woman."

"What a horrible thing! Why?"

"There are nerves, you see, that connect the eyes to the brain. These would begin to snap in smoke. Such a volume of blood shot into my head to douse them that my heart could not endure it."

"Are many young men this way?"

"Don't laugh!"

She: "A girl, if you looked at her this way..."

"Usually, she would run."

"If not?"

"She gets caught up. There's nothing like a woman's eyes catching fire!"

"Oh! You make me nearly lose my breath. I've never heard anyone talk like this."

Myself: "Now, you see, I don't have this problem any more. I'm stronger; I can stand in the presence of beauty and return the gift of speech. I can gaze at the most beautiful woman as you would gaze at the sun if you could endure it, until I am filled with light."

"I wonder if William feels this way when he looks at me?"

"That's not possible."

"Why not?"

"Has any man ever known such a strange, rare feeling?"

"I see," she smiled. "But don't you think his might be more powerful? By your own description, they soften with the years."

"How old did you think I am? Did you answer that?"

She: "Come, sir, you're old enough to be my father, and you know it. Will you promise me something?"

"Anything!"

"Will you always be my friend?"

☙

Fortunately, that conversation never took place except in the shadows of my imagination.

Chapter Five

A lonely cello was chased by its thrilling consort of violins out of the candlelit windows and into the night. I stood on the brick walk outside the door, taking in the breath of summer wisteria, and watched where every note vanished among the stars in pursuit of the lovely moon, while pondering the tragedies of the constellations. The harp and grand piano began their gentle interpretations of the lost musical phrases, and I turned from my lonely position among the stars to the more brilliantly clustered candelabra of the great ballroom, and to that which they illumined.

In a white dress, in the arms of William Stuart, she waltzed over the floor within the circumference of tall windows and mirrors. Together they turned and leaned into the steps, spinning weightlessly in the music that embraced them. I had no idea who taught her to dance like that; nor had I realized how the ancient Graces invoked a language that poets must interpret.

The moment the piece was finished, she and William were on either side of me, each taking an arm in answer to the applause that followed them. Before they could catch their breath they were introducing me to the crowded guests, names that had been legends in my childhood. My handful of other students made a line behind them, eager to initiate learned conversation in the presence of the older generations. Latin and Greek phrases were punctuated by jokes on genteel manners.

"What was it that Aeneas whispered to his father with respectful awe?" said a white-whiskered gentleman with spectacles. The students hushed. "And Odysseus to his mother in tears? I've forgotten the lines. But it is delightful to see the high literature passed on to the young in the original language!"

Catherine gave a curtsy, and said to me, "This is Mr. Morgan, from Memphis, and his wife. I'm sure you know of him."

"Your students cling to you as to a demigod," his wife laughed. "Can you supply my husband with the prophetic verses his failing memory seeks?"

I shrugged. "Spoken to the dead, in a dead language. 'All hope abandon, ye who enter here,' said Dante in his new Italian dialect, a language as beautiful, and just as dead! Have you not read what our contemporary poet writes?

> *Come Muse, migrate from Greece and Ionia,*
>
> *Cross out please those immensely overpaid accounts,*
>
> *That matter of Troy and Achilles' wrath, and Aeneas', Odysseus' wanderings,*
>
> *Placard "Removed" and "To Let" on the rocks of your snowy Parnassus...*
>
> *Those ancient temples, sculptures classic, could none of them retain her?*
>
> *Nor shades of Vergil and Dante, nor myriad memories, poems, old*
>
> *associations, magnetize and hold onto her?*

27

"Fear not O Muse! truly new ways and days receive, surround you,

I candidly confess a queer, queer race, of novel fashion...

"Or have you refused to read Walt Whitman?"

Catherine leaned on tiptoe to my ear, pressing that white dress gently into me to whisper, "You are not going to win students for your academy by shocking the guests;" and she glided away. I could tell she was pleased.

Mrs. Morgan was less amused. "There is to be a play this evening, I understand? Is it your own composition?" I bowed, saying nothing more. "We will stay, of course," she said sternly. "Everyone will be here to see it."

Emily Stuart emerged from the crowd, and William hurried to take her arm. "It's a fine poetic drama, mother," he said eagerly. "Did I tell you? I'm to play Lafitte!"

Her blue eyes danced on her son and turned to me like sapphires in the sun: "Shame on you! Converting my only son into an outlaw!"

The two men escorting her stepped forward at these words like they wanted to arrest me. I laughed; but I could tell I didn't like them.

"You remember the Donaldson brothers, don't you?" said Emily. "They've taken over the business at their grandfather's bank."

"That's who that is behind those gray beards? How could I forget? I wish you could have seen," I said to William, "the fights we used to have in the woods behind the fence! You remember that, don't you?" I said to the wrinkles behind the gray whiskers.

"How could anyone forget?" said one.

"Two against one!" I said, grinning. "I'd say I did all right."

"We remember everything," said the other, returning my grin. "We remember grandfather's stories of the old country, where our clan won lands and cattle from your clan."

Emily sighed: "I thought this ancient feud would have ended by now."

"It ended," I replied, "when the bank swindled our house."

"Your father's preaching wasn't winning many converts," said the first again.

"My father..." I glared at them while the years wavered before my eyes. I saw them as they had been, boys in the primeval wrath of my bloodshot eyes. Behind them stood my father in the years when I'd still loved him. I swallowed, blinked; and my father stood there as I'd never seen him: white-haired, white-bearded, and in a suit of clothes he could have never owned.

He was standing next to Catherine, who had returned with him on her pretty arm.

"Look who has come to see your play," she said merrily.

I stared. The great ballroom went silent.

"Son," he began; and his voice joined the silence. Then he mastered himself and said, "Son, I'm glad to see you."

I turned for the door.

⋙

Outside, I thought I would be alone with my own chaotic reflections; but Lady Wells was waiting.

"Sit down, Mr. Thompson."

I did. She remained standing. "You have the pride of an idiot," she said. "You think that because everyone has come to see your play that you are the man of the hour, do you not? You have forgotten that none of this is due to your own efforts. I have arranged and guided the whole affair for reasons you do not entirely understand. Let me remind you that you are a servant in my house. When you speak to persons of high degree you are to speak with respect. Your manner towards my guests has been far too familiar for their liking, or for mine; your speech has been inappropriate, do you understand? You will need to work diligently for the remainder of the evening to win a favorable reception for your work."

❧❧❧❧❧❧

The vast stables could not contain the number of carriages that continued to arrive throughout the evening. Sleek coaches, the latest European molded steel with highly polished lanterns and running boards, were scattered under the oaks and watched by stern drivers and stable boys, the youngest of whom had better manners than mine.

In the great ballroom was an audience that surpassed my expectations, both in numbers and in the degree of their elegance. I stood in the middle of the polished floor and wondered what half-swallowed words could escape my dry tongue:

"The opera boxes of Memphis, Vicksburg, and New Orleans have been emptied for a playwright that has not been seen on any stage", I said, bowing. "I hope you will not be disappointed when I tell you that tonight's drama is entitled, 'The Natchez Treasure'."

A murmur of delight moved through them like a breeze, so I went on:

"It is not my purpose to reconstruct works already written and criticized. I am not here to give a mere versification of my novel, Jean Lafitte, or to respond to the many articles which it inspired. Nor do I intend to further examine the life of an American hero, a life for which there is no scholar yet born with the resources nor the enlightened understanding to reveal the full value. I do not wish to inspire the search for his treasure, whatever it was, legendary or otherwise. Indeed, the story is circulated in riverboats, taverns, and newspapers that it has already been found."

Again, a murmur. "According to this story, its gold was used to adorn the unusual steeples of the churches in Port Gibson." I found my father in the audience and smiled. "The symbolism of those very unique steeples inspires rumors of their secret architect and the anonymous donor. For example, one of these is fashioned as a giant hand pointing at the heavens, which has been interpreted as a secret Masonic gesture." My father's expression was unreadable.

"I myself have nothing to say of that. I have taken an entirely new direction. I have concentrated on an unknown character, one which I mentioned only in passing in my book: one who played a vital role in the unfolding of the inner life and conscience of the pirate.

"Lafitte's career as a liaison among men of revolution has been discussed. He disguised this dangerous activity by posing as a bounty hunter, apprehending international criminals and collecting government rewards. His greatest capture, of course,

29

was Napoleon, whose escape he intercepted on the high seas. Not only did he collect the rewards of all nations for this, but he also secretly looted the wealth with which Napoleon had fled – and this was nothing less that the treasure of all the crumbling medieval kingdoms of Europe.

"Many secrets of this last meeting with Napoleon have never been brought to light.

"Among the captives taken was one whose life became the key to Lafitte's own mind. This was a French priest, a prisoner of Napoleon's, who had gone to the Holy Land as a pilgrim, and had spent many years there. He was a prophet, said to understand the secrets of history and the hidden destiny of America. In Jerusalem, he had known masters of every religion and initiates of the Knights Templar..."

The audience was in my hand. No one breathed. The elder Donaldson brother, however, stood, trembling, and said quietly, "Now that's just too much to divulge in public, sir."

"Why, sir," I said as quietly, "won't you have a seat?"

His brother leapt like a lion, overturning chairs and their finely dressed occupants. Both hands tore into my face like claws, rolling me hard on the polished floor, while he screamed, "You know where it is, don't you!"

☙

In a way, it was the best moment of my life. My fist in his face felt better than anything. It was like a sweet morning in spring when you lift a shovel above the earth, then thrust. It breaks the crust and penetrates; you thrust it deep, and the soft soil gives way. Or think of an old gourd sitting in the garden since last fall - its rind is tough, but inside it is completely rotten. You turn your shovel, aim between the largest warts, and let fly with all your strength. Once you break the skin, a terrible smell escapes with fermented juices that spurt into the air. The cheekbone, just beside the nose, gave way like that. Rich internal spurtings of blood filled the whites of his eyes just before they rolled out of the light, and he fell.

His older brother stared over him a moment, then looked around with a terrified glance and fled through the garden door.

Ignoring the chaos of the great ballroom, I retreated to my quarters to wash my hands and face. In the mirror, I saw her butler standing in my door.

"Shall we start the play now?" I joked. He was not smiling. He held up a small bag.

"Here is your monthly pay," he said. "You are to pack your books and papers immediately, and then I am to take you into town; and you are never to return here."

Chapter Six

In the tavern, alone and happy at my table by the window, writing, wondering how I could have so completely forgotten the contentment of a social outcast!

"Over there," said the innkeeper.

"Thanks," said Gerald.

"Well, my old friend!" I said. "How thoughtful of you to visit me here!"

He held up my whiskey bottle in front of the window. "I didn't know you could drink this much."

"One of the skills I perfected in California."

"Are you writing a new novel?"

"Yes; my greatest work!"

"This is how you start it? What a pile of notes and maps! Will this be the title, here? 'Freemasonic Intrigues and the Revolution of the Southern States'. That's insane! You think Masons are behind the talks on secession?"

"A controversial theory," I said, smiling. "It should sell some books, if I used that title!"

"That's the strangest idea I've ever heard! It's an argument over the issue of slavery, nothing more – even if the landowners call it 'states' rights'."

"You could look at it as a feud between rival economies, though," I said. "When an agricultural economy is dominated by the economy of the Industrial Revolution, slave labor becomes necessary for market competition. The irony of the moral issue of slavery is that it's really no different in the Northern states, where factory conditions for adults and children are not much better than slavery!"

"If it came to war, who would I be fighting for?" Gerald wondered aloud. "The large landowners? It's something to think about! My long days in the store are almost like slave labor for them anyway, with nowhere near the profits they bring! But why bring Masons into it? The lodges of the North and South will follow the desires of their memberships."

"And just like that," I laughed, "you have explained the whole mystery of Masonic intrigue!"

"You explained their political philosophy of revolution in your novel," said Gerald. His face assumed a seriousness I had not seen in a long time; it was an expression that showed itself only in our most earnest conversations. "Their goal in founding these new independent republics is to achieve the intellectual enlightenment of all men, in an ideal brotherhood."

"That is well said," I confessed.

"Your story implies that Lafitte discovered some secret of the New World. It was linked to a fantastic belief in an ideal but lost civilization, like that in Egypt, where Masons think their teachings originated. In the New World, this legendary civilization was called El Dorado; in it was the Fountain of Youth. This was what Ponce de Leon was

31

actually looking for; and Cortez, too, until the lust for gold took him over. And the same was true with Lafitte himself, right? At first, he was hoping to find out what the Spanish had actually discovered, some secret of El Dorado; until he also became so wealthy and powerful that his motives degenerated."

"I see that you read carefully," I said with a note of amazement.

"It was an exhilarating adventure," he admitted. "And there was a commentary in the Memphis newspaper. It made an interesting comparison between the fiction of Lafitte's revolutionary ideals, and George Fisher's actual involvement in the independence of Texas, Mexico and California. Now there's this talk of states seceding from the Union. But I don't understand; when does this revolution end, and brotherhood begin? How can such world-wide destruction lead to enlightenment?"

"You can read the whole affair when I'm finished," I said. "I can't explain it now."

"What was it like in the Wells plantation?"

"It's nowhere as grand as the quarters in this house!"

Gerald shrugged. "With your powers of description, I thought you might be able to tell me about things I'll never see. I tried to talk my wife into letting you have the corner room in our house. The boys like to move into the attic for the summer anyway, but..."

"I'm not her favorite author, I suppose?"

"I was very excited when I was reading Lafitte!"

"You didn't let her read it, I hope?"

"She didn't want to, so I tried to tell her the story."

"No, no; tell me you're joking!"

"The fineness of your language escaped her."

"With the wages I brought from the plantation, I can stay here as long as I like."

"The rumor is that you've found something new about the treasure."

"If that's the rumor, I'll be receiving some visitors," I said.

"Maybe I shouldn't be seen here."

"Maybe. You don't want to help me find it?"

Gerald stared at his own hands on the table. "I think you might not be joking." He was silent for a moment. "It's an interesting thought, I admit. You have a way of drawing people into your incredible dangers, don't you?"

"You're right."

"I say what I think, that's all."

I swept my pages together and dropped them on the floor. "I've never known anyone like you! I wish I could put aside the complexities our times have written in my mind, to understand the simple truth of who you are to me!"

He had been right to be angry with me. When I left home, he represented everything that was to be left behind and never again thought of. He was just an acquaintance of youth, no more than an ordinary person: straightforward, honest, hard-working and unassuming. He had no sense of adventure; but he always had an ability to forget himself out of concern for others. In the years of separation, he was not forgotten. He became linked to my thoughts of home. Home, of course is an island in the mind, hidden, guarded, a mirage that expands in the silence of suffering. When one harbors no clear hope of father or mother, a person like that becomes a solid wall in one's memory, behind which everything reliable about home is sheltered.

And this was no mirage, after all, that had matured into a man – and not the fantastic kind that made its appearance in my books. Now he was staring at me with that old look.

"You really are in trouble, aren't you?" he answered. "Whatever it is, I don't want to know. If there's any help I can give you, I will. But don't misunderstand me. Whatever prison you're destined for, other than the prison of your own thoughts, I won't go there in your place."

"It has always surprised me, though, the way you see me! Maybe you're right. Maybe my paths are more dangerous than I like to admit. But maybe the reward is greater than you can imagine."

"I don't want anything," he said. "But I've let the Donaldson brothers know that you can be found here. That's what you wanted, isn't it?"

"We'll see about that! They financed your store, I imagine?"

"I want no part in your arguments with them. They think you have the information they want. Do you need me to do anything else?"

"Yes."

"What's that?"

"Come see me when you have time."

"I will," he said standing.

☙

As the door swung behind Gerald, a pretty young woman came in wearing clothes, too warm for the weather. Without removing her oversized sunbonnet, she stared at the innkeeper and bashfully dropped her head. He shot a glance at me, shrugged, and returned to drying and stacking his pewter mugs. The girl took some slow and erratic steps in the direction of my window. She had my attention completely. She surprised me with such a sudden and direct stare that it took a moment to recognize her.

"What are you doing here?" I said.

"I'm looking for my teacher."

"I have nothing to teach you."

"May I have a drink?"

"No!"

"I will," answered Catherine. "I'm old enough." She tasted delicately from my own glass.

"Your aunt," I began.

"Would like to see you hanged," she finished.

"For your own sake, you should not be here."

"My aunt needs to learn about the modern era. In the North, women are beginning to assert the rights of their citizenship."

"This is what you learned from me."

"I can't help it, neither you nor I."

"I don't need to point out that your life and future under your aunt's direction are more valuable than anything you will find in the world."

"I don't intend to abandon either what I am or what I've become," she replied. "I

33

would not exchange my breeding or position. But I know that you are the secret of my nature."

"If I knew the secret of your nature, I'd be a rich man."

"What is it about you? I feel lost since you've come."

"Yes, have a drink. I insist." I called the innkeeper over for a second glass.

"It's true, isn't it?" she said, gazing out the window. I answered nothing. She stared at me hard and said, "You do care about me, don't you?"

"It is said in every word that I write."

"I'm so confused! I feel so strongly..." she shook her head.

"What are the plans for William's education?" I said vaguely.

A light jumped into her eyes, and their bewilderment was gone. "He's a fine piece of a man! Don't you think? Do you approve of him? Tell me that you do!"

I stared at her in disbelief.

"He doesn't know I'm here. When I tell him where I found you, he'll be sure to come! Neither my aunt nor his own mother will be able to talk him out of it. He doesn't want any other teacher. You see," she reached suddenly for my hand. "If only you were my father! You could be his, too!"

"You'd better go now."

"Did I say something wrong?"

"No," I said. "I think you said it right; except I can't be someone I'm not. But you'll recognize those men that just came in, and they'll recognize you if you're seen with me!"

"I won't leave!"

"Then wait at the bar."

She took her glass, with the whiskey in it, while the innkeeper was pointing me out for the Donaldson brothers and laughing, "He's bringing in the business at this hour."

"Who's the girl?" they said.

"None of your business," I answered.

"Oh, she's with you, is she? And are these your notes?"

"Maybe," I said.

"Character sketches for your drama on the treasure, I suppose? Or notes from which could be drawn a new map?"

"Or maybe we've got guns in our shirts," I replied. "It's been a while since this town has seen an old-fashioned shoot-out."

They looked carefully at one another for a moment, then said, "We represent the local chapter of the Masonic Order. We're supposed to have that treasure."

"You're opportunists."

"We were appointed by Fisher to search for it. He wrote us, before he died, that you would be bringing some information."

"You expect me to believe you?"

"We can prove it," they said, standing. They showed me their hands, while their fingers went through certain strange motions.

"Are these gestures supposed to mean something to me?" I said.

Again, they looked carefully at one another and sat down slowly. "If you were an initiate of the higher degrees, you would have known these signs."

"Initiates! You're pirates, like Lafitte; that's why you're interested in treasure." I spat, and missed the spittoon. "Fisher believed in an ideal to his death. He wasn't motivated by personal gain, like you are. Every time he acquired wealth, he renounced it and moved west, inspired only by his mission. You are pirates!"

"The Lafitte you wrote about is fiction. We know some things about the real man."

"The fiction I write is about real men, what makes a man do what he does. You don't understand Lafitte, do you? He was no hero! He was a man who couldn't understand the condemnation of his own heart!"

"Your task in this piece of writing, many believe, was to define yourself, not someone else!"

"You're so right! You think it does not also define yourselves? I want nothing to do with you, your plans or your purposes."

"You think very highly of yourself, but you could learn some things from us," they said. "You don't even know the source of the philosophies by which you live."

"I will give some thought to that," I answered. "You are dismissed."

They didn't leave. Instead, they looked at each other again, and then at me.

"We'd better explain some things to you," said the younger brother. "We will have to tell you why we are interested in this so-called treasure. What we have to say will sound incredible to most people. We think, though, that you will understand us clearly.

ৡৡৡৡৡ

"The American Revolution took place against a background of world revolution. The goal of these revolutions was set in place by the international Masonic Brotherhood.

"Our purpose, as defined by the Rosicrucian Manifesto at the dawn of the seventeenth century, has been to abolish monarchies and to replace them with the rule of the philosophical elect.

"Our greatest hope has been to establish a new nation, freed from the slavery of crown and of religion. It would have no creed other than the inner meaning of all religion. This hope has been very nearly realized in the divine establishment of America – a special nation on a new continent, ruled by people with democratic ideals under an inspired and enlightened leadership. This is the New World of Francis Bacon's Utopia! The Great Seal of the United States, as you must know, is none other than the capstone of Masonic symbolism, the so-called All-Seeing Eye above the great pyramid of Egypt.

"The divine fate of America, however, remains unfinished and unknown. The prophesies of the unknown founders and guides of our Order have always concerned this: after the government of the New World is established, the key to its final purpose will be revealed.

"The divine directives will be found in a secret tomb, as in our Father Christian Rosencreutz' tomb was found those directives which led to the founding of the Freemasonic Order and the publishing of the Rosicrucian Manifestos. The new directives will be found with the secret archives and the keys to understanding and enlightenment!

35

"Fisher was sent here by our brotherhood to complete the work of revolution in the New World, which he accomplished. It is believed that he also knew something which would lead to the discovery of the buried archives.

"It is believed that this secret information is what Lafitte buried.

"Lafitte was more than a hero of revolution. He was searching the high seas and the shores of the old world for the key to its ancient mysteries – the mysteries which, we believe, are to be revealed anew in the divine establishment of America.

"It is believed as well that this priest of Lafitte's was the emissary of the mysteries for whom he had been searching. His writings would have given the inner meaning of Solomon's Temple, which is the crowning mystery of the Masonic Order. The guardians of that secret, since the time of the Crusades, are the Sacred Order of the Knights of the Holy Temple in Jerusalem, otherwise known as the Knights Templar. They had been trained and sent on the holiest of missions, to take the ruins of that sacred Temple from the control of the followers of Islam. Instead, they were instructed by their own enemies in mysteries greater than they had imagined. These are the ones who sent instructions on the divine plan for America!"

Here he went silent, waiting for me to speak.

"You are not looking for treasure, then, but for profound answers?" I said.

"The hidden meaning of history!" he replied.

"I see. Touchstone of the alchemists?"

"The secret of sublimation and the great transmutation!"

"That's what I was afraid of," I said. "When everything you touch turns to gold, you will be the most miserable of men. The true foundation of Masonic philosophy, as I have understood it, is not world revolution, but interior revolution, the formation of the new man. The transmutation of metals as well is an allegory, representing the emergence of the spiritual man out of the gross material consciousness bound by the senses. Did I misunderstand?"

"See?" said the older brother to the younger. "I told you he was one of us! Listen," he said to me, "this priest that Lafitte captured off a plundered vessel is our guide to the treasure, and George Fisher knew it. We believe you are closer to essential clues to its existence than you realize! Don't you understand what we're saying? Lafitte was ransacking the ports of the ancient world for records of its lost tradition – the secret of the pyramids, and the environs of great Alexandrine library which burned in the early centuries! And yes, he did finance his inexhaustible research with robbery, and yes, his archaeological methods did approach plunder! In his chest, according to the legends of the Lodge, was the altar table of Isis engraved with precise instructions for her rites, as well as the records of our Father Christian Rosencreutz. These and other things he was instructed to bring to America for hiding until the revolutions were complete.

"The one piece of instruction he lacked was provided by this priest. When he was captured on his return from the Holy Land, he was an enlightened man. According to Napoleon, from whose ship he was taken, he had encountered some great truth in the tomb of the Savior. He had lived among holy men and had become one. He was clairvoyant, knowing all things. That's why the Masons believe he was carrying the secrets of the Knights Templar!"

36

"Interesting," I admitted. "You learned all this from the Masons?"

"Not from the Masons, no. George Fisher was in correspondence with the Archbishop of Paris, who regarded this priest as a schismatic and yet respected him."

"And you want to know what I might have found out about this priest?" I said flatly. They said nothing, but stared at me intently.

"If that's what you wanted," I said, "you might have been kind enough to sit still for my performance at the plantation! You acted like juveniles that belong in jail. Have you any idea what kind of position and salary you ruined for me? Now what! You want the full research and final plot for your private audience, and expect my simple cooperation? You're out of your minds; but that's nothing new."

"We can make good all your losses for you," said the older brother, shaking his head at the floor.

"You think so? How?"

"There is no position or salary you could have had in this world," he said, "that could possibly compare to the attainment of this treasure!"

"Then you don't understand the magnitude of wealth that the Wells Plantation commands," I challenged.

"We do," he said with disgust. "The financial power of the entire banking industry in this country is feeble in comparison with her possessions!"

"Is that so?" I said, as though considering the thought. "The banking industry should contrive a war somehow, so that her estate could be taken as plunder! If everything else were lost, it would still be worth it."

"She herself doesn't know how great an enemy her family has been to our Order; more reactionary than the Catholics of the Holy Roman Empire! Fisher knew; he married into it so that he could destroy it!"

I stood and turned to the window. "What do you want me to tell you, then? That I wanted to write the drama of the mysteries, veiled in perfect symbolism? That I, too, believed the story of Lafitte's death was one of the Masonic legends, an allegory of the translation into immortality? That I followed George Fisher to the California Land Office, where he ended his life robbing the Spanish Land Grants for the greedy Yankee squatters? That in my delusion I believed that in his California Land Office I would find the vault of the ancient archives translated to the New World – or at least some clue to where it was hidden?

"Listen carefully, then, while I invest you with the truths which I discovered!

"Lafitte, too, believed that this priest knew of some great mystery, though he appeared an ordinary man of religion. His religion was old-fashioned; he demanded Lafitte's repentance, commanding him to give his treasure to the poor. Lafitte tolerated him for a while, hoping to gain knowledge; but their stormy relationship deteriorated, and Lafitte had him hanged.

"It was Lafitte's remorse over this deed that killed him. He died of a painful venereal disease, a miserable exile, wishing he could be shriven of his sins by the one he had deprived of life!"

After a moment, the older brother said, "Well. Perhaps there is still more to this story. Think about it. You refer to a relationship of conflict between Lafitte and the priest. We know there are two branches of the Masonic Order. We are of the Scottish Rite. The Knights Templar are the highest degree of the York Rite."

"You assume there is conflict between these branches?" I asked.

"More ancient than the feud between your family and ours in Scotland," he answered. "Older than that of the War of the Roses, between the white rose of Lancaster and the red rose of York! This is a power struggle that goes back to the time of the Crusades, and it's bigger than the feuds between rival revolutionaries in the old countries over the destiny of America."

"You have no idea what you are saying!" I whispered vehemently. They looked at each other and smiled.

"What if we told you that the Masons of the York Rite are mobilizing the opinion of the industrialized states of the North?" said the younger brother. "We of the Scottish Rite are continuing the work of revolution by preparing for the secession of the Southern States."

"That's insane," I said.

"Lafitte knew of the conflict within the secret societies, all of which knew that he had some great mystery from the Knights Templar of the Holy Land," he went on. "That's why he remained in hiding! He was to bury that secret until the time of its preordained discovery. Our instructions are to find it."

"Fascinating," I said. "I wish you luck!"

"Do you understand the promise that the Masons hold out to you?" said the older brother. "We need your help."

"It is yourselves who completely misunderstand the goals of the Masonic Order," I answered dryly. "I am to give a public lecture on the subject, if you wish to attend."

"What!"

"Yes. In the Natchez Masonic Hall."

"You will be killed, if you attempt to divulge such secrets!"

"On the contrary, you will be murdered if you try to prevent it. I have permission from the Grand Master to give this talk in memory of George Fisher, to increase local membership. They are counting on my reputation to bring men in. Fortunately, you've failed to ruin my name completely; and now, you have a reputation of your own, you know."

They scowled. "Which Rite are you of?"

"I cannot reveal that."

"If you are of the York Rite," they frowned, "you should know that there is a war coming, greater than any this country has ever known!"

"I see. Will you kindly leave now?"

Like dogs, tails between their legs, they crept out the door.

Catherine walked slowly to my table. Her glass was empty. Her eyes were wide and frightened.

"It's nothing," I laughed. "A conversation between men who don't like each other."

Her voice quivered. "I had no idea. You are like a wise man that walked out of legend. It's dreadful."

I stared at her in astonishment.

38

"My dear," I said after a moment, "did you like the taste of your whiskey? Will you be able to find your way home?"

"Don't tell me," she answered, "that I don't understand you."

Late afternoon sunlight, through the window, burned the table between us.

"Who was Christian Rosencreutz?" she said.

Chapter Seven

"Christian Rosencreutz was born the poor son of a noble lineage at the end of the fourteenth century. He was given into a monastery at the age of five to be brought up. Dissatisfied with his education there, as a youth he determined to undertake a pilgrimage to the Holy Land with a companion. The fellow traveler, however, died during the perilous journey that it was in those times. He himself, disabled with an illness, was delayed at Damascus, where he was thrust upon the mercy of certain philosophers, who healed him and continued his education.

"From these philosophers he heard of the mystics and Kabalists who lived in the desert city of Damcar. Giving up his desire to visit Jerusalem, he arranged with a caravan of Arabians for transportation across the vast sands. At the age of sixteen he arrived, and was greeted as one who had long been expected.

"He was instructed in the secrets of the Arabian adepts, learning their language and translating a secret text into Latin, which he later brought to Europe. After three years in Damcar, he departed for the fabulous city of Fez, where Arabian magicians taught him to communicate with the elementary spirits of nature.

"At the age of twenty-one, he returned to Spain, bringing with him the mastery of the secret arts from the mystical East. He began to visit the learned men of Europe with his wisdom. From them, he received nothing but ridicule; so he retired into a house in Germany to pursue the ends of knowledge.

"After years of study, he became determined to disseminate the great secrets in his possession. He sent to the monastery of his youth for three trusted brethren. These he bound by an oath and taught.

"This was the origin of the Fraternity of the Rose Cross, or Rosicrucians. Its founder was motivated by a burning desire to elevate the arts and sciences of his day to the level at which they were capable of performing according to the wisdom and vision of the ancients, and to the degree which his studies in Arabia had shown possible. He organized its teachings and prepared its secret language, engaging the brethren in what the Rosicrucian histories called 'a comprehensive dictionary in which all forms of wisdom were classified to the glorification of God'.

"Their success in the highest achievement of wisdom was quickly seen in the large numbers of sick who came to them for healing. A larger house was built for the Order and dedicated to the Holy Spirit, and the size of the brotherhood was doubled to include eight members. All were unmarried, dedicated solely to their work.

"At this time, the brotherhood dispersed to spread their teachings throughout the world. First, they bound themselves to an oath to accept no compensation for healing the sick; to adopt no dress other than that of the country in which they abode; to meet once each year at the House of the Holy Spirit, or, if they were unable to do so, to represent themselves by an epistle; to each find one candidate to succeed himself in the Order; and finally, to keep the work of the Order secret for a period of one hundred years.

"At the end of the first year, they met in the joy of knowing that their wisdom was being spread to the benefit of mankind; and so their work continued. When the first member suddenly died, they resolved that their tombs should remain secret. It is believed that Father Christian Rosencreutz prepared his own tomb shortly after calling the remaining brethren together for his final instructions. It would be more than a century before that tomb would be discovered.

"This occurred when one of the later members of the Order decided to add a large chapel to the House of the Holy Spirit. On one wall was a brass tablet with the names of the original eight members engraved in it. This he wished to remove to the new chapel. As he dislodged it, the nails by which it was fastened broke the plaster and revealed a strange bricking pattern within the wall. He widened the break and discovered a door that had been sealed in the wall. Upon the door was written, in Rosicrucian cipher, 'In one hundred and twenty years I come forth'.

"He called out to the other members. Reverently, they removed the bricks and entered a room. It was seven-sided, infused with a mysterious light in the ceiling whose source could not be found. In each of the seven walls were vaults containing the original documents and instructions of the Order. In the center of the room was an altar. Examining this, they moved it slightly and discovered the brazen cover to a vault beneath it. Inside it they found the miraculously preserved body of Father Christian Rosencreutz in the robes of the Order. In his hand (according to the Rosicrucian Manifesto, in which this story is contained) was 'a mysterious parchment which, next to the Bible, was the most valued possession of the Society'."

"He was a saint, then," Catherine said quietly.

"That depends on what you mean by that word," I answered angrily. "A holy man, he was. The Church did not canonize him, but declared war on his followers and attempted to destroy them. For this reason, the Rosicrucians remained a notoriously secret society. Only by the publication of two Rosicrucian Manifestos were they known. Meanwhile, an entire generation of Protestant idealists, inspired by the very possibility of the mystical illuminati of the Invisible College of the Rose Cross, were hanged, burned, tortured and executed in various ways. This was called 'The Thirty Years' War'. Did we not cover that period in our history?"

"But that's strange," she insisted. "Too many features of his life are just like those of the saints – at least, those saints of the Church in earlier times. The writer of these Rosicrucian Manifestos must have known that. It reminds me of the incorrupt relics of my own namesake St. Catherine, or the other virgin martyr St. Lucy, or St. Nicholas himself, and a hundred others that my aunt read to me when I was little. Their perfect, peaceful faces are visited by pilgrims even today, after more than a thousand years – they are not hidden away. They are kept in the altars, and many have seen them. I will bring those books if you want to read them – the stories are wonderful. The presence of divine light reminds me of that which surrounded St. Columba when he was alone in prayer, or the light which led to the discovery of the body of the martyr-king St. Edward, not to mention that which burned itself through the mind of St. Paul, or that which was seen in the face of St. Stephen during his stoning, or in the trials of martyrs, and at the culmination of St. Anthony's temptation!" She had become so animated in the memory of these stories, that for a moment I wondered if I were going to see such light descend on her. "The prophetic wisdom of vision and foreknowledge belongs to the lives of most of the saints of the British Isles. Everyone knows it, doesn't he? This is nothing new. These are the features of the life of a saint."

"Well," I said after a moment, "I don't know. I've never heard these things. I've never understood the Church's twisted logic about its own saints, or the fictions in which, like splendid vestments, they have buried them. There are many who think that both Christian Rosencreutz and his Order are also fictional, or maybe allegorical. If so, he is a symbol of the true Christian. That much I understand. His name means 'the Christian of the Rose Cross', and the course of his life, legendary or otherwise, reflects this idea. His symbol, and that of his brotherhood – the rose blossoming at the intersection of the cross – is the symbol of the inner meaning of the equally fictional, or allegorical, crucifixion of Christ."

"What a dreadful thing for a man to believe!" she said in obvious concern.

I laughed. "When you speak of such a thing as illumination, you don't even know what you're talking about."

"That's exactly right," she said. "No one can understand the illumination of the Holy Spirit, not even the saints on whom it rests. It proceeds directly out of God in unspeakable, supernatural grace, acting invisibly, but powerfully, directly upon the heart. That's how it was described, I think, in the book of St. Adamnan, describing the vision of St. Columba – or maybe it was his own – I can show you the manuscript."

"It really is amazing," I admitted, "what is to be found in your library. I have a list – where is it? Here. If you would be kind enough to lend me these books, without your aunt knowing it, of course..."

"I don't know how often I can come here," she said anxiously.

"And you may bring me whatever other books you may think are necessary for my own education," I added, smiling wryly.

"I will have William bring them," she said, standing. "He would love to see what you're working on!"

Chapter Eight

Outside the Masonic Hall on Saturday night, the religious of every denomination in Natchez were awaiting my appearance, carrying protest signs like they do in the big Northern cities during political rallies. This was something unknown in the South. The phrase-craft was not smart. Instead of posting clever messages with a few well-chosen words, the placards were burdened with sermons. There were no margins and no clean endings, as though words had spilled off the bottom corner. The general message, if one could make sense of it, was that Masons were men who corrupted the meaning of Scripture while planning revolutions, and, like the den of thieves in Natchez-Under-the-Hill, would be wiped out by God.

My father's entire congregation from Port Gibson was there, but he was not to be seen. My commentary on Port Gibson architecture had made me famous. There had never been so many people in Natchez. I walked through the crowd smiling like a celebrity.

Inside, the hall was even more crowded than Wells Plantation had been for my play.

ა-ა-ა-ა-ა-ა

"Tonight, I have been given permission to open for you the door of the temple of the mysteries.

The silence was thicker than the crowd.

"It is only a glimpse of the interior that I will be able to reveal, since one must prepare his understanding and character to receive sacred truths. Also, it is only the forecourt that I may show. The Holy Place within I cannot open, while of the Holy of Holies within that, I cannot speak – except to say that its secrets are symbolized even throughout the outer courtyard which I am permitted to show.

"The secrets of the craftsmanship of the master builders, or Masons, is most fully symbolized in the building of Solomon's Temple, which was the great temple of the mysteries in ancient times. It was surpassed only by the Great Pyramid. The Masonic legends surrounding the building of Solomon's Temple, such as the legend of the death and resurrection of its master architect Chiram Abiff, indicates the nature of what is called "The Great Work". This means that the building of the perfect temple is an allegory, signifying the extent of sacrifice necessary for the interior resurrection of the spiritual man, with the goal of philosophical illumination.

"The Masons' craft has passed down through the generations not only the art of building, but also the 'freemasonic' or philosophical interpretation of its meaning. This is revealed in the passage of its thirty-three degrees of enlightenment, represented by the thirty-three steps leading to Solomon's Temple, as well as by the thirty-three years of Jesus' life. The perfection of all spiritual illumination is seen in the figure of Solomon himself, whose wisdom is not just legendary. His power over the elements

43

and his conversations with angels and demons are well known.

"Of course, this implies a different interpretation of the Biblical text than that which has been given to us by the churches."

Here I allowed some silence for effect, staring boldly at individuals in the audience. Some met my gaze with open anticipation; others squirmed and looked about.

"Certainly," I continued, "the writings gathered in our Bible are most remarkable documents. The numerical values hidden in the combinations of Hebrew letters – where every letter is also number – and the inherent intelligence in the very forms of their alphabet of fire – where each unique brush-stroke represents a tongue of flame – these clearly reveal that the Law of God was indeed written by none other than the Divine Mind. Of the tens of thousands of studies on these texts, however, only a handful have indicated the profound depths of the esoteric teachings locked in the Jewish mysteries of Adonai.

"The original form of these Scriptures is lost. Our existing Bible presents a perverted state of divine teachings. In the prophets, many separate and mutilated texts are brought together under one or another name. The Johannine writings, shrouded in a veil of mystery, are likewise prophecies of the Universal Mind written well before the Christian era and later attributed to the man Jesus.

"While lamenting these errors, which many scholars today are beginning to accept, we know that the secret and original doctrines have been woven into the books of the Hebrew Torah, and are incorporated in Masonic rituals.

"Masonry is old, indeed, as the world. Early Masonic manuscripts now in Scotland affirm that the craft of initiated builders existed before the Great Flood. Its members were employed in the building of the Tower of Babel, and in the story of that tragedy is enshrined the most terrifying of the mysteries. The origin of the craft is attributed to the children of Lamech. They are said to have built two pillars, one of marble and one of brass, and to have written the primordial sciences on them. These were found after the flood by Hermes, wisest of the Egyptian sages, who translated their writings into hieroglyphic form. It is said also that Enoch, who walked with God, built an underground temple of nine vaults, one under the other. In the deepest, he hid a golden triangle in which was written the name of God. Hermes found this also, and emulated its design in the building of the Great Pyramid. Moses, the Egyptian initiate, transcribed these mysteries into the secret doctrine of Israel, known as Kabala, giving the instructions for the temple of the mysteries in the form of prophecy. Solomon, in building that temple, became the greatest of all initiates.

"Nevertheless, let it not be thought that such mysteries originated with men. Before the fall of the angels, God taught them to Lucifer first and then to Michael, and then to the lesser orders of angels in lesser degree. They are symbolized in the order of creation. Angels bestowed their secrets on Adam while he still lived in the pristine state of paradise. Both Lucifer and Michael in turn communicated with him. It was Lucifer who fully developed the ideas of the exalted mysteries, while Michael remained silent unless asked for an explanation.

"The Creator-god, Elohim – which is a plural form meaning 'gods' – created man 'in our image'. Even in our Biblical account of Genesis, this clearly shows a polytheistic origin of religion. Christians limit their 'gods' to three in their conflicting notion of a monotheistic Trinity. The secret doctrine of Israel, however, expands the number of Elohim to seven – one for each 'day' of creation – teaching that their work was limited to dividing the heavens and creating the inferior universe. Their spheres of existence are the emanations of the Demiurge who formed the first matter which now imprisons the spirit of knowledge latent in man.

"Adam, the first man, understood clearly the nature of the creation in which he stood. His being was purely spiritual. His sight was not obscured then, because his spirit was not yet fenced in, as it were, within the surroundings of a universe of material substance. This is the denotation of the word 'paradise' as 'enclosure', without, however, erasing its purer connotation as a place of primordial knowledge. Of the loss of this inner condition we will speak in a moment, understanding that it is to his state of natural philosophy that we must return if our existence is to have meaning.

"The Adam of the Kabalistic diagrams rises through the four worlds. As both man and God, he stands with one foot on land and one foot in the sea, tall as the titan Atlas holding up the universe in the concentrated effort of contemplation. His feet, then, are in the lowest world, this world of matter and the elements. The sun itself resides in his solar plexus, while the planets are hurled in orbit around his mid-section, which is in the lower heavens. With his hands, he holds the ring of the zodiac which encircles his breast. This is the upper heavens, the third world. His head, towering above all creation, is fixed in the Unmanifest. These are the same four worlds which divide the Kabalistic tree of the sephiroth from the roots to the upper branches, as symbolically revealed in the Tree of Life in paradise. This is to say that the structure of the universes and the interior structure of man are identical.

"Adam was at first complete in himself. The first principles of the philosophers of Greece were embodied in him – the Pythagorean monad or the 'One' of Parmenides, as well as the Platonic idea of the perfect man before the division into male and female. In alchemical engravings he is depicted as the divine androgyne, half man and half woman. After the division into the sexes, the one became two; and by this mystery and the loss of his original self-contained completeness he was driven from paradise. The sleep of Adam, then, represents the total descent of the mind into matter. Eve – 'matter' – is the darkness of the mortal creature.

"The fall into matter was the demonic workmanship of the creator of the inferior universe, called by Plato the Demiurgus, but whose name in Kabalistic texts is Jehovah. The secret of his name is the great secret of Kabala. Neither the Demiurge nor his creation participate in immortality, but this is no longer known to the darkened mind of the fallen Adam. How will he be redeemed? By the descent of the immortal Nous, or spiritual mind, through the process of philosophical enlightenment. His initiator will be none other than his apparent enemy, the serpent who guards the tree of the knowledge of good and evil!

"I apologize for the extreme depth and complexity of this introduction to our doctrine. I will try to make things as simple as possible. Are there questions so far?"

From the back corner of the room came a meek voice: "This is most enlightening. Thank you!"

I smiled, glowing with the pleasure of my words, and he went on: "Before this very clear introduction tonight, I never realized how thoroughly the European Secret Societies embodied every heresy of the first millennium of Christian history!"

Everyone turned around to look at him, then at me. The murmur that rose was like waves against a shore, threatening storm.

"Actually," I replied boldly, "we believe that the heretics were in possession of great and hidden truths which the Christians were zealous to destroy!" My voice was thunder, and the aftershock was a silence of fear throughout the room.

His small voice filled that silence. "As well as you seem to understand the Scriptures, I am surprised you don't know the interpretations of the Church Fathers."

"The book of Irenaeus of Lyons, Against Gnostics," I replied, "as an uninspired, self-contradictory treatise, weak in its foundation of thought, is typical of the writings of these Church Fathers. Nevertheless, it remains our most complete record of the Gnostic secrets of the early centuries."

My antagonist answered only with a defeated sigh.

"Since the first century," I continued, "all books of secret philosophy begin with critiques of the Christians. These arguments are not against Christ himself, that great initiate who in his boyhood travels learned the mysteries of all lands, from Hindus, from Greek and Phoenician mystery schools, from druids and from the more mystical Jewish sects. But they are against those who appropriated his name and assumed his following, discarding all who do not agree with their own interpretation."

"The nature and person of Christ himself," my antagonist interrupted, "was the mystery which none of the mysteries could penetrate."

"That is what these august Fathers believed, isn't it?" I agreed. "Yes. I believe you must know my own father. Did he send you here to torture me?"

This was followed by tentative waves of embarrassed laughter.

"Let me explain something about Masonic philosophy," I said to him. "It requires an intimate knowledge of all the ancient Greek philosophers; not merely Plato and Aristotle and the more well-known of their predecessors, Heraclites and Parmenides and Pythagoras, but also the systems of such deep thinkers as Anaxagoras, Thales, Solon, Xenophanes, Zeno, Democritus. These were mystics and idealists whose sciences cannot be understood without initiation into the mysteries they guarded. True masonry requires familiarity with all the mysteries of the ancient world, and the nature of their temples and rituals. It requires an understanding of the ancient sciences of alchemy, astrology, and numerology, which differ radically from our modern understanding of the sciences of chemistry, astronomy, and mathematics, just as the arcane philosophies carried a tradition of mystery and initiation which is foreign to the over-rationalistic nature of modern philosophy.

"This is the background necessary for the study of ancient thought, which the Church Fathers attempted to dismantle. The word 'orthodoxy' and its relation to Christian doctrine is vehemently opposed with deep and careful consideration by the Secret Doctrine which is kept in Masonic interpretation of the Scriptures. Only in Masonic Initiation itself is the fullness of truth! The Church of Rome is the greatest heretic!"

My voice continued rising with the importance of words. "I quote the Rosicrucian

Manifestos: 'God, before the end of the world, will send a flood of spiritual illumination over the earth; but the world must first sleep off the poisoned chalice of theological vision.'

"Now. Are there other questions?"

"Yes." A man my own age, well dressed, stood: "No one needs to be reminded of the advances in science and civilization that have been made since the time of the Dark Ages. Yet you seem to imply that ancient philosophies possessed a wisdom that is lost to us. Does Masonic philosophy believe that the myths of old contained truth, while it is our idea of progress which is a myth? If so, I am confused. What is true philosophy, and what is simple madness?"

"That is an interesting question!" I said eagerly. "The greatest thinkers have always had more respect for the thinkers of the past than we realize, looking upon them reverently as fathers. Beyond that, however, few today remember that the progenitors of modern science and philosophy, Francis Bacon, Descartes, Isaac Newton, and Christopher Wren, were initiates of the Rosicrucian Order. Elias Ashmole and Robert Fludd in England gave the order the name of Freemasonry, making it more visible than it had been. Newton was deeply involved in alchemical studies. The ideal of the advancement of learning, which has become a doctrine of our modern era, was championed by the very founder of the British Royal Academy of Science, Francis Bacon. This greatest advocate of the empirical method of observation, experimentation and discovery – the cornerstone of modern science – was also author of the New Atlantis, a mythological re-telling of the ideals of the Rosicrucian Manifestos.

"These men understood the ancient sciences. They understood that science, even as we understand it, is a form of magic, to the degree that it participates in the transmutation of forces. The physics of the ancient Greeks, on which our theories are founded, were steeped in mysterious philosophies on the nature of matter and its emergence from the darkness of non-being into the light of reality.

"The mixture of fire and water to produce steam, and the shaping of metals in huge furnaces into parts to be moved by the released force of steam, all the aspects of the Industrial Revolution, were known already in the alchemical laboratory, including the effect of such a revolution on the thought and indeed the very nature of man.

"A locomotive speeding across the prairie is a transmutation of time itself, a magic spell on the deep mind of man. Whether for good or for evil, it takes place according to ancient formulas no longer understood, or even thought of, in practical applications. The Masons who know these things are the careful planners and builders of our age.

"The supreme magic of ancient science, however, concerned itself much less with the outward forces of nature than with the inner nature of man himself, which was its focus. The alchemical allegories of transmutation actually refer to the mental and physiological process of enlightenment. When this is achieved, it is said that the initiate, represented as an alchemist, has refined the elements of his nature to a spiritual condition known as 'achieving the philosopher's stone', which has the legendary power of transmuting all base elements into gold – that is, into the true spiritual nature.

"In Masonic lore, the alchemical process is enshrined in the legend of the casting of the molten sea in the courtyard of Solomon's Temple. Alchemy and Masonic initiation are also linked in the story of the Chemical Wedding, where the seven days of Creation represent the re-creation of man in the seven days of that alchemical ritual.

"As I said earlier, the thirty-three steps of Solomon's Temple represent the thirty-three degrees of initiation followed in Masonic ritual. These are understood to involve an interior psycho-physiological process which raises the spirit-fire up the thirty-three sections of the spinal column, through the seven plexuses, the nerve-and-muscle centers of the body, to the pineal gland within the brain. When this occurs, a flood of light, energy, and understanding invades the entire consciousness of a man, who is then regarded by the wise as 'enlightened' and 'regenerated'.

"A still more esoteric allegory referring to the interior magic is the strictly Rosicrucian interpretation known as 'removing the rose from the cross'. This has to do with the freeing of the spiritual man from physical limitations, and is connected to the legend of the crucifixion. According to this, there are three nails that attach the crucified spirit to the body. I am not permitted to say more about this.

"The profound loss of man's innate nobility as represented in these symbolic sciences, which were concerned with the building of the interior man, was never intended to have been the result of the scientific revolution. This has been instead the result of an unreflective use of scientific advances, which is not the philosophical life. The intended goals were quite different, as given in the Rosicrucian Manifestos. These were, first: the abolition of monarchal government, and the establishment of the rule of the philosophical elect. Second: the reformation of science, philosophy, and ethics. Third: the discovery of the universal medicine, the panacea, otherwise known as the Elixir of Life.

"These are the goals, as re-stated in Bacon's New Atlantis, that were established as the divine plan for the founding of a new nation in America.

"Divine guidance has been seen at work many times in our young history. I will give one outstanding example.

"In the late afternoon of July 4, 1776, the representatives of the colonial Congress had fallen into silence. Jefferson still stood, having just finished reading his masterpiece. That remarkable treatise, freshly penned, the Declaration of Independence, lay unrolled on a polished table – not, as it is now, among the greatest documents of the human spirit, but as a pledge to the impending sacrifice that freedom would require. The setting sun painted the bricks of the walls and streets in fire, and the light fell through the windows as brilliantly as a crimson river of blood. The silence was ominous. The signature of one's name here was the equivalent of a sentence of death before the English Parliament and Crown.

"The sun touched the horizon. At that moment, a voice, remarkably similar in tenor to that of the bell in its tower, rang from the door. They turned to see a tall silhouette in the blazing light. He began explaining the content of the Declaration's words in rising phrases, his hands climbing the flashing air in gestures, the shadow of his finger stretching across the room as though to touch the table and its unrolled parchment. Kindling fire in the minds of his listeners, he then blew it to a roaring flame of understanding. His final words rang like the swinging bell: 'God has given America to be free!'

"With that, he sank into a chair, while all other men rose. Name after name was swiftly added to the wide margin underneath the writing. They then turned to greet and congratulate the stranger – but he was gone.

"This is not unlike the appearance of other illuminati, known and unknown, who, at crucial turning points in history, have guided events toward a divine purpose. As the destinies of nations have been re-shaped in recent centuries, such appearances have increased. We believe that the institution of a new republic on the American continent has been the work of divine guidance, the fulfillment of which is yet to be revealed."

Overcome by the effect of my own words, I fell silent, looking down. There was nothing more to say.

Nevertheless, a young man in the front row stood and spoke: "Your belief in the great destiny of this enlightened Utopia is in sharp contrast to reality, with forebodings of civil war!"

It was one of William's cousins from the school. I perceived the larger unspoken question beneath his words. He was angry, I think, for the failure of the Wells academy. I smiled at him knowingly:

"If the masses decide on a course of action that is not to the benefit of all men, the philosophical elect will withdraw into obscurity. This may indeed occur. An immense cloud darkens our horizon. Perhaps we may do no more than to take some advantage of this period of calm before the storm. Do you realize, then, what an extraordinary event this is tonight, to so openly speak of great secrets?"

He was still standing. "I haven't asked my question," he said. "In order to overthrow monarchies, it has been rumored that not only did the philosophical Freemasons engineer the American Revolution, but they planned the French Revolution and those in the rest of Europe as well. The coming revolution within America, with states asserting their sovereign power in separating from the Union, would naturally seem to follow in this course of world revolution. On the other hand, the leaders of the Union loyalists are themselves known to be Masons, espousing their own ideals of unity, brotherhood, and peace. Is this to be seen as a schism between parties of Freemasons? Is the Brotherhood divided against itself?"

He was answered with murmurings from every corner of the room.

"Yes," I said after a moment. "Yes. This has always been.

"There are true Masons, and there are false Masons. There are illuminati, and there are sorcerers. The struggle between the two is as ancient as that which exists between good and evil.

"In England, the Wars of Roses over political control of the crown involved also an essential philosophical difference. The two parties, each with an emblem of a rose on its shield, were involved in the greater European struggle for control of the secret societies. This conflict was inherited by the struggle for the independence of the Scottish Highlands with the institution of the Scottish Rite, and its separation from the York Rite. In America, the practitioners of the York Rite in the Northern states, like the Lords of England, are consumed by passions of political control over a more rural and independently-minded people. America was never intended to become a world power like the colonial principalities with ambitions of empire! It was supposed to be the focus of revolution.

"The first settlers in the Southern states were the political enemies of the English crown, exiled to the Carolinas. These were followed by hordes of Scottish immigrants during the English scouring of the highlands. These had been Catholics, fiercely loyal to their traditions of Columba of Iona, Aiden of Lindisfarne, and Cuthbert of Melrose. These traditions had been older than those of Rome forced upon them by the medieval church, and certainly older than the Anglican domination now forced upon them by the successors of Henry the VIII. The Scots reacted by forming their own Presbyterian church, in the same way that the oppressed but ancient Welsh churches became hardened in their own fervent Methodism.

"The theology and hierarchy of these churches, popular in the rural South, if one looks closely into them, are guided by Freemasonry."

The younger Donaldson brother broke a vein with his shout as he leapt from his chair: "Who gave him permission to say this?"

"None other than a deputy of the Knights Templar, the enlightened guides of the entire Masonic Order, if you must know," I answered calmly.

"Do you expect anyone here to believe you?" said the older brother, still seated. "You and I know very well the nature of the old feud. You will not be taking control of this lodge so easily."

Several men had risen by this time. They looked at one another threateningly, and then at me.

"I told you he would betray the lodge," said the younger brother. "This is like his lies of Lafitte and his treasure."

"Lafitte!" gasped someone else. "He was hiding out in the South, hiding from the federal government..."

I smiled. "It all makes more sense now, doesn't it? I only wish we could know what that treasure was."

The younger Donaldson brother put his hands over his ears. "Do we have any control over what is said in our own lodge?" he groaned.

The sheriff stood and stared at him, then leaned back and crossed his arms: "Your Lodge?"

The sheriff was a man who rarely showed himself except where there was trouble. I always believed, because of this, that trouble was what he wanted. I noted the position of the door, and the easiest access to it. The elderly stranger, though, had begun to walk into the crowd, and his presence had a quieting effect.

"Please, gentlemen," he said softly, "I will tell you the truth." Everyone shut up and stared at him. "It is true," he said, "that there have always been conflicts of power among the secret societies, and that this has been a closely guarded secret. Of all their terrible secrets, none has been kept so hidden as that of the extreme confusion that has resulted from the disbanding of the Knights Templar in Jerusalem."

"Sir, whoever you are," I said, "that's a rumor I have not heard."

"The larger number of us abandoned the Order when we began to learn that we were heretics. This was the secret that was known to Lafitte's priest, and this is why Lafitte had him silenced."

The sheriff whipped out his gun: "Take him! Bind him! Gag him!"

"Why?" said the older Donaldson brother; and the younger sank into his own chair and, as though to continue his brother's thought, said, "The secret's out."

"He knows were to dig for it, idiot," said the sheriff. "Or, if not, he can tell us who does!"

In one moment, the entire content of my well-prepared lecture was forgotten. The Masonic Hall erupted in a volcanic brawl, a thick confusion collapsing inward as every man's fists worked to be first to grab him. Some men were crumpled under knuckles, others rose to the occasion with vigor – some even flew violently through the air, but not by the force of their own will. One crashed against the post of the low stage, broke it, and fell unconscious. The stage limped forward and I slid into the crowd, joining the fight out of pure anger.

It wasn't long before I was enjoying the blind passion that gave muscle to my arms and chest. When gunshots started, though, I was afraid they might be for me. I hadn't thought to bring my pistol. I scrambled for the door on all fours. The sheriff was behind it, firing into the ceiling, but other bullets whistled by the ears. The sheriff stepped out to give me a glare. I didn't wait for his instructions.

No one knew what became of the stranger that night.

Chapter Nine

Spring was getting tired. Its flowers wilted in the Mississippi heat. I, too, had grown weary of its promise. I was content with my corner of exile in the dark saloon. The cool recess of the dark, expansive room, with its ceiling of low beams, welcomed me to the place where I had first learned to escape from the devouring world, with only my own burning thoughts for companions, setting them down on paper like flaring torches to show my way.

A tavern by the San Francisco wharfs had become my home in California, because it reminded me of this one. What a place of distractions that was! Adventures born in every hour – most of them doomed – swept me into the fire of real literature that had nearly cost my life. I met men whose characters I would sketch for my portrait of Lafitte. There were the saloon girls, too, who fought for my company because I was tender towards them, and because I crowned and canonized them with poetry.

Here, though, it was as peaceful as a hermit's cave. I could concentrate on my work. Besides, I was on the trail of the one adventure greater than all the others. I stared at my growing pile of notes.

It was in a tavern under the hill, in the remnant of the old Natchez that had itself been a wild frontier town, that I had been initiated into the seriousness of this legend of the treasure. We were halfway through one steaming mound of crawfish, and another of fried catfish, flanked by cornbread bathed in butter and black beans in gravy. We were drunk on ale as brown as the river. The topic of treasure had begun as a joke, but as the Louisiana boatman kept talking, his voice quieting into tones of increasing solemnity, we all sobered up.

He had known Lafitte's cabin boy. Now he's an old man, he had said, living in the swamps of Louisiana where a river passes through a chain of three lakes before emptying into the Gulf. Many nights he had sat on the old man's porch over the moonlit river, hearing tales of pirate adventure.

He had described one night on a low bank where a bayou, lazy in the cypress swamps of its wide mouth, quietly emptied into one of the lakes. Lafitte sat on a chest, serenely running his fingers through his beard and taking long draughts of Belgian ale from a stone jar, then looking out over the dark waters. Behind him, a hastily piled earth embankment concealed the twelve cannon off his ship. It was after his heroics against the English in the Battle of New Orleans, at a time when the U.S. government was no longer an ally, but an enemy. A warship had been pursuing them in the Gulf. They had made this unknown escape from the sea into a muddy, bracken river which, after some miles of strong current, opened into the three successive lakes, each with mysterious borders of swamps and bluffs. On this shore of the innermost lake they had disembarked and made their defensive stand. The place is now called "Dead Man's Lake", because there Lafitte sank the U.S. schooner that was pursuing him. Earlier, he had sent men to bury a treasure in the darkness of the swamps. They had gone with lanterns into the cypresses, marking them with Roman numerals. In that chest had been deep mounds of Spanish doubloons, enough to fill the U.S. treasury for many years. But whatever lay in the chest on which Lafitte sat, he would not be parted from it. His men had stayed their distance from him, glancing at him now and then with fear. The lanterns were extinguished. The universe was dark. The naval ship lay out in the lake, still and black against the lesser shadow of the sky. Phosphorescent lights danced among the cypresses where the men with lanterns had gone, then wandered out over the lake where fog came up...

The old man had seen the treasure many times, always closed – a great chest, large enough to hide a man. He had seen many smaller chests, filled with gold and jewels thick as gravel. Whatever was in this one was far more valuable than anything else. He had been with Lafitte when it was lowered into the floor of the Natchez warehouse.

"You're crazy to be telling us this," said Johnny.

"Why?" he said. "It's not there now. You're Masons, aren't you? I thought you'd knowed it already."

We stared at each other, uncomfortable and embarrassed, wondering how he could have known this about us. We had become neophytes just the night before. Following the ceremony we had stayed up all night, carousing in good Masonic fashion after speaking vows of the highest ethical character. We drank until we found ourselves flat on our backs by the river, staring up into the endless rifts and canyons of thick stars, comparing our future lives to the constellations of heroes. I was thinking of Denise and missing that recent moon. As the sun came up, we escaped the inquisitive stares of the early dock workers by retreating into a little-used warehouse piled with broken bales of rotting cotton. Johnny scared off the mice with his vomiting, then looked up into the dark eyes of the black-haired Louisiana man, staring down from under a strange hat, his wrinkled pants discolored to the waistline with mud stains that wouldn't wash out. He smiled, congratulated us on our initiations, and invited us to breakfast.

"It was in that warehouse where I found you," he said.

When the cabin boy was sixteen, he said, they came and took it out, then buried it somewhere else. Some things had happened while it was in Natchez, he said. There were murders, gunfights in the streets and on the docks, and assemblies on the hill where the Masonic Hall was later built. And something else happened, but Lafitte wouldn't tell him what it was.

"So I asked him myself," said the boatman: "Where is it now?"

"Buried," was the old man's answer.

"Where?"

"I know what the place looks like – or did then – but I don't know how to get there."

"How can that be?"

"He blindfolded us on the boat. Three days we paddled blind, then carried it maybe two hours blind. There was only two of us."

"What did the place look like?"

"An oak."

"Tell me more."

"Nope. Nobody alive knows where it is. Best that way."

53

ભ

The next day, the Louisiana boatman was found by a side-wheeler, drifting dead in his boat. His throat was slashed, his tongue sliced down the middle.

That's when I decided to leave town. It had been in my mind anyway. I was terrified that I had become a Mason. I didn't know who was friend or enemy. My movements would be watched, freedom limited – the opposite of what I had hoped for when I joined the lodge.

In California, I kept to myself for some time. It was easy to do there. When I found George Fisher, I spilled my story in desperation. From him I learned of the treasure's real importance, that it was something inconceivable. What, he would not say – perhaps because he did not know. Under his tremendous influence, however, I was reconciled to the Masonic Order, raised through its degrees, and encouraged to publish the story of Jean Lafitte and to begin gathering the evidence from the four points of the compass. I was entrusted with locating the treasure.

As far as I knew, I was closer than any man had been since Lafitte died. All evidence so far had pointed in the same direction: some valuable document, note, perhaps even a map, somewhere in the library of the Wells Plantation, if I had any idea in which volume to look – in which marginal gloss, which heavy, hollow spine, or under the delicate endpapers glued down. I spread my notes across the table like a hand of cards, and stared at the pile that remained.

I wondered if this was where the trail would end, in a pile of useless papers in the quietest tavern in the world – not at all like that noisy one in Natchez-under-the-hill where my search had involuntarily begun. Maybe it was better this way. Maybe the cabin boy had grown old in that wisdom. I turned my gaze toward the serene window.

Out in the street, there were men enough for a posse.

The sheriff stood in the door: "That's right, stay there. I'm going in alone!"

My alarmed gaze swept their faces. A handful of deputies; the rest of them, Masons.

The sheriff stood over my table: "That was quite a riot you started."

"Damn it, it was a good lecture. I said just what I was supposed to, and said it well; and you know it!"

"I mean, it was even better than that scene you staged at the Wells Plantation," he said.

"Why don't you set your barking dogs on the scent of that stranger?" I offered. "Without the witch's ingredients he threw in, the pot would not have boiled."

"Can't find him. Don't even know where to look. Thought I'd have better luck with you."

"If I'm going to jail," I said, "I guess I'd better gather my notes."

"No need for that."

"What the hell! Am I supposed to be looking for a map, or not? I've still got access to Fisher's papers, even if I can't get into his library myself."

"I know that. I'm not going to jail you."

I gave my blood a minute to settle, and said, "The Donaldson brothers are out there. They won't be happy unless you come out with me in handcuffs."

"I can handle those jokers!" he laughed. "They think they're hot shot, because they

54

own the bank. My interest is in this unknown Templar you just mentioned. He's our best lead."

"I agree."

"The way he responded to you, we think he has more to say."

"That has occurred to me also."

"Do these things really happen? It was right out of the Masonic legends, wasn't it? The mysterious appearance of the unknown Illuminati! We must be on the right track. But if we kept you in jail, he wouldn't try to come to you, would he?"

"I appreciate your consideration."

"Oh, it's great having you around," he grinned. "We haven't had this kind of excitement since the old town was taken away. And Lady Wells has things under her control since Fisher left. She gives more money to the Department than the other plantation owners combined."

"Much of it goes right to the Lodge, I imagine?"

"I'm sure she knows there's nothing she can do about that. On the other hand, we have to keep a semblance of law and order. As soon as you hear from the stranger, you'll let me know?"

"Count on it. He knows where to find me, I assume, since everyone else does. It's getting hard to think."

"You want to be left alone?" he said, tipping his hat. "I can arrange it. No visitors, not even news reporters – unless they see me first."

"Really," I said quickly, "I don't want to be that much trouble to you. Innkeeper! Do you plan on clearing these dishes?"

"Do you plan to pay me?" he responded.

"I paid you already!"

"Last week's room and meals, yes; but what about this whiskey tab? It's getting expensive."

"There'll be plenty to pay with, believe me, as soon as the river goes down and my things arrive from California."

"It's down. There are boats at the wharf. Is yours late?"

"Here," said the sheriff, giving him money; and to me: "That's from the same unlimited source as your previous wages. As soon as you learn anything..."

"You'll be the first to know," I said.

Chapter Ten

After that, I was left alone.

To tell the truth, I was glad to be alive. The lecture in the Masonic Hall had been a more dangerous risk than anyone imagined.

In an Order whose teachings were veiled in secrecy, the lodges lived in terror of their secret hierarchy. Strangers would sometimes appear who knew the signs that gave them access to the higher rituals. If the rituals were not then performed according to strict correctness, severe reprimands were given, sometimes with ominous threats. Strange new teachings were given which the lodge leaders were required to disseminate according to the degrees of the members, on pain of punishment. In a few months, they might receive a visit from another unknown man outraged at the innovations in the teachings and rites, demanding to know their origin, and condemning the previous visitor. The lodge itself was held accountable for this confusion. Local leaders sometimes went mad.

If I had invoked the authority of a hierophant who may have been purely fictional, I was playing my hand for the highest stakes, simply for the purpose of finding out if anyone knew who was really in charge of the local Mississippi lodges. The answer was the one for which I was least prepared.

If the mysterious stranger were to be believed, no one was any longer in control of the Masonic Order at the highest levels; and the power struggles in the local lodges were the result of a more widespread confusion than I had realized. This meeting with the sheriff confirmed it. He would not have spoken with such blatant confidence otherwise.

But how could it be that the ancient and solemn Masonic Order had fallen into such decay? Long ago I had become disillusioned with Masonic intrigue and leadership. I had more than once wondered if the Illuminati, the wise but unknown guides behind all great destiny, were indeed only legend. Still, I believed in their ideals! My life, like the life of George Fisher before me, had been dedicated to the search for this key to the secret destiny of the New World. Nothing that the Donaldson Brothers had told me was new; only I never believed that they really cared about such things, or were even worthy of such secrets of knowledge. The sheriff was convinced that the treasure consisted of material, not spiritual, gold. But I sincerely believed that it was of a different value altogether; and I truly believed that I had been appointed by Fisher to find out what it was. This was more important to me than the actual possession of it.

Moreover, I was determined to succeed, whatever the cost; and I was convinced that I would.

How could it be that now, when the secret purpose that Masons had carried for centuries was about to be revealed, at the dawn of a new era, that the venerable edifice of the Masonic Order itself was falling into dust? Of course, I reasoned, just because it had always been reported that Knights Templar were the highest Initiates in Masonry, that did not mean that it were in fact so. Perhaps the true Illuminati were not to be found even there; perhaps the Masonic Order itself was nothing but a facade.

Also, I was aware of the ideological split within the Order, and had been warned that this would soon come to a crisis. Fisher and his followers believed fervently that secession of the Southern States was necessary to the cause of revolution, that the Union was no longer worthy to uncover and inherit the secret destiny of the New World.

What if, instead, this were simply further evidence of chaos and dissolution?

It had admittedly been embarrassing to have claimed the supreme authority for my speech, only to have had in the audience one of the Knights Templar of Jerusalem whom I had clearly never known. Nevertheless, it was a most important piece of evidence to have uncovered.

Whatever the current condition of this solemn Order, of which I myself was a high initiate, the need to pursue the secret of this treasure was pressing. Perhaps it was even more urgent than I had realized. There was nothing more I could do, for now, other than to turn my attention to the notes I had collected, and my studies of them.

೮೩

There was plenty to think about.

But shadowing it all was the mystery of Catherine herself, and the nobility of her lineage surrounded by books and manuscripts such as I had never known to exist. That alone was too much for me to understand.

Also there was this problem: that everything she represented so clearly to my heart stood in conflict to the revolutionary activities of Freemasonry and its own claims to an impossible antiquity, with its history of schisms and power struggles ugly as the scandals of the churches. All this thoroughly defeated by a woman of such deep beauty that it suggested that humankind could contain an element of something pure, and, for the most part, forgotten. I began to understand Fisher's perplexity in his marriage to the young heir of the Wells Plantation. It troubled him to the end of his life.

Perhaps I was now prepared to understand the state of mind in which he recorded his notes. Slowly, I dug through them. His collection of letters from Lafitte – where had he plundered these? – and his own correspondence with Knights Templar in the Holy Land, cross-referenced to books and manuscripts in his library, many of which I had already studied.

How were all these things interwoven? What was this thing for which I was searching?

An intuition had begun to seat itself deep in my thoughts. As often as I dismissed it as a thing unconnected to anything other than my own ancient confusion of feeling toward women, it remained, twisting its roots into my heart and growing. I had begun to believe that Lady Wells was the one who would know the direction in which my search should lead, if only I could humble myself before her and unburden my thoughts. I wouldn't even know what I would be supposed to ask her. Perhaps, like the perilous question in the Grail castle, it would be the most obvious, if only I could bring myself to speak it. "Whom does the treasure serve?" Or something to do with the veiled matter of faith, and its loss. This had been her principal concern, and the one from which I had been most happy to free myself. I had no desire to believe that it had anything to

57

do with the mystery of Lafitte and his treasure. But I knew that it did. The importance of his priest proved it; and since it is in the power of a woman to make things of the heart understandable, I sat speechless in the conviction that for myself, as it had been for Fisher, Lady Wells was in possession of the map toward some profound answer. And her beautiful niece was my pure Grail maiden. In her hands, the mystery would be unveiled – though I could not trouble my reason to see how that could be.

I was almost ready to believe that my secretive, slow plunder of her library, carried out through the agency of William and Catherine, had not escaped her eagle-like attention. On the contrary, it would not have amazed me if she controlled the information that came my way.

In this perplexity, I turned to the two most remarkable books that had yet come into my hands.

∞

They had been given to me for the purpose of a comparative study between the two. Fisher had alluded to them in his notes. One he had studied as a boy in Austria and had never seen since. But its memory haunted him, increasing in his fevered mind through his last days, when he thought he was still a youth in the presence of God in the incense of the church, and in the presence of holy elders whose minds were so focused on God that they had no care of this earth and its problems. In the paradise of plainsong, he said, they spoke with the divine Presence. He could not remember that book clearly enough to quote it, but he retained the general nature of its contents. It was a book that revealed the nature of their hymnographic conversations, though he could not understand it until he was near to death, he had said.

These books, Fisher said, survived in their only remaining copies in the archives of the Knights Templar in Jerusalem. And here they were, in my possession.

Gerald had brought them one morning. An old man he'd never seen had come into the store early, before it opened, and left them with instructions to give them to me. Gerald had described him as small and pale, with a meekness such as he'd never seen, but gentle-voiced.

The first was a massive Greek Bible with marginal glosses in Greek and Latin, commentaries from centuries of Church Fathers as extensive as the text itself. The other was Irenaeus of Lyons' *Against the Gnostics*. Its marginal glosses were every bit as impressive. They included a complete text of the ancient Masonic doctrines, through detailed analyses of Irenaeus' condemnations of the various Gnostic teachings.

Again, I read the letter that had been included with them. It was a communication that I had neglected to mention to the sheriff. He would not have been able to appreciate such books anyway. This was the letter:

Unlike Father Christian Rosencreutz, Father Honoratus was not hindered by Arabian mystics from reaching the goal of his pilgrimage in the Holy Land. This was the name of Lafitte's confessor, named after that founder of the ancient Lerins monastery off the coast of southern France.

In the sacred crypt in the middle of the Church of the Resurrection, which was built fourteen centuries ago around the tomb of the Savior, he met a monk from the desert of Mt. Sinai. There he spent three days without food, water, or sleep, listening while the old monk fervently unfolded for him the history of the first millennium: labors of the apostles, lives of martyrs, the population of the desert by miracle-working ascetics, the holy teachings of brilliant and highly-educated hierarchs, and the equally sacred discourses of illiterate monks, taught by God alone. He illustrated a burning vision of the primitive church, forgotten by Western historians after the split between the eastern and western churches, but still living in holy places in the East. The monk proved convincingly how the Western church fell away from this sacred inheritance in the second millennium. Western theology lost the mysteries which Christ himself had handed down through his apostles, replacing it with scholastic arguments influenced by Aristotle. Such theology became estranged from the essential Christ-likeness of earlier Fathers. Western thought began its irreversible march into the wasteland of rationalism, while the Western soul, thirsty for mystical experience, turned eagerly to the inheritance of all those teachings which had come under the Church's ban. These, then, became the doctrines of the secret societies.

Father Honoratus had heard these same arguments many times, and had received them with skepticism. Somehow, touched by the day and place – for this meeting took place in the celebration of Easter – his understanding was transformed by them. He went with the old monk to Mt. Sinai for some months, and returned with a book by a certain John Climacus – whose name meant 'John of the Ladder' – on the divine ascent of man to God. He said he had been granted a glimpse of its goal.

He was the first of our Brotherhood to denounce our Order. He was very patient in explaining his reasons to us. I was among those who opposed him. We plotted his death; but in the night, he fled to sea.

This was many years ago, of course. I was little more than a youth, yet one of the highest initiates in the world – so I was told. You will see for yourself that these books are stamped with the seal of archives of the Knights Templar in Jerusalem. It should be obvious that no one could have smuggled them from that place, unless that Order were in some degree of dissolution.

Nothing will make sense to you until you begin to grasp the contents of these books. Understand these, and I can show you more.

The idea of a complete commentary on the Scriptures had been first conceived and executed by Origen in the third century, according to an introductory note to the first book. Many copies had been written with much labor, but all had been lost. Next to this note was a handwritten entry in the margin, explaining that Origen's Platonism had cost him his reputation at the hands of later Church Fathers, who then replaced his interpretations with their own. Origen's had been destroyed or left to rot, except for the one remaining in the Jerusalem archives of the Templars. Its shelf location was given in red ink.

This commentary had been printed in Venice in the fifteenth century at the insistence of Byzantine exiles. Its only Latin commentaries for the Old Testament were those of Ambrose, Gregory the Great, and Augustine. The Greek commentaries were very full, however. Ephrem the Syrian and Basil the Great on the seven days of creation, Gregory of Nyssa on the life of Moses. Origen's commentaries survived on the wanderings in the wilderness and on the three books of Solomon, culminating with the Song of Songs. For major events in the lives of the patriarchs and prophets and the entry into the promised land, there was given as commentary the insertions of much hymnography by liturgical poets. These I found to be of astonishing poetic quality, rich in complex meters. I found myself wishing I could hear the musical settings.

The New Testament was as large as the old because of the number of commentaries. Most of these were by Chrysostom, 'the golden-tongued'. His depth of understanding and his rhetorical grandeur really took me by surprise. There were others by desert monks, simpler in tone but of astonishing depth. Latin commentaries were confined only to the most ancient of Western Church Fathers. There were substantial portions of Cassian, and sprinklings from the fathers of the Lerins monastery. A few sayings and hymns by Columba and a handful of Irish saints had apparently made their way somehow to the Byzantine scholars, but these were very few.

So it was that I began to read the writings of the Fathers themselves. Like Athenagoras, who began his study of the Scriptures in order to refute them, or like one of the hundred philosophers summoned to debate with Catherine of Alexandria, I began.

When you're in study like that, you are not aware of time.

The sun sits in a corner of the narrow window and fully illumines the table and the open pages on it. The pen quill moving in your hand sits as though dipped in the very light as you bend to record certain thoughts, and your heart and mind are united in a full illumination.

Time is still. You are not aware that in a moment the sun will disappear from your narrow window. You are not aware that it moves; or, if you are, you don't notice that each moment, each fraction and degree of its universal arc is not eternal. Because, you see, it is; but it is we who are never fully present to that moment.

The entire book lies open before you. Right now, you have this page; this thought finds its full focus in you. Every page, one to the next, will unfold its secrets to the climax of the final page; and then you will have the understanding you need to pick up the next book, to appreciate its first page, to let its question sink into your mind so deeply that you must begin again to read, begin again to search more deeply, because you are being led toward...

And the sun is gone.

But the books are still there, and the pages. You will still be there when the stars are going by the window, one by one... fighting sleep to get a grasp on one more chapter... if it slips into a dream, who knows... if it will awaken a search in a new direction... promising refreshment in searching...

The dinner dishes are pushed to a corner of the table, dinner half eaten, long cold. You need that space for both books open, and your notes.

Again, the question: "Would you like to get these dishes?"

Again, the reply: "Would you like to pay me?"

Chapter Eleven

"You've heard? James Thompson is back in town. James Thompson! Causing more trouble than before he left!"

That was a voice I had forgotten! It flooded me with memories and overpowered them all. Like the greatest of rivers tearing at every country it passes through, that voice ripped my carefully studied thoughts in half. I threw my pen against the floor, stared at the ink it splashed across my boots, and went immediately to the door.

I leaned in its shadow and gazed at Denise's father as he talked to a small crowd in the street.

"I thought we'd got rid of him! I thought California would be far enough away that he'd never come back." Already he had them muttering excitedly, with the talent that only a true preacher possesses.

"Why in the world would he ever dream of coming back to a place like Natchez?" I offered.

His audience hushed into an embarrassed silence, but he rose to the occasion, ready to enter into debate with the stranger in the presence of all. His informants had failed to warn him, I guess, how I looked in a beard.

"Have you not heard the rumors?" said John Matthews. "He made Natchez famous for this legendary treasure. Now he's come on a mission to confuse everybody about it. Even the Satanic Masons are beginning to regret his return!"

"Satanic?" I smiled. "Are you sure? They're a men's society, nothing more. Their rituals are harmless and meaningless."

"Sir, you never witnessed their highest initiations."

"Well, no," I answered. "They keep them secret."

"And well worthy of secrecy and shame!"

"You're a preacher," I said. "How would you know?"

"I was liberal-minded when I was younger. That's when I knew James Thompson!"

"Was he always such a scoundrel?" I asked.

Everyone else had made excuses to leave. He didn't even notice we were alone on the street.

"Not at first," he replied, after reflection. "I thought he might become a preacher, like his father; and I thought he might marry my daughter."

My heart was twisting from its sodden roots in pain, but I only studied the ink under my fingernails and said, "What happened to James Thompson?"

"I don't know, really," he said sadly. "He was crazy for my daughter, like she symbolized something more for him than she was. I knew her better than anyone, of course! I knew her – he never really did. I understood her, and she understood him perfectly – but he never even knew himself! I sometimes wondered – you know, a woman can be an exalted mystery to a young who lost his own mother at such an early age."

I had to smile again; it was the only way I could avoid the wild rise of emotions. "That's profound psychology, sir. I think you could be a true pastor of men, with an understanding that deep."

"He was a complex young man," he went on. "I was like a father to him! His own father had too little patience with his wild ideas. He's somewhat of a fanatic. James had once admired him. I tried to reconcile them. I was the only one he could talk to. I listened to him, prayed for him, and said little. I knew what was in his heart."

"There are very few men," I said, "who could display such wisdom as that. I'm sure your influence on him was profound."

"But he was such a bad influence on my daughter!" He retorted angrily.

"Your daughter..." I said, and took a breath. "That's too bad. She married someone else?"

There was no answer. He was lost in his own thought.

"Is it true," I said gently, "that no one knows what happened to her?"

"I know!"

Exploding in a frightened ecstasy of promised knowledge, my heart wrenched free of its moorings and floated free, drenching my limbs with ruptured passions, while I spoke with detached clearness, "What?"

"She went into a convent in New Orleans."

"A convent! The daughter of a preacher?"

"Her mother was of French ancestry. That's why the girl was named Denise, the feminine form of Dionysius, the Areopagite, whom the French believe was the first bishop in Paris."

"A Protestant preacher, married into a Catholic family!"

"She was the one who converted me from the madness of the Masonic doctrines I clung to in my youth. At that time, we were closest to the parents of James, when he and Denise were born..."

"A convent! Why a convent?"

"To heal her heart."

"This James injured her that badly?"

"It was not just that. It was also myself. James injured her, yes – the worst injury, so I thought, when she became pregnant with his child. But it was not the worst. That did not come until the alienation of her proud father, disowning her..."

"With child! My child?"

"Here I was talking with the devil himself," he said, "and didn't realize it!"

"What happened to the child?"

"After twenty years of abandonment, you ask me this?"

"And you, abandoning your own daughter, and don't know what's become of her?"

"Which of us is the worst?" he said with a deep sadness.

"How could you be so heartless?"

"Me? She was in love with you!"

"Denise did not love me!"

"You couldn't tell? What kind of fool are you – or is youth so blind?"

"I will help you find her," I said desperately. "When is the earliest boat to New Orleans?"

He stared at me, unblinking.

"We could leave tonight, by horseback," I wept.

His hand came up toward me. At first, it was in a fist; but it opened, and he took my arm in his shaking fingers. "We don't know where to go. I would have to write letters, and wait for answers from my wife's family – if any would come. I've been alienated from them as well, all this time. When I disowned my daughter, they did not. They kept her in their protection and saw to her needs, becoming principal donors to the convent, as I think I remember. My wife hardly dared talk about it, and soon after, broken by sorrow, she died..."

Quietly crying and bent with years that must only be unutterable, he stood in the dust of the street in such desolate solitude that I brought him in and gave him whiskey. He didn't know what it was. He must have been used to drinking water. He spit it all over the floor, washing out the stains from my pen, and stared at the books on the table.

"Church fathers!" he said incredulously. "You?"

I shrugged. "How many convents can there be in New Orleans? We leave tonight."

He shook his head. "It's a strange, sprawling city, with many hidden alleys and many secrets that will swallow your whole being."

"Like San Francisco!" I laughed.

"Older than San Francisco. Much larger. Holier – and more wicked! It's better to wait for answers. These are the writings of these Church fathers? My wife's family revered these names, though I don't know that they ever heard any record of their actual words. We Protestants, you know, we preach against the veneration of their relics and their doctrines – these are their sermons?"

Through his tears he drank in paragraphs at one gulp, as though his broken mind were suddenly able to grasp things inconceivable. "These are amazing! These are like hymns you would hear in the court of heaven! Can I have another taste of your drink? Just a drop, for the sake of education?"

Chapter Twelve

Catherine, in the disguise that everyone knew by now, came into the tavern in a high state of excitement.

"I found the letters! They do exist, like you thought, and I found them: George Fisher, to the archbishops of Paris and Austria, and the Patriarch of Jerusalem! I found them in one of his Bibles – isn't this what you wanted? You don't seem interested!"

"I'm tired, that's all."

"You've been in study all night?"

"Study?" I said vaguely.

"What's wrong? You look as though you haven't slept."

"How can I sleep, when poetry itself is my pillow, and my thoughts rest on dreams of the world as it was in the beginning, with her?"

"You've been thinking of Denise."

"How did you know her name?"

"You told me!"

"She's the reason I left for California, and she's the reason I returned."

"What happened in California?" she said, dropping the letters on the table and herself into a chair.

"Already I've forgotten that I came to find her, distracted by this search for a meaningless treasure. Can I have forgotten my own heart? Why are you crying?"

"I don't know!" she answered. "I want to hear about Denise, but I don't know why! I want to know her need to be deeply loved by you, helpless as a girl wanting to be kissed and held in a way that men don't understand!"

I gazed at her with quiet, indefinable feeling. "This reminds me of the way my saloon girl would talk."

"How can you make such a comparison?" she said with such angry tears that I was appalled at myself. She raised her arms as though searching for a handkerchief that was not among her present costume. Then she sat erect and drew her long sleeves across her eyes in a fashion that completely disarmed me – as though her tears were the most intimate revelation of her nobility. Composing herself, she said, "She was not as young as I? Your San Francisco girl?"

I dared not answer.

"As young, then," she concluded, "but not as innocent. Tender and passionate?"

"I gave her what she asked, and tipped her well."

Catherine looked away with obvious scorn.

"But it was Denise I loved. The girl did not know that – and she would not have cared."

"She must have been a stunning saloon girl."

"But at one time," I said, "a girl, just like you. Her tears were as real as yours, when she trusted me with her story."

Catherine settled herself to listen.

"She was born to a hard-working pioneer family, but her earliest memories were lit with a simple happiness. Her father died when she was very little, though; after that, life was hard and tragic. A stepfather came into the picture – one who never cared for her. His lack of affection in itself caused damage, it seemed, but it was worse than that. One night, when drunk, he raped her. She was not yet twelve. At first, she forgave him; but when he did it again, she had to run away. Nothing mattered to her anymore. Life in saloons was the only survival.

"When I came into her life, as she told me, it was better for her than it had been. It was never love, but it was a brightness in the gloom for both of us. Access to her soul, though, that was a difficult journey. Many nights, we sat by the window, under the moon in tall California redwoods. I listened to her talk until she wept in my arms like a child, so beautiful and innocent, this saloon girl.

"The first time I heard her story, I, too, wept deeply and bitterly, without knowing why. Later, I realized it was because her story reminded me of my own. I remembered my mother, and the inconsolable retreat of my own feelings for life after she died.

"Often, I wish I still had that girl, with her tears on my shoulder's wound. In those moments I cared about nothing else – except to return here to find out who I am!"

Catherine provided the proper effect by relapsing into tears.

"My God!" I whispered, staring at her. "I forgot to whom I was speaking!"

"Yes," she said, "like the drunken stepfather. It would be good for you, I'm sure, to drain less whiskey on any given night. Come, sir, do you think I did not know this about you already? I read your book!"

I felt my head drop; I watched my hands come up over it like a burial shroud.

"But what I don't understand," she insisted vehemently, "is what happened between you and Denise. And I don't think you do, either; and if you don't know what became of her," she said angrily, "why are you sitting here and doing nothing to find out?"

My hands moved down to my chest, and I groaned.

"What is this wound you mentioned?" she added.

"I'll tell you another time!"

She stood to leave. "I'm to be married in two weeks. Are you coming to the wedding? My aunt knows that I won't be happy unless you come."

I stared at her thoroughly; and she at me through wet eyes. And with that she turned and went out.

ଙ

Late that night, when I was alone in its deepest hours, I went into action. Catherine was right; no longer could I sit musing in despair. I was unredeemable. Again, another night for which there will be no forgiveness, saying what should not be said, silent on what should be spoken. She will never come here again. She will not want me at her wedding! She will never want to look at me again. It was time to do something about it.

And so I went into action, sweeping bottles off their shelves behind the bar and onto the floor.

Chapter Thirteen

The next morning was Sunday, and I celebrated the Lord's Day with my pistol in the wooded pasture out back of the tavern, setting up whiskey bottles on the fence posts and stepping back a half acre to take aim. The repeated sharp crack and echo, with its comparatively silent explosion of glass, this was my sermon, inspired by last night's conversation.

I was sure I'd bring an angry congregation to chastise me for interrupting the Sabbath rest. Some things you can get away with in San Francisco, they would sing, but this is not done in the deep South. By noon, though, I had been joined only by William and Gerald with their six-shooters, standing by my side and taking aim at the targets. We were hitting about eighty percent when Emily came up the dirt road.

I had seen her coming. Her hair uncovered was a torch in the sunlight, and when she stepped into the shade it was like smoke. She stood and watched a moment, knowing I was aware of her presence. She was a handsome woman.

"This is what you teach our scholars?" she said.

"If you want to see them defend their honor, and their women, children, and lands," I answered.

"There's a war coming," William said with enthusiasm.

"What part will you take if it comes to that?" she quizzed me.

I holstered my weapon and turned to her. "One thing I never want to do is to kill a man. If one takes up the gun at all, the intent is to kill. Another thing I don't want to do is to die in a war. Some men know how to die in war, I suppose. These are the two choices of the gun, as I see it – both of them decided already, both of them horrible. The only thing to do is to take up the gun and learn it. Then it can be used without having to think."

Without a thought I turned, drew, and emptied my barrel. Five bottles leapt in fragments into the sunlit air; the sixth remained in its place.

"Damn," I said.

"I've heard too much," said Gerald. "It's going to happen. It's not to defend the slave-owners that I'll fight, but because north of the line they think we're a race of devils to be wiped out. It'll be a full invasion. They'll burn the towns, you watch. Then it's prime Mississippi land for the taking. So I'll fight alongside the slave-owners."

"You really think they'll burn the towns?" said William. "Everything?"

"Would there be any reason not to?" said Gerald.

"Decency!" said William.

"Have you ever seen a war?" I said to William.

"No," he admitted. "Have you?"

"I've seen plenty," I said, "although not that. I've seen enough to know it can get worse than you could imagine. There's never been a creature more monstrous than a man, when he gets in a killing mood. That's why you keep him in jail – so he doesn't

66

infect the whole society. Such laws are abandoned in war. The normal boundaries of behavior are removed. The criminal in every man is let out. One nation breaks out of its borders like a pestilence spilling down over all peoples. We'll see it for ourselves, when we stand in the meeting of two such armies."

"Stop," said Emily. "You're scaring me."

"In the North," I went on, "they say they're concerned for slaves. They say they're victims that should be freed. I don't know. I don't own slaves. Could be there's some truth in it. But it won't turn out that way. It will be the lower-class population on both sides that will be the victims in this war."

"If I didn't have something from my father," said Gerald, taking aim, "I'd have to sell myself into slavery. That's how they've got this economy locked up." He fired, and hit his target. "It's no wonder so many give up the family land and go to Texas or California. Then who gets the land? Nobody matters but the plantation owners."

"You're nowhere unless you can buy slaves," I said to Emily. "Don't try to sell cotton against the slave-owners! Don't try to grow anything, unless it's just for yourself. So who are the slaves? Who will fight this war for the gentlemen officers? We'll get a taste of the slaves' existence, believe me!

"Think about it," I went on. "Except for the color of skin, they're not different from us. When a new one comes from Africa, they have to keep him locked up like an animal for a while. Why? He's not an animal; but what he was in the jungles, I don't know that I would ever understand it. This is how we teach him to be like ourselves: lock him up like an animal. Then, it's remarkable how quickly he adapts. He gets a little language, and suddenly he has a personality, a deep, honest person, sincere – I mean, if he's treated well. Too many are not. Some are unspeakably mistreated. They will break out one night under a full moon, and we'll die horrible deaths. The old people have feared it for years, and they still talk about it in whispers. But we'll be saved from that fate by this war."

"Well," said Emily, "I've brought you some things."

"What things?"

"Food, new trousers and a jacket, boots, fresh bedclothes."

"What's wrong with my jacket and trousers?"

"Nothing," she said tactfully. "When you change into the suit I've brought, I'll send a servant to launder the ones you have on. I want to see you in the clothes I've brought, and I need to take measurements for the tailor."

"What's this about?"

"The wedding."

"You don't really think she will allow my presence in her Episcopal Church!"

"A scandal, I know, but it will have to be borne."

"What stance shall I assume while you measure me?"

Blushing in her unique manner, with the color racing in delightful rivulets, she said, "It will take some time. Besides, I want to talk to you privately."

"You'll tell him your idea about our tutorial, mother?" chatted William.

"What chance in hell is there for that?" I said.

"I know they visit you, James, whatever her aunt may think of it. And their schooling is in disarray since the academy was abandoned."

"Oh, I don't know, mother," said William, taking aim. "I think it's going splendidly!" He missed his shot.

"What does Lady Wells think of this?" I said.

"She disclaims any control over your destiny or your influence on her niece."

"But the money will come from her?"

"There's no need for suspicion!" she laughed. "I will never be able to measure your imagination, but I need to stretch my tapes on your arms and waist."

"Shall we go to the saloon then?" I said.

"That's not what I had in mind, I suppose."

"Then where would you suggest? Your place?"

She appeared lost for a moment.

"To the creek?" I said.

She laughed and took my arm. "I suppose the inn, as we'll call it, will have to do!"

⋑

The tavern reeked of whiskey still drying on the floors. "How awful!" she said.

"It's not always this bad," I assured her. "I quit drinking last night."

"Well, there's benefit to that!" she said.

In my tiny room at the top of the stairs, she sat me in the strait-backed chair that was the only furniture other than the bed, and wrapped my wrists in her cloth measuring tape. "For the cuffs," she laughed.

"Then I must confess, as long as I'm your prisoner, that I understand what you want," I said. "You want some degree of control over my influence on your son and his fiancée."

"That experiment failed," she said firmly. "We won't try it again." She was silent a moment. "But there is something else. I want to speak to you about Catherine."

"That's what this is about!" I said, wiping the tapes off like cobwebs.

"She has become confused and withdrawn since you've left the plantation," said Emily.

"Is that so?"

"Don't pretend the innocence of an idiot! Do you understand what this means?"

"It doesn't matter. She won't come seeking my counsel again, after last night."

"What happened last night?" she said with alarm.

"I told you already; I gave up whiskey. You've seen the evidence."

"It looks like that decision was sudden and violent," Emily observed.

"She wasn't here when it happened."

"She was here last night?"

"Don't worry; I was careful to act like a gentleman," I said, wishing that I had indeed been more of one.

Emily was not deceived. "I think you might have been drunk!" she said.

"I think that might possibly be a fact, but it will never happen again."

"What are your feelings for this child?" she demanded, coloring deeply as soon as she said it.

"I fail to understand," I answered with irritation, "what my feelings have to do with anything! Have you spoken with her this morning?"

"She was elated."

"This morning?"

"She made her mind known, as to the cut of your new coat!"

Now that put things in a different light.

"Everyone loves the girl," I replied with a sigh of relief. "Should I be different? An extraordinary beauty, with intelligence; and her thoughts would have been my own, if I had kept my soul in its pure state."

"Even if you hadn't fallen off the edge of the continent, your thoughts would not have dared the heights of purity which are natural to her!"

"Alright then," I said. "What else?"

"William hasn't taken notice of the change in her. He's confident of her love, but he doesn't yet have the understanding of women."

"Yes," I said. "But she worships me."

"I'm not implying that you, on the other hand, do have such an understanding! But until you came, she did not know that there was something lacking in the very foundation of her life – something so essential that, without it, she feels like less of a person. I think I know what that is."

"I'll admit everything," I interrupted. "I adore her in a manner that I've never experienced and do not understand. I'm ready to accomplish any deed of proof to convince her. If I had to leave to obtain for her the mythical Natchez treasure, I would, if I could understand what is the wealth I seek in her. I would die in repentance, if I knew how to, in that search! A search, not for material wealth – she doesn't need that – but for a sense of worth, some secret of meaning in her, that can be found nowhere else. I've begun to understand that what she is - and no one else knows it – that she – " but here words failed me, and I could not continue except in silence.

"It's very simple, if you understand women," said Emily. I stared at her with my whole attention.

"Think about it for a moment!" She spoke with an unusual earnestness. "Think from her point of view, if that is at all possible for you. Can't you understand why she is desperate to have an older man in her life?"

"She desires wisdom and experience; she wants to have someone to open new worlds to her inexhaustible curiosity, of course."

"What you represent to her is the figure of a father," she said.

I must have stared like a lunatic. Something in my expression changed hers.

"If only you knew how to be a father," she said desperately, "and how one feels for his child! If only you could appreciate how deeply your own father feels for you! Can you at least try to imagine what it would be like for a girl to grow up without a father's love?"

I tried. First, I remembered my saloon girl; but then I thought of Denise, betrayed by her father in her hour of deepest need. That's what she needed, I reflected angrily. She didn't need me; she needed him. But that wasn't true, either. What she needed was a better understanding from both of us.

"I'm afraid I cannot pretend to be something of which I have had no good experience. The only fathers I can think of are worth nothing, except to be rescued out of their hands!"

Emily sighed: "How could I have hoped you would understand? It's too bad; this is what limited your success as a teacher."

"What would you say, then," I smiled, "if I kidnapped her on the morning of her wedding and went back west? I would accept no ransom!"

Visibly upset, she gathered her tape measures into a wad in her basket and turned to go. "I should say," she said with a trembling voice, "that it would be a great mistake even to think of such things!"

"You're right," I admitted in an entirely different voice. "Sometimes I say things for effect – things that are far from my heart. I don't know why. It's the weakness of an actor, I suppose."

She was staring back with genuine astonishment. I myself was surprised I said it. It was a revelation to me that Catherine had not been entirely disgusted with my behavior; and I guess I did not want Emily to be angry, either.

Ω

At that moment we heard the innkeeper's footsteps downstairs. Swiftly they crossed the floor and fell off. This was followed by the heavy thumping of his weight ascending the stairs two at a time. The door was taken off its hinges as he came through. Emily stepped back toward the wall, but he didn't seem to notice her.

"What have you done?" he said to me, out of breath.

"Add a little liquor to my bill," I answered. "There won't be any more."

"You broke half my bottles of whiskey! Have you any idea how much that costs?"

I shrugged. "Send the bill to the sheriff."

"I will!" Like a madman he ran through the room, throwing my possessions onto the bed. He picked up the chair – with me in it – and hurled it against the wall. He gathered up the blanket by the corners and threw it with my things out the door and over the railing to the floor below, into the sticky pools of evaporating whiskey. I went next, rolling down the stairs while Emily screamed.

"Don't ever come back in here!" he yelled.

I picked up my hat and tipped it to Emily, who stood at the railing staring down with wide eyes. "As soon as I find a new address, I'll send a note for the new clothes," I said.

Chapter Fourteen

One more time, I read George Fisher's letters to the archbishops by the light of the dying campfire. Again, I searched their veiled replies concerning some pearl of immeasurable price which the French priest had brought from the Savior's tomb. I pieced together the fragments of their narratives until I understood the sequence of the violent interruptions of his return journey from the Holy Land. First, he was intercepted by the fleeing Napoleon, who had been searching the seas for his priest, and then by Lafitte, who was hunting down Napoleon for the bounty on his head, as well as for his vast plunder. Napoleon was turned over to the European authorities, who, in return, allowed Lafitte to escape with Napoleon's treasuries, and with the priest.

The campfire collapsed into embers, leaving me with only my thoughts. I lay in the tent with the flaps open, staring up at a fresh new moon and thinking of her.

If only she could be here with me! When had this desire to possess her stolen upon me? When had it overwhelmed every other thought? Perhaps it had been there from the first. Perhaps I saw it answered in her first glance, unless I misinterpreted that look of recognition in her eyes.

But what would I do, really, with a young woman like that? This was not a girl like those I had in California; nor did I want them anymore. Innocent and trusting, I delighted in this girl. What did I want, other than to simply look at her, to listen to her speech and the nature of her questions?

To hold her... how? To watch her go to sleep like a child! In no hurry to see her become more of a woman, I desired to guard her growth from any unholy influence – my own included. Why? She, for her part, demanded these things of me. She was not unaware of my faults; her very presence commanded them to stand far off and no longer trouble me...

If this was what I wanted, to give her what was best of myself, what was this but a desire to raise up, to support all goodness – to truly educate? And how had such a desire come with so much power? Was this the mysterious yearning of ancient wisdom, the transmutation of desires into the rare substance of the alchemist's quicksilver, so that I could pour my purified soul into her and stand back to watch what the new mixture would become in her eyes?

And if this was what I truly desired, why would I want anything more than the life I had in the Wells mansion? Was there any way to go back to that existence, or why was I glad to be free of it? These were things I could not understand.

But she would not be fulfilled in the freedom I had found in a place like this. It was good to be alone here, to think. The bear and the panther would leave me alone, and no one else would dare come. But a woman wouldn't like it; unless...

If she were here with me – because it was clear that she wanted me in her life – but I had to face the fact that she was not going to leave her youthful suitor behind. William. A fine young man, Emily's son – raised better than I had been raised. Catherine certain-

71

ly was able to attract the most intelligent and gifted of youths. He also would be able to raise sons and daughters better than I would. But not in a place like this. You could not have children here. The panther would not leave a child alone, but would stalk it for prey. This place would have to be tamed and homesteaded, no longer a deserted wilderness. They would have their house over there, beyond the fields, which would all be farmed, and my cabin could be here... would that be so bad? It would be a good home – but not for a woman like her. This was a place too removed from the world.

The silent protection of a place like this, where singing waters crept shyly from under rocks at the base of a ridge of sharp boulders, not steep but densely wooded, was meant for only a few. Someone had been here before. My campfire was not the first. Maybe a robber, maybe the last remnant of the Natchez tribe of Indians, or maybe the runaway slave whose serious, gaunt-faced ghost breathed on me in dreams. Or maybe this was the hidden site to which the treasure had been removed. I had already dug under an oak. Wisterias in its branches, which had exploded blooms into late spring and still fell in shrapnel of fragrance in the first dawn, were thick as dangling ropes.

The delicate moon approached her gateway in the low hills, where the chaste goddess of the wild-lands must be racing near the goal of her hunt. Respecting her distance from the tumult of my own heart, I shared somewhat in her ecstasy, simply in the understanding that absolutely no one knew where I was.

Here, where there was no possibility of seeing Catherine, I touched her in my solitude more intimately than if she stood before me. I could love her from afar, until my heart was purified of the sickness of its desires – until her image blended with the vague face of my young dead mother, Denise's yellowed photograph, and the piercing afterglow of the moon's brilliantly slanted horn running away between the trees. Its light fell across my pillow, and I fell asleep weeping almost convulsively, drawing my clutching hands close into my chest. Catherine looked invisibly upon me, first with the sorrow of Denise, and then with the unremembered eyes of my mother – a strange and consoling resemblance.

When the sun woke me, it occurred to me that another benevolent hardship of my new existence was that there was no liquor, and no way to get it. I learned to love the taste of water fresh from the rocks. I lived by hunting, and by gathering abundant greens. In the fall there would be pecans.

The thought even stole upon me that I had begun living the ascetic life of the hermits – except without prayer. I began to wonder what would be the taste of its solace. The thought stayed with me all day. As afternoon deepened, I was overcome with an intense sorrow that I had never known this invisible God to whom the saints prayed so fervently that He lived within them. In my sadness over His absence I could almost feel Him touch me, stirring perhaps a deeper heart in me than I had known to exist.

α

I was not aware in these thoughts of the way in which I was summoning her. But in the day that she appeared, I was not as surprised as I pretended.

"How did you find me here?"

"I don't know!" she said. "What are you doing?"

I was crossing a meadow when I got caught – but by the one I had hoped might catch me. Her expression was terrified. It must have been the Indian bow I had found and re-strung, or maybe it was the way I carried it. The arrows, and my hands, too, did have a bit of blood on them.

"I'm poaching," I said, setting down my bag and bending to open it. "Would you like to see the prize?"

"No thank you!" Then, in a softer voice, "What is it?"

"A splendid hare!"

"You killed it?"

"Yes, I did! And I'm going to skin it, and cook it; and then, my dear, I'm going to eat it! It will be the best thing I've had..."

Her eyes, which had been huge, softened into pools in the distance. "In how long?" she said.

"In a couple of days."

"Are you terribly hungry?"

"My dear, it's not as bad as that!" I could see in her whole face that she was as glad to see me as I was to be looking at her beauty. "I've told you about the life of the gold-rush pioneers in the mountains. I've lived this life enough! It's not bad at all. Actually, it's rather delightful when you get used to it."

"Where are you staying?"

"On your property!"

"Where?"

"Now if I tell you, you won't send the sheriff after me, will you? I doubt even he would want to go there." I pointed to the hills beyond the fields. "Have you ever been up in there?"

"No," she said.

"No one goes there except the panthers. It took them some days to get used to me. They are very territorial, you know; but they respect a man's determination. Up there is a beautiful grotto in the rocks, the headwaters of your creek. No one's been there since the Indians, unless it were some renegade like me."

"How did you find it?"

"By walking."

"I miss you terribly," she said.

"Yes, well. I've missed your bright presence more than I can say."

"I wish..."

"Yes?"

"I mean, I wish I could tell you how much I feel."

"To love me as much as if I had been your own father?" There, I had said it now; but I was a little surprised by the bitterness in the words.

"You don't know what it's like to grow up without a father!" she said, close to tears.

"I'm sorry. That was insensitive of me. George Fisher was already gone when you were born, wasn't he?"

"He was not my father."

"That's right," I said. "I never thought about it. He was your uncle. Your father, then – who was he? What was he like?"

"I don't know. I don't remember anything except the feelings of a child, too big to know what they are, too deep for words. What are you thinking?"

"I was remembering the feelings of a child. I was remembering my own father, a long time ago. And I was imagining you as a small child."

"I always thought you knew everything," she said; "but these are things you could not have understood."

"I will be leaving soon," I said.

"Where are you going?"

"I don't know yet. Some journey beyond the world, to find the answers that will destroy every mistake I've made."

"You seem like a different creature," she said. "Your eyes are almost transparent!"

"Like a firebird," I suggested a little too proudly, "rising from the ashes of a fire I've never been able to endure!"

∞

The next time I saw her, it was very different. I assume she had been looking for me again. There would have been no other reason for her to have come that far back from the river. It was even farther from the house than the place of our first encounter. But she hardly noticed me. She sat crying, holding a newborn colt in her arms. The mother lay dead nearby. It had strayed beyond its pastures to give birth, had broken through the fences and kept going.

"My voice is a stranger's voice," she said gently to the colt, "and yet I understand what you feel, abandoned at birth. It is not a crime to be born, is it?"

I attempted to comfort her, but walked away with unnamed feelings of grief.

Chapter Fifteen

Blackness upon blackness, deeper than the tomb, and eternal silence – but I was not afraid. I knew where I was. I stood in the tomb of Christ, and it was the eve of Easter. Invisible faces crowded in on all sides, silent, waiting, warming the doors of hell with their breath. The patriarchs and prophets in one corner, behind our first forefathers Adam and Eve, were awake and present. The darkness was never so visible.

Light leapt in the confined altar of the tomb, spreading out as the thirsty candles leaned forward to drink from the triple candle-stand in the bishop's trembling hand, while the song of God's rising ripped through the curtains of the universe. One candle was in my own hand, bright as the unknown power in my breast. I stared into the brilliant altar built into the tomb of rock, and saw indescribable gold and treasure glowing in intense light which increased into the explosion of sunrise.

The scene changed then, as they do in dreams, and now I stood by his tomb in the dawn of the first Easter. There was a young man standing next to me whose clothes were too bright to see. Voices in the dream were approaching, and the hand of light reached out –

I awoke in disoriented wonder. The linen walls of the tent, burning with sunrise, surrounded my waking consciousness on all sides, as voices continued their approach. I ran out and stood half-naked in front of Catherine, William, Denise's father, and Gerald.

I knew immediately, without having to be told, that Lady Wells had discovered my presence and had sent them. I could not have believed that Catherine would have betrayed me by telling them where to find me. Before I could speak, though, Denise's father, beside himself with excitement, said quickly, "I have received a reply from my letters. We know where to find Denise."

He had not yet finished speaking when Catherine said, "The treasure is a real thing! It's not a legend at all – and we know where to find it!"

She had not spoken the last word when Gerald broke in: "You will have to leave here immediately. Lady Wells is very upset."

As soon as he said it, William finished, "We are going with you!"

"Where are we going?" I said, bewildered.

"To find the treasure!" said William. "She gave us the map. She's had it all along!"

"Do you mind," I said, looking down at myself, "if I get some clothes on before we go?"

☙

We sat on the mossy rock under which the quiet waters originated, in the shade of three immense, bent oaks, while each took his turn to explain.

"It's a good thing we didn't go to New Orleans, " said Denise's father. "She's not there. She wasn't happy in the old convent, so they sent her to another one near her mother's childhood home on Lake Charles, on the other side of the Louisiana swamps.

My wife's family had an estate near a convent on a bayou there, which had a hospital, grounds known for lush beauty, and a reputation for healings. After Denise was placed there, the family gave part of the estate over and became the principal donors for the convent's expenses.

"There were initially some reservations about sending her there, according to the letters I received. Liturgical practices there had come under the censure of the bishop in New Orleans. The nuns had adopted the dress and chant of the Greeks while corresponding with a spiritual father in Jerusalem. The bishop was lenient enough to grant them the practice of the Eastern Rite Catholics, but he kept an uneasy eye on them. They had become convinced of Greek theology; their manner of speech was different, and it was said that they had learned to think. While this troubled the bishop, the Freemasons from New Orleans were so fascinated that they had started making frequent visits. None of this concerned the family, however, and they saw how glad Denise was to be there."

"I've never seen my aunt so upset as when she heard this," said Catherine. "Her actions have never been irrational that I can remember. She paid off your bills and summoned us together – even Gerald, who was terrified of her presence – gave us money to finance the journey, and then gave us the map. But I want to go, too!"

"You can't go," said William.

"Why?" she challenged. "You're going, and even the wedding is postponed, while I stay home and wait?"

"It's too dangerous," he said.

"All that means is that my aunt doesn't want me to go. I can make my own decisions as well as you! Your mother doesn't want you going, either. She says that the Donaldson Brothers will follow you and try to kill you. I don't care. I want to go."

"I've never seen a woman so agitated as Lady Wells," said William, returning to the subject. "First she screamed in a high voice, listing the principles that one lives by, only to find out that one had been doing everything wrong. She could never have known what Providence was placing in her way, she said. Then she started throwing books in the fire. 'Your historical writers are all wrong!' she screamed. 'A man thinks he can write history, as though an original interpretation, a new view, something revisionist, makes it so! Like all revolutionaries, they belong to the fire of hell!' she said. 'History has been written. Men don't know how to read it!' None of us had any idea what she was talking about. Then she gave us the money and the map."

"And she gave me a sealed letter for the nuns," said Gerald. "She said she had called me because I was the only one she could trust with it. Can you believe that? I didn't think she even knew my name!"

"The strangest thing of all," said William, "is the way the map corresponds to the description of the grounds and environs of the convent. I've studied them together, the map and the letters from Denise's family. The bayou on which the convent is located is called Contraband Bayou, because of the local legends that Lafitte's treasure is buried there."

"Let me see the map!" I said. It was Catherine who untied the ribbon and handed me the scroll.

"Yes, I've seen this," I said. "And I have studied it carefully, knowing that I need the keys to its meaning."

"This is the same map that was brought into my store many times, after your writings about Lafitte became famous," said Gerald. "I never took it seriously."

"It shows a remote country staked out in three portions, each more inaccessible than the one before," I said, pointing. "Within their boundaries, you see, it shows the coordinates of six treasure-caches, each more valuable than the one before. I had begun to assume that it was not a map at all, but some allegorical diagram of Gnostic mysteries.

"And I still think it might be that. First, the sunken wreck; then the Spanish doubloons from the high seas scattered under the water; next, Napoleon's wealth, buried in a sweet-gum grove where the trunks are carved with Roman numerals. Then, strange tomb-like vaults containing jewels or, perhaps, half-living corpses, perhaps Lafitte's own tomb; then a vault containing a prophecy; and finally, something mysterious of inestimable value. But," I said, looking up at William, "if you were right, these are the boundaries of the three successive lakes along a river emptying into the ocean, while the inmost lake leads into the entrance of Contraband Bayou near the convent. That," I continued, abandoning myself to admiration, "is an excellent study. It appears that you have become a finer student of literature than I could have imagined."

William, with a perfectly transparent self-confidence, simply returned my stare.

"Give me the sealed letter," I said with authority.

"No," said Gerald. "She warned me that you would try to open it. If I deliver it still sealed to the nuns, she assured me they would help you locate your treasure more quickly."

"Well," I said, "I guess we'll have to go, then. Whatever we find will just have to be worth the search!"

"It will be," said Catherine. "My nurse Sarah has told me more about the treasure. Her grandfather saw it while it was still in Natchez. I've asked her about it every night, until finally she told me everything. He knew where it was the whole time that it was in the warehouse, but never dared to go near it. When he saw Lafitte's ship at the docks, though, he knew it was going to be taken away. He slipped into the warehouse at midnight. The pirate who was watching it on fear of his life was in a drunken sleep in which he stammered the curse of Lafitte.

"When he pried open the lid, he was so amazed at its richness that he dared not disturb it. It was a kind of wealth that was indescribable, such treasure as has never been seen in this world! The thoughts he had while gazing on it, according to what Sarah could remember, would never be understood.

"After that night, he and his wife valued their poverty and their simple lives, even when their family fortune was lost in the flood that took their warehouses, and Sarah was given into the service of Lady Wells. They left the dangers and cares of riches to the insane world and were content. But once, before he died, he visited Lafitte and made a vow under the oak where it was buried. But I don't care about that. I want to go with you so that I can help you find Denise."

"You can't go, and you know it," said William.

77

Catherine stamped, stared hard at him, and walked away beyond the shade into the light.

"What kind of coincidence is this," I said, "that where she is, there also is this treasure?"

"And that's another thing," said Denise's father. "Denise always knew something about the legend of Contraband Bayou, having heard it from her mother's earliest memories."

"Denise is your treasure," said Catherine from her distance of light. Turning, she held out her hands, which were filled with sunlight in their prophetic gestures. "I've known that all along."

"You told Lady Wells about myself and Denise?" I said to her father.

"I told her everything, of course," he answered, "when my messenger returned to deliver the letters to her house."

"To her house? Why there?" I said.

"That I don't know," he admitted. "He was such a little old man, I worried that his frailty would prevent him from completing the journey. He convincingly assured me, however, that he would bring the reply if it were God's will."

Gerald held a hand at the level of five feet. "This tall?"

Denise's father nodded.

"A thin beard, sad eyes?" said Gerald. "He's the one who brought me the books for you."

"Is it possible," said William, "that this convent may know the secret of Lafitte's priest?"

Chapter Sixteen

Two roads, branching from the end of the Natchez Trace, are passable to the southwest corner of Louisiana, where the dark waters of Contraband Bayou drink from the clear waters of Lake Charles. One road is by land; the other is by water.

The land route is the wagon road into Texas, across the Louisiana hills to the Red River. There it joins the Old Spanish Trail, El Camino Real, coming up from New Iberia alongside Bayou Teche, crossing the Vermilion River into the oak forests of the central Louisiana prairie to the first pine-covered hills at Ville Platte. There it continues on to the Red River and Natchitoches, the site of the first French fort, the oldest settlement in the Louisiana Purchase. From there, the Old Spanish Trail continues west to San Antonio and south to Mexico, then north again at last to its final frontier in California. All roads branch from this one, like spokes from a wheel. The one to Lake Charles turns south at Alexandria, alongside the creeks and streams that cut through thick forests to feed the Calcasieu River. This was the affordable route. It was not, however, an easy journey; but the passage of so many settlers since George Fisher had opened the way for them, had at least made it not so dangerous as it had been. Enough small towns with French names had been scattered along that way so that one could find an inn before nightfall if he traveled with determination and haste.

The other route, pleasant, swift, and far more costly – the one Lady Wells had chosen for us – went by steamboat to New Orleans, transferring there to a small ocean-going schooner into the Gulf of Mexico. The ship would then turn up the broad Calcasieu River, through the widening of its lakes to the deep freshwater port of Lake Charles.

This port, the steamboat captain told us, had been built by a handful of Creole plantation owners for the export of their acres of rice and sugar. Denise's father answered that his wife's family had been one of these, with the large white house at the bayou's mouth, the plantation of Charles Sallier, for whom Lake Charles was named. The captain replied that the port had since been expanded to serve a booming business in the other rich resources of the area – sulphur mines at the head of the lake, salt domes in the marshes to the south, and inexhaustible timber for the building of New Orleans. Also, he said, a cooperative of Cajun farmers ran a prosperous store in that port, with corn, poultry, unlimited wildfowl and seafood, furs, seasonal greens, homespun cloths and hand-carved watercraft. Gerald then began a friendly debate with him, comparing the prosperity of his own store at the end of the Natchez Trace.

While the brilliant shores of the Mississippi glided past the windows of the steamboat, we sat in the luxurious parlor smoking cigars with the captain. He had come down from the pilot-house, eager to entertain anyone connected with the legendary matron of the Wells Plantation. "Imagine a southern aristocrat demanding to be addressed by an English title! No one has dared that since the Revolution – and she gets away with it!"

Then he informed us of a third route to southwestern Louisiana. A small boat could make its way across the swamps by the extensive maze of interlocking bayous. It was not a journey for any man. A trusted guide was necessary, since once inside the swamp a passenger was at his mercy. Cajuns don't think and act like other people, he said. Their sense of time, determined by almost indiscernible currents of silent waterways long disconnected from any tide, was impossible to understand. Their minds, too, were calmly disconnected from reason, as a result of living whole years in such deep shade of ancient forests that they never saw the path of the sun. Their only direct light was an occasional haunting of the moon or some glaring, unknown planet appearing in rifts of ground-fog, and they lived entirely by superstition. It was not wise to go into the swamps. It was a country in which a man could be lost forever.

The New Orleans transfer occurred too quickly to satisfy the curiosity in myself or William, but both Gerald and Denise's father seemed glad to leave that city in the wake of a ship. "I've not been here since before you were born," I said to William; "and it's grown since that time." Denise's father answered William's constant questions with only a troubled silence. The river traffic alone was more than I had seen even in that which poured into the San Francisco Bay during the Gold Rush.

By the time the Mississippi's tremendous currents surrendered themselves to the Gulf, we were almost out of sight of land. There was only a low profile of almost non-existent shoreline – a strip of beach protecting vast coastal marshes from the vaster sea. Here it was the height of summer, the long days of heat in June. The air was an oppressive steam. The schooner was not large enough to house quarters under the deck, but we slept there anyway, in the cargo hold from midmorning to sunset, and gathered on deck under the stars.

White stars, and a paler white moon when it appeared, drowsy, a half-closed eye of light until it climbed into cooler regions of the heavens and seemed to widen a little – these stirred me on the first ocean night to challenge William to a duel of love.

"Describe, if you can, your feelings for Catherine. Include your finest words for the presence of her beauty, her intelligence, and her subtlest qualities. I will counter you with my own memories of love – mere recollections from a scrapbook."

William laughed. "I'm a student of literature, and you're a poet. What chance do I have? And this is your other advantage: I am assured of the love I left behind, while you are burning so brightly for the one you seek that you've drawn us all into the adventure! How can I compete with that?"

At the suggestion of lost love, I took fire and began to speak, remembering Denise. Her father went pale as a ghost of the moon, William trembled, Gerald stared with wonder. Everyone agreed that I won the contest of words; indeed, I burned with such inspiration that I thought I might not survive. The schooner's first mate proposed that we drink to the health of the muse who drenched me in sweat. They did, as convinced of poetry under the stars at sea as if they sat in the presence of long-journeying Odysseus, hearing his stories in hexameters as powerful and regular as sea-waves.

Did it matter, after all, if in my defeated heart I knew it was William who had won the girl? Perhaps I had something more. Perhaps the stars that were guiding these winds were bringing me to the end of a quest of twenty years. Would she still be waiting there? Would so many years of suffering and loss be enough for her?

The second night was too calm. The sea lay like a mirror of stars. William began to recite The Ancient Mariner from memory, inspiring fear. The schooner's first mate related tales from the Sargasso Sea and Caribbean Islands. Then Denise's father, in an icy voice that seemed to come out of the mirror of water, said, "These stories reveal only a glimpse of the horror that creeps through those regions."

The silence that followed this statement was terrifying. The ship sat motionless, its sails limp; even the stars seemed frozen in place. No one dared a question.

He began to speak, slowly, in another man's voice, as though in a trance. In New Orleans he had seen religious customs from the Caribbean mixed with those from Africa and the remnant of the Aztecs from the American jungles, chanted in a bizarre midnight mass in the crypt of a church. It was the revels of Mardi Gras on the eve of Lent. The streets overhead were filled with masked revelers; but here the true meaning of carnival, "feast of flesh", was unveiled.

He was presented to the master of ceremonies as one of the most prominent young initiates in the entire Masonic Order. The master grinned at him, then proceeded to the sacrifice, where the victim was an island girl.

"Yes, that's right," he said coldly. "Don't think it is only the blood of chickens that they sprinkle on their doors when the demon of death, screaming in the night, comes to drink! I saw the inconceivable murder in the presence of silent spectators who dared not stop the crime. I heard her desperate cries to heaven; I saw them rise like steam from her spilled blood as it ran to fill the stone chalice. Then her little slaughtered body was carried, accompanied by torches and screams, to the tombs."

Beyond the doors of a vault, he said, the procession entered a network of tunnels. Many of these were entered through the mouths of grinning masks painted brightly on the side walls. He thought at first that he had entered the demonic counterpart of the catacombs, until he recalled that there were no such layers of rock as those supporting the ancient city of Rome. Under New Orleans there was hardly enough dry ground to dig a basement for any building. Such tunnels there were an impossibility. He had never since discovered any evidence for their existence. Even the church was later found to have no underground crypt! Its graveyard was filled with above-ground vaults, since any coffin interred in ground would have simply floated to the surface. And yet he had gone into that cavern of unthinkable horrors and had witnessed conversation with apparitions to which the Creoles offered reverence. At the site of interment, he had witnessed a second sacrifice, similar to that described in Poe's Cask of Amontillado, which likewise occurred at Carnival.

"You are not going to tell me, I hope, that this was Masonic ritual?" I said.

"These were not Masons," he answered. "We had been brought, however, to see a living example of the kinds of ancient traditions from which our most secret rites had been borrowed. Only a few were allowed to witness that night."

"I had no idea you were that esteemed by the hierarchy, Mr. Matthews," I said.

He came out of his trance with a laugh. "Call me John, for heaven's sake! You're old enough now, you know, to call me by my first name!"

I was as astonished by this sudden warmth of response as I had been by his tale, and I stared at him like I had never seen him.

"I had been chosen, without my knowledge," he went on, "to be the one who would challenge the hierophant himself."

"You?"

"I've known secrets more terrible than Lafitte's," he said, focusing his eye on me with strange, exotic humor. "I saw the hierophant that night, seated on his throne!"

"You're inventing this story, aren't you?" I responded. I did not know what to think.

He chuckled, took out his pipe, and ignited the bowl with too much intensity. "I was involved in a struggle for power. Fortunately, they became disappointed with my progress. I was still bitter with disappointment when I met my wife. She saved me from that life, by her prayers, and by her quiet example."

"How can this be?" I challenged. "Do you know how rarely it is, when someone is that involved with Masonic secrets, that the Order will allow him to leave? I myself, for twenty years, have been afraid to attempt it!"

"It was a miracle that they let me live, having seen the things I've seen."

We watched the smoke from his pipe curl upwards toward the brilliant constellation of the dragon, wrapping the north star in his coils.

"When I told this tale to my wife – she is the only one who has heard it, before tonight – a spiritual war began. It would be difficult to describe. The house was filled with unseen powers that one could feel. Even my unspoken thoughts were being examined by powerful, disapproving demons. It became terrifying to think. My wife withdrew into prayer. After some months, she made a journey to visit the nuns she had grown up among. It was the same journey we are making now. She returned full of peace, which settled on me also. After that, the Masons no longer troubled me or took any interest in me at all, even when I became the most outspoken preacher against them in the South. My wife attributed it to the intervention of a holy man."

As he said this, there was a whisper of a breeze, not so much that would be noticed except on so still a night, and only by those who might be awake and watching. The sails responded with a loud clap as they spread themselves. With a shudder, the ship began to glide.

"When I was young, I discussed with you my interest in Masonic doctrines," I reminded him; "and you never mentioned any of this!"

"By those years, I was master of myself," he answered.

"I would say so!"

"There were many things I could have said to you that you would not have listened to."

"I suppose not!"

"But with my own daughter, you see, I failed completely. In effect, I sacrificed her – to my principles. The one for whom I would have been willing to give everything..."

He was close to tears, so I changed the subject: "These nuns, then, have that much influence with the Masons?"

"What that influence is, I don't know. In New Orleans, I learned that many of the Masons were frequent visitors to that convent. Some of these renounced the Order, speaking of a certain transformation of mind as though it were miraculous."

"I think I understand," I said, remembering my own studies of the old Biblical commentaries. "Was George Fisher one of these?"

"George Fisher was seeking his answers in a different direction."

"What was the answer he was seeking?"

"You know as well as I."

"I was not aware," I said, "that you knew anything of the working of George Fisher's mind!"

"There are many things we never discussed," he answered.

Dawn came up in increasing breezes, spreading their purple sails of glory across the vast skies and pushing us gently toward our destination. The sun, in a white band of humidity on the horizon, immediately spread its heat across the sea. As it climbed the tropical degrees of its furnace, we sought shelter in the ship's bowels. Only the first mate remained on watch, tending sails and rudder. The others collapsed in the shade of such fevered dreams that, had the first mate slumbered at the rudder and fallen overboard, none would have known until, the following night, they observed the shifted latitude of the constellations.

For myself, though, there was no rest. Suspicion, sleeping since I was sent on this impossible errand – indeed, since the first dawn I learned of the treasure with its murders and intrigue – suspicion had been roused from its hell to rage in my dissociated recollections. Long ago, in the first night of my initiation, I lost faith in the Masonic teachings; and long before that I lost faith in the Christian doctrines which they claimed to correct and replace. Not even then had I thought Masonic perversity could be as extreme as had been described tonight.

I rose, shifting the bulk of sacks under my shoulder, and lay down again. Snores and groans drifted through the dark hold where men lay on the various levels of shelving planks for cargo, connected by ladders, while bilge water sloshed below.

It was evident that Denise's father – John Matthews, as he would now have me address him with new familiarity – knew more about both the Masonic Order and the nature of this voyage than I had realized. Why he had chosen to reveal to Lady Wells the nature of my relationship with his daughter, and why it had upset her, would be matters for my wildest conjectures. Most likely, she desired to rid her niece of my influence completely. But there would have been deeper levels to that conversation, many things, as he had just admitted, that he had never told me. Yet not even to him had Lady Wells entrusted her letter. Its contents were unknown to any of us.

Gerald snored gently in the level just above me. I stood and stared directly into his sleeping face. The letter was in his shirt. I turned to locate the forms of John Matthews and William sleeping in other levels, the one in moans, the other in soundless innocence.

Like Hamlet on the ship to England, I stared at my Rosencrantz and Guildenstern. Having tried his friends, and having found them false, he exchanged his destiny of death with theirs. I reached toward Gerald's breast –

What should I suspect in Gerald, my oldest, most honest friend? Too sensible to trust himself to my adventures, here he was on his way with me to find the treasure, at the summons of Lady Wells, carrying secret instructions concerning my fate!

William, my rival in love, I trusted completely. Yet why should I? He was more thoroughly under the control of his fiancée's aunt than he could realize. As for John Matthews, I would not be surprised to find that he secretly hated me still, and would sacrifice my welfare for news of his daughter. Indeed, his role in these events had become inscrutable.

Yet they were all three better men than I, worthy of many virtues I had never claimed to earn by any struggle – and I was sure they knew it. With utmost gentleness they were taking me to some distant and secure prison where the world would be safe from my marauding passions: a locked room in a convent; a room no larger than a treasure-chest; a locker in the sea to keep companionship with Lafitte's ghost, and to hear the endless recital of his murderous adventures until he wept with remorse!

My hand trembled over Gerald.

What was the poison in the ear that killed the sleeping king of Denmark? The poison in the ear, symbolic of the demon's whispers? Suspicion was the poison that destroyed that kingdom! The list of victims: Polonius, the innocent Ophelia, his friends Rosencrantz and Guildenstern, the queen, Laertes, and then the prince himself were sent into that gulf. The usurper, Hamlet's uncle, killed only himself; all the rest were murdered by a brooding suspicion that Hamlet himself brought to its terrible fruition. Something rotten in the state of Denmark. This had been my own brilliant analysis of the masterpiece; and yet I had no control over my own heart. I was not the hero Hamlet was – suspicion had ten times more power over me, and for less reason was I infected.

A column of light penetrated the darkness, fell on my hand, and momentarily blinded me.

"All hands on deck!" yelled the first mate, who had thrown open the hatch. Gerald woke with a jump, seeing my hand an inch from his shirt, and every tortured thought in my face.

"She warned me you would try to do this," he whispered.

We had entered the outpouring current of a river at high tide, at the peak of its battle against the waves. Our sails held onto a cross-breeze, just enough, with the right maneuver, to make possible our headway against that flood. All hands were needed as we tacked severely, leaning from shore to shore. Skillfully the little craft cross-threaded the warp and woof of the river's current and the rolling tide, making slow but steady progress. And so we reached the calm of the first lake. Now we relaxed under an easy sail and gazed at the wide skirts of the Louisiana marshlands.

The first is the largest of the lakes, large as an inland sea, where waves run smooth. Its shores were endless reeds or low banks of shell. Portions of sky were clouded by populations of waterfowl.

The second lake was small enough that all shores could be seen at once. It was adorned with clay bluffs, on which grew sweet-gums and moss-covered oaks. These bluffs were well settled with fishermen's houses and crude docks. Lower shores were broken by the influx of bayous. There were sandy islands, too, the refuge of egrets, and, probably in times past, of pirates.

I can't say that my mind was entirely calmed by these peaceful lakes. Having seen the greatest of rivers in flood, so much greater than any imaginable power, I understood too well the geography of these varied shores. This was no more than a segment of the

Mississippi's mighty legacy. One who has known whole towns clawed down from their heights by that cataclysmic torrent, can look at a map and see into the layers of its history. The intricate waterways of the southern half of Louisiana, including the borders of Texas and Mississippi, will show how the courses of the major rivers were decided in years of flood. There the muscular current reversed upon itself, strong as the will of a wrathful god overcoming itself, suddenly as a forking thunderbolt gulping forests in its ravenous mouth. Where there had been a quiet swamp – itself the forgotten memory of an ancient river course – in one afternoon this was changed into a channel as deep as the earth, drinking continental waters in one moment. And here, too, this wide lake under a quiet sky had its brief centuries when it was the thirsty gaping maw of the serpent Mississippi. Who knows? Perhaps even the Gulf of Mexico was once a continent in its path!

My mind, then, as long as the undercurrent of its fears threatened, was not completely calmed by the increasing beauty of these lakes. Their dark shores developed suggestions of my suspicion. Perhaps I was simply in need of sleep, that I saw pirates in the shadows, that I expected ambush from my own ship-mates. My mind was not calmed by the unique loveliness of these lakes; but it was charmed.

This was especially so as we came into the third lake, the smallest, but with the clearest waters. In places, springs could be seen welling from its depths by the pure action of its sweet waves.

A busy port dominated the lake bank, just where it turned into the river with waters dark, deep and swift. On the main dock were the store and post office, with schooners at the wharves. This was flanked by other low docks with warehouses, a ship-building establishment, and a sawmill with steam-operated saws. From that point on, the lake shores were deep with grass and flowering bushes. Forests of oak came down on many sides. Plantations stood under some of the oaks; their lawns seemed to have been arranged by nature. Beyond one row of these, at the side of a small bayou that siphoned off the lake, was an unstockaded military fort. The stars and stripes flew proudly, though its log buildings appeared to be little more than a historical relic. The only wall was an earthen bank – such as the Indians built in forgotten eras – at the intersection of the lake and bayou.

To the north, the river began again, coming in again at a bend of a mile or more of brilliant white sands. On the far west side of the lake, beyond the entering flow, enormous piles of logs surrounded a string of more sawmills.

The first mate thanked us pleasantly for our help and company, and asked if we needed directions to our next destination.

"The bayou to the convent is not difficult to find, is it?" I replied.

"That's where you're going! I should have known. There's saints in that place."

"What do you mean by that?" I asked.

"Oh, you'll see for yourself. Listen! This is Lafitte's territory. That's Dead Man's Lake there – that embankment at the entrance to Contraband Bayou – where he sank the government ship. Used to be, no one dared pass that place. Lafitte's curse. The nuns changed that. They went into the river of hell itself, and redeemed it. A holiness is there like no one's seen in a thousand years."

We searched the port for a small boat to rent. When it was discovered we were going to the convent, we were given one rent-free, already loaded with supplies for the nuns. It was a pirogue: "a pea-shell of a boat," said the store-keeper; "it can float on a heavy dew." It was equipped with a pole for shallow water, and paddles for deeper water.

"This is something I've never done!" I said, taking the pole and standing at the rear.

"Then you'd better let me do it," said Gerald.

"It can't be that hard," I said, and promptly went overboard. The water here was less than two feet deep. The mud was at least as deep as that, and smelled strongly of decomposing vegetation. The other men laughed merrily as they helped me back into the freely tilting craft.

"You'll look presentable at the convent," said William.

"A smelly beggar covered in dried mud," added John Matthews.

Gerald took up the pole and, as so often before, proved his proficiency in silence.

"You've done this?" said Mr. Matthews.

"Not since I was a boy; and then only with flat-bottomed boats, " Gerald replied. "The balance in this is more delicate. The feeling is about the same, though, as a sturdy flat-bottom tossed in the treacherous Mississippi. There, if you fall out, you won't come back up again."

We passed the white house where Denise's mother had grown up. If I fell into a silence that no man would dare disturb, her father's was an intolerable weight. He shook; his face was paler than its white-washed walls in the strong sunlight. We passed the embankment where Lafitte guarded the treasure hidden up the bayou from the American gunboat. Then we turned into the bayou itself, where Denise disappeared into the convent twenty years ago.

Chapter Seventeen

Summer on the bayou!

The drifting boat, unmoored from the world, as it seems, so effortlessly moving – while the lazy sky wanders through fragrant steam toward distant white towers of thunderstorm gliding in from the Gulf. Now the dark water slides through reflected balconies of shadow: steepled cypresses, anchored by immense gnarled knees growing outward like the hidden base of an iceberg, where the water lays so still you would not know it could be water; great live oaks with magnificent muscled arms; magnolias that drop their blooms in full sail to disturb the dreaming mirror with a wave. Whatever other current exists is in no hurry to tear itself from the perpetual noon of high summer.

Now the forested swamp mysteriously gave way to shores with lawns, fenced in with tall, subtropical blooms. In them were houses, formed of gray cypress planks laid horizontally. Shaded porches along their fronts ended in rough stairs that led to sleeping lofts. Corn gleamed in the sunlight of back pastures. Livestock slept under the trees; chickens muttered in the heat; children sat barefoot on the steps or were gathered on the docks that terminated the path from every door. Clearly, the water was the main road through this village. Everyone stared at the strangers and spoke an unintelligible French punctuated with laughter. It seemed to be a scene more idyllic than Longfellow's Acadia, from which the ancestors of this people had been exiled. More than any exiles since paradise, their homes gave an idea of the first home. Gliding upstream, we made our way as though in a dream toward the source of memories and hope.

Around a bend, we came within sight of the grounds of paradise, planted in a convent.

The expansive lawns under immense oaks, beyond a fence of finely wrought iron, with gardens perfectly placed among them, made no other suggestion to the mind; but the suggestion was immediate and powerful. The centerpiece of these lovely grounds was the large white hospital with its tall Victorian windows and its exquisite Creole galleries and stairs surmounted by a slender bell-tower. It seemed a place where one could be healed of every bitterness since the first doubt.

In my step onto the dock, the weakness of my knees was due not only to the transition from a floating surface to one which did not yield beneath the thrust of feet. My heart must have been in the surface of my eyes as I stared. Beside me, the tread of Denise's father sounded heavily. He stepped onto the dock with the eyes of a man climbing the executioner's platform.

A few steps led to a landing with a gate under a bell. Gerald reached for its rope and pulled. A young and lively nun ran from the well.

"Au nom de Dieu, messieurs, que voulez-vous?"

She was robed in black instead of white. Her large eyes under thick black eyebrows held in them a mystery, a hint of something in the blue of the sky I had never seen when

87

I looked into it myself. I don't know what it was in her that could have reminded me of Denise; but I was overwhelmed with the thought that this could have been my daughter.

Denise's father attempted an answer in French, which she had such difficulty in understanding that she switched to flawless Greek. To this I gave an equally incomprehensible reply so that she frowned and ran off to the gatehouse. With one quick glance finding it empty, she swiftly curtsied in our direction and vanished into the gardens.

"They speak formal continental French," explained Denise's father. "I assume they have no difficulty communicating with the local Cajun dialect, which means my accent must be wretched."

She returned with two stately figures in black, tall and graceful, in whose faces were no signs of age. They carried simple knotted ropes in place of rosary beads, but the practice appeared identical: the fingers moved habitually from one knot to the next, while the repetition of a prayer could be seen in the concentration of the countenance.

"The mercy of our Lord Jesus Christ be with you," was all that one would say.

Her eyes were calm and dark as a bayou; but hidden light danced through them as though they had robbed paradise of its secrets. Perhaps she no longer remembered what color her hair had been when she first concealed it in tonsure. Perhaps she no longer gave thought to what color her hair had been; now, the eyebrows were silver.

Gerald handed her the letter through the gate. There was nothing I could do to prevent it. She opened it so that the two could read it at one moment. They stood in the sunlight, reading my sentence at the gate to eternity. They looked at each other for a moment, then at me. I remembered that I was wearing a mask of river mud.

"Yes, I thought so," said one to the other, who then looked directly into my soul and said, "Our abbess told us to expect you. Come with us."

I went through that gate and stepped into another world. Thrilling bird-songs and chirped responses became audible in their distances of sunlight and shade. Even the riot of questions that had assaulted me outside the gate mysteriously vanished. How the abbess could have foreseen our coming, what swifter messenger had preceded our letter – which she herself had not yet seen – what the letter might say about the curse which Denise's father and I carried in our hearts, or whatever else might already be known concerning our purposes and secrets: all this no longer mattered in the incomprehensibly sweet fragrance of those paths. The two nuns walked before us in unpretentious dignity of soul, immaculate and on fire with unworldliness, wholly involved in a flame of virtue which was visible in their movements. I had not known that it was possible for a human creature to carry such an angelic presence; but the ground itself knew it, and yielded the soul of beauty in rows of azaleas and roses, walls of camellia blossoming in every hue of flame, chambers of shading magnolias, and well-placed pecans with high branches from which the sunlight was hung.

A different kind of mind was revealed in me as I followed them. Questions, shaken off like dust on the dock, were replaced by invisible vistas of knowledge following one another in swift succession, indiscernibly, but in fullness. I could not have said what it was that I then knew, except that the meaning of every struggle was somehow made clear.

In the shadow of the hospital, another gate led into a second lawn of oaks. In a distant corner of this field was a small chapel. Beyond it, black granite and white marble tombs burned in the sun or sat pensively under the oaks. By this gate we waited while a much older nun, bent and tiny, crossed the lawn from the chapel. We waited in silence until she spoke a blessing in Greek, at which the two bowed. As she neared I could see more than a half century of wisdom in her face. Her bright eyes, serious but more alive than any I had seen, peered deeply into my mind.

One of the two nuns who had brought us remained, the other being dismissed. A conversation then took place in quick formal French in gentle accents, which was translated by our silver-browed guide.

"Please accept our poor hospitality, but understand that men are not allowed beyond this gate except in very special circumstances of need. The nuns have their cells in the forest beyond the chapel.

"The small chapel was built to house the reliquary of our spiritual father. We know that his relics will be found. Meanwhile, he protects us and grants his blessing, as he stands in the presence of Christ. Let me tell you about our spiritual father. I am the only one who is old enough to remember him.

"I knew him in Poitiers, in France. I was a girl then. He often came to our convent to serve liturgy and to hear confessions. He was very popular throughout the country. He was friends with the archbishop of Paris. He knew the king himself before he was beheaded. Artists, philosophers, poets, politicians enjoyed his conversation; and we, too adored him. Freemasons asked his advice. He was a cautious supporter of the revolution before it got out of hand. But when the cathedral of Tours was blown up by the revolutionaries, and with it the precious relics of ancient saints, he abandoned his native land in sorrow and made his pilgrimage to the Holy Land.

"At that time we, too, fled to New Orleans; but we remained in correspondence with him, as did all the changing leaders of France. Napoleon came to power and argued with him. During this time, we became aware of the change in him. Eagerly we read his descriptions of the life in St. Catherine's Monastery on Mount Sinai, and in others near Jerusalem. He began to provide us with the ancient writings of the desert. As he became a holy man, we also miraculously became his obedient daughters. It was a difficulty, however, when he made his break with Rome in order to become an Orthodox monk. He did not immediately advise us to do the same. We must think of the welfare of the faithful whom we serve in this region.

"You know the story, of course, from this point: Napoleon's fall from power, his flight from Europe, his seeking for our Father Honoratus on the high seas. Fr. Honoratus himself had foreseen the time of return from the East according to prescience. You know of their meeting and their interception by the pirate.

"When Lafitte brought him here, we came also. Three of us came first. We built the first huts in the forest, then a crude chapel. The pirate allowed us to come to our father for instruction, as long as we met under his eye. Lafitte also listened, with a brooding pensiveness. But that is a hard way to follow the illumination of the Gospels, and the murderer in the habit of his passion could not abide it. As you know, our holy father confronted the pirate's conscience, demanding he give his riches in repentance to the poor, and seek his treasure in heaven. No longer able to hear this good advice, Lafitte attempted to stop his mouth in death.

"It was at this time that our convent became permanently established in our father's memory. You can see how these grounds have flourished since then. It is because of his blessed presence that the hospital heals so many.

"Lafitte tried to erase the crime from his heart by concealing the body where no one could find it. Despite our tears, he would not tell us where he buried him. But Father Honoratus had already forewarned us of all this. He prophesied that his gravesite would be found by one who had lost a great treasure, and had come to find it."

Stunned by this old woman's reading of my heart, I confided desperately, "That is not what we came here to find!"

"Are you James, the author?" she said.

"How do you know my name?"

"We know nothing of the news or writings of this world, and we know that these things are not linked to our true identity. Your name is taken from that of one of the three of our Lord's most intimate friends during his life in our flesh. Here is what you must do. You have the map that Lafitte left. You will have to follow the trail of his buried treasures, which is the trail of his repentance, known only to God and to our Father Honoratus. The search will be splendid and terrifying. It is not for us to make this search, though we greatly anticipate its conclusion. Great riches will be found with our father's relics in his sea-chest from Jerusalem, marked with Greek letters and a Greek cross."

I sat stunned by this description. It was similar to many I had read of the treasure that at one time had rested in Natchez.

My thoughts were interrupted by another man's voice: "Our first concern is for one of your nuns, who was sent here many years ago. I am her father…"

Fiercely the old woman answered: "One who has taken the monastic tonsure is dead to the world! She has no father but Christ, no husband, no brother but Him who writes her new name with His own blood in His book. The old name is forgotten!"

"Yes," he answered quickly, "and that is right. He is the only father and husband worthy of such a one. Nevertheless, for the sake of a father's heart of sorrow, since no one comes into the world without a father except for the first man and woman, and except for their Redeemer Himself, tell me. Her mother was born on this same shore. To this same shore, her father abandoned her, and has no right to see her again; but tell me. Is she well?"

"Yes. She is our abbess. Last night, she told us you were coming. I cannot take you to her."

"She has become a solitary of that degree?" her father asked softly; and I added:

"How could she have known of our coming?"

"Our Father Honoratus himself baptized her when she was born," the ancient nun answered. "Though she never met him again in this life, she became his greatest disciple through prayer. By the time she died, she had become a prophetess, like him."

"You spoke of her just now as though she were alive!" gasped her father.

"She is alive. She is often seen walking the grounds at night, or in the church during long services. Last night, she told me to expect you. She told me that she has prayed for you both unceasingly; and I can tell you that her prayers are powerful. Now you are here. She gave me her blessing to allow you into this gate to visit her tomb. Come with me."

Only he and I were allowed in to see the inscription on her stone.

I was first to break the crucifying silence: "What happened to the child?"

"It was given to adoption in New Orleans," was the answer.

"And now," I said, "the child won't be easy to find, I suppose?"

"A healthy girl, of sound mind, we were told. The circumstances of her upbringing could be known, if you wish, from the New Orleans Sisters of Charity. It will be no difficulty to send for information."

We were left alone at her graveside, in the shade of two oaks, into which abundant wisteria had climbed from the fences, spilling mild perfume. The inscription on the stone was simple:

GERONDISA
DIONYSIA
Kyrie eleison

Her father leaned on the earth and wept, inconsolably – wept, to tell the truth, for both of us. What I felt, perhaps, no man had ever felt. I felt as though I were beginning to understand. From within the little chapel, where the nuns had gathered for the hour of Vespers, drifted thrilling plainsongs in Greek inter-modal melodies with chanted responses from psalms. As my quickening mind began to pick words and then whole phrases out of the Greek, I remembered that these were the songs that had been inserted as commentaries in the Greek New Testament – songs whose melodic settings I had not really hoped to hear. They gave sublime power to the meanings of the words; and I took fire from within the embrace that Denise had so painfully prepared for me.

Chapter Eighteen

"First, you will find the sunken wreck in the marshes south of the lake," the old nun had told us as we were sent from the main gate. "Then you will know where to go next. Ask anyone where the ruined ship lies. Everyone knows the spot."

"As you see, gentlemen," I said to William, Gerald, and John Matthews, "the old nun's predictions, uncanny as they seem, are not always accurate."

We sat at a table under the side porch of the store, where the heat was barely endurable. A ship with folded sails sweated at the docks, but the sailors were dreaming down in its hold. Even the birds did not stir from their shade. The usually noisy pelicans glided in silence under the docks, and the multitude of waterfowl were gathered under trees along the bank, since the fish themselves had escaped to cooler waters in the depths of the lake. The store, however, was never still as long as the sun was up. Fishermen and farmers, wives and their children, made up for the general calm by the incessant clashing of their unexpected use of the French language and their unique accents of laughter; though even these did not now stray from the store's dark interior.

We knew that we were the topic of their conversations. The storekeeper, an American, one of the locals who because of his business with sailors spoke both English and French, was happy to keep his customers informed of our quest. Upon the hour, throughout the day, he had visited our table to give reports of information and lore, and to make his sales of breakfast, lemonade, and beer as the hours progressed.

"Someone will know where it is," Jim Hodges the storekeeper had assured us that morning. "Lafitte was a pillar of our community. It was his constant trading at this spot that allowed my father to become prosperous enough to open this store. It may have been smuggled goods and slaves that Lafitte brought us in exchange for fresh meats and vegetables, but without them, survival would have been difficult for many in those days. You see how the sawmills and shipyards surround my store?" he had pointed out. "This is the kind of shipbuilding and commerce that followed Lafitte's career!"

"Everyone knows about the sunken wreck," Gerald said now. "It's just that no one knows exactly where it is. Every man's grand-folks had an idea about the spot; but none of these agree."

"You can see how the legends of a locality will define its people," said William. "Their legends carry more weight than the facts. The names given to places, on the other hand, survive until the history of their origin is almost forgotten. That's why ancient poets gave so much attention to the lore of place names. But no one seems to know of any marsh, bluff or river-bed named for the sunken wreck. The wreck itself is nameless in its own legends. It only makes the old nun's pronouncements more enigmatic."

"Everything she said was startling," I admitted. "She said that the priest's gravesite would be found 'by one who had lost a great treasure, and had come to find it,' then without reservation indicating that I was that person! I felt she was implying there was something that was in my own hands at one time, the value of which was unrecognized.

She appeared convinced that this was what was meant by a prophecy the old priest had made before I was born! Then there is her description of his coffin, which matches every description I've ever seen of the treasure-chest in George Fisher's papers, in the Freemasonic lore and even in the descriptions of those who claimed to see it while it was in Natchez! Taken altogether, these things make no sense."

"I've never been in a convent," said William. "Are they all like that?"

"No," said Denise's father. "That one is very unusual. I doubt there is another like it west of Russia and the Balkans."

Gerald looked around. "But this store reminds me of my own. Everyone who comes in likes to talk about this fabulous treasure, but no one knows any reliable source of information. Everyone knows there is treasure on Lafitte's ship, but no one can agree on where it sank. In my store, everyone who came in had a map and wanted directions, but none of the maps were quite the same."

"Yes, I've been thinking about that," said William. "I've wondered if a study of the variations in the maps might yield anything interesting; and I've found that it does."

"Will this put me to sleep?" I yawned. The heat had made me drowsy.

William grinned. "We've looked at many maps now. Gerald provided some and drew some from recollections of others he had seen. You have described two that were in George Fisher's possession, which I have sketched, and Mr. Matthews has brought the one from the Wells Plantation. I've studied all these, and have found there are four basic variants; and that of these four variants, two are of one kind and two of another.

"Variants One and Two, as I call them, seem to be literal maps of treasure sites, while Variants Three and Four appear to be more symbolic. The common feature of all the maps is that they show always six sites distributed over three regions. Here, I'll show you."

He opened his satchel, removing his journal. From this he unfolded a series of sketches showing composites of the maps. These took up the whole surface of the table.

"That's quite a bit of work!" I whispered.

"Here are the general sketches of the first two variants," said William, "with their six treasure sites. In Variant One, the order of the first three sites is always the same: first, the sunken wreck; next, a group of strange, tomb-like vaults; and third, a grove of marked trees. The treasure concealed at these sites varies among the maps of Variant One. In the sunken wreck is always a treasure-chest, but what is in it differs: Spanish doubloons, or jewels, or some kind of writings – specifically the ship's log or Lafitte's journal, to which great importance is attached. If the old nun's prescience could be trusted, I suspect that such papers might provide a key to the maps.

"The tomb-like vaults contain Spanish gold in every version. Its value is inflated, in some versions, to include the greater portion of the entire wealth of the New World.

"The third site, that of the marked trees, differs in the kind of grove that is to be found. Often, it is an oak grove; but sometimes it contains sweet-gums instead. The number of trees is consistent: six, marked with Roman numerals. Under the sixth tree is to be found the trunk which contains Napoleon's wealth.

"It is this consistency of the first three sites that encourages me to classify them together. This consistency breaks down for the last three sites, which contain vaults with more mysterious contents, such as a prophecy or something else of inestimable value.

"Variant Two, as you see, lists the same treasure in different sites and in a different order. The consistent feature of Variant Two is that the last site listed is always somewhere along Contraband Bayou – it is the treasure for which the bayou is named.

"Now it is remarkable, don't you agree, that in all these variations there is such consistency as I have noticed in these two classifications? One is inclined to think that it is not accidental, and to wonder what this might mean. The puzzle is not less interesting when Variants Three and Four are studied.

"In the maps of Variant Three, each site is listed merely as a clue leading to the next site. In these, the monetary value of each treasure is not its actual value. Each is symbolic. The unveiling of its meaning leads both to the location and the understanding of the next site. It seems that an interpretation is needed to understand these maps, and one is led to believe that this would be provided by cross-reference to some other document. My belief is that this might be found in Lafitte's journal, if that could be located. James would have more to say about this, since it is the study he has involved himself in for many years."

With my most silent astonishment I stared at William, who answered with a trusting smile.

"Where did you learn this kind of disciplined research?" I demanded.

"From you," he answered.

"I pointing out no more than a few fundamentals," I said.

"But I was listening; and when I studied your novel again, I could see how you applied those principles. So I went into the plantation library, and started practicing."

"Variant Four is similar," William went on, "but with this difference: the treasures are listed in ascending values. Each is more precious than the one before. In these maps, it really appears that there is only one treasure, all the rest being no more than symbolic pointers.

"I have not seen a single map that does not fall clearly into one of these four classes.

"How do we account for these astonishing circumstances? Was there one original map from which the others were copied, perhaps by memory, and were the variations due to scribal errors by men who were far from scholarly? Or were variants perpetrated from the beginning for the purpose of keeping the treasure concealed? The existence of a map in the first place means that the treasure was intended to be re-located, but by whom? Was it for Lafitte's own purposes, or did he intend this inheritance to come into the possession of someone else?"

"You should go to the university," I observed.

"Lady Wells thinks so, too," he answered. "She is applying to the University of Virginia for me."

"Of course! The best one in the South," I said.

"Stories linking Lafitte's activities to those of a secret society, in the light of these observations," William added, "become more intriguing, don't you think?"

"Not as intriguing as what we have already encountered," was John Matthew's strange response.

Ever since we had come from his daughter's grave, he had been silent and withdrawn. I noticed, though, that he was listening to William's dissertation.

"What are you thinking?" I said to him.

"I'm thinking about what the old nun revealed to me last night," he answered.

"Yesterday afternoon," I corrected him. He was disoriented with grief, and perhaps still in shock.

"No," he said. "You were all asleep in the guestrooms when she sent for me. It was past midnight. Questions were swarming in my mind, deeper questions than I had ever known. As though she knew it, she sent one of the nuns to find me. The hospital was asleep, but the nuns were singing vigil in the chapel. I was led to her room.

"'I know of the depth of your involvement with the Masons,' was the first thing she said to me.

"I replied that neither I nor her mother had ever discussed that chapter of my life with Denise.

"She told me that there were two things that Gerondisa, as she called her, prayed for unceasingly to the end of her life. First, she prayed for two men whose misguided actions guided her into the monastic paradise. Second, she prayed for the relics of the priest to be found. By the time of her death she was certain that the answers to these two prayers had been joined into one.

"'Will you tell me,' I asked her, 'what it was that the Masons from New Orleans were interested in, when they visited you here?'

"'The truth,' was her only answer.

"'But were they looking for something in particular on these grounds or in your possession?' I persisted.

"'They wanted to engage us in theological debates,' she answered, 'based on what they knew of Lafitte's arguments with our Father Honoratus. We were not very patient with them. After a certain number of visits we would no longer allow them into our gates unless they submitted to Holy Baptism. As it turned out, that was what they desired. Cleansed and illumined, they were free men.'

"This was the last thing I expected to hear; but as she was saying it, I had a vision. It seemed I were standing inside the chapel where the other nuns were singing. I saw the stone sarcophagus within the altar. It was closed, and I knew that it was empty, but the presence of sanctity that came from it was so strong that I could think of nothing else. In the moment that the vision was gone, I realized that I had seen it by looking into the old nun's eyes. The sanctity I had seen was in her. While her face remained as serious as it had been, there was a smile of intense beauty in her eyes. She then gave me a blessing for the journey we are about to undertake.

"I told her I did not want to leave the side of my daughter's grave.

"She only responded by warning me of certain things."

"What things?" I said.

But Denise's father fell back into that brooding silence. In that mood, he seemed incapable of an answer.

Hodges, the storekeeper, came out to our table with a Negro who was carrying the biggest watermelon I had ever seen.

"This won a first prize ribbon!" he laughed. "Don't eat too much of it at one sitting!"

"This heat does not inspire hunger," I replied; and Gerald added, "How much does it cost for a slice?"

"No, no," laughed Hodges at the Negro, who looked back at him and laughed heartily. "This one's on us!"

As soon as my knife bit into the rind, its juices squirted a powerful scent of rum.

"How do you get liquor into a fruit still on the vine?" I asked while my thirsting teeth and greedy tongue were already lost in the barbed taste of that fresh bait.

"We won't reveal all our secrets in one afternoon!" he said. "But this man can show you what you came to find. He belongs to my business partner, Jacob Ryan."

"George Ryan's the name," said the Negro.

"He knows more of the history of these parts than anyone," said Hodges. "The Indians, all the first settlers, the Cajuns – he's known them all!" he said over his shoulder as he hurried back to his store.

"That's right," said George Ryan. "And we's all refugees in this port, not jus' my folks from Africa. Them pioneers, and Cajuns from their Canada. Even the Injun tribes here was pushed west from they's homes in K'tucky and Tennessee, and the Mississippi too.

"I knows 'em all, and how's they su'vived, how's they built here.

"I built this store m'self, and the dock it sits on. I built that sawmill right next door there, and from the logs it spits out on the shore, my boys and me built half the town yonder. I ain't built no ships – ain't no ship carpenter – but I built the raft we used to float the courthouse here from up river, when we moved the county town from Marion to here on Charley's Lake. A small boat I can slap t'gether s'good as any cajun's. I'se be going out in the morning to check the master's crab-pots, and I can show you where that old shipwreck was.

"Ain't nothing there now, but my grandma knew where it was f' sure. She called it the ghost ship. She was mighty afraid of Lafitte. He was the one that brought her in a boat o' slaves from Africa.

"I was born on the old homestead on Rose Bluff, six miles downriver, where the Pujo place is now. That's right near where that ship went down. Used to see a rotting mast leaning out of the water, with a piece a' crow's nest. You's wouldn' notice if it wasn't pointed out – seemed like any other dead cypress with 's roots rotting away. Grandma 'membered a piece of the rear end with the cabin, all in weeds. They was a hole right at water level, where them giant water rats went in and out. She was awful scared by that. Even if there's nothing left, I still shudder to go near the place! Mr. Hodges, he already talked to the ol' man, says I got to take you there; and I do whatever he says."

Chapter Nineteen

Out of a fog as thick as a mass of wet cobwebs – so coldly did its droplets cling to one's face – leaned one dead cypress trunk. Its height was interrupted by a single broken limb, from which hung torn rags of Spanish moss. Neither sky nor water could be separated out of the gray dawn. Neighboring cypresses, barely discernable beyond, disappeared in curtains of formlessness; but there was no shore here. The lake ended in swamps that stretched for miles.

"It wasn' the place to bring ships – too shallow," said the Negro.

"You're sure this is the place?" I said.

"I told you there was nothing," he replied.

"Like everywhere else," I said.

"The mast was over there," he said.

"That tree could be its ghost," I suggested, as though we were gazing at a framed oil canvas, painted by one of the Romantic symbolists.

"My crab pots will bring up a piece o' gold from time to time. Grandma 'membered somebody bringin' up a piece a' lifeboat – or maybe was a coffin – nobody was sure what it was."

"I've heard lore of a sunken chest," I suggested.

"Tha' was found. Good cypress wood, like that tree there, covered in lead. Never rots. Perfect condition. 'Ol man Prien fished that up. He's strange in the head. Everybody knows his stories! Says he was Lafitte's cabin-boy. Nobody believed it, until he went and pulled up that chest, right where he said it was!"

"What was in it?" said Denise's father.

"Tha's 'nother thing! It was just what he said it would be! Books. Ship's log. That's what he says, anyway. Not many 'round here read, 'cept some of the masters, and them nuns."

"Is he still alive?"

"He's not too far from here, on a bayou off the lake. You go ask – everybody knows about him!"

A crowd of shadows, emerging in the vague distance of limitless mists, began to take the ghostly shape of cypresses. They drew some suggestion of a shore to the undefined horizon of waters.

As we floated in the middle of that undistinguished gray, the changing shape of fog molded itself for a moment into the form of men in a distant boat. Their unrecognizable faces were all turned toward us.

As soon as the apparition revealed itself, it was gone.

"Did you see that?" said William with alarm.

"Hush!" whispered Gerald. "Be still!"

We heard nothing except for the absolute silence of fog.

"Not a sound," said Gerald after some minutes. "Not an oar, not even a wavelet slap-

97

ping the underside of another boat. Did we all see the same illusion?"

"Tha's a sign," said George Ryan in a low voice.

"What?" I asked.

"Ghost of Lafitte." he replied. "Whether guiding you or opposin', I wouldn' wanna know!"

"Perhaps we should ask ourselves," said Mr. Matthews, "what we are risking, and why?"

"I thought we had come this far because you wanted to," I answered. I was beginning to fear that such traveling companion, who had been one of the few men I had trusted in my youth, was a complex personality of volatile emotions. Besides that, my skin was still crawling in fear from what the Negro had said.

"But tell me," said John Matthews, "why should we care anymore about Lafitte's treasure! What is it worth? Until the nuns mentioned it again, you had forgotten it. It is Denise's child, not treasure, that I would be searching for! What about you?"

At this point, I would have thrown him overboard if others had not been there to witness it.

"You wrote the letter, did you not?" Gerald replied for me. "To the New Orleans convent?"

"Yes; the nun assured its delivery."

"Then why should we not act according to her request in this search, while we wait for a reply?" Gerald answered sensibly. "Why is there even a question? It would not be wise to disappoint both her and Lady Wells!"

"The question," said Mr. Matthews, peering off into the fog, "is what are we risking. Do we even know?"

"What did she warn you of?" I insisted.

"I can't tell you," he said stubbornly.

The silence became tense, until George Ryan broke it with a booming laugh: "Lafitte's ghost can wander the swamps and frighten all the fish he wants to! It doesn't matter. Everyone knows that what he really wants is to return to the convent, beg forgiveness, and be at peace!"

This, which was meant to put us at ease, only caused deeper silence and terror.

Chapter Twenty

At the south end of Lake Charles, where its clear waters enter the vigorous deep-water turn commanded by the shipyards, the Calcasieu River regains its identity. Throughout its lower lakes the river current remains well established in deep channels; but the freely dreaming waters often wander from this main course. Expanding in shallow lakes as wide as the regions of sky they reflect, they explore every detail of the coastal lowlands, entering bayous that emerge in surprising backwaters or are lost in uncharted swamps.

Prien Lake, the second of the lakes, was named for one of the first settlers on its shores. These shores are brilliantly washed by sunlit waves. Any shadow from their sprinkling of pine forests, with an occasional giant oak standing as large as the world itself in the axis of its own shade, keep its distance from the bright marshy banks. Every mile of its shore is an original landscape, ingeniously sweet, accented by tiny cottages. These seem to have grown as naturally as trees out of the shell banks, sitting at the end of long boardwalks. It was for one of these in particular that we searched.

We were looking for the oldest living member of the Prien family. It didn't matter that he had been orphaned, was possibly illegitimate, disinherited in his infancy, discredited in age. Nor did it matter that members of that family complained he had claimed a surname that had never been his. Anyone could tell us where to find him. Everyone had always known that he claimed to be Lafitte's cabin boy. In recent years, more had come to believe him.

The curving shore entered the wide mouth of a sunny bayou so innocently that it was only after some turns that we realized we were no longer on the lake. By then, we knew we were looking at the house that, all through that day's hot journey, had been so thoroughly described for us.

An oak to one side, ancient as the universe, spread its depths of shade. One half of his porch, immersed in its shadow, was dark as the cave from which dusk emerged at the beginning of every night. At the other extremity of the same long porch, glazed windows gave back to the sun an image of light as intense as that of the water at his dock. It was on that end that he sat today, a bent silhouette against the blazing window, smoking his pipe. The local population, as we had heard, liked to calculate the weather according to his position on the shadowed or sunlit half of his porch.

"Pere Prien?" I inquired from his dock. He sat motionless. I wondered if he were alive.

"We're looking for Prien," I said again; "the one that everyone says was Lafitte's cabin boy."

"Maybe he doesn't speak English," said Denise's father, translating my announcement into French.

"Maybe he doesn't speak at all," I said. "Maybe he's deaf."

We looked at each other and moved up the boardwalk. Without moving his head he reached out for a rifle by the side of the window. We stopped.

"I've known about you since I was a youth," I said. "There was a boatman, a river trader that came to Natchez, who told me your stories. I've wanted to find you for twenty years. Don't shoot me now!"

I waited while Denise's father translated into French.

He waved the gun, dipping its barrel into the intense sunlight and making it burn.

"Maybe we've got the wrong person," said Denise's father.

"I understand you've found Lafitte's journal," I said. Denise's father translated, and he cocked the gun.

"No," I said; "he understands us perfectly.

"They say you are the only one," I went on recklessly, " who might remember where Lafitte's treasure was buried. But what I have wanted to know is this: if even you might know what it is!"

Denise's father, standing next to me in the aim of stranger's rifle, turned to me in disbelief; but I kept my gaze fixed on the old man. This was what I had come here to find out. I wasn't going home without the answer.

John Matthews cleared his throat and provided the translation. This time, there was an angry reply in Cajun French.

"He demands to know how we know these things," said Denise's father. "I can't quite make out the dialect. I can't tell if he's worried about what we know, or if in fact he wants information from us."

"I'm very interested in everything you could say, but that's not why we would dare to stand in the sight-line of your gun," I said.

I paused, waiting for the translation.

"We're here," I added, "because there is something that the nuns want us to find".

αβ

"Ah, well, why did you not say this thing already?" He said it, although in a strained accent, in perfectly understandable English, putting the gun aside and standing. "Do you walk in the way of the saints?"

If the clearness of his speech was unexpected, the actual thing he said was more so. I had to laugh, "I know nothing of such things as saints."

"No matter. They sent you to me! The time it has come! So many sunsets they have gone down in the winding coils of this here river like on fire, until all they were swallowed up in its big watery mouth, while I've sat on this here porch thinking. And do you know what it is I'm thinking? All them sealed-up chests we shoved into that earth and covered up! I remember them, every one now. And you know what it is I'm thinking? It was all strange, but maybe I understand what now it was all for. And here you are! The time it has come."

This speech so stunned us that we stood in the quiet sunlight, not knowing how to respond.

"It's not exactly that the nuns sent us here," I admitted with embarrassment. "They did not make any mention of you precisely".

"Are you feeble-minded now? Do you not understand a thing in front of you? You come here under their direction, yes? Long years they have told me they would send someone, and the day it has come! Long years, and I been sitting on this here porch thinking. And do you know what it is I'm thinking? Things like no one could dare hope to think, things beyond all thinking, and just lately them thoughts they have been a-growing! We will set out at the dawn. Hope you won't be too weary now. Tonight, rest here. Rest well. There are many trails in that there water to follow, many buried things to dig up, and, at the last, one which passes 'em all!

"Come on up here, sit down, sit down, rest yourselves now! I'll tell you everythin' about that there treasure, anything you want – everything, I say now, that can be known. You understand now, there's mystery – a mystery to make us called to find some thing mighty deep and strange, more than anything one could dare hope to think."

As each found his own spot in the shade of his porch, we discovered our weariness. We watched the sun go down, and the silent dusk fell like a dew on every side while he told his story:

🜅

"Even before them last burials now, conducted with secrecy like ritual, Lafitte he had hid so many treasures that not even he could remember. By that there day, though, he had perfected his system of the mapping, which only he could understand you see. Some he taught to myself.

"Now I was taught by him in the marking of a spot to find it again. The marking of trees and hidden trails, of course you see, them there are signs that only will last for just some seasons. Myself I carved the numberings into them sweet-gum trees on Niblett's Bluff. I was a boy that time; by now, the bark it has closed around and hidden those numbers inside the growth. And land itself it has changed. Not only is it trees I would find hard to remember. Settlements they have grown up. Swamps they are drained some for farms. Nothing looks like it did when I was that there boy. And also, also, there were diff'rent burials in the same, or similar like, places – these are confused in my remembering mind. Treasures buried before that there meeting with Napoleon at sea were one kind; afterward it was like a different thing now. Even the most richest thing that we had hid before that, when we dug it up and dug it under again, it was like to have a different meaning for him. Napoleon's riches, and them grave-vaults which they were filled with the Spanish gold pieces, we buried this while Napoleon's priest he was still alive. At that day then, we thought there could be nothing richer, nothing in the world. After that priest had his death, Lafitte's mind it worked in a different way, and the things he hid had a different way to them too. I didn't understand then, not at all. I was made to know only that he meant them to be found again, and only when certain things were come to be that I didn't know of you see. But that's why he taught me that there science of maps, see: like how to measure off the big signs of the earth here, the measurin' of rivers and the placements of their forests. And these are only things that will last for just some seasons, so he showed me how to find a place by the stars, exactly you see as one takes a position at sea."

"He was as learned as you have imagined," said William to me.

"Great fiction," I replied with some awe, "is a poor copy of a great man."

"A great man," old Prien went on, "a great man he suffers the greatest fall, not easy to understand – unless you could have known that there little priest that he had his

101

pirates murder. What a terrible black day that was! It changed him, Lafitte, surely in a way even he did not foresee. Like that there ancient mariner, you see, he started looking for someone who could understand the thoughts he began to think, them things wrote down in his journal."

"You read poetry?" said William.

"He taught me to read, yes, Latin and Greek and good-sounding French; and he taught me how to speak and act in the presence you see of gentlemen."

Sunset burned its way into the horizon. The river with its broad lakes and ribbon-like bayous spread themselves in light under the breathing indentations of their dark banks, revealing, it seemed, an intricate map of the underworld from where the sun gazed up for a moment before turning its attention to the revelations of another day. A few stars quickly hurled whole constellations out across the skies, until the thick tapestry of the Milky Way fell all the way to the horizon even before the sky had finished drinking the splendors of sunset from the water.

Fireflies had begun to swarm from the cooling dampness of the grasses, illumining here and there the intricate curl of a leaf with their brief torches, when he rose and stooped into the darkness of his cabin to light the lamp. Immediately he returned with it, and also with a massive volume tucked under one arm.

"This is it now!" he said with a boy's eagerness. "Packed in lead under the lake mud all those seasons, in perfect shape see!" Sitting, he threw it open on his knees, and the light splashed across pages darkened with ink to the margins: red-lettered dates, bold entry titles, sketches framed by neat paragraphs, frantic scribbling between the lines and crowding every border.

"This page it reads about Lafitte's talking with Napoleon, when he cut off his escape at sea. This is it just exact. I was there then. I heard every word."

And in flawless classical French, he read.

Mr. Matthews began to translate, slowly stumbling over the words. William suggested a word or two to help. Finally, William took over altogether, translating as rapidly as the old man read. I began to realize that perhaps William had already learned a great deal more than I knew, before he even came under my instruction. The translated text was as follows:

"Is this the end of the revolution?" I said to the Little Emperor. "Is this its defeat?"

The general stared at me with fevered eyes I had never seen in his face, and he answered me: "The revolution was doomed from its beginning."

"This is delirium," I remarked.

"Take its torch from me, if you wish," he said. "Take everything I've saved. Only let me escape, with my soul."

"You have the documents?" I demanded.

"In that chest," he replied.

"You have the treasures of the Old World?"

"All there," he said. "Take them. In another generation, no one will understand their worth. To sort them out of the worthless piles of gold and jewels in that chest will be a task that will drive a man to madness."

"And you have on board the master of the mysteries, as certain signs have led me to

believe?" I demanded.

"There is no such master," he answered. "The secret brotherhood has disbanded. I have only this poor priest, who was himself one of the wisest men in Europe. He can tell you that story himself."

In anger, I demanded this priest. Napoleon wept, the little wretch, begging me to take everything else except for the priest. It amused me. I took everything, indeed, and had the great Napoleon placed in chains in the hold, promising to deliver him for the price of his bounty.

Prien looked up from the page. "He could be the gentleman's gentleman, when the agreement it was to his liking; and he could be the cruelest of all them pirates.

"I remember watching him write this down you see, sitting on that there chest in his cabin at sea, gazing out at that there porthole for long times as he wrote. The chest it was carved with Greek letters – it's that one we will be searching for, that one the Father Honoratus he had from the Holy Land. I never was told what was in it, but Lafitte he was very much troubled in his mind with what was in there. He seemed to be thinking more things than ever, though I had seen him sit like that many times in days before.

"He had sat in just that same way just two weeks before now, right by our campfire. That crescent moon of this here Louisiana summer it swam over the waves in one hundred mirrors like – it showed a thin light in them shadows of cannon lined up on shore. Big Latin books were open in front of him that was under a low-burning lamp now. His fingers ran around an Arabian astrolabe – fine piece of brass that was I remember it – and he was staring up at them stars. He had that same look, thinking things. The U. S. gov'ment schooner that had chased us up the Calcasieu it sat out on the lake, dark. Alligators broke out in them waters, brute mad as they chewed on them bodies of them all killed dead. The men grumbled: 'How long do we hide in this here backwater?'

"That War of the 1812 it was all over, and we had been under full pardon by that there President Madison because that we had helped win it for him at New Orleans. But that pardon though it had some hard restrictions you see. The new gov'ment had treaties that they forbade us plunder Spanish ships. Now this you see was what which had provided for our living and fame. Even the Caribbean gov'ments they began to frown down on our smuggling, that which was so accepted normal like before the war. The men wanted out on them high seas, battling galleons. Myself, too, I thought that the most splendid life. I thought Jean Lafitte he was master of all things, the way he shaped men and things by his own will. That was long seasons back ago.

"'Up until now,' Lafitte he told to them grumbling men, 'you've been privateers, sanctioned under papers with the seal of France, and by the colonial enemies of Spain, too, to attack and board Spanish galleons. Their spoils have been your legal right. You've been smugglers, operating in territories where excessive and unfair tariffs have made smuggling a necessity of life. You've upheld the honor of France and her colonial citizens as well as your own. Those days are over. If you continue in this life, you have no choice but to become known as pirates. You will be hunted criminals. If captured, you will be hung.'

"Arsene LeBleu he growled: 'It's a little late for this history lesson. The U.S. government,' he said it as he spat down on that fire, 'took all our winnings before the war.

103

Maybe you don't remember that raid. You escaped into the swamps; but I went to jail.'

"Lafitte he leapt onto his feet, and his sword it was on the vein of Arsene's throat. The reflected campfire it seemed like to roar up in his eyes. 'I gave half of what was left to get you out,' he said in just a whisper.

"'And they took it gladly, didn't they?' said Arsene, not even afraid, not a little. 'Everything Spain had stolen from the shores of the New World went into the U.S. treasury, and they called us pirates! Their pardon didn't extend to the return of our wealth. The more we questioned their plundering of our ships and storehouses in their own courts, the more they frowned on our continuing presence in New Orleans. Now they hunt us down as a way of life. They've established garrisons up and down the coast, hoping to catch sight of us, hoping to get what we've got left. We're their richest source of revenue. And they call us pirates! That's why we're hiding here. What's left for us but to pursue the occupation they've forced upon us? A life of dangerous ventures is better than one of hiding!'

"Lafitte he slammed his sword into its sheath and turned his smoldering eyes into them heavens. 'You're in for more adventure than you could want,' he said.

"He pointed up into them stars. 'Do you see, ' he said, 'between those fierce stars of the lion and the softer stars of the virgin, there, riding on the southern horizon as though rising out of the sea, Argo, ship of the hero Jason and the adventurous Argonauts? Think of the exploits that constellation has inspired you toward, in all your nights at sea as you followed its daring course! Now, see, above its mainmast, Mars is burning!'

"It was like the same light we had just seen in his eyes, like a smoking meteor coming on that starry ship, as like it wanted to swallow it up in flames.

"'And there,' Lafitte he went on, staring into the stars like as though he could read the language, 'near Regulus, the brilliant heart of the lion, Jupiter and Saturn seem near to collision.

"'I'll tell you why we are in this unmapped wilderness – neither land nor sea, like the twilit boundaries between two worlds! There is a treasure to be had, greater than any we have seen. I've been waiting for the moment to go after it. Meanwhile, I've been looking for a new base for more hidden operations, and for the place to hide this treasure where no existing government will ever be able to find it.

"'The night has come for us to set out to intercept it. We break camp this hour. By dawn, we will be on the seas.'

"I thought, that night, that he was the master of the universe!"

❧

"Lafitte really talked like that?" William said at the pause of this narration.

"Like what now?" answered the old man.

"That precise and exquisite language! I thought it was just the rhetoric of the author. What I mean, is the manner of his speech in James' book..."

"Why, what book is that?"

"My research on Lafitte," I replied. "I will send for a copy."

"You done research, and hain't talked to me?" laughed the old man. "I don't know, this is the nearest I can put his words down in that English. His speaking it was always straight, but French it's a poetic tongue you see; and them Lafitte brothers they grew up in a family that had education. I got some too, from them; but I got more from them there nuns. You wrote a book about Lafitte, hey? Is it made-up legend, or is it like truth then?"

"You will be able to tell me," I said. "Were you going to tell us more?"

Chapter Twenty-One

"Out on that Gulf then, and on across that big Atlantic, we followed the wake of them planets as far as they would lead before them skies they clouded up. By then the signs they had gotten dangerous. The pressure dropped, dropped deep. That kind of a storm it was building that no sailor in his mind would be on them seas – 'cept that what Lafitte he had been reading in them heavens drove him on to that prize. His men, they were eager for action, they gave themselves up to their captain and laughed at them rising winds.

"We had been following that there Jupiter bright in his rising you see, as he sailed past that old ship of Saturn like a ghost-hull, with them sagging sails of his weaker light. It was that there kind of late summer twilight that keeps on to brightenin' in front of a full moon a-rising. As soon as her great big orb broke out them waters of the east though, it was bothered by the rising, right next to it too, of that angry a-frowning Mars.

"With these lamps of heaven all still beaming outside the window, I found him in his cabin.

"'How do you read them stars like that?' I asked him. 'How can you see destinations now, how can you tell times for startin' out on a voyage?'

"The wind it was getting furious out there, calling them clouds from every dark horizon. The ship it was tossed to the edge of its sound timbers on every climbing wave; but he paid no mind, he explained everything to me. Oh, my mind it was stirred; it soared like the rising wind! Jupiter, Mars, Saturn he showed me to understand them – treasure, but more than treasure – death, burial, and something all unthinkable beyond.

'And you can see a treasure that will have to be hid where no man knows it?' I went on in more questions.

"'No man but maybe you, my boy,' he replied. 'You must be able to remember everything. Destinies may depend on it.' I shuddered you see. 'And there is something more in this journey, something in the stars I've not dared mention to anyone. I am going to meet my guide, and the guide for which the secret brotherhood has been waiting.'

"At that moment, them clouds, which had been dropping down over all them stars, closed over them heavens and put them out! Even that sturdy rising full moon, filling the seas with light stronger than any beacon ever burned on land, it was taken away. We went on our course by compass, lost else-wise in all chaos of waves torn off by wind and darkness. Then, an awful silence, an eye in that there building storm was torn out from the east, revealin' the moon now, which sat right there blood-red in eclipse.

"Mars it seemed even brighter, sitting by that there eclipse! Wholly wrapped up in angry fire, and it seemed like to spill blood over the moon's face. And just then as that moon's feverish forehead it began slowly to climb back into the light, a wall of clouds put out all vision again.

"Lafitte turned to me, and he said, 'Remember this. I dare not record an eclipse like

106

that in any ship's log.'

"Oh yes sir, we went out on deck and stood in windy mists that screamed in the increasing coming of that there storm. No longer we could not even read the compass that led us into a dawn so dark you see we could not tell drenched air from them climbing waves and them down-lowering clouds.

"Lower and darker, them clouds, rushing like overhead churnin' waves.

"Just before rain began like the unloosing of them firmaments, like God Himself let down the great wet sails of His own Creation I tell you, we saw masts on that southern horizon. It was right there where them stars of Argo they had disappeared, like as if Lafitte he had foresaid, that's where she'll be, boys. Now that there it could only be a ship desperate, fleeing her pursuers into that there storm.

"Now when that we saw that there ship you see, the men they remembered that Lafitte's word it was good, that he had made all their good fortune. That there bounty on the head of Napoleon there you see was half the wealth of this here world. And then besides that we found on that ship riches like had been forgot since the downfall of them kings. We thought it a greater taking than any thing we had seen – but now that was because we did not understand the worth of what we had taken already before. Which was richest you see – Napoleon's treasure, or all them Spanish pieces of coin we had? Which was the measure then of that there Old World? These here were questions later in Lafitte's mind, when he thought of them Inca gold art things all melted down in bars for carryin' to Spain, and them men and whole civilizations dead you see before they came even into our hands.

"And there were stranger riches on that ship – old, old writings and things.

"It was them there writings, I do believe to this day here, for that the U.S. gov'ment had been chasing after us.

"It had reasons besides, many, to chase us down. There was all our robb'ries that they had led to that there War of 1812. Them British you see they were right mad; they blamed that there American navy for our success with all that smuggling. Even after we helped out Gen'ral Andy Jackson in that there war, there was suspicion about all our doings. It was not only our treasure that they wanted – which was enough there to finance that whole Fed'ral treasury for some years now.

"Them old writings which we took now, them there were thought to be important for what they called that there world revolution. I never saw them writings, but I have heard them Masons talk. What they say is them old papers or parchments or tablets, or whatever, they were supposed to be with Napoleon; but by that time that he was handed over, they had gone missing. They suspected now that Lafitte he took them for himself. If them there things been handed over with him, them Masons say, the gov'ment would have left us to be. But then they go and say that by this season that U. S. had become a nation no longer trusted by them revolutionaries.

"And then you see there was the strange prize of all – that there priest. Himself he was a leader of them French Masons. And here he was, coming from Jerusalem with his locked chest.

"My first seeing of this meek priest was that it showed he was most insignificant a little man. No one could have seen before that his death it would make such a mark on

Lafitte, and myself too, and this here whole region.

"On that there return from sea, the priest he was quiet. Lafitte questioned him all about his things found out in the Holy Land, again and again. He just looked down at the deck while his fingers they ran like little mice around that knotted rope in his hand. Now he would not even answer Lafitte's questions about that there rope – the prayer-rope it was, as we found out later – and so Lafitte he took it, and locked him in the hold. That there priest he was not even bothered about that. Lafitte would go down to visit in the dark, but could not get him to speak. Concluding that he had gone deaf or mad, he left him down in the dark hold.

"But then after we got back to this here land you see, them nuns from New Orleans they came to him. That there's when he started teachin' them that Greek. Now Lafitte he was not fooled by this. He knew that the French it was his native language and theirs too. He had a mind to put a stop on this here teaching. The priest then turned to speak right out to Lafitte's mind, ruthless too and right exact. He said this – he said to repent him of his doings, and to give up all his riches to them poor.

"And that's when Lafitte got that there feeling to bury them treasures.

"These swamps they were all uncharted at them there seasons. Lafitte he began to test us our skills to hide and recover things. He would take us deep into them floating prairies of marsh to bury a chest in one them unknown shell-banks. These here was what we did with all them Spanish gold. When that we proved ourselves by finding them again, we got sent to bury more. He would put that blindfold on us, or take us into them swamps by night now, expectin' us to maybe remember the turnings and the miles. Only Arsene LeBleu and myself we was able to prove ourselves that way.

"After the death of the priest you see, we dug them up again and brought them all into a just few spots. I was sent to hide that map. Then we buried that there treasure which was more than the rest, under that oak of the hanged-man's noose.

"To the end now, Lafitte he spoke often of that there noose in all scattered out kind of words. It began as a joke see, a play on his words.

"That there little old priest always finished up his teachings by sayings of that Greek word nous. He would make it out in French by that there word 'mind', but it was like he would shine when he said it. It seemed like that he was meaning the mind in a turn of illumination; but always he said it while holding his hand to his heart, as like as his mind it was in his heart. Lafitte he thought that he was part insane. He would grab the prayer-rope out the hands of one of them nuns, and hold it upside down you see. This prayer rope it was a circle out of knitted yarn woven with a hundred knots, and a woven cross hung from it. This here it is my own, you see, hung 'round my wrist. Each knot it is a little prayer, that's all, which kept repeating, you see brings the heart and mind, I tell you, to the shining shores of prayer the which it don't never stop."

Here, for the first time, old Prien was silent for some moments. We dared not interrupt him with any question.

"Laughing, now you see, Lafitte he would hold the prayer-rope upside down, with that loop of knots hanging under the cross. You could see in Lafitte's mind he was looking at a hanged-man's noose dropping from some tree. 'Is this your nous?' That was his joke.

"Then came that there terrible black day when it was no more any joke. His wrath it could go beyond control you see. He marched that priest deep into that there swamp where even he had never been before.

"Many men his black anger it had murdered. This, it was his last.

"He was not the same you see after that. Things he did, commands he put us up to, they had always been all quick-like, strange maybe, but his men they loved them there hardships for all the sudden fortune that he brought them with such mastery. Now, you see, it was not like that. His mind it walked in ways that the men began to question that there loyalty. This was the beginning of the things that led to the hiding of that map.

"The map it showed signs for finding again that one most priceless buried thing. Compared to it you see, the others they meant nothing. That was the chest brought by the priest from the Holy Land. I heard it said that in there was the elixir of life; a drink from the fountain of youth in the Blessed Isles. Some said that it was what Columbus he had come looking for in the legends of the New World. Sailors they said that Columbus had been named for Columba the visionary, that there first of the voyaging saints. Some of them there Irish saints they had come far as America back in the seasons of centuries long before, looking for paradise along an ocean-road of miracles. Every mariner he knew them there tales, and he was driven by them dreams!"

Here, I had heard enough of old Prien's tales. I could no longer restrain myself: "Incredible. This legendary treasure, for which the wisest men have been searching for centuries, half a millennium, for which men have been murdered and wars have been fought, turns up now to be nothing more than the bones of a priest."

"No, it could not be that!" said Prien in an odd tone of voice. "That had not crossed my mind then, not in all them things I was thinking! Do you think it could be now?"

"What, then, am I not understanding in these events?" I said to the others who sat on the porch with me.

"We did not tell him what it was that the nuns sent us to find," William answered me.

"It's true," said Denise's father. "Their description of his lost coffin in every way matches that of the treasure."

The old man gave tongue to an expression that seemed to be a mingling of Cajun French and Greek, as though his astonishment were beyond the reach of language.

"You see," he said, "Lafitte he had made a habit of protecting them buried treasures with corpses of men that they would not bend to his will! In them there graves that they were guarded by skeletons were his most precious winnings. Tomorrow you see, if you have the heart, you will see some of these yourselves. Laughing, Lafitte he called them his scarecrows; but his men they vowed that they had seen ghosts guarding those chests. His second captain Dominique, he was hero of that there Battle of New Orleans, he was so disturbed by this that he consulted a Caribbean priestess. She said now that Lafitte he had learned an old rite, that them there spirits a-guarding those chests they were not the ghosts of dead men, but demons, powerful ones."

Denise's father also was disturbed at hearing this. He stood and walked slowly to the edge of the porch, staring out into the darkness.

"I believe that there was about that season that Dominique and some them others of Lafitte's men they left him," said Prien. "They became respected citizens in New Orleans you see."

"Yes," said John Matthews, "respected leaders in the New Orleans Lodge. The Masonic compass and square are engraved on their tombs. They were still alive when I was young."

"When he was a young and angry man," Prien went on, "he challenged many men to their deaths at dawn, with saber and pistol you see. Only a few saw those duels, so he said. It was a darker duel I think, and one there that even his own men feared, that he won against those demons – if indeed it be that he were the winner."

"Do I understand you, though?" I interrupted. "Are you implying that there was something else in that chest other than a heap of bones?"

"A heap of bones!" Prien replied. "What you know about anything?" He stood, stooping, and walked his porch like a man shedding his years with every step. The lines fell from his face, and his eyes moved more quickly. I don't know that I have ever seen a man that inspired.

"Flesh and bones bedewed by that there oil of the holy blue fire!" he said. "Sacre bleu, for sure now! Do you nothing of what that means? I never thought of it! No wonder we thought he had lost his mind! That there it would be a thing worth searching for!

"Now what else was in that there chest that the priest brought from the Holy Land, that Lafitte he thought worthy of this priest guarding it in death? Something more precious than anything he had ever seen, ever. He never told what it was."

"We have the map, if you want to see it," I said.

He laughed heartily. "That there map, you have got it? How much did you have to pay for it? Let me see!"

William gave him the stack of papers. His face grew somber as he leafed through them.

"Yep sir," he said, "these are all them forgeries. I should know now. Myself I drew the map.

"His men they had gone away from him by that time he was satisfied with all them re-burials of his chests. His hair it had gone from black to a steel gray. His hand it had begun to tremble, and they thought sure he was gone mad. Arsene and myself we were all that stayed. Us he was teaching to make maps. Arsene was best in the mapping of these parts. He knew them better than anyone; he was native here you see, descended from them first LeBleu settlers.

"Now my first map it was more complicated than any of these here you see. 'Not good enough!' he shouted; 'You don't understand what you're doing!' Now I had got the idea of mapping them rivers and all them deep swamps, I had got it good; and he wanted it that good, but more disguised you see. So that there is when he taught me that science of symbolism. Now then, that was when I got to begin to see into his mind. Land forms they started to take on deeper meanings you see. New countries, deep in the mind, they began to show themselves to me.

"After a few more re-drawings, he was satisfied with my map. He gave command to have it hidden.

"Arsene he was greatly angered by this here idea. He formed that idea that the map should be his, and also all them treasures to which it led. He it was who made them forgeries; and later he got rich selling them. Lafitte he had guessed that Arsene would act in this way. It seemed to be part of his plan.

"'These maps are useless, then,' I said.

"'Each has some reflection, in its own way now, of that there original,' he replied.

"'That being so,' I said, 'some kind of key to the right interpretation would be needed.'

"'Even with that first map that would be the case now,' he reminded me. 'And here is the key.' He lifted up the journal from off the floor, where it had fallen during his narration.

"We had just buried that last chest now. Only Arsene and I we had made that journey with Lafitte, and we were blindfold. Arsene then he left for his own home. I was alone with Lafitte, when that there ship went down. He'd just written the last page in this here book when it sank. He seemed to think it kind o' funny you see. That was the last I saw him, ever."

The night had grown silent. The thousand voices of the swamp had grown weary with the hours. The crickets had ceased their symphonic decrescendos of the cooling air. The tremendously numerous sopranos of the tree-frogs, the distant bass of bullfrogs, even the occasional but startling refrains of the owls, had fallen off until it seemed inevitable that even the night creatures must sleep. The dance of the fireflies was forgotten, and the stars themselves began to fade in pillows of mist.

Our minds alone were unable to rest.

"This is a story far stranger than any I imagined," I said.

"What a weird quest this is," added Gerald. "Have we any idea how to proceed?"

"First, I suppose, we will have to study the journal," suggested William.

"Perhaps we should consider not following this venture at all," said Mr. Matthews. "It's nothing but trouble. It will lead us into more trouble than you think."

"How do you know?" I said.

"I've encountered enough intrigue for a lifetime already," he answered enigmatically. "This will surpass them all. I'm not sure I want to be part of it."

I studied his face, and tried to answer a number of suspicions that had been secretly growing in my mind concerning Denise's father.

"If Lafitte had not indeed gone mad," said William, thumbing through the journal, "he conceived a definite plan for leading a particular type of person to the finding of this chest."

"That's right," said Prien, "and the time it has come now for us to find it. I understand it better than ever I have before. This here is how he intended: that there stack of forged maps; the things of his thinking as put down in this here writing; my remembering as a guide; and then someone would come you see, by way of them nuns that learned that there holiness from the same priest he killed, to lead us to that chest! It will be a great adventure, greater than any I have seen even. And I could tell some that would amaze you now.

"Rest tonight! Rest well. Tomorrow now I will show you a strange graveyard rising

111

out of the marsh, lead roofs of sunken vaults. There, according to this here writing, our search begins.

"It's late. We should sleep."

But from that hour until the dawn came up in fog, he kept us entranced on his dark porch with the recital of more stories than I care to relate.

Chapter Twenty-Two

"His journal is divided into three sections, written in elegant French," said William. He sat on a box in the rear of the pirogue with the pages open on his knees. The sun was still high, though beginning to wheel toward the west, and the pages as he turned them flashed in the light like the wings of gulls that dove to investigate our boat.

It was Prien's largest, bigger than any pirogue we had seen, but built in that style. In the first hours of morning we had loaded it while Prien like an angry but experienced seadog barked rapid orders, his mind racing through every circumstance that could possibly be encountered. Provisions for three months were crammed within its narrow confines. One could see that he had loaded many holds beyond their limits. Small arms were stored under the seats while the old man whispered prayers. These were concealed behind fishing equipment, hunting traps, and tents. Empty strongboxes for the retrieval of treasures were hidden within boxes of grain. There was even a light canvas and rig for erecting a sail if necessary. In spite of these extensive preparations he had us distribute the weight so that the little boat floated superbly. It glided over the water as easily as a leaf, and even if we moved in our seats the balance was hardly disturbed. Two men on each side of the boat worked poles or paddles while one rested. This left William free for the moment to read through Lafitte's journal.

Prien turned to look at him, and laughed: "You now, you're the picture of that there young gentleman-scholar hisself, when he first came into these waters!"

"The overall tone of these writings is one of penitence," said William. "The first section is the journal of his career. It contains the narratives of his crimes and his buried treasures. This includes the list of the six treasures buried along the Calcasieu River, but it is often vague about what they were. Most of his stories are in the form of digressions concerning his travels in the bayou country between here and New Orleans. The treasures buried there are more explicitly chronicled.

"The second section of the journal is more reflective and philosophical. It gives more information on the nature of the six treasures, but only in enigmatic fashion. The third section is the strangest. Its title indicates that it will reveal the locations of the six treasures. Instead, it merely lists his major trading routes throughout Louisiana and the Texas border. Actually, it contains more of the teachings of the priest and his nuns than anything else.

"His sudden shifts of thought are incomprehensible to me; but I had no idea he could be a philosopher of this degree."

"Yep sir, he was like that now," said Prien, "but more so near the end. His last days there, no one understood him, and them there were the days he spent writing that. He made right sure that I knew where this here journal was before he disappeared, but he said that I would not be understanding it until I got old." Again, he laughed: "I guess I still got some seasons to go now!"

"What seems clearest," William continued, "is that Lafitte's reflections on the teach-

113

ings of the priest are to be the theme of his journal from the beginning. Here, let me read the introductory pages:

One afternoon the elder was teaching the nuns in the shade of his favorite oak on the three stages o http://wiki.kcls.org/tellmeastory/index.php/A_Tooty_Ta_Ta f the Christian life.

"Many of the holy fathers speak of these three stages of the transformation of the human creature into the divine. In the words of my spiritual father on Mount Sinai, these are: first, purification of heart. This is difficult and even impossible without divine assistance. Only those who follow the Lord's commandments are able to achieve it. The second is illumination of the heart, which occurs miraculously once the heart has been purified. In the final stage, one is immersed in the Vision of God, in which the human person becomes God-like, deified. It is not wise to say too much about this state, except to say that it is illustrated, at least in one or more moments, in all the lives of the saints.

"St. John Cassian received this tradition directly from holy fathers of the Egyptian desert who were the disciples of St. Anthony the Great. He then brought it into France in the fourth century. He spoke of these three steps as 'the three renunciations'. The Christian, obeying the commandment to leave everything and follow Christ, renounces first all worldly goods, then renounces all earthly attachments, and finally renounces even every thought in order to receive the revelations of the blessings held in store for those who believe. He speaks likewise of the three kinds of monks. He is speaking of these same three stages of the Christian life, as you see, from very early times, from the desert fathers who understood the sacred gospels, and from the divine teachings of the visionary Paul, who saw Christ in the throne of heaven and labored to establish His true teachings.

"St. Gregory of Nyssa, whose elder brother St. Basil also spent several years observing the life of the Egyptian desert fathers, writes of these three stages as the spiritual ascent of Mt. Sinai in his Life of Moses. There the grace-filled and God-beholding patriarch is understood to be the type of the perfect Christian. He speaks of its lower slopes, where determination to climb is begun; of the higher slopes, where God was heard to speak out of the miraculous burning bush; and of the summit, where he spoke with God face to face as to a friend, in the midst of the roaring fire that reached into the heavens and engulfed the mountain yet did not consume it. He speaks of the mountain of vision likewise in his treatise on the Sermon on the Mount and the divine blessings known as Beatitudes. This is the same St. Gregory who spoke also of the tremendous and fearful responsibility of calling one's self a Christian.

"St. John of the Ladder, who lived in the monastery of Sinai in the sixth century, speaks of the Christian life not as an ascent of three steps, but rather as a ladder that leads into heaven. The twenty-six steps of this ladder are the spiritual virtues. Nevertheless, my holy father on Mount Sinai saw no contradiction in mere numbers. The ladder referred to is the ladder of vision which Jacob beheld in a dream at Bethel. The twenty-six rungs of the ladder refer to nothing other than the labors of purification and illumination which lead to the vision of God. I have seen for myself venerable and holy men who have labored to ascend the three slopes of Sinai and, seeing the mystical ladder set up on its summit, have begun the terrifying ascent into the presence of God..."

The old priest trembled as he said this, and I truly believed that I stood in the presence of one who himself had seen God, impossible as that may be. However, as was my habit, I laughed out loud and derided him. As always, he took my derision to heart as

114

though it were something he deserved, which he certainly did not. As though my insane judgment were as precious as the things which he himself taught, he turned to his nuns and said, "You see how you hold me in great honor; but he is the only one who sees me as I am."

Not a man of us moved his oar. We drifted in brilliant, sun-multiplying waves that moved with a gentle but authoritative current.

"This is the most astonishing introduction to a piece of writing that I have ever seen," said William after a while. "First of all, it implies a clear insight into the nature of Christianity in early centuries, which in itself is astonishing. We are given summaries of the writings of different teachers in different centuries, probably with widely divergent writing styles and rhetorical skills, who in the images of conflicting metaphors present an identical teaching on the nature of the Christian life. Further, these teachings in every case assume a penetrating, even prophetic understanding of the entire vast body of Biblical writings in all their prolific divergence, as though all books of Scripture comprise one consistent teaching from beginning to end. What I find even more amazing is that these Biblical teachings were so diligently followed by those who were writing about them that they themselves were completely transformed by them. If I understand the goal of Christian life as these teachers have outlined it, the extraordinary visions of Paul, said by the apostle himself to have been indescribable, were intimately familiar to them!

"This is the way Lafitte has chosen to introduce his journal, setting the tone for what will follow. Clearly, then, the three-fold division of its contents are meant to mirror the three-fold division of the spiritual life of these ancient fathers of the desert, practiced even to this day on Mt. Sinai and taught by this priest. Apparently Lafitte, late in life, took these words to heart. We are led to believe that this journal of repentance will hint of a purification that leads to some kind of illumination, if not to something even more extraordinary.

"You will recall that the consistent feature of the maps in all their variations was the distribution of six treasures over three realms, which we had come to believe were the shores of the three lakes along the Calcasieu River. At the same time, we remained convinced that there was an allegorical meaning as well to the three regions. Have we not indeed discovered the key to the maps?"

∞

I suppose it had already occurred to me that it was absurd to think of William simply as my best student. Even at his age he was already a better scholar than myself. Of course he did not possess the kind of fantastic imagination that I was known for. Nevertheless it was clear he had his own imaginative gift. Without it, he would not have such extraordinary ability to see into the heart of the matter at hand, focusing on the question to be researched.

In every way, if one were to be truthful, William's character was superior to mine. He was as trustworthy as Gerald himself. Other than a touch of the pride common to youth's first discovery of its powers, he was almost entirely lacking in arrogance. Never did he fail to defer to his elders. No doubt this was the result of a sound upbringing by

115

attentive parents. That was a world I had never seen.

It occurred to me that I knew nothing of the home in which he had grown up. I had never known his father except by reputation. Even of this I knew little, except that he was among the wealthiest plantation owners. I knew he was not educated, but obviously he had desired that his son should be. What kind of man he had been, I could only infer from his son.

And concerning his mother, what, really, did I know about Emily? Except for her splendid face and form, well preserved into her late thirties, and the immediate effects of an out-going good humor, I had never studied the woman. I knew nothing about her, except that she seemed to understand me quite well – including my ugliest faults, of which she appeared to be quite patient. Who she was, and how she thought, I had no idea, except, again, as these things had somehow influenced her son. That son was an admirable young man, promising to mature into the best kind of Southern gentleman.

These reflections caused me to wonder what Catherine saw in me at all. Certainly nothing to rival her fiance. And yet there was no denying that there was something in her nature that mirrored my own... something hidden...

∛

I was shaken from these thoughts by the voice of old Prien. He had also been staring at William, and, apparently, weighing his comments with high regard.

"My boy there," he said, "everything you said there is just right. That there's the way I read it too, though it took me a right few seasons more to get to that understanding. But now did you never really know the thinkings of them fathers and mothers of the Church? My own spir'tual mother, one of them nuns now, has taught me 'bout these things for many seasons. But I forget. There was a season when I too was unlearned of blessings and miracles and things of faith, and them powers of all heaven!"

Denise's father, however, was staring at me. "William appears not to know of your multi-columned Biblical commentary! You never showed that book to your brightest scholar? What kind of a teacher are you? It was the finest book that ever came into your possession, and you know it!"

There was no need, of course, to reply to such an accusation. John Matthews knew he was right. "Does the journal say anything about the treasure of the sunken vaults, or why they would resemble tombs?" I said to William.

"Yes, it does," said William. "It is marked as the second treasure-site after that of the sunken wreck. Lafitte's notes on it are more extensive than those on any other site. It is the only place where he clearly identifies the nature of its hidden riches."

"You see how he has studied the journal and the maps," said Mr. Matthews to me, "and how much he has helped us to understand them, even though you've handicapped him by not showing him the most valuable writings you have found! If he had read that commentary, he'd have understood the whole Biblical tradition of the Church by now! He already understands it better than you do!"

"All right!" I said. "I brought it. It's packed in my trunk. I thought it might be useful somehow."

"You have a writing on Scriptur's, writing by them holy fathers?" whispered Prien.

"The whole text of the Bible," answered Mr. Matthews, "with patristic interpretations in every margin."

"Oh!" said the old man. "My own spir'tual mother she spoke of such books, and sure desired to see one. Can I look there?"

"You said Lafitte taught you Greek?" I replied.

"Well sure, and I been around them nuns long enough to get comfortable with a little Greek when I have to," he replied.

I dug into my trunk and handed the immense volume to Prien. William surrendered the journal to me, then sitting beside him, together they began to read from the first page of Genesis. Tears rolled from the old man's eyes.

Gerald held out one oar as a rudder and gazed into the broad skies, surrendering to the gentle current. John Matthews sat brooding by himself, and I was left alone with Lafitte's journal.

The pages of the manuscript were written in a handsome but informal cursive. Only the bold red headings were in a formal lettering style, and these were few, with the largest at the head of each of the three sections. There were no page numerations or table of contents, yet the entries on the six treasures in each of the sections were easily located. Those on the sunken vaults that we were approaching were, as William had warned, extensive. By comparison, the only thing written about the sunken ship was this:

What is the sunken wreck? A ruined life; the wreck of history; the fallen soul: the pirate's career.

The writings on the wealth hidden in the sunken vaults began with the enigmatic sentence:

The tombs indicate the nature of their contents.

This was followed by a lengthy and detailed narration of the progress of his crimes, beginning at his childhood fascination with his older brother Pierre's tales of privateering. He told how the crews of captured ships were thrown into the sea. This was followed by the account of Lafitte's first duel. I glanced over other memoirs with marginal interest, until I became increasingly alarmed at the number of men he killed, and the cruelty of his killings. By the time he became the iron-handed despot of a kingdom of smugglers, the nature of his executions were nothing short of horrible. Many of those whom he found unfaithful to his own interests were interred among the tombs that also contained his buried gold. These unpleasant narratives ended with the following paragraph:

Many crimes lead at last to one great crime. Murder and pillage is the pirate's career. When I was a young and zealous freedom-fighter for the cause of France against Spain, taking spoils from the enemy as my rightful reward, or even after I had become accustomed to killing Spanish priests, whom I always considered spies, I would never have believed that I could end my career with the murder of a holy man. Yet I might have foreseen, when I intercepted these marble tombs hewn by a Spanish stonemason on

117

order for the New Orleans graveyard, and used them to conceal Spanish gold in order to frighten the superstitious, that they would become the symbol of my legacy.

Underneath this paragraph was a bold red title, "The Buried Treasure". The entry under this title read simply:

At one time, nearly all the gold of the Spanish Main was collected here. This was the greatest of treasures before the capture of Napoleon's wealth. Later, a greater treasure was placed in one vault and removed to another site.

Turning to the second part of Lafitte's journal, I found that his reflections on this particular treasure were by far more interesting than I would have thought:

Spain itself at one time had been the lost treasure of Europe. It was the last bastion of the Old World when the Renaissance spread over Italy, France and England. Cut off from the world by the rainy Pyrenees on one side, where the last stronghold of Arian Goths were found, and by the fog-bound pillars of Hercules set between two oceans on the other side, from which came the farthest reach of the invading army of Islam defeated at last by El Cid, it remained firm and timeless in the uniqueness of its own culture. But the corruption that had already crept into the Roman Church, in power struggles for the papacy, came with terrible suddenness into Spain, ripping through the high clergy and new theological faculties in the fierce hatred of Inquisition, under which my own family was persecuted.

Spain entered the new age with all the greed of world domination when Christopher Columbus was presented before Ferdinand and Isabella to say: 'The route to the fabled riches of the East Indies is not by land, as Marco Polo chronicled, but by sea; not east, but beyond the western horizon, beyond the limits of sunset where only the blessed have gone.' There they found a civilization unknown and ancient. They robbed its treasures, not understanding them. Stripping its temples of their gold, they built a Spanish empire in the New World, itself a vanishing dream. The value of the Old World is lost, and the new is valueless, as gold is valueless in itself – but our minds are darkened, and don't see this.

This vast collection of Spanish doubloons, comprising nearly the entire wealth of the New World, is a mere shadow of the wealth that the first explorers came searching for. They were looking for paradise, and they actually believed that it might be found here.

The Irish traditions of the Blessed Isles west of the sunset were well known, and especially St. Brendan the Voyager's account was read and re-told by wandering poets. Ponce de Leon was passionate to find nothing less than the Fountain of Youth described in these tales, and Cortez ransacked the jungles for El Dorado, the city of gold. He was convinced that a utopian, enlightened civilization, known in American myths as a city of the sun, was the inspiration of the cities he found among the Aztecs and Incas, the pueblo cities carved into the cliffs, and even the mound-builders. Finding no such paradise, he became content with stealing their gold.

This degeneration of desire is representative of the thorough corruption of Spain which I grew to hate, neglecting, however, the corruption into which this very hatred led myself.

"There now," said Prien. "That there bright shore."

The sun, racing toward the broad, burning vapors of the humid horizon, threw its strongest colors opposite against the eastern shore – a deeper blue into the lake and sky, and every palette of green into the bank.

"We'll have to row for it," said Prien. "You don't want to walk on that there shore after the sun it goes down!"

The others grabbed the four oars and dug vigorously into the waters, leaving my hands free. I turned to the third section of the journal and read out loud:

A low shore on Big Lake; a ruined graveyard, the place most feared by all the local peoples. Some of the fierce Attakapas were said to offer sacrifices here before I came. Among them was the fabled chief Quelqueshue, 'Crying Eagle', for whom the River Calcasieu is named.

"Yep sure, he chose that there place already long known for murders, for this here treasure," said Prien. "He knew that only a pirate would open a tomb; and if he did now, he'd be as likely to find the rottin' corpse of another pirate who'd already tried the robbery."

At that moment, the sun entered the haze stretched over the west, and was dimmed.

"The way them tombs looks is right fearful now," Prien added. "I expect I should maybe warn you before of them stained marble slabs dripping with all them seasons o' death. Them lead roofs is all broke, them crosses up on top are scattered and in pieces, and they lean into that there marsh every this way and that sinkin'. It's a fearful sight enough; but I got to warn you of them legends of hauntin's. I got to warn you 'bout that there, 'cause some of them hauntin's was seen by folks I knew."

By such swift degrees was the sun stepping down into the haze, that dusk came up at an alarming rate, thrown over us like increasing shrouds.

"Is nothing more written about this site?" Mr. Matthews asked.

"Only a marginal note," I replied.

"What does it say?" he insisted.

I read:

The most flawless of the tombs, which is now the vault of the mysteries, was removed.

"Yep," said Prien. "Arsene and I floated it upriver on one them big flatboats. That was the journey for that he blindfolded us now."

"Fascinating!" said Mr. Matthews. "He mentions the vault of the mysteries! There must be something more about that somewhere in that journal. There's nothing else written?"

"There is a reference to the teaching of the priest," I said.

"Well, read it!" he said vehemently.

"Seven seals in heaven, terrifying, a book unopened until the end of time, yet revealed to the youngest apostle, the one who lived to the greatest age," the honorable father said to me just before I had him hung. These words he said not as a judgment upon

119

my crime, but lovingly, as though he were giving last instructions to one of his own disciples.

"The seven seals!" said John Matthews. "Six concealed treasures, whose meaning is veiled, and the seventh is the vault of the mysteries! Don't you think it's curious that he would dare to make such a comparison?"

"I think it's curious," I said, "for someone who has denounced the Masons and grumbled at the undertaking of this search, that your interest in the legendary vault of the mysteries has so suddenly awakened."

"Whatever was in that there vault," said Prien, "ever'body wanted it now: Masons, them pirates, priests, even nuns. But tell me now – my eyes they are not so good anymore – one used to make out them busted crosses a'top of them tombs by this here distance. What do you see now?"

"I don't see anything," said Mr. Matthews.

"Nor do I," said Gerald.

William continued to look, saying nothing.

"Them weeds maybe they'd have overgrown them all by this season," said Prien. "We'll beach on the sand now, and have a look around."

"There's no sand here," I informed him.

"Ah but of course there is! The sandbar it is all overgrown too?"

"There's no shore at all, as far as I can see," said William.

"Marsh grass and then inland marshes," added Gerald.

"Why that there whole shore is gone then!" gasped Prien.

"Well then," I said, "there's more gold to be found in the mud under these waters than in the California mother lode."

Chapter Twenty-Three

"The trail is erased," said William.

Prien stared into the trembling green refractions, as though trying to read the waves as they drifted into the marsh grass, suggestive of a shore that no longer existed.

"You're certain this is the place?" said Mr. Matthews.

"These are them shores I know best," said Prien, "since we first ran into the mouth of this here unknown river under that darkness and fog, bein' chased by them there warships."

"Whatever we were to recover here is gone," I said.

"What might we have expected?" said Gerald.

"A mass o' gold, sprinkled over with dead corpses," said Prien. "It's good I think to find that gone. Only thing that mattered, it was taken away and put somewhere else now."

"Lafitte's trail of treasures," I said. "How can it lead to the vault of the mysteries, if the trail is erased at the very beginning?"

"He'd a' known that the tides would take this shore," said Prien.

"If none of the treasures have any importance except for the last," said William, "is it possible that we are searching in the wrong place?"

"There must be something in the journal somewhere that refers to that final chest, what it is or where it might be," Mr. Matthews insisted.

"Only a brief word near the end," said William; "this:"

Only a blind man will find it.

"That's right now!" said Prien. "I'd a' forgot he wrote that! By that season there that he blindfolded me for that last journey, I'd mastered them blind marking of turns, that there measuring of miles. I could find them things again, even them buried things. And besides now, he kept on teasing me in that there journey, as though to sharpen my notice. Many seasons have I thought upon that journey. It led upriver now. I could feel us making way against the current. I do believe we must have buried it near Arsene's place now. If we go by night, I think I can find that there place!"

"We should go straight to the goal," said Mr. Matthews.

"By this here midnight now, we could enter the first of them turns that I recall," said Prien.

"But not tonight!" I groaned.

"You have never been so close to the thing you've sought for twenty years," said Mr. Matthews. "Is there any reason for delay?"

"It's just that it has been so long since we've had a night's sleep, that I'm not sure I can tell the sun from the moon," I answered.

"Well now," said Prien, " you don't want to sleep nowhere near this here place."

The last shadow of darkness fell on us as he said this, and immediately a ground fog rose from the marsh in which we floated. One moment, we saw it begin to glide out over the lake; but it quickly rose to the level of our eyes and blotted out our vision.

Who can explain fear? In the moment that the world vanished in fog and silent darkness, our minds were suffocated in such an irrational terror that if one more shade of night fell on us before we moved, it would be the final shroud of death.

Blindly, we backed out into the waveless expanse of invisible water under invisible air. Our poles feeling for mud and taking the depth, we crawled toward deeper water away from that bank, like a desperate water insect creeping back from the black reach of a great spider. The hairs of its legs brushed against our cheeks. Into deeper water we shoved the mud away until our arms were into water to the shoulders. As long as we could reach bottom we still had feeling of some differentiation among the elements when none were visible; but when the bottom fell out of reach, we drifted with no orientation. The water was visible only when balls of faintly luminescent swamp gas broke its surface, a sight which only terrified us further. They rose slowly into the air and shattered into distorted fragments that drifted in our wake. There was not a man among us who did not believe they were ghosts. They seemed about to stretch themselves into distorted faces when we broke clear of that fog.

A remnant of dusk was still on the west, and along the reflections of the far shore. The evening star burned brilliantly, and stars were swarming out of the other skies. The fog was no more than a low ribbon on one horizon; but shreds of swamp gas broke out of its limits in crowds that seemed to watch our departure.

৵৵৵৵৵৵

All that night we labored against the current. Just before dawn we camped on a sandy island, sleeping soundly through the long summer day. We broke camp at dusk and struggled through a week of nights into the headwaters of the Calcasieu River.

Even after moonset, our guide knew the backwater of every bayou and the varying current of every mile of open river. For us who knew nothing of this river country, the journey by darkness to the source of so many interwoven waterways could have been an expedition into the underworld, always chased by erratic globes of luminescent gas like the dim lanterns of damned souls.

Night is that much deeper in the swamps.

Its uneven darkness stretched like the primeval waters out of which the massive worlds were moved before the first light was formed. We drifted through waveless dark waters that went on forever. Instead of horizons, there were the shadowy suggestions of mossed masses of cypresses like cobwebs left by the spiders of night.

The old moon began to rise over one oak on solid ground, next to the dark frame of a house; and just as the surface of water began to shine, dividing darkness from darkness, the fog raised itself and drifted in the anemic color of the moon.

"That there was Arsene's house," said Prien.

"They call this a river?" I said.

"The Calcasieu," he said.

122

"There's no shore. The water goes on among the trees. Where could you have buried a treasure?"

"If you go far enough into them there cypresses," he answered pointing, "you come to land. Maybe a gentle rise, maybe a bluff."

We shoved our poles against the shallow bottom, moving in that direction.

"How can there be this much freshwater on the face of the earth?" said Gerald.

"Fresh?" Prien laughed. "This here's so stale with rotting leaves now that it's no clearer than this in sunlight."

"What I mean," said Gerald, "is that there is no salt water mixed in from the sea. Where does all this water come from?"

"From the Mississippi, in times long forgotten," I answered.

"The Mississippi is half a thousand miles east!" he said.

"In unrecorded ages," I answered in poetry, "it has changed its course over the entire southern half of Louisiana, draining the continent from Appalachia to the Rockies and farming its rich territories on the continental shelf."

Gerald stared into the opaque water. "You make it sound like these waters could rise up and overwhelm everything."

"You've seen it yourself, when the floods took half the town from the hill under your store," I reminded him.

A large disturbance of water announced some creature by the side of the boat.

"What was that?" said Gerald.

"Maybe a gar now," said Prien.

"Gar? What's that?"

"Oh, he's an old fish now, prehistoric I once heard Lafitte say. Leather-skinned. Jaws they are as long as the body – three foot long to each part now, six feet all full grown. But now maybe it was just a gator."

"Just an alligator?" said Gerald, alarmed.

"Are you sure we are not in the river of hell?" I joked.

Swamp lights, drifting in and out of the trees, seemed to follow us.

Gerald said, "I know you'll think I'm crazy if I tell you something."

"No," I assured him, "we'll just think you haven't had enough sleep."

"Some shadows came out of the fog after us, when we came away from the vanished tombs on the lake; and I think they have been following us ever since," he said.

"Shadows?" I asked.

"In dusk, they looked like shadows," he replied. "But at night, I keep thinking there is a light that doesn't look like the other lights. It doesn't move like swamp gas."

We turned to stare at the lights that had been following us from the distance.

"You remember at the sunken ship, we saw a boat in the fog with two men in it," he said. "We all saw it, right? Their faces were looking directly at ours. I can't get that out of my mind!"

Among the faint glowing spheres that followed us, it did seem that there were two, more than the others, that revealed a pallid suggestion of faces.

"If they followed from them tombs now," said Prien, "I'd say it's a good idea they not catch up with us."

The boat's bottom dragged on mud, and would go no further.

"I think this here might be the place," said Prien. "We'll have to wade."

"Besides gar and alligators, what else can we expect to find in this water?" I said.

"Them snakes they will hear you coming and swim away," Prien answered. "Just don't step in no moccasin nest now."

"Why, what will happen?"

"Just don't do it," he repeated.

"How can I tell to avoid one?" I said with a trace of panic in my voice.

"Well, there's only one way, really," he said. "You have to feel the mud with your hand. When you find a hole, reach in, gentle and slow. You can stroke the belly of any creature now in just such a way that they like it. If it's a fish now, you can tickle it to sleep, then grab it and pull it out. If it's a snake, you let it go."

"You're making this up," I said.

"No, it's called hand-fishing. Choctaws taught me to do it. You coming, or not?"

We kindled lanterns and jumped out, leaving William to guard the boat. He crouched in the dark hull, his young face refusing to show fear, and promised not to light his lantern until we shouted for him.

Our lights revealed the grotesque wilderness of half-submerged cypress knees through which we picked our way, the invisible mud sucking our boots from our feet.

The moon was searching with us, but the fog was against us. When we came to land, Prien gasped to see a grove of oak trees. As soon as we stepped into it, a swarm of giant water rats charged us from the trees.

We turned and ran, slipping, splashing and screaming as no less than a hundred angry nutria swam after us. Our cries awakened William's lantern. I don't know how we made it to the boat before we were eaten, or how long we beat them off of the boat with our oars before they gave up the chase; but we never went into the swamps at night again.

ౖ౿ౖ౿ౖ౿ౙౙౙ

I woke to a strange sight – the sun, just out of the trees, bathing the sky in light. I had not seen it since that weird odyssey upriver began.

The serenity of its rising was the more disorienting because of the dream from which it had pulled me. In its first warm embrace I thought that Denise's hand was on my shoulder. She was whispering urgent directions which I did not understand. She was dressed like the nuns, wrapped in black. There were wrinkles in her face that filled it with austere beauty, but it was the concentrated power in her eyes that I did not recognize. Her eyes and brow were accentuated by highly developed facial muscles which I had never known could exist in the substructure of a human face.

"Did you not reveal to my God your desire to see my face as it has been interpreted by the years? Were not those your own words? Remember, then, that He will hear your prayer!" Small rays of light ran from her wrinkles until her face was filled with tiny suns, becoming painfully bright – and that was how I found myself awake and staring at the face of the morning sun.

The other men began to stir from their hollows in the open boat as the sudden heat drove sleep from their bodies. We had tied to a tree in the open water as soon as we escaped the terror of the water rats, and, lulled by the chanting of the old man's prayers, had fallen into exhausted sleep.

"The fog has completely vanished?" said Gerald.

"It's been a week since we've seen the sun," William yawned.

Now as we stretched and slowly sat up, one by one, we fell into wonder at the vision before us on the opposite side of the river.

We were in a deep outside turn of the river, across from a low bluff that sloped gently down to a sand bar. Against the forest beyond that bank, fiercely illumined by sunrise, was nothing more than a simple Indian settlement of wooden lodges and more temporary leaf-thatched dwellings. Perhaps it was the utter peace in which its elders sat on the bluff; perhaps it was the easy grace of the women coming down to the water or the laughter of children, or the degree to which all were completely unconcerned at our existence; or perhaps it is only in the most vulnerable moments of first awakening to the splendor of morning that one can have any recollection of the original innocence of mankind.

Perhaps, again, it was something else, something entirely indescribable.

"I had forgot now," said Prien, "that this here tribe has its trading post in these parts."

"You know them, I hope?" I said.

"Very well now," he replied. "Their spir'tual mother among them nuns was the same as mine."

The elders on the bluff, having heard our voices, stood and called us in greeting.

"The nuns allowed them to continue in this state of existence?" I said.

Prien laughed: "Do you see anything wrong now in their way of life?"

"Not at all," I admitted. "But it is not the way I've seen the natives treated by the California Padres."

"Them nuns they instructed them in prayer, and other than that did not mess with their lives," he said as we neared the sandbar. "Before them nuns came, we both fought and traded with this here tribe. These elders now I have known them since their youth, both before and after they submitted to the sayings of them nuns, and I can tell you this here: I have lived on them there convent grounds, and I have lived in this here village. They are not so different as you think."

George Ryan the slave came out of one of the lodges and roared with laughter to see us at Prien's side. He joined us as we sat with the elders in the shade of an oak overlooking the riverbank. The women brought us a breakfast of wild rice and fish in shallow baskets. There were also steamed wild greens and boiled nuts with a delicious, delicate flavor. This completed, the elders sat in silence and waited for Prien to speak. He used their language. They appeared to regard him with reverence, listening with heads bowed. He spoke for an hour. They never interrupted, but now and then supplied brief answers which he seemed to seek. At intervals, George Ryan would speak abruptly, and this was always followed by outbursts of laughter from all; even the women would turn their heads and laugh. After one of these interruptions, Ryan turned to us, and, so that we would not miss the joke, explained, "These chiefs here they want to know why you didn't bring a good supply of meat and pelts, when you found so many o' those plump river rats!"

A long silence followed Prien's speech. Then the elders, one by one, began to reply with gentle voices, deep with humility. These discussions lasted until noon. At that time, we rose and with all the village gathered in front of the main lodge. There, where the tribal totem would be expected to stand, was a cross of lashed logs. Men and women sang a meditative chant in their native cadence while children skipped through the edge of the crowd.

After this, Prien led us in silence to the boat while the village watched. He untied it himself and stared at it. I wondered if he were going to abandon it to the river. Gerald, however, seemed to understand him better; he got in, and we followed. Prien shoved off from the sandbar and hopped in. The current quickly took us into the turn.

It was a long time before Prien began to talk, but no one said anything until he did.

"I told them why it is I am looking for that there chest," he said. "I said what it might be. I told all them rememberings of that journey to bury it. Arsene LeBleu he was Lafitte's only loyal captain in them later days. He had ideas for that there map you see; them ideas was all in his forgeries. Well since this was the country he knew best, I always thought that final journey it led near the place he had settled. Well but them chiefs there they showed me my rememberings did not fit these here waterways of the upper Calcasieu.

"And they asked this: why search for the end of the trail without following the trail. Now I explained my readin' of that journal. They had me recite long pieces of it. They showed me that I misunderstood the meaning of the lost shore of them tombs."

"What was their interpretation, then?" I demanded.

"Well they did not give one. Instead, they asked the results of my search upriver. I told of them nights of fear since we came away from them tombs.

"Well they reminded me of the life that was taught by them nuns, when we worked by side with them, puttin' in all them nice gardens. We were showed the way of prayer and the way of them good virtues. Now first of them good virtues see was what they called perfection of obedience. They showed us clearly in this here way how to avoid such dangers as we have found in recent days."

"All your life you have lived in dangers!" I interrupted.

"Not all my life now, no," he answered; "only them few quick years o' youth, before I learned how it is not only, see, to avoid them powers that destroy a man, but even that way of blessedness was open to me, if I just chose to follow after it."

"I think your earlier life was the better adventure," I proposed.

"Well now that's because you know nothing of the dangers even along the way of blessedness," he replied calmly. "But that is the way we will have to follow in this here adventure, not the way of our own making! That's where I misled us, forgettin' this here journey has been started on out of obedience to them nuns."

"I don't think you understand the nature of my search," I said, taking up an oar, "but you are our guide. We will have to follow your intuitions. What's the next site listed in the journal? Niblett's Bluff, is it, all the way back down at the bottom of the river?"

"I don't think you understand anything at all too well," he said to me. "Why did you come to them nuns in the first place?"

Conscience smote me like it had not since I was a boy, and I did not know why, and could give no answer.

Gerald spoke for me: "We came with letters of commission to search for this treasure. "

"Letters!" said Prien. "From who now?"

I found my tongue, and it moved: "From the widow of George Fisher. He was a Mason who spent much of his life following the mystery of Lafitte's treasure."

"Not just a Mason," said Mr. Matthews.

"What, then?" I said to him.

"Don't tell me you never knew that he became the Grand Master of the American Lodges!" he replied.

I said only, "I never knew that you could have had information like that!"

"And so that's why you wrote this book on Lafitte?" Prien interrupted. "Well now, I'll just have to take a look at this book. What did them Masons believe was in that there chest?"

"They really don't seem to know, do they?" I said, looking aside at John Matthews.

"Their belief," said Mr. Matthews, "was that the incorrupt remains of Father Christian Rosencreutz, along with the secret archives of the Rosicrucians, had been brought from Jerusalem and given into the care of Napoleon. During Napoleon's escape after his defeat, they were transferred to Lafitte to be hidden in America."

"Oh, I see," said Prien. "I have never heard this tale exactly, but it makes sense of the way Lafitte he treated that there old priest and his trunk, at the beginnin' of things."

I was staring at Mr. Matthews. I could not believe that even an ex-Mason would dare to divulge such knowledge, confined to only the narrowest circle of secrecy! He calmly answered my stare and said, "The old nun in the convent assured me that it is nothing but a myth."

"She told you that!" I said.

"A Gnostic myth she called it," he said. "It was a word that came off of her tongue with disdain; and I have to agree."

"A word for the secrets of true knowledge," I replied, "spoken with disdain!"

"Come, James, do you really believe those counterfeits of mystical doctrine?" said Mr. Matthews. "You read Ireneas of Lyons! Do you really believe that an evil god made this world, and that our souls can only reach enlightenment by freeing themselves from our flesh? That the material world exists only to entrap and darken our spiritual intelligence? You cannot deny that this is what the Masons teach!"

Prien whistled. "Is that what them Masons think now?"

"Not only the Masons," I replied calmly. "This is what the ancient Greeks believed, as did all the Indo-European doctrines: Egyptians and Persians, all the religions of the Far East, and probably even the Druids."

"You read the commentaries on Genesis!" said Mr. Matthews. "The flesh and the world were created perfect and good; decay and death were not part of the original Creation, and were not in the constitution of man. The tragic separation of body and

127

soul in death is due to the Fall of man. The Fall is spiritual in origin; it is not the fault of matter and flesh, it is a result of pride."

I shrugged and said only, "I don't see why the Church's interpretation is superior to that of all others."

Prien decided to get more involved in this discussion.

"Well, I'll tell you why then," he said. "Look here now. That there same God that made ever'thing out of nothin' you understand, ever'thing good and right in the beginnin'; when it got corrupt from that there pride o' angels and men you see, well He's the one who came into the flesh Hisself to make it good again. Now that there was God, not some angel, and man, not no spirit. And that there was not pride; that was humility, real Divine humility, with love and power you see. And He gave new Divine Energy so that folks could be like Him. Now Lafitte, he looked all his life for them there 'lluminati folks, never saw nor heard of even one. I bet you hain't never seen one neither. But wonder-workers and healers now, I've seen 'em, and so have you now, that know them things of the Spirit that no one else could know. And that there's the difference. You know the tree by them fruits from it, you do."

"That's what the nun was telling me," said Mr. Matthews. "That's why she called the life of Christian Rosencreutz a myth. She assured me, though, that its prototype exists in the lives of the saints. She described the incorrupt remains of the great saints Nicholas and Lucy, which she herself had seen in the churches of Italy. She compared the lives of many saints, which I had never heard before, to details in the story of Fr. C. R. C., pointing out that the inventors of his story were familiar with the lives of these saints. She showed me how the Rosicrucian myth was an attempt to recreate the vision of a true Christian church by western Europeans, who no longer saw living examples of that sanctity."

"The Rosicrucian myth! The old nun said that!" I repeated.

"You seem surprised," he answered. "Listen: she told me the life of Saint Catherine the Great, the young philosopher of Alexandria; and I can tell you, it far outshines the story of Fr. C.R.C. She said the maidenly beauty and miracle-working power of the body of St. Catherine on Mt. Sinai was seen by Father Honoratus. On her finger was the ring which Christ himself, appearing in a vision, had given her. She said that Fr. Honoratus' hand had trembled when he told her this, because the monks had taken the ring from her finger and had allowed him to hold it for a moment. That was the moment that transformed him. He came away wrapped in the fire of Mt. Sinai, which never left him since that time."

"Did she say what is in that there chest that Fr. Honoratus he brought from the east?" Prien asked.

"She doesn't know." John Matthews answered. "The only person that opened it was Lafitte, when he placed Fr. Honoratus' body in it."

"That's why the nuns want us to find it," said Gerald.

"They directed us to begin the search for it at the site of the sunken ship," said William, "without telling us where to find it, what we would find there, or anything about you or the journal."

"That's the way they are now," said Prien. "You will see it for yourself how them things turns out if you follow their direction. They won't tell everything. They don't take your own decisions from you, and they let you discover them things yourself. I never doubted that they sent you to me now. But something there is I don't understand: how did this widow of a Mason know to send you to them nuns in the first place? How did she know about them? Had she heard of them from somewhere?"

"That came about strangely," said John Matthews. "If she knew about them, she said nothing until I began to search for my lost daughter." His eyes searched me as he let the words fall on me, and did not apologize for the pain that ripped me open to his gaze. Gerald and William took up oars and pretended with all their strength that they could not hear.

"Did you believe the nuns would know her fate?" said Prien. "They know many things mysteriously!"

"She had became one of them," said Mr. Matthews.

"Your daughter! One of them nuns! You did not tell me that now," said the old man.

John Matthews sighed and lapsed into silence, staring into the vigorous currents as they divided, rose against each other, and fell around a fallen tree submerged in the clear waters. Gerald, with his oar's quick action avoiding collision with the broken trunk, was glad to avoid that conversation. A turtle, sunning on the one branch that broke the foaming surface, met my stare, and, startled with what it saw there, dove.

That left Gerald to explain: "We arrived at the convent to find her deceased."

"I see," said Prien when the waters took calm after the turn. His oar rested on his knees. We drifted.

When he lifted his oar to guide us into the next turn, he spoke: "I've never raised a child now; and surely, you know now, I've never buried one. But I can tell you this: if your child is buried within the fences of that there convent, that's more extraordinary than any treasure can have been buried anywhere. The Eldress Dionysia herself, planting climbing roses with me one day in the soil of that there cemetery, told to me some of the wonderful, sorrowful and terrifying things of life and death – things I would not dare repeat..."

"When you call her an 'Eldress'," said Mr. Matthews, "what do you mean?"

"It means that she was among them wisest of the spir'tual fathers and mothers of old times and all times – that she walked into eternity with them now, passin' back and forth between the doors of this life and that one there after death. It means that she – like your daughter, sir, like you and I and every person, required to pay her debt now to our first fallen ancestors with death – that neverth'less she lives, sir, she lives. I have proof of that now – proof I can't right show you."

"That night we stayed in the convent, the old nun showed me the icon in her room," said Mr. Matthews. "It was called 'The Joy of All Who Sorrow'. In it, the Mother of God was cultivating a garden where blossoms rose from the acts of the martyrs and the tombs of the suffering faithful."

"How many other things did she tell you that night?" I said with suspicion.

"So many!" he confessed. "The whole summer would not be enough to tell about them! How can I describe that interview? I don't even know how many things she really said, or how many I thought she said; it was as though the heavens opened their speech in my heart while she sat silent..."

"That's right!" said Prien, "that is what it is like now to sit in front of an Eldress!"

"I think I understand," said Mr. Matthews.

"That there Eldress Dionysia now, she was my spir'tual mother, as she was for many – and by that, sir, what I mean is, that she like gave birth in spirit to children of that there paradise in which she lives. Last night, she spoke to me in a dream, warnin' that I was following a wrong and wanderin' path."

"Yes," said John Matthews; "I had a similar dream."

"Everything she said to me was confirmed now by them tribal elders. But tell me, sir, your daughter – which one was she? What was her name? Perhaps I knew her!"

At this point at last, the man's breast could not contain his heart; it burst in a moan that continued in deep-voiced sobs. Pelicans in the tall magnolias, answering his cry, bent over the nests of their young, tearing their breasts. River currents broke open in commotion, and the boat spun between whirlpools of a deep bend. His eyes, mirrors of those whirlpools, flooded the face until all of its features reflected light.

Prien spoke in awe: "Now I recognize that these eyes here in you are the same that I have known! Strange it is now, to see one person's eyes so reflected in another's. Dionysia – she was your daughter? I find myself in strange company now, angels and men! This is a stranger journey than could have been thought – showin' marvels more than the old tales!"

ॐॐॐॐॐॐ

The next turn revealed Arsene Lebleu's house. The homestead stood abandoned in its oaks, overgrown and lonely, but no longer ominous as it had appeared by night. Beyond it, the river divided, wandering into the lowland backwaters and bayous we had entered the night before. We passed the broken dock and a weather-beaten boat swinging in the current from a taut and fraying rope. No one spoke, but our thoughts were probably the same; we wanted only to slip past that region before its night creatures woke.

"Now, that there's most interestin'," said Prien.

"What's that?" said William.

"That boat," he answered. "It hasn't been there so long."

"So long as what?" said Gerald. "It looks as old as the river to me."

"It hasn't been there as long as just a few seasons, to still be floating. There's somebody in that there house."

At the fork, we followed the current into the deeper channel, opposite the bayous we had entered the night before. We heard a noise behind us as we swung into the curve, and we turned to see two men stepping into the boat on Arsene's dock.

"Are those our ghosts?" I said.

"They sure are," said Gerald.

Mr. Matthews tore a page from his own journal and occupied himself in rapid writing, while Prien dug out the spyglass from under his seat. The rest of us broke out the oars and clawed into the current. Prien turned suddenly, focusing the glass as quickly

130

as he would aim a rifle, and said, "Those are no ghosts!"

I was not less afraid to hear this.

"I caught him right in the eye," chuckled Prien as he dropped the scope and reached for his own oar; "just as he was focusin' his own glass on me."

Mr. Matthews rolled his scribbled page into an empty cider jar and set it out on a wave, smiling. "This will be evidence if they are ghosts or men!"

"What are you doing?" I said.

"If they turn aside for this, it will give us more time."

"Good idea." said William. "Is there a place ahead where we can hide and let them pass?"

"There's a cut-off that joins up with that other channel," Prien answered. "We go through that anyway, but where they would expect us to continue downstream on the other end now, we could turn upstream instead and return to the fork. They'll never find us after that."

William shoved his considerable vigor into his oar, leading the boat suddenly into to a watery stand of cypresses where the current was taking the cider jar. "Let me off in these trees, and come back for me later."

Without waiting for an answer he stood, grabbed a low branch, and swung himself into the tree. He was immediately out of sight between the thick branches and the heavy draperies of moss.

The cut-off came up suddenly to the left, straight and narrow, and the river poured into it in surprising volume. It led through a drowned forest no more than sixty feet before joining the river's opposite leg. Here the current turned angrily, softening its mood as it expanded into the wider channel. Turning upstream of the cut-off, we found a wide and lazy bayou with hardly a current, one of the many abandoned courses that would eventually silt up and become nothing more than swamp. We easily made our way up it, digging the water for speed, and recognizing the forbidden backwaters we had visited in the night. We came to the fork just in time to see the other boat slip into the cut-off and speed out of sight.

William dropped into our boat as we glided under the trees.

"The Donaldson Brothers," he said.

"What did they say when they read the note?" I demanded.

"Nothing," said William. "They made gestures to each other and paddled off."

"What did you write?" I said to John Matthews.

"Just a note," he said.

"What did it say?"

"What difference does it make what it said? The purpose was to throw them off our trail."

"Why are you answering me like this?" I said quietly. "If the Donaldson Brothers are following us, our lives are in danger."

"I suppose you are right about that," he replied.

I jumped up and stood over him, yelling, "You knew before we did that they were following us!"

"I had a suspicion."

"Did you talk with them before we left Natchez?"

"Why would I avoid talking with them? I've known their father since the time I was a Mason."

"Since the time I thought you were my father's friend, not theirs?" I yelled louder. "I saw the cryptographs you scribbled on that note!"

"I wasn't trying to hide them from you," he said. "I was only getting rid of the brothers. We'll see if I succeeded or not."

"Yes," I said, returning to my seat. "We'll see."

After a sullen moment I added, "Were you my father's friend, or not?"

"I am a better friend to him than you are," he said. "I had nothing to do with your disinheritance or any of your disagreements with them. I never got you into any of your troubles, did I? Did I get you into this one?"

Whether or not it were wise to trust such a complicated man as John Matthews, we never did encounter the Donaldson Brothers again during that journey.

Chapter Twenty-Four

The river unwound and opened its lakes, wider and wider, until the horizons were all water. The days had grown longer, and it seemed the sun could stretch the limits of its own horizons no further by the time we rowed into the inland sea that is the lowest lake of the Calcasieu River. The unbearable heat of the summer solstice was magnified by the huge mirror of water; but Prien assured us that before sunset we would step into the deep shade of a grove.

We rowed by turns across that endless afternoon, taking frequent rests and drinking water. William, John, and Prien read out loud from the Biblical commentary. They had developed a habit of this during the journey back down the river. They seemed content in nothing more than its words and the simple fact of their own existence, drifting on the slow current of blinding water. Gerald, too, had begun to ask questions. Although he was always satisfied with the simplest answers, he appeared to continue thinking them over. Having already read the entire volume, I listened to their conversations and said nothing, until the sinking sun revealed the outline of a low hill on the shore.

"Napoleon's treasure is no longer buried on Niblett's Bluff, I suppose," I said then.

"All of it was in that there grove, carefully marked and mapped," said Prien. "I don't remember everything that was reburied later you see. The map now, if it could be found, that would show us."

"In all variants of the maps we have," said William, "this bluff is the focus."

"We're not going to enter that maze of documents again, I hope," I said. "It's more complex than the network of bayous; and I didn't see how they helped us find our way out of those swamps!"

Prien chuckled. "Don't put much faith in Arsene's forgeries now."

"If they are only forgeries," said William, "how do you explain the consistency of the four variants? Isn't it possible that he, like yourself, struggling to remember the complexity of later burials, was attempting to sketch the layers of Lafitte's own thought?"

"You make some right powerful sense there, young man," said Prien.

"In the variants where the listing of sites is consistent, Niblett's Bluff is always the third of definite, recognizable sites, the next three being more enigmatic. In variants where there is no order, Niblett's Bluff is the only one that is always listed. In the variants which emphasize the three regions over which treasures are buried, this bluff is the gateway between one region and another."

"Yes," I said, "where each treasure-site is the clue to the meaning of the next. If that were so, you would expect that we would have learned something at the last one we visited. Let's go over what we found at the tomb-like vaults: absolutely nothing. Not only that, we went all the way up the river and back, finding absolutely nothing. From this, one might conclude that we will continue to find the same."

"Are you getting tired of your treasure-hunt already?" laughed Mr. Matthews.

"And what about you?" I replied.

"I'll follow your suggestion," he said; "let's go over the list of our discoveries. First, we found that the legendary Natchez Treasure is historical fact, that it is buried in this region, that my own wife and daughter knew about it. Then we found my daughter. We discovered that she had become not only the abbess but a prophetess as well, and that she had foretold our coming to find it! The nuns – who became her disciples – instructed us to locate Lafitte's shipwreck. We found it. At the time, we may have thought we found nothing but open water at the site of that discovery, just as we now think we have found nothing at the second site. However, we found not only the treasure it concealed – Lafitte's own journal – but we found it in the hands of the only one who could explain it to us. He has become another of the prophetic abbess's spiritual children: Lafitte's cabin boy, who witnessed the events which the journal describes, and whom Lafitte himself seems to have been intended to have become the guide to its pages."

"Nobody could make up a tale like this!" I admitted.

"We can't complain, then, if the search encounters some difficulties," he said. "What does Lafitte's journal say about Niblett's Bluff?"

William opened the manuscript across his knees.

"In the first section of the journal, the narratives of his crimes, this:

The great betrayal: The Masonic Brotherhood works in ways often inharmonious to the laws of nations. The trust of the Brotherhood itself is inviolate. There comes a time when even that trust can no longer be taken for granted. Great betrayals will take place. Honored counselors will become hunted criminals, as when I sold Napoleon for the price of many pounds of silver.

"Among his reflections in the second part of the journal, he writes only this:

What was Napoleon's wealth? He gained the world, and lost his soul.

"Finally, to locate the treasure, in the third part, he writes:

The number of trees corresponds to the number of treasures."

"What was Napoleon's treasure? Do you remember?" I said to Prien.

"Not too clearly, now," he admitted, "As great as it seemed at that there time – crown jewels of them European kings I think, gold pieces, too, minted by them dynasties all long dead, and some other things – their worth began to seem like less, you see, when we saw that there was also kings' sealed charters, there was Roman vellums, purple-dyed they was, and some things from old Egypt, stone tablets and little statues. I guess I remember some them things right well then after all, hey? Then there was that there locked trunk belongin' to the priest you see, that we never got opened; and that priest himself that was all mystery, more and more all that there time. And Napoleon's treasure itself, you see, in all them trunks he had, it was of such a natur' that whatever you could imagine to be the thing of most worth, there would be something there in another chest which showed itself even finer now."

"In Arsene's fourth variant of the maps," said William, "the buried treasures are listed in ascending value. Each is more precious than the one before; and the finding of the last is the only thing that matters."

"Young man," Prien answered, "you have stumbled across the meaning of our goal, in that there last chest!

"To the young Jean Lafitte now," Prien went on, "disinherited you see, a boy brought up fairly poor now, it was a quite a treasure to seize a ship of goods. He used to recollect these here things to me hisself. By that time there he came to be king of smugglers in all them Barataria swamps down under New Orleans, there was no one who thought there could be a man in the New World could ever be richer. They said there was nobles in the old country who had less land and wealth. Then you see he got more ambition to go steal all the gold of the Spanish main. He thought now there could be no bigger treasure in all the world. But Napoleon's, now you see, it was, it was bigger than that. Only a man who saw it would believe, now. And there were writings in that treasure which were thought now to be worth more than all the rest. And that's why we supposed you see that whatever was in that there priest's chest from Jerusalem, we thought it must be greater out of comparin'. Then there was that priest hisself, and the way he was that was so different from anything. This here's the key to Lafitte's thinking. He would lay aside his treasures as something more valuable caught his eye. The last steps of this here repudiation it got difficult for him, though. It wasn't something he volunteered for no more." The old man held up Lafitte's journal. "And this here is where it gets hardest to understand it; but this is just what it's most important to understand."

"That explains it, then," said Gerald.

"Explains what?" I said.

"Think about it," he said. "From what we have seen, it seems there are no material treasures remaining along the Calcasieu – only symbolic ones."

We did think about that as the bluff and its grove floated on the horizon, nearer and nearer as the sun reached down to the waters of the opposite shore.

As we prepared to disembark, William said to Prien, "Have you any idea what we might find here now?"

"Once we are standing in that there grove, I think I will have to dig through some memories," the old man replied.

"I ask because it seems that the journal brings us to this point, and no further," William explained. "The last three treasure-sites are not listed."

೮೩

The setting sun burned against the face of the low bluff as we climbed it. We walked into the tall and leafy sweet-gums. Their shadows fell from the southeastern sides of the trunks, stretching ten times longer than the height of the trees themselves. The grove itself was brilliant, with the shadows congregating far in the distance.

"Twenty-two trees," I counted. "Does this mean we are looking for a full twenty-two treasure sites? That would mean we have only just begun. This is the third we have searched; only nineteen more to go! I thought we were looking for six treasures. I thought the last one was in a grove of six oaks, underneath the one with the hanged-

135

man's noose."

"That is right now," said Prien. "This here is not that grove. And you're right about that, too, that this is just the beginnin'."

"Look," said Gerald. "The shadows of these trees are pointing toward another grove over there. Aren't those six trees oaks?"

"Imagine that now!" said Prien, walking in the direction of the shadows. "Imagine that! We just happened to come here just on that there midsummer's day!"

The old man could walk fast, and we were out of breath keeping up. The sweet-gum shadows swallowed us as they advanced before us in a pointed wedge reaching for the oaks.

"On that summer solstice now, the shadow of that there tallest sweet-gum will point out the tree!" he said with excitement in his voice.

The trunks and knotted limbs of oak burned fiercely in the last light of the sun, while the elongated shadows of the sweet-gums bore down on them like the bearers of dusk. Their tip of racing shade touched the great roots of one and began to climb its trunk just at the moment that the immense horizon put out the sun.

"There!" cried out Prien, breaking into the limping run of an old man. He embraced its bark with one arm and thrust his other into a knothole, pulling out a stone jar. He uncorked it, and twisted out a tightly rolled map.

"Too many things to remember," he said, shaking the scroll at us, "but this here will make me remember them all!" His fingers overcame the leather thongs that tied it, and it unrolled in his hands.

We crowded his shoulders to have a look.

Its correspondence to the contents of the journal was immediately clear. The waterways of southern Louisiana were meticulously drawn in three colors of ink. In the bayou country of the central part of the state were shown the final locations of all the buried treasures in black ink. These were cross-referenced to the account of crimes committed in those places as listed in the journal. The locations of the six treasures along the Calcasieu were in blue; and, as Gerald had noticed, there was no treasure left in those places other than the journal and this map. The last three of these six sites were located along Contraband Bayou. Finally, gold ink marked three churches: the convent of the nuns, that of the Sisters of Charity in New Orleans, and the Church of St Martin on Bayou Teche.

"Interesting," I said. "He shows the entire Barataria basin blank."

"We're supposed to follow that there trail of his crimes," Prien whispered, "all the way from the start!"

"That's where the treasure is," I said, smiling.

He rolled up the map quickly and spoke to the sky: "I don't want to do this now!"

We stepped back from him. A change was coming over his face. Intense emotions were rolling over his forehead.

"That darkness of them acts in them there swamps is not a thing I want to go back to!" he said to the sky. "I was there when he did them things. I helped him. You know now I turned away from that life, you rescued me out of that there. I do not want to remember!"

Tears erupted violently out of that face. He ripped the prayer-rope off of his wrist and began shaking it against the sky. He walked back toward the sweet-gums, crying out: "I'll do it alright, then, but you have got to go with me now! If you do not go right with me, right along with me now, I won't go there, not no-how!"

He continued gesturing toward the sky like a man who had lost his mind. This is what we would have thought, perhaps, that he had lost his mind, had we not seen what we appeared to see. We all saw something; what it was seemed a little different to each. We discussed it later, around the campfire, before the old man had yet returned from his fevered dialogue with the open heavens. Gerald said that a few stray shreds of the vanished sunlight seemed to fall into his face and fill it up with light. William saw it in the tears, as though the whole sky came down into a few tears: he seemed unable to say it any better than that. John Matthews wouldn't say what he saw; he just stared at the others as they tried to describe these things, while he nodded his head in agreement. I didn't see anything like that, but what I saw was something I had never seen before. I saw a man in transformation, a man entering a vision. I had no trouble believing that the sky into which he was shouting came down into that transformation and planted itself there. Whatever he had learned from the sea, whatever he had learned from the nuns, whatever he had been musing over all those years while sitting on his porch in prayer and contemplation, I saw it all ignited in one moment of spontaneous combustion.

We let him go. We returned to the boat, and brought out provisions for camping.

We ate in silence while the midsummer evening slowly grew dim. When the first star showed itself, Gerald said to William, "Do you remember what you were reading in that commentary this afternoon?"

"When Moses was staring into the burning bush," William replied, "and was transformed by whatever it was he saw there, until he could hear the voice of God."

"I was thinking about the nuns while you were reading that," said Gerald. "I was thinking about the way they look at you whenever they speak to you."

"I was thinking the same thing," Mr. Matthews agreed.

"And yet we have just seen the same thing happen in someone who is really just a simple man," Gerald added. "It's amazing, really."

"And then you think about those nuns again, about how calm they are," said Mr. Matthews, "and you wonder if what we just saw happen to Prien might be something they are actually accustomed to!"

"Who could have imagined," Gerald mused, "that such wonders could be contained in a human frame?"

"Think what their elder must have been like!" John Matthews offered.

"And did you hear," Gerald pursued, "what Prien said about Denise?"

No one answered, though we all knew what the question meant.

"Now this is what has been bothering me all these years," Gerald went on. "I always knew Denise was the kind of person who could become someone remarkable..."

"You saw that, so young?" I replied skeptically.

"Sure I did," he affirmed. "I could never have imagined this, of course; I never knew such things were possible. But from the time we were children, it was obvious that she had a unique understanding of others. That was what attracted you to her the most. Am I wrong?"

Again, I had no answer to this.

"So this is what has been bothering me all these years," he said, "while you were off in California getting rich and famous and making a mess of your life. It was not hard to see into the heroes of your own stories, and read how you yourself were falling apart."

"You've always known me better than I thought you did," I admitted without any sarcasm.

"I am not saying the stories were uninteresting. They were fascinating. But it was painful to read what was happening in your own mind while you were out in the wild West, living hard and free from anyone who cared, and writing whatever came to your mind for all the world to see. Like you were some kind of new intellectual rebel; but I kept wondering what your rebellion was all about."

I sat quiet and sullen, wondering how much worse this was going to get before it was over.

"Because I remember when this all started," said Gerald. "Suddenly you were talking about it all the time. We were seventeen years old or so, you were reading Lord Byron, and you found something there that stirred up all your bitterness. You remember?"

I stared at him hard, waiting like a murderer before the judge to hear the court's decision. To tell the truth, I was curious to know what it would be. Like a man who has tried hard to believe his own lies, I actually felt some hope that the truth was coming.

"But the way you started thinking then was driven by anger, and all that anger was about one thing. You started believing that you had been poisoned by some terrible childhood. But I knew it wasn't so bad."

This was all he had to say? "What do you know about it?" I challenged.

"It was never as bad as it was for the people you wrote about. I thought about this a lot, you know. It was as though you had to exaggerate your own disappointments. I know there were disappointments. It was a tragedy to lose your mother at such a young age; I know that nothing can replace that loss; but it was never as though your father was so completely unequal to the task! I remember when you were very close to him, when you idolized him; and I remember when you turned against him."

"You were very hard on your father," Mr. Matthews agreed; "and you still are."

"Are you going to try to convince me that my father is not an idiot?" I replied to the fire.

"That's the kind of exaggeration that Gerald meant," Mr. Matthews answered gently. "These are the views of an adolescent. You need to look at them now through the eyes of a man. Your father knows he made mistakes. He knew it then; we used to talk about them. No man is above mistakes; but he never made one so catastrophic as the one I made, with my daughter..."

"But this is still not the thing that has bothered me all these years," said Gerald. "I never understood why you ran away from Denise; and I still don't understand it. That was your big mistake. I could see even then how it would have changed you, if you had submitted to her influence. I think you could see it, too; and it frightened you. That's why the wound in your chest never healed."

"You should have said something," I admitted with lead in my tongue.

"I think I would have, if I had thought you would listen," he said. "I think she felt the same way."

I glanced up. My features must have been filled with a glowing heat from the fire. William, who had been staring at me with wide eyes, winced.

"Then why are you telling me this now?" I replied to Gerald.

"Because I'm beginning to think," he replied with that softened frown of honest introspection so unique to his face, "that she's going to have her way with you yet!"

I watched the flames roll into embers. I didn't even notice that no one else spoke until William, still with some embarrassment in his voice, attempted to change the direction of our thought.

"Do you remember how the steamboat captain cautioned us about going into the swamps? He warned us about trusting ourselves to a guide; but I think we can trust this one."

"I think so too," said Gerald. "But I'm not sure he wants to go there himself."

"There's no communication with the world outside the bayous, is that right?" said Mr. Matthews. "It's a world beyond the world?"

"That's what they say," I affirmed moodily.

"I think it's best to go, then," he said.

"Why?" I said with sudden attention.

"I'm afraid we may still be followed," he said. "If we go deep enough into the bayou country, they won't know where we have disappeared."

"They?" I said suspiciously. "You mean you think the Donaldson Brothers might still be following us?"

"I think the entire Masonic Brotherhood might be looking for us," he said.

"I never told them what we are searching for," I said. "Did you?"

"No, but they have been watching you with a thousand eyes."

"And how do you know that?" I said.

"I never lost my wariness for their secretive skills," he answered.

I was about to question him more about this knowledge of their skills when Prien walked out of the darkness. His manner was composed and peaceful. He sat by the fire in silence which we did not interrupt.

"When Dionysia she taught me how to pray," he said after a while, "she warned me about a time, you see, when I would really need to know how to do it right. She taught me, you see, them prayers for the dead, too; and she wanted me now to pray for that there soul of Lafitte. That's when she warned me that there was going to come a time of hard trial for me, and one that she could not save me from. But she promised now that it could heal me. This is it. To have to look at my own crimes now, that would crush me I think; but that is what I have got to do. There are them twenty-two treasures you see, in Lafitte's favorite hiding places, around near all his trade routes. Do you know now why we have to uncover them?"

"Twenty-two treasures," I repeated. "Are you suggesting that we are going to actually find something, after all?"

"Yep sir, likely so. May be even we might see some that gold buried after Fr. Honoratus he told Lafitte to give them there riches to the poor."

"If we do find that," said Mr. Matthews, "are we to carry out those same directions, as the Elder commanded? Are we to give that gold away?"

"If we do now, we will sure understand some things," Prien affirmed. "That there pattern of burials it will be clear, and this now it will lead us to the priest's own chest you see. It will happen, you'll see; just in the way we were led to this place here, to come just on that one day that I'd remember where I hid that there map."

I was lying on my back and counting the stars. Each was a diamond of incomparable value. And I was thinking of the number of treasures buried in the bayou country. Twenty-two: equal to the number of mystical paths between the branches of the Kabbalistic Tree of Life! Lafitte would have known that. It occurred to me that this could be a trick, if he wanted to mislead the Masons who would surely come looking for that map. Nevertheless, I would have to find an opportunity to search this document for alternate meanings.

Chapter Twenty-Five

The rising of the morning star leads the procession of first light that comes over the east, while the mockingbird's finest solos are hurled from the quiet branches. At that hour, we were already breaking camp. By sunrise Prien had led us to a shore of so much marsh it could not be said to be a shore at all. We floated into an endless fire reflecting the huge exploding disk of the sun as it surfaced through cattails and bull-rushes. As soon as the sun broke free and its blinding light across the water subsided, we found ourselves in a maze of saltwater ponds connected by narrow arms of shallow water. These led at last into the brilliant wide lane of Grand Bayou, stretching wave-lessly straight into the ascending skies of the east. The marshlands on either side to every horizon were disturbed by the commotion of a thousand kinds of waterfowl; and one could see why that was. The fishing nets were remarkably easy to fill.

When the sun climbed to its higher altitudes and its suffocating heat descended, the birds hushed and withdrew from the sky, and Prien set up his rigging to stretch the sail low over our heads for shade. We leisurely dipped oars in the steaming water, mak-ing our way down that perfect ribbon of water toward the blue horizon, while Prien explained the course of our journey east.

"We go right across them there deltas o' seven rivers coming down from the north. We are not far from sea now, and all them marshes and bayous they connect one to th'other. The whole bottom of Louisiana can be passed through in this way now. Not, though, in no straight shot east as in this here watercourse! This one it's strange and different that way. There's a-many turns ahead of us, and different kinds of country too that we'll see now."

Within a few hours, just as he had predicted, the bayou broke into two winding channels. We took the southern branch, lazy as the noon itself wandering through floating prairies, at times within sound of the Gulf's roaring breakers. Here the trawling nets scooped up every variety of clamshell, shining fantastic shape of crab, and dark gleaming oyster.

The channel narrowed and then unexpectedly emptied into a vast expanse of deep marsh. Floating islands of all sizes, and wide peninsulas of water-rooted reeds with no visible soil broke down into open water, going on forever, horizon after horizon. Fish could be seen darting through the sunlight under the boat and diving into the deeper shadows. Some were larger than the boat.

We slept that night in our floating cargo. Prien pulled down the canvas to keep the mosquitoes out; but their constant humming, louder toward the dawn, invaded our dreams and often woke us.

On the following day, we broke clear of those vapory curtains of tall marsh grass. Prien explained that we were entering the Mud Lake chain that drains the confluence of Bayou Lacassine and the lower Mermentau River. Here we were surprised by the shade of a forest of large oaks. As far as the eye could see into their deepening shadows, tremendous trunks dropped their stout arms to the ground, resting there like burdened elbows before lifting great mossed fists of leaf.

Eagerly we climbed that bank into the shade. Before we could rest, though, Prien set us to work. I was ordered to clear the ground for a fire ring. In doing so, I found earth composed entirely of shells. William and Gerald brought fallen branches and dry leaves for kindling. Prien pulled fire from a flint. John Matthews brought a pot of salt water and set it to boil. William went down to the boat for a frying pan and a cup of lard while I watched Prien fillet a flounder and roll it in powdery corn flour. The shellfish went whole into the pot of boiling water while other fish were buried in ashes with whole ears of corn from our stores. Still other parts of our catch were left smoking over the smoldering fire on screens of green branch-work.

Then we sat to satisfy our hunger, extracting the sweet meat of crustaceans from the transmuted color of boiled shells, the tender flakes of fried flounder, and the roasted fish and corn.

"Are we staying here long enough to eat everything?" I said.

"The smoked fish they will keep; the rest we trade tomorrow now," answered Prien.

His voice had become such comfort to us, that we lay on the ground in the shade of that grove to listen.

He explained that we had come to Grand Chenier. Chenier was the name for those fertile ridges of shell rising out of the marsh. Some were begun by storm tides, then built through the centuries; others chronicle the bends of powerful rivers that once came through here. This was the largest. The forest was one of Lafitte's favorites, until he murdered a man here. It was the first time he killed a man so that he would not tell where a treasure was buried.

"That's exactly what Lafitte says here," said William, opening the journal, which he had brought up from the boat. "In the second part, among his reflections, he writes:

The ritual performed in this grove was the beginning of my possession by evil passions. Murder and covetousness robbed my eyes of their own ideal.

Prien shuddered while William turned the pages to read the entry in the last section. "He says this of the buried treasure

It should never be found. It was buried in a wooden chest in the shell reef, between the trees and the shore, which the waves will be certain to remove. When the chest is dissolved and the reef washed away, jewels and gold will appear among the shells. By then they will have been washed of their crime, when no memory of the deeds performed here will tarnish them.

Prien dug his fingers into the grit of broken shell and raked through them, bringing up a dark doubloon. He smiled. "This is the place all right. I wasn't sure now I recognized it."

I jumped to my feet. "If we dig, we'll find more!" I said.

"Maybe, maybe not," he said, dropping the gold piece back into its groove and covering it. "I suspect that them tides would have done damage here more than along that there Big Lake. I seem to remember now that this here beach was right larger."

"Well, it's more than we found at the site of the treasure vaults," I said, sitting dejectedly.

"Lafitte seems to have been fascinated with the hope," said Gerald, "that his crimes might be washed away."

Prien nodded thoughtfully. "What did we find now, at that there haunted graveyard where all that Spanish gold it had been hid?"

"Nothing," I reminded him.

"For myself now, who saw terrible things, there is you see no treasure that could have been found, either here or there, that could have been more precious."

"I don't really want to know what happened here," said Gerald. "But according to what Lafitte wrote, he seems to have thought that it affected his character for the worse."

"That's right," the old man answered. "Lafitte began privateering as a freedom-runner, friend of the people he was: an idealist like, believin' in the promise of this here New World. He saw hisself a friend of the U.S. democracy, and an enemy of all that Imperial Europe. Organizin' the pirates that filled them swamps down there around the mouth of that Mississippi River, he got rid of crime 'gainst the French colonists. He was one of the great leaders of that there time. He got control of all that contraband movin' from the Gulf and Caribbean, and all the way down to South America, all from his headquarters on that there isle of Grand Terre. His plunder off them Spanish vessels was seen by all us French colonists now as an act of just war 'gainst Spain. And it was them Spanish colonies down in South America wantin' independence that gave Lafitte them legal papers to take Spanish ships you see as spoils of war.

"But that there big fortune got from privateering, and them profits of trade with the new wealth of sugar planters you see, that got to corrupt him. First, he got that taste for gold, for rum and for women; and then it was greed beyond all bounds now began to take him over. He looked for bigger treasure. He got that taste for a life of crime, schemin' and murder. And so he got skeptical then of his own ideals you see. Well, them Masons in New Orleans, they started comin' round him awful mad, saying he got to remember his mission to help the New World promise. It was that news of Napoleon, though, that shook him out of that there dreamin' always after riches."

"Yes," I yawned; " and his controversial obtaining of Napoleon's wealth, and his mysterious disappearance with it, caused the legends which made the world go crazy!"

I think he replied to me about that statement, but I don't remember what he said. I must have fallen asleep in the shade.

❧

Before dawn the next morning, Prien found me digging in the shell banks.

"Find anything now?" he said.

"I can't even find the one you threw back down!" I said.

He was about to reply. Instead, he shook his head and chuckled.

"How can you just reach into the ground and find a piece of gold, and I can find nothing?" I said.

"If it were meant for you to have it, you would reach into them sands and they would all become gold coins for your sake now. What good would that do, if you got to be skeptical like Lafitte in them there darkest years? If you want gold now, we might find it. Not here."

ᥣ

From Grand Chenier, as we entered the lovely wide course of the lower Mermentau, it was evident we had come into another country. Oak and pine forests were separated by wide flowering wetlands in a mingling of beauty and light.

"I don't remember it like this now!" Prien said. "I remember storms and winters, fog, and looking for places where to hide."

Fishing villages marked the river's entrances and exits through Lower and Upper Mud Lake. "These here are them Cajuns," said Prien, "that are all unknown to the rest of that there world. This here's no bustlin' port like Lake Charles now. We'll stop at the village on Grand Lake."

He took the opportunity of the pretty setting of those wetlands to explain to us the story of the Cajuns. He began with the settlement of Breton farmers in the idyllic coastal valley in southeast Canada which they named Acadia, after the pastoral myths of Greek Arcady. It was the same as Longfellow's story, with their cruel expulsion at the hands of the British, at the conclusion of the French-Indian Wars, before the American Revolution. Transported to all coasts, the exiles at last found welcome in French Louisiana. Here, families scattered from the Carolinas to the Caribbean islands were re-united and began a new existence. Finding the Mississippi and the banks of Bayou Teche already settled by colonial planters favored by the crown, they spread throughout the uninhabited bayou country. Where no suitable bank remained to be farmed, they went into the swamps to live by fishing and hunting from houseboats.

"We are a peace-loving people now," said Prien. "We don't worry 'bout money. We live off of what's here, right in the land." And he continued to describe what had always been the rural, pastoral – one could even say bucolic – society of the ancient Bretons.

ᥣ

On the docks at Grand Lake, Prien was greeted by name. We were made to sit on the shaded porch to exchange news and discuss items for trade. William explained that the store-keeper was asking for news of the nuns. Tiring of a conversation I couldn't follow, I wandered into the store. Nets, wooden hooks and supplies were all handmade and of respectable quality. Corn, rice and peas were stored in bins, and of course the fish was fresh. A spindle and loom transformed small piles of cotton into cloth. I wondered if the rum in stone jars was local, and what it was like.

That thought led me to realize that I had not tasted whiskey in more than a month. It occurred to me and that I felt sound in body and fully awake in mind. A window that opened in front of me to the simple houses lining the water, and the quality of light out on the lake, confirmed the growth of this revelation. I returned to the porch, quietly acknowledging a sense of gratitude for Prien and his leadership in an adventure into a world of grace and beauty.

Prien and the store-keeper were concluding their trade with jokes, while William and Gerald unloaded baskets of fish from the boat. Gerald was staring at me curiously. Prien told me to return inside for jars of salt and dried fruit from the shelves, and a string of smoked sausages. Gerald came in to help me.

"How are you feeling?" he asked quietly.

"Fine!" I said. "Never better."

"I saw you staring at the rum."

I gave him a hard look. "You were right."

"What's that?"

"Everything you said to me last night."

"Well, I feel badly about it – thinking out loud like that, when I should have kept quiet."

"A real friend," I acknowledged, "can only keep quiet for so long."

"True," he admitted simply.

"But you were right. Things were never so bad for me. Why did I need a mother, when I had a friend like you?"

He answered with a confused look.

"So," I said, "we have what we need now. We'll leave the rum where it is."

Now he smiled. We returned to the dock and climbed into the boat, while the storekeeper tossed down ropes of garlic and dried peppers for lagniappe, 'something extra'.

Guided by the sun, we crossed the expanse of Grand Lake. We reached the east shore by sundown and made camp. The following day we progressed through shallow marshes filled with reeds I had never seen. Thick stands of pine trees not far off warned that we were near higher ground. We squeezed through a narrow channel where the boat scraped bottom into White Lake, which, according to Prien, would be the last of the great lakes. We kept within sight of its southern shore. After several miles, we turned into another maze of bayous filled with forested cheniers.

"Them waterways they have changed," said Prien, who seemed to have trouble finding his way. "This here country is more filled with folks than it was; but it's glorious now, hain't it?"

The small farms crowding those cheniers were indeed pretty. Corn was beginning to burst into silk, and the climbing beans still flowered while dark pods already hung in their shadows. Cows and sheep kept the marsh grass down in places. Cotton, covering just enough ground to provide local clothing, was laid in between other crops to give the charming impression of quilt-work fields, from which songs rose now and then. Children were everywhere. When a man floated by in a pirogue, Prien greeted him in the name of the nuns, which always won approval, and then asked for directions. By nightfall we had come to the settlement of Pecan Island.

ଔ

The sky was still clear and full of light, but shadows were stretching their covers over the ground when Prien climbed a dock and said with uncertainty, "I think this here is the place."

He stood on the planks, staring into the darker shadows of the porch. There were silent faces in them, staring back. A dog took a few steps toward him, ears and tail erect.

"Papa Prien!" A girl broke from those shadows in a run. She leapt in a cannon-fire of Cajun phrases against his torso like a child who was accustomed to jumping into his arms, but was now a few years too old for that. She was about eleven, with dark eyes and volumes of black hair spilling from a blue scarf that dropped a single white star over the back of her hair. The light that flashed in her eyes had no hint of wickedness in it, but rather showed rapid movements of pure delight, perfectly tempered with an

145

innocent wisdom. I had never seen anything like it.

She turned to me and curtsied. Her quick eyes assessing my character, she abandoned her accent for flawless classical French. William, being the more proficient in that tongue, replied for me. The sight of that intelligent and handsome young man sent a smile exploding through her eyes, which did not diminish while she studied Gerald, whose silent qualities appeared to delight her just as much. As her eyes traveled to John Matthews they sobered with deep understanding, and she bowed to him respectfully. He responded with a formal French greeting. He and William having replied sufficiently to her, she turned again to my silence and overthrew it with an astonishing display of perfect Greek.

"Have I come, like Odysseus, to the land of wonders, then?" I replied in Greek nowhere as good as hers. She cocked her head, searching through my words, picking them apart as she repeated them to herself, and then with no more reflection she straightened her head and said, "You will find us as hospitable to strangers as were the men and women of every land to that hero."

Then she pointed at Gerald: "What about him? Where is he from, and what language does he speak?"

"He knows only English," I replied.

She put her hands on her hips and frowned at him, shaking her head, swinging the black hair from its kerchief. Gerald laughed, and so did she as she took Prien's old hand and led us to the house.

"This one goes to school at the convent," said Prien. "Claudette is her name. She is home for the summer."

Her father stood and smiled to take each man's hand as Prien gave the French form of our names. The mother, holding a sleeping baby, remained in her rocking chair, as did the elderly grandfather on his stool. Prien and Claudette entered into a rapid conversation with the father and grandfather while the mother laughed. Leaning against the door, a boy of about five years on crutches listened with shining eyes. Suddenly the grandmother emerged from the house and chased us in to the table. Claudette lit lamps around the room and began to carry plates to the table, talking all the time. If one thinks of a mockingbird flying from branch to branch and constantly switching songs, at one moment answering the jay in its own coarse language and in the next whistling to the breeze or singing to its mate, he will have an idea of Claudette.

"Papa Prien tells mama I am the exact image of herself when she was my age, but the personality is completely different," she said to me in Greek. "Grandmama remembers when Prien was with the pirates. Does he tell you his stories?" This last question she posed again in Cajun French for the man himself.

Prien chose to comment on that in English. "She is the expert on my adventures. She loves to hear them, but as soon as I finish she lectures me in detail on how I should have acted instead according to the Gospels."

"What is he telling you?" she said to me in Greek.

"He says you are an expert in the Gospel precepts," I answered.

"By God's grace and your prayers," she said with shining eyes, placing a steaming plate of rice and beans and a mug of water before me.

The room that overflowed with conversation in several languages was plain and comfortable. It was not as small as a settler's cabin, yet not much larger either, with a table and sideboard, straight wooden chairs around the hearth, which were dragged to the table, and a spinning wheel. The kitchen was off the back porch, and the beds, as always in these houses, were in the loft. The hand-crafted furniture was without adornment, but strong and polished smooth. The finest piece was the rocking chair, which the father had brought inside and set in its place of honor near the window. There were no wall decorations other than lamps set against round pewter reflectors, and a cloth in one corner with a prettily stitched image of the Mother and Child. This, like the curtains, the tablecloth, and the quilted pillows on the rocking chair, filled the room with the refinements of a woman's presence.

We stood while Prien uttered a prayer, and then our hands went out to the meal. A simpler one could not be imagined, but secret ingredients made it savory. As eager as we were to eat, the three generations of inhabitants in that house were as eager to engage Prien in conversation.

"Are they talking about the nuns again?" I asked William.

"I think so," he said. "It seems like everyone knows about them, and no one has ever seen anything like them. There are too many words in this conversation, though, that I cannot recognize."

"Our speech now, it comes out from a mixing of them Injun words and sounds with that there French," explained Prien. "Our way of life, you see, it's that same mix. 'Bayou' now, that's a word from them Injuns, bayuk, for 'stream'. If it were not for them Injuns, we would never have learned to live right so well in this here country."

"Your English is so proficient," said William, "that I forget these are your people."

"Lafitte himself now, he took care of my education," he answered. "I can talk that there French right polished and gentleman-like if I have to now; but my learning it was never refined like his was."

Claudette had me put this in Greek for her so that she could turn it into the language of her family. They demonstrated their disapproval of Prien's self-assessment, and she agreed, giving their judgment back in Greek: "Compare the life of Prien to that of Lafitte, and everyone can see which is better."

Mr. Matthews and William were able enough to follow this part of the conversation in French and Greek that they thought it important to translate for Gerald.

"I've been thinking about that," Gerald said to Prien. "For a man to have seen so much robbery and murder, and then to have turned out as you have – that is something that you never see in human nature."

"You yourself now, are maybe right keen to make that out," Prien responded. "It was a changing did not come out without slow hard hurt. For my fistful of years with Lafitte now, I paid with them tens of years in suffering hard work. It was them prayers of them there nuns, and their hand at the helm of my soul, that's what saved me now. If it wasn't for Eldress Dionysia, who watched over me, I'd not have ever knowed no different life.

"She told me that there story of a robber who tied up St Martin of Tours in a cave. 'I could kill you,' says the robber; 'hain't you afraid of me?' That there great saint he replied now that he was afraid, but only for that there robber's soul, and he sure explained to him why. Now that there writer Sulpicius, he wrote down the life of St Martin, he said he had that there story from the robber hisself; he got to be one of St Martin's monks.

"She told me this here story now. Moses the Black, he was the fiercest murderer that ever lurked on them banks of that there Nile. St. Macarius of Egypt, though, he made him into a different kind of man. She talked out all the sides of his story now, while I worked for her in them gardens. Mighty soothing it was to hear that; it was like a voice with a hand of healing inside it. She didn't not ever stop from telling these stories: like them labors o' St Mary of Egypt, who watered that there desert with her tears; or the thief of Mt Sinai, he demanded God's own judgment against them monks, unless now they took him in and gave him a way to change his life; and it was him that turned out their best example of repentin'. Yes sir, that Dionysia she filled my mind with new visions now; and she still does."

As I gave this in Greek for Claudette, and she in the Cajun French for her family, she came close to my ear and whispered, "You know, the nuns regard Prien as a righteous man."

"What do they mean by that?" I asked her.

"You don't know?" she jumped back in alarm. "What are you, a fool?"

William, recognizing that word, laughed.

Prien turned to the others in their own Cajun dialect. "He's asking about the health of my brother," said Claudette to me. "There is a doctor from Paris in New Orleans who thinks he can heal him, but we don't have money to pay him. The parish priest in St Martinsville has requested the Sisters of Charity in New Orleans to donate the funds, but even they may not have enough."

Prien sighed, and appeared to change the tone of conversation. Claudette leaped up with a squeal and ran to hug him. She stood next to him and said to me in Greek, "If you have finished your business by August, he says you can take me with you, when I go back to the convent for school!"

"Tell her that's not possible," said Mr. Matthews. "It will be too dangerous for her."

"Why, what danger?" I demanded.

"I don't know yet," he said.

"You really think now them Masons they are dangerous?" said Prien.

"For now," said Mr. Matthews, "we are safe; but I have no idea how we will ever get back to the convent."

"That there," said Prien, "is not a thing you need worry over. Them's ways that no one knows. But I suppose now you might be right there. We can't take Claudette."

"What are they saying?" Claudette demanded of me; but Prien told her himself.

"Why, what business are you on?" she said to me.

"Tell her, now," Prien nodded.

"Tell her what?" I responded.

"That we are searching them bayous for Lafitte's cargoes."

I did. She translated for her parents, who again engaged Prien in a dialogue in their own language. The conversation was lively until something Prien said made them fall silent, their faces filled with awe.

William leaned forward. "I think they are discussing the location of a shipwreck," he said. John Matthews nodded. Claudette, as though hardly conscious of doing so, began to translate the conversation for me:

ଔ

The father: "Everyone knows the story of the treasure of Pecan Island. Only the children believe it anymore."

The boy: "If only we could find that, papa!"

Prien: "There was a ship that ran aground near here." (It was wonderful to hear Prien's native speech translated into pure flawless Greek by the girl – as though hearing his true voice for the first time!)

The grandfather: "Sure enough. Many years it lay rotting on the bank, before these houses were built. I searched its hold myself. There was nothing in it."

Prien: "Do you remember where it was?"

The grandfather: "No. I have forgotten about it."

Prien: "There was nothing in it, that is true, until we deposited a precious cargo in what remained of its hull."

The grandfather: "I stripped its decking of wood planks for the porch of this house. It was very near here."

Prien: "Try to remember where it was!"

The grandfather: "You see for yourself, this house is not new. How can I remember, so long ago?"

Claudette: "Don't you remember when we dug the garden the first time?"

The grandfather: "Every spring we dig the garden. You were not alive that first time it was dug."

Claudette: "Well it was the first time I dug a garden, I can tell you for sure. We found something wooden in the ground, don't you remember? You said it might have been a lifeboat, or it might have been a chest – or it might have been a coffin. That was the first time you told me about the old shipwreck. We never disturbed that spot again after that. It was beyond the edge of the cornfield."

The grandfather: "That's right. On the bank of the bayou. I remember now."

Prien: "The treasure of Pecan Island is right in your own yard! God has given you money for the doctor, and more."

Claudette: "I know where it was! We'll dig it out in the morning!"

Prien: "Well, I don't see why we can't do that."

ଔ

By the time Claudette began to help her mother to clear dishes from the table, she had fully succeeded in engaging Gerald in conversation. William was their translator. Both men had already surrendered entirely to her charm; and so had I, watching their interchange with delight.

"I can tell you are a father," she chimed, spinning in place and pointing directly at Gerald.

"The father of a red-haired son," I answered for him.

"And now," she said, "you must have a red-haired baby girl."

"I think I must," he laughed.

149

"And you, handsome prince," she chirped to William, climbing up on his knee and putting a hand on his shoulder; "tell me about your princess! How did you rescue her from terror, and when are you to be married?"

"I don't know that she has ever known fear or danger, unless it were in a book," he replied.

"Oh, she really should have a little more romance in her life then; but of course you will keep her safe. I must be the flower-girl for your wedding. You will not have one son and one daughter, like this poor man here," she said, pointing to Gerald, "but you will have five sons and five daughters. And I," and she placed her finger upon her own breast, "I will be their teacher and governess. Is this agreed? You shall not leave until this is agreed."

While the conversation diverged in that direction, Gerald, with the assistance of Prien as translator, had turned his quiet thoughtfulness toward the older generations. Clearly impressed with the girl's precociousness, he seemed to be searching for clues of the same unusual intelligence among the adults of the family. Whether he were answered with modesty or with some language or cultural barrier he could not penetrate, he seemed to be fumbling his questions. Claudette, however, showed that she was still following everything that was said.

"The nuns informed my parents that I had unusual potential," she announced in Greek. Prien laughed and nodded, and I translated for Gerald.

That was when I noticed that Mr. Matthews sat outside the circle of lively talk, morose and silent.

"What's wrong with him?" Claudette queried me in Greek.

"My guess," I replied in the same language, "is that he is sad, because he is thinking of his own daughter." In the confusion of tongues in that crowded little room, I forgot that Greek was one that Mr. Matthews knew.

"What happened to her?" she asked with a touching gentleness.

"She died."

"Oh," she breathed. "How old was she?"

"About my age," I admitted.

The room went quiet for a rare moment.

"I remember when Dionysia died," said Claudette at last. "She was about your age, too. Did you hear about that?"

No one replied.

"You probably didn't hear about it," the girl continued, "because the nuns won't talk about it – but it was most amazing, really. It was almost like she didn't die at all. Her face was full of joy and peaceful, and then it became bright – really bright, like the sunrise, but whiter, with a light that made you think you were walking in heaven. And she was saying the most wonderful things... and then she fell asleep, but we could still hear her voice! Do you remember, Papa Prien?"

The old man evidently understood her perfectly, but he replied in his own tongue.

"That's right!" She jumped to her feet. "I remember that, too. I had forgotten she said that, because it didn't all make sense to me. When she blessed us at the end – oh, but the words of that blessing were wonderful and powerful – she also blessed her father and her daughter, and the man who would have been her husband. You remember how surprised we were?"

I am sure that Mr. Matthews' face must have betrayed his understanding at that moment, but I couldn't see it. In my mind I was staring at Denise like I had never seen her before. I say that I saw her in my mind, but I can not really say what I saw. My sight was blinded by tears, in which I saw only the light of the lamps, and in that wavering sense of growing light, her, standing by her death-bed and looking at me. The expression in her eyes was not what I would have expected; it was like nothing I had ever seen.

"Oh!" Claudette whispered, staring at us with wide eyes. The astonishment in them lasted only for a few minutes before she shook her head and moved toward a corner of the room.

"This calls for celebration!" she said, handing a fiddle to her father and, to her grandfather, a beautiful old accordion.

The tunes they played and sang were of a kind of music I had heard only in New Orleans. Claudette then stood to sing long sections from a French translation of Evangeline that took us well into the night. I could not follow the language. But I knew Longfellow's heart-rending narrative well enough to understand the girl's lively pantomime. We watched her interpretation of the hero's long search for the betrothed maiden from whom he had been separated during the British occupation of Acadia, with the sundering of families due to the suddenness of forced exile. This was the story of a man who was faithful to love, not a man like myself. But I could not help wonder whether the cunning child who sang it was conscious of the parallels which the story suggested in relation to my own. He found her at last only on the death-bed – his, not hers – and only after she had transformed the disappointment of her life over into acts of mercy for God, having entered His service as a nun.

These thoughts were enough to trouble me, for the rest of that short summer night, with confused dreams of who I was, and what I was really doing. The atmosphere of home into which we had been welcomed awakened a feeling that suggested we were part of a family. The revelation of our relationship to the beloved former abbess Dionysia appeared to cement that feeling as a fact in the eyes of our hosts. To be part of an untroubled family, though, was a new idea to me – or one very old, buried since the earliest memories of childhood. Disoriented in a maze of half-thoughts, wondering what was the dream and what the reality, I failed to make peace with the restless pillow that was given to me that night – until at last the kiss of sleep, in the form of a black robe bending over my thoughts, sent its pure and unknown comfort.

☙

Even before the mockingbird is disturbed from its nest by the first dreams of the light that sits on the east, dividing the dark earth from the fading stars, its throat is disturbed by weak notes of involuntary song that escape from its sleep. One chirp falls from its nest, then another, until suddenly it finds itself awake and singing full soprano. The earth is still dark, but the sky has gone faintly into color, softly glowing in a hint of blue that has erased all the stars except for the one that heralds the sun.

Even before those first spasms of song had disturbed the mockingbird's peace, Claudette had roused us from our dreams of riches, tugging our blankets on the porch

151

from beneath us. We rubbed our eyes to see her piling picks and shovels in the yard, then returning to her father's shed for more. Prien laughed and walked out to choose one.

We started digging where Claudette pointed, at the edge of the corn patch over the bayou. By the time the sun was up, neighbors had begun to gather to ask why we were digging out good corn. Some of the elder neighbors remembered the ship and began to offer recollections about its location, until our trench expanded in both directions along the bank. Soon the whole community had brought its shovels to assist in the excavations. "It's for the crippled boy," they said, shoving their knees into the work. The cornfield was in real danger of extinction when the old woman walked up. Her hair was so white and frayed it was almost invisible. Shaking on her cane and stepping painfully, she stopped at an oak near the family's dock. Everyone stopped to watch her. She counted paces toward the cornfield, then jabbed at the dirt with her cane and spoke.

"She says that is where the broken mast lay," said Claudette, who stood next to me, absolutely black with earth.

Everyone converged at the spot with shovels. A few inches of leaf loam covered a layer of gravel, and then we were digging in soft sand.

By late afternoon, the remains of the schooner, lying on its side, were completely uncovered.

Much of the hull was rotted, but the tiny cabin was beautifully preserved. The windows were broken out, the brass was tarnished, but the paint was still visible in streaks. The mast had been removed, probably for someone's roof beam, just as the deck had been taken off to provide lumber for the house built by Claudette's grandfather.

Prien showed where the chest was deposited in a mound of sand, underneath a section of deck that remained near the cabin. He remembered putting it there during a storm, after the deck had been removed and the ship lay almost buried. By the light of lightning-strikes they had covered the rest of its hull with broken branches and sand, to make it appear as if the storm had done it. Prien retrieved his gun from the pirogue, shot the lock off of the chest, and allowed Claudette to throw open the lid. She pushed with all her strength, but it was too heavy. Her father and I tried to help her, but it would not move until a pickaxe was applied for leverage.

The opened chest, three-quarters filled with gold, broke off bits of sunshine and hurled them into our eyes. Every tongue let go of some stifled utterance – every tongue except for Prien's.

One corner of its cavity held books, neatly packed. Claudette pulled one out and gave a yelp of delight. It was an old Greek volume, sturdily bound, splendidly printed. Others were manuscripts on vellum, elegantly lettered, adorned with brilliant miniatures.

"These are the Elder's books!" She screamed.

"They were in that there chest that he brought from Jerusalem," Prien explained with a stern expression I had ever seen. "Lafitte he took them out of that, to make room in it for something else I think."

 og

By lamplight, late that night, we sat at Claudette's table, deep in the study of the

152

Elder's books. We had just begun to repack them, in order to send them with Claudette to the convent when she returned to school. The task had been dropped as soon as we held them. The gold in its chest, too, had been hardly touched. The doctor's fee, even at double what had been asked, had raked only a little off the top, and the villagers had accepted nothing. The boy was being prepared to journey with his father to Vermilion Bay, where they would be transported to a cargo ship for New Orleans. The baby and the grandparents were quiet in the loft, but sleep was not able to touch our minds.

I had already perused the contents of those books. Brief lives of saints were arranged in neat blocks of text, introduced by stunning iconographic miniatures. These glowed with deep, brilliant color, executed in lines of composition so bold they might almost be called abstract. A better way to describe them, though, would be as an idealization of beauty in line and color that is a unique characteristic of the Greek mind. Each tiny composition was arranged around a strong focus from which it seemed to radiate. Most often, this center of focus was the face, which burst from the painting in an expression of powerful interior concentration upon the ideas – perhaps one should say the present realities – but of what burning inspiration, I could not say. Other compositions, which were not frontal poses, formed his or her posture around the act of writing, or some act of charity. Still others showed an indication of worship, bending the whole body in strong gestures toward the revealed throne of Christ or His Mother.

Plainer than these beautiful manuscripts were the simple books of wisdom-sayings of the desert fathers. The language of these sayings was likewise plain, but powerful in simplicity.

I spent most of my attention on the liturgical texts, which I had seen only in small excerpts in the margins of the Biblical commentary. These unillustrated volumes, ornamented only by an occasional initial letter and by the inserted lines of red-lettered instructions, were the most beautiful books I had ever seen. It was not just the delicate elegance of the Greek letter displaying itself in its most natural, dignified robes, whether that of the excellent type founders of Venice or the superb but subdued penmanship of professional scribes, though this in itself was extraordinary. As the eye traveled over them, it drank from the splendid arrangement of these letters in lines of verse that sang silently in their impositions on the page. Headed by brief notations that gave the tone or melody, the variety of meters and rhythms on any one double spread of opened pages suggested a richness of song excelling the choral odes of Pindar. But more than that, it was the suggestion of ideas in each line of verse that forced my breath into a dizzying climb beyond the brink of thought. There I tasted poetry more brilliant than the quick sketches of glory in which Homer clothed the epiphanies of the gods. I remember hearing some of these verses sung by the nuns; and I wondered how they managed to remain incarnate while they chanted in their little chapel.

Gradually I became aware that Claudette was reading aloud to me from the Biblical commentary. She was quoting the eloquent John Chrysostom's explanation of the Sermon on the Mount, with his warnings against covetousness. Seeing that she had my attention, she re-filled my mug from a pitcher of fresh water. I drank, and, wholly under the spell of her child's voice, listened.

"You see," she said, "why you must give this gold to the poor. Father Chrysostom explains it right here, in this sermon on the value of love. Even if you obey all of Christ's commandments, you are still no more than an unworthy servant, having done only what you were commanded to do. Think about that! Who has been able to follow all of Christ's commandments, except for those to whom he gives the power to do so? And yet, Christ says clearly, if we give away all our riches, and all possessiveness as well, and then turn and follow him, we will have reward in heaven. But it is not the gold itself that has this power. As He says, even if we give a cup of water in His name, we will not lose our reward."

"You are telling us to give this gold to the poor, and yet you will take no more than what the doctor demands of you?" I said to her.

She laughed at that. "What makes you think we are poor? We have everything we need! I'll tell you where you can give it. Our church in Abbeville has become far too small, and the parishioners have no money for things like architects and builders. You should try to make good time so that you get there for the Feast of Peter and Paul tomorrow night. You have never been to a vigil, I think?"

"I don't know what that is," I replied.

"Good," she said. "The feasting afterward will also be like nothing you have ever seen!"

Chapter Twenty-Six

Midsummer, when it settles its broad canopy across the sky, and it sets the hot sun like a victory flag over the pole of the year, seems permanently camped in place. Until well into the following weeks, one day appears to be as everlastingly long as the next. That sun was well established along its high road before we entered the boat to begin our way down in the water, following toward the east.

The way was no longer as lonely as it had been. Other families in pirogues were on the water toward Abbeville for the feast. Prien exchanged lively shouts with them. He was perfectly at home, even relaxed. Gerald and William, too, seemed more at ease since the two nights in Claudette's hospitable little house. Even Mr. Matthews, though still resigned to his silence, looked peaceful.

There was occasional talk, but thoughtfulness reigned among the shadows and slow currents of the bayous all through the long hours of that day. William and Gerald and Prien traded reflections upon the Scriptural annotations; but these ruminations seemed less heavy with awe than they had been before the events in Claudette's home. Instead, such thoughts seemed now to inspire in my companions a strange brightness of hope.

I let them read, and I let them talk. I kept the paddle, trying to shove off the gloom that settled on me. For myself, the past two nights had bred a far different mood. My heart was heavier than it had ever been, perhaps, since the first day I stood at my mother's grave. It was not just the loss of Denise that gave that burden. Everything that Gerald had said about the direction my life would have taken, had I accepted her – had I even once understood my own feelings – had begun to open vistas of sad lost worlds in my mind. The most poignantly distressing of these, however, was one I had never considered before. I had never known how to consider it: what it might have meant to see a daughter grow up under my eyes!

Nor would I ever have thought about it at all, until the living presence of little Claudette danced into my soul like the slicing of a sword sharper than any Lafitte had ever weighed in his hand.

What had happened to my own daughter? Since I had learned the news, I had not thought about it. What did she look like as a child, and what did she look like now? What was the nature of her personality, and how had it been formed among those with whom she had grown up? How might she have prospered in her true home if I had been there? And what kind of creature would I have been, maturing in such an environment, taking thought and responsibility for others?

The same gloom that had transfixed John Matthews the night before, as he meditated in sorrow upon his daughter, had now taken possession of me. Never would I be able to think about the daughters of men in the same careless way again. That foreign and unknown object in my breast had grown so heavy that I was not sure I could live with it.

155

The painful transformation in my thoughts must have shown something in my face. Gerald kept regarding me with brief glances of concern.

ೞ

We came to the village of Abbeville at the sinking of the sun.

Fields and houses surrounding the town were eerily deserted. The whole population was found in the town square in front of the tiny church of St Mary Magdalene. Vespers was being sung for the commemoration of the martyrdom of Peter and Paul.

We joined the crowd outside the windows to hear the slow Latin chanting of the priest and his choir. Responses were joined by parishioners familiar with the music and words. Prien, too, knew those phrases. When the service was concluded, instead of departing, the crowd stood still for the solemn beginning of the Matins service, which then went deep into the night.

Weary and famished as we were, we stood while the stars moved into their places and the old moon awoke. The patient constellations walked across the sky while one hymn of prayer faded into another.

At last, near midnight, we received the priest's blessing to depart. Moving with the crowd away from the church doors, we found that a bonfire had been lit in the little town square. Musicians were tuning their instruments, and even the fragment of a warm-up tune inspired girls to practice dance steps. Frogs' legs, battered and fried, were set out on benches to one side. There were platters of lamb and poultry from the farms, alligator steaks, and shellfish stews so fragrant one felt nourished by the steam alone.

Tired as we were, no one thought of sleep once the music had begun. Prien talked with everyone, spending the brief hours before dawn in gathering information on the descendents of men he had known in the area. News of Lafitte's treasure started to go around. Some of the people of Claudette's village had come, and they gave lively accounts of its discovery. He took crowds down to the boat to show them the chest of gold.

"Is this wise?" I said. "Shouldn't we stay to guard the boat?"

"Anyone who wants some can have it," he answered. "Why not?"

Instead, the whole village brought their old priest, Father Antoine, down to the bayou.

"Your prayers for a church large enough to shelter us," they said.

The old man wept. "No," he said, "it was the prayers of the people that accomplished this." He spoke in French, repeating himself in Latin. "You say little Claudette demanded you bring this here? I consider that child already as wise as the nuns. Do you make this journey under their guidance and with their blessing?"

"We do," Prien replied.

Again Fr. Antoine wept, and told a boy to bring holy water from the altar. The sun was coming up as he blessed the boat, the chest, ourselves, and the crowd. Then he said, "We need only a small portion of this."

"What will we do with the rest now?" said Prien.

"What was Lafitte's will?" said Fr. Antoine.

"Other than this here journal, he left no will," said Prien.

"What is in the journal?" asked the priest.

"The record of his crimes," Prien shuddered, "written with grief."

"Then it is clear what should be done," answered Fr. Antoine. "Find those who were wronged by him, follow the route of his crimes, and offer recompense. Then take this journal to the priest at St. Martinsville. He knew Lafitte as well as anyone in these parts, and he will want to see what is written. I should tell you that he has one of the rarest treasures that Lafitte brought to the New World. I can't tell you what it is. Tell him that it was I who told you this."

We camped in the town square, comfortably dreaming of Paradise throughout the hot journey of the sun across the waters of the sweating sky. Our dreams were broken by strange conversation, as it seemed that more people came to see Prien than in the night before. I thought that I heard someone say that Abbeville, named for its abbot, had grown up around the hermitage of a spiritual son of the nuns.

"Is all this country under the influence of the nuns?" said William in one of my dreams.

"That's right now," Prien answered from some distance; "and it has changed this here country to something right splendid now; and that there is a thing to see!"

Perhaps it was not a dream. "Everyone wants some of that gold," I said drowsily, not knowing what I meant.

క్రీక్రీక్రీక్రీ

Abbeville, on the Vermilion River, brought to an end the miles of prairie that divide the waters of the Calcasieu from the series of bays that drain the lesser tributaries of the Mississippi. We had avoided all those wide central prairies by way of the more southerly coastal marshes. Now, we turned north into the rushing Vermilion River. Prien assured us that its turns would lead to the shaded gates of the bayou country. We threaded our way upstream through its powerful currents, guided by two books.

"Go and sell all that you possess, and give to the poor, and you shall obtain treasure in heaven; and come and follow me."

Those were the words that the elder Honoratus spoke to me – the words that shook my world and changed it. And watching my countenance fall, he added these:

"It is easier for a camel to go through the eye of a needle, than for a rich man to enter into the kingdom of heaven."

"To think of a camel performing a circus act like that!" I said.

William had both books open, one on each knee: Lafitte's journal on one, the annotated Bible on the other. Turned to the pages on the gospel of Matthew, he read:

Some say that "camel" is not the animal, but the thick cable used by sailors to cast their anchors.

157

"That comment, it says in a note, was by Theophylact, Bishop of Bulgaria," William added.

"That's right now," said Prien. "Lafitte he never had no doubt about that there meaning. He'd seen for hisself that tough rope made in that part of the world now, and it was out of camels' hair. That's a fact now, just like this here treasure is a fact; and how we got it and what we're supposed to do with it now, them there's facts too. No arguing that. The awful burden of this here gold is his, not ours. But it's up to us now to lighten that burden for him. That now, that's how we're going to purify our hearts you see. This here big book now," he thumped his hand on the massive commentary, "everything written there, and everything written about what's written, it's all about one thing. But that one thing, you see, that one thing it's not easy; it's harder than hauling that there rope through a needle's eye. But this now, this is going to make it easier, you'll see!"

"The three sections of Lafitte's journal," William replied pensively, "were modeled on the Elder's teachings. On the first pages, remember, he wrote down what Fr. Honoratus called a transformation of the human creature into something God-like. The first step of that transformation was called purification..."

"That first step now, that one's the hardest," old Prien interrupted. "I was there when he said that you know. He said it can't be done without help from on high there. Well, that's what help we've got now you see. And I'll tell you something else about that first step now. It never stops, it doesn't. Even when that great light it comes into this here heart and a man begins thinking things beyond all thinking, and them thoughts they keep a-growing, that there purifyin' in the heart it doesn't stop."

William and Gerald and John Matthews were staring at him, like moths at a flame. They stopped whatever they were doing or thinking and leaned toward him, as though toward one who had already penetrated the third heaven of the Elder's mysterious teachings.

"But this here giving away this treasure, you see," Prien said, "and this searching out the things all broken by another man's crimes, it's going to help like you can't think. I know it now. This is not just like paying the price for them awful deeds. Not at all! We'll see this here gold changed into something mighty fine we will. We'll see tears dropped from beyond the grave now, drops to cool a tongue in them flames even. This here it's going to change our minds completely, turning 'em toward..." He fell into a silence of pure joy, looking up into the light.

"Yep," he said after a long silence, "I'm right glad to be a'doin' this after all. I was mighty afeared o' this here visitin' the place of all them crimes; but when I begged that there help from on high there... you'll see, it'll change everything!"

William returned to the journal still open on his knees. "Following that entry, where Lafitte recalled the Elder's counsel to give everything away, he writes this:

Two ships, unusually rich, captured off the coast of Texas, I brought into Vermilion Bay, not wanting my men in Barataria to know of them. I was circumspect in my watch over my own crew because of the value of the cargo. One was a man-of-war, commanded by officers from the best families in Spain. These officers I threw overboard at sea, keeping only their subordinates who signed a pledge of loyalty to myself. The man-of-war was escorting an illegal slave ship from the ivory coast of Africa.

I determined that the slaves were to be conveyed to the master of Liseaux Plantation below Vermilionville, which lay up the river. I had already promised him such a number of slaves that I did not know where so many were to be found. He would also want the rare Spanish wines on board the man-of-war, but for these he would have to pay the price. Having come across the whole number of slaves he had asked for so soon, I now planned to increase my price for them as well. These were young and strong, men and women, who, after I released them from their chains in the reeking hold, fed them with fresh grain and meat and put them ashore under the trees of Marsh Island, looked to me as to their savior.

I began to search the village at the mouth of the Vermilion River for a guide to take me upriver by way of the backwaters. As word spread concerning my presence, I was approached by the local priest. He was out of wine; and since the divine service could not be celebrated without it, he begged me to procure some as quickly as possible. I immediately conveyed him to my hide-out on the island and showed him the cases of wine. We opened one and tasted the contents. Then I told him the price. It was twice what I intended to charge the planter. I was not fond of religion at the time. He said that he had never seen as much money as I demanded, but that if I were willing to take cattle for one case, he would gladly impoverish himself for the sake of serving the liturgy. He then led me to the guide I needed. This was an orphan boy in his care, a boy who knew the swamps. The boy informed me that these parts were not like Barataria, where alternative routes were as available as the air; but what there was, he could show me.

"Them swamps now that that particular guide led him through," said Prien, "they are right over here." He pointed into a breach in the natural levee, where a damp wilderness of cypresses receded into shadows. "I haven't been in this here country for forty years now; but them things they will always be fresh in my remembering."

"Were you with him then?" said Gerald.

"Yep sure; it was my first journey with Lafitte," Prien answered. "I was that orphaned guide he wrote about there.

"My mother, you see, she went and ran off with me from that there slave revolt in the Dominican Republic. That's when the French were all murdered, and that there island it was re-named. Haiti they called it after that. My mother though, she died of fever in a storm on the sea. I remember that there night she died; nothing else before I came here do I remember now. I remember her dying and the frightful waves, and her saying that my father he had been a sailor, and had seen storms like that now many times.

"And that there is what I told Lafitte too. 'Is that so,' he said; 'and what was your father's name?' Well I did not know that. 'Your mother's name, then,' he said. 'I, too, grew up from childhood in that island.' I said that her name it was Allisandra.

"'Yes, I knew him,' Lafitte he said then. 'His name was Victor Prien. He died bravely at my side.'

"Now I did not know that my father he served with Lafitte. He had been killed during the taking-over of one of them there ships of gold. That now you see is why Lafitte adopted me like as his own son.

"Who knows? Maybe we have got some of that same gold here on board with us now."

159

Every man returned to his own silence. Mine was overshadowed by dim memories of my mother, reaching out of her grave. I could not bear to look at any other man on board. Denise's father and Catherine's young fiancé, I knew too well, would be deep in the shade of thoughts I would not dare invade with my misery. I felt more impossibly alone than an orphaned boy. He, at least, was innocent of the cause of his poverty.

William, after a while, again picked up the journal and resumed reading:

I was not as welcome in this region after killing the owner of the Liseaux Plantation in a duel. His death was the ruin of his family, which degenerated into poverty.

All those who perished in duels at my hand were victims of my pride, which, according to the Elder, is more destructive than covetousness and murder, being their cause.

"I almost ran away from Lafitte that very morning now," said Prien. "I had never seen a duel you see, and it scared me right bad. That whole thing, it was Lafitte's own fault. He asked a bigger price for the slaves than Messieur Liseaux had expected, much bigger. He was right you see saying that Lafitte had become a pirate, even though he said it kind of like a joke. Lafitte now, he was mad, mad. He had always thought that there it the worst insult."

"This gold is to be deposited with the heirs of Liseaux, then," said Gerald.

"There's the house now," said Prien, pointing out a sunlit bank coming around a quiet turn of the river.

It had fallen, except for one wing which remained and seemed inhabited. The front lawn, however, was covered by a village of tradesmen. We tied up at the dock, and Prien asked for the descendents of the property. We expected to be led to the remains of the mansion, but instead were shown a small house like any of the others. He introduced himself at the door, holding a brief conversation with a middle-aged blacksmith and his wife. They led us to the old lady next door.

The conversation, which took place in Cajun French, was essentially this: first, Prien asked if she recognized him. She gazed at him a long time. Then, as though she had forgotten herself, she asked us to come in to her table. She served us tea with slow difficulty, but with grace. Again, Prien asked the question. She confessed that she did not remember if she had met him. Of course, said Prien, who was only a boy when he had come with Lafitte. That name she recognized. She smiled and nodded, saying nothing. Prien asked who lived in the main house. She said it housed a chapel and its priest. There followed a conversation concerning the nuns, as always.

Prien called for the blacksmith, and told him to have a notary come to him from Vermilionville, which lay around the next turn of the river. He was informed that the town had grown, and had just been re-named in honor of the late Marquis de Lafayette; but the notary was summoned.

"The family has fallen into that there poverty of its neighbors, you see," Prien explained to us. "Them planters now, they live in a world above them Cajuns. The widow she says she is all right this way. She misses her husband now, but she knows he would never have been happy with simple things, the way she is."

"Did she not consider you an unwelcome enemy?" I asked in surprise.

"She has prayed for Lafitte all of her long life now," answered Prien. "Them nuns they showed her how this is the way to think of enemies. I convinced her to take Lafitte's gold, more for the sake of his own rest now, than for her own!"

ᙅᔑ

That night, at a lamp on the widow's table, the notary copied out the parts of Lafitte's journal which mentioned the murder of her husband, as well as those which discovered the location of the gold we carried. The notary stacked all the gold pieces, counted it, and recorded the incredible sum. She divided the largest part to be given to the Church of St John the Evangelist in Lafayette, and had this amount recorded by the notary. She designated donations for church property, and donations for the poor. "You yourself would have received from such a donation when you first came here," the widow said, smiling at Prien.

Of the portion that she retained, some was set aside for a new roof and other improvements in the chapel, and some was to be given to its priest for the poor. More was to be used to re-build the house as a hospital like that of the nuns. A tiny amount was set aside for the inheritance of her children. The rest was paid to the notary for the sizable task of writing documents transferring ownership of property to the villagers for the land of their houses and fields.

All this amazed us, and we left her house in silence.

Going down to the boat, where we had made camp, we found the widow's son, the blacksmith, waiting for us.

"We have a room prepared for you," he said with perfect English.

"We're fine here," I replied. "There's a hint of a breeze along the river."

Prien gave me a stern look that told me it was not my place to refuse. "But of course, we will accept your hosp'tality now," he said.

The blacksmith smiled. "Believe me, it is much cooler down in the bottom of the old house. You will not regret it!" His English was not that of a blacksmith, but rather that of the heir of a good family. He was evidently well educated, at the least.

The old servants' quarters were dug a few feet into the ground below the main floor. Windows at ground level let in the breeze. The large room was nearly bare, the paint was almost gone; but there were clean cots, and lamps on a table. William sat down in the circle of light and began furiously to write.

"What's in that book now?" Prien asked.

"Have you not noticed he's been keeping a journal?" I answered for him.

"So many things have happened," said William, "I am afraid I may forget."

"That's good!" said the old man.

"It's because of his notes in there," I said, "that we were able to make any sense of Arsene LeBleu's maps. We will probably find a clearer understanding of our wanderings in that journal than we will in our own minds."

"And so many thoughts," William said with his youthful enthusiasm, "inspired by Lafitte's writings, and also by that book of Scriptural commentary, which seems to be a guide to everything, absolutely everything! Thoughts of new and strange things, worthy to be written down and remembered! I thought it might be a good idea."

Prien nodded and went out into the night.

John Matthews stared after him for a moment, then said to William, "May I read through that some time?"

"Anytime you wish," said William.

Mr. Matthews stood and followed after Prien.

"The old men have thoughts of their own," said Gerald quietly. Then he turned his gaze upon me.

"And you," he said quietly. "What's been going through your head?"

"My head?" I laughed. "An empty breeze from the ocean."

"I know better than that," he answered. "Look: William needs to write, Prien needs time alone for contemplation, and Mr. Matthews needs to think things through. I think you'd do better with all that's happened if you talked."

I avoided his look, but could not escape it. It was the first night we had spent indoors since Claudette's house. We both remembered the influence of that home; and we could feel it in the gentle hospitality of this place as well.

"You've been thinking about the daughter you never knew, haven't you?" he said with acute perception.

I sighed and nodded, and suddenly the tears came. At least they made no sound to interrupt William on the other side of the room, in his circle of light.

"Just the day before yesterday," I said when I could speak, "it was all I could think of. But it was too much for me. By today, I had already put it out of my mind – until you saw fit to remind me! Isn't it enough that I have nailed myself up into years of emptiness, without you having to make me look again at all the damage my thoughtlessness has done?"

Gerald was not a man to employ forethought in conversation or to use clever techniques to coax confession. He was so genuinely astonished at this admission that he retreated to his own cot, staring at the floor.

"I assure you," he said, "we are going to find out who she is. Are you going to be all right when that happens?"

That was something I had not really considered. Such a real possibility surprised me with a strange, vague fear.

Gerald, reading my face, said, "Well, you had better prepare yourself. Mr. Matthews will not likely rest until we are introduced to her. That reminds me to ask you: try a little harder to show less distrust toward him."

"You're telling me that you trust him?" I replied. "Completely?"

"I think you misunderstand him."

"You will at least admit that he is a complicated man?"

"Perhaps. He has been like a father to you."

"That is supposed to make me trust him?" I laughed.

"Yes. Your mistrust of your own father has become nothing more than a bad habit. You may call it distrust; but really it looks to me more like basic disrespect."

"You think so?" I replied coldly. "If you were willing to admit John Mathews' complexity, you would have to bear in mind that his motives are complicated. What if some of these are not in our interest, and are not to our benefit?"

"You think he might still be working for the Masons?" he said with exasperated disbelief. "Even at this point, you think he is capable of selling his daughter and grand-daughter for some secret treasure?"

"You don't understand how dangerous the Masons can be."

"You're right about that; but I think he does understand, maybe better than you."

"Maybe."

"If you remember, you didn't even trust me, when I was carrying that letter to the nuns."

"That was different."

"Was it? I'm afraid it might be the shadows in your own conscience that keep bothering you!"

Our voices, during this dialogue, might have become a little louder than we intended. William looked up from his writing; but his face was calm with his own reflections.

"When we were in Claudette's house," William said, "I remembered what it felt like in my own home, when I was her age."

Apparently, both Gerald and I thought it safest to let him speak without interruption.

"My mother enjoyed entertaining guests in the parlor. Writers and artists liked to gather there. Discussions were lively; anyone was welcome. That's why Claudette's house reminded me of those times."

"And your father?" I prodded.

"That's just it. My father didn't say much; but his presence was always felt. My mother was always happier when he was in the room."

"I've never heard you speak about your father," I said.

"He was not a man of much speech; but he was kind and gentle, and always had a smile for me. When he took me with him out on the plantation, it felt wonderful to be by his side. That's when I really learned about the world. He taught me how to communicate with the horses and cattle with touch and sound. I could tell he was thinking about me when he looked over the fields and managed the workers. He would do something a certain way, then give me that gentle smile, as though to say, That's how you do it, son. His blacks were unusually comfortable with him. He could even go into their homes and sit down at their table, and it was as natural as anything. Of course he took care of them; and they were more skilled than normal. Some of them he taught trades himself, and some of them, he let them teach him. And then he would give me that smile..."

After saying this and thinking about it for a moment, William returned to his writing, as though we weren't even there.

૭૪

On Sunday, we followed Prien to the service at St John's in Lafayette. Afterwards, we walked the church grounds with the rector. Having informed him of the widow's donation, our charge over Lafitte's treasure was finished. He was ecstatic, and took us into the crumbling cemetery, pointing out his plans for gardens and the restoring of tombs.

"There are graves here that are older than anyone remembers," he said.

"Oh!" said Prien, staring toward a shady corner of ruined and overgrown vaults. "I didn't know now that she was here today! I did not see her before in that there church."

"Whom do you mean?" said the rector.

"It was one of them nuns," said Prien, squinting.

"No, I don't think so!" laughed the rector. "You know as well as I that nuns never travel outside their convent without permission of the bishop, and His Grace would certainly never permit that. You are aware, I assume, of the controversy that surrounds them?"

"Controversy!" repeated Prien. "That has never come into my mind now!"

"They would leave the Church of Rome and join the Orthodox Greeks if they could," said the priest. "For all I know, they may have done so already. It is a serious matter. All the people of this country go to them for advice. And what can I do? The advice they give is good; and no one can overlook the number of influential Masons they have persuaded to leave that Order and join themselves to the Church. Perhaps it is for the sake of the people that they remain under obedience to the Bishop of New Orleans, who is good enough to understand the difficulty of the situation and allow them to practice the Byzantine Rite. What else could he do? When he threatened to excommunicate them, they were so unmoved that he began to suspect they had already severed that tie. They remain in correspondence with monks on Mt. Sinai. I should not even speak of this. My predecessor was too supportive of their counsel, and so was exiled to the tiny parish in Abbeville. The bishop keeps his eye on my church! You will not see one of the nuns here."

"It was Dionysia, then," said Prien, advancing toward the broken vaults. "What graves are these here?"

"There is no record of them" said the priest. "They were here before the old church was torn down. As you see, they are unmarked."

"That's right now," said Prien, "I recognize them. Has any man dared look into the cracks of these vaults to see if they are filled with bones now, or maybe with gold?"

The priest laughed. "Are you joking?"

"I myself moved them here from them shores of Big Lake," said Prien, looking at me. "I would not have recognized the place now." To the priest he said, "The Eldress Dionysia must want that there Bishop to dispose of this wealth as he sees fit."

The priest's face contorted with amazement. "Open the vault," Prien said to me. I did not even move.

His hand reached under the lid and found a latch. The crack, as it appeared now, was part of a broken door. It shuddered with the weight of gold behind it and fell down, spilling the loud coins across crushed weeds.

No one knew what to do.

Someone was calling from the cemetery gate. We saw the Liseaux blacksmith, the widow's son, walking toward us. His face shown with tears.

"My son, what is the matter?" said the priest, translating his own words into the local dialect. The answer was brief.

"The widow has died in the night," the priest explained to us. He turned, staring at the gold still trickling out of its vault.

"There was a wise woman!" he whispered with fear. "She kept nothing for herself; and when her soul was required that very night, she had secured for herself treasure in heaven!"

◌

At Lafayette, we turned from the river into the swamps and bayous of the backwaters. There Prien found the water road into the heart of Louisiana.

The bayou country is a tapestry of waterways spawned along the lower Mississippi. It begins in the belly of the state, just underneath Alexandria. There, Bayou Teche separates itself from the Red River and follows its own dreaming course through the shadows of oaks and cypresses for more than a hundred miles to the Gulf. Only a few miles separate the source of the Teche from that of the Atchafalaya River. This turbulent river vaults into lowland forests just above the confluence of the Red River and the Mississippi. The peaceful Teche is thus pursued by the parallel course of the devouring Atchafalaya, more deadly and tumultuous than the Mississippi itself, and so deep that no man has thrown down the knotted rope long enough to find the bottom. Its dark but blossoming swamps, wider than the Florida Everglades, become whitewater oceans when the Mississippi overflows in early spring.

Far down the muscular coils of the Mississippi, Bayou LaFourche turns aside from the river north of New Orleans. Although its source is so far removed from the others, it nevertheless follows a course parallel to theirs and only a few miles to the east. Its tributaries complete the delicate lacework of interconnecting bayous from the Teche to the swamps disintegrating into the subtropical islands of Barataria Bay. These waters and their territories form the vast delta that drains the lower Mississippi, and records its most recent historical wanderings.

Prien remembered the way with astonishing acuteness. In places, there was no more than an irrigation gate dividing one bayou from another, since the marshy pastures between them were the most convenient for flooding a rice field. Finally, an eastern loop of an unnamed bayou wandered close enough to a tributary of the Teche that we only had to walk the pirogue across a cornfield from one to the other. Of course, Prien knew where this cornfield was, and the old Indian trail that led through it for ancient food-gathering journeys.

Thoughtfulness reigned; and its rule increased. Other than occasional references to Lafitte's journal and our continued reading of the Biblical commentary, the journey proceeded in silence. An awe had fallen on us. For one thing, Mr. Matthews seemed to change before my eyes as he slowly began to comprehend what it was that his daughter had accomplished. His severe eyes softened whenever he briefly questioned Prien about the character of Denise, and he received the answers with grave humility. It almost appeared to me as though the two older men were becoming as of one mind. I could not help wonder how far such change might go in a like man Mr. Matthews; my anxiety about his motives was not entirely relieved.

William, too, entered this thoughtful silence. He would look up from his reading out loud as though he knew what question would be asked and what the answer would be, and then would return to reading or to quiet contemplation. Gerald said nothing at all; but his eyes showed that he was focused on the same mystery of the reigning quiet, and was gathering unspeakable things out of it.

I sat by myself, uncomfortable with my thoughts, uneasy with the giving away of

165

incredible wealth, forgotten for decades, and not entirely reconciled with the kind of person Denise had become. At last, I made an attempt to overthrow that silence.

"Where are we going now?" I said.

"St Martinsville."

"And why is that?"

"Don't really know," said Prien. "Even when I was a boy now, that there Church of St Martin it was more revered than that big cathedral in New Orleans there. That gift that Lafitte gave to the Church of St Martin is not wrote down in that there journal; but he said a thing of it when we moved them vaults of gold to that there graveyard in Vermilionville. He said it was a secret even them Masons they didn't know. Dionysia now, she was awful close-mouthed about it. She wouldn't even say why she could not speak of it. Whatever it was, they had somehow convinced Lafitte to bring this thing from France, after the revolution."

"We are no longer looking for treasure, then?" I said.

"Don't really know what we are looking for anymore," smiled Prien.

"Good," I said. "I thought I was the only one that was confused. I forget what we started out after, and why, since we have already given away greater riches than I ever had hoped to see."

"What's the matter with you?" Denise's father came out of his silence with a vigor. "That you should care about treasure at all anymore! Have you forgotten what you've already lost? My daughter loved you to the very end! She didn't have to, you know. You certainly had nothing to offer for her sake! Even entering a sanctity which was like nothing we knew to exist, she loved you. It's unbelievable that a man could be as unworthy of such a love as you are. Even now her prayers are guiding us! Are you blind?"

I have never seen a man as angry. His face was pale, he trembled to the roots of his hairs, and his eyes were on fire. Even my father in the pulpit, roaring from the pit of hell when I was a child, had not frightened me as much. No one dared to answer him. No one dared to speak at all.

I must admit that the sermon was effective. I spent the remainder of that day in the agony of self-examination, while we passed through an endless series of loops and cutoffs. Again and again we turned into ponds that looked like they could have been the same we visited an hour earlier.

These twisting lanes of water, narrow and without current, were sometimes floating gardens that bloomed in an almost total lack of direct sunlight. Where the sun did penetrate, it created rooms of dazzling beauty in those halls of shade. Draperies of brilliant vines made golden walls in the sunlight, adorned by hanging towers of purple and silver trumpet-like flowers opening their lips to the light. At other places, where the walls and floors of our passageways were bare, we could have been in caverns deep within the earth. Great gray trunks grew out of bare mud banks, and brown water sat between the gigantic cypress knees that came out of its stillness.

∞

"Did you see that?" said William, suddenly alert.

"Lafitte's ghost again?" said Gerald.

"The nun that led us through the convent grounds," said William.

"Where?" said Prien.

"In the shadows along that bank, I think," said William, pointing; but as soon as he said it, I saw her, too, disappearing with a quick walk into a narrow waterway between the cypresses. Even after twenty years, I knew her walk. It was Denise.

"I've never been down that way now," said Prien, "but that's where we're going."

"You saw that, too?" said Gerald. "It looked like she was walking on the bayou, as though the water were a path of polished gravel!"

The swamp she led us into was concealed in peaceful chains of shadow that fell from towering cypresses. Our oars in the water were the only sound disturbing that nest of shade. We brought them in and drifted, joining ourselves to the silence until she was seen again in the distance, quickly disappearing into a shadow as dark as her robe, and we followed.

The fierce midsummer sun, burning somewhere above that forest, threw just enough light here to distinguish one shadow from another. Silence ruled those shadows; but the thoughts that fired up in our hearts as we followed her into that silence, might perhaps have been ignited nowhere else in the world – unless, as William had been reading earlier, one had been following the ascent of Tabor into that explosion of light in which Moses and Elijah stood.

I was stunned to catch myself thinking such thoughts.

"I don't think anyone has ever been in here!" said Prien.

"How can she make herself visible in these shadows?" wondered Gerald.

She turned, and we saw her face. It was the face I had seen in my dream. Like oil that drips from a cracked lamp, light ran from the wrinkles in her face, flowing like tears that spilled into the air around her and floated toward us on a breeze that carried a fragrance sweeter than morning dew. The light intensified until her features disappeared. We saw, where she had stood, that light reached into the swamp from an opening between two trees in the distance. We followed it, coming out of the shadows into the sunlight that poured itself over the graceful turns of Bayou Teche.

The rivers that came out of paradise must have looked like this one.

The oaks that lined its lush green banks were grown to their most perfect form before that species would allow decay to break down their strength. Massive trunks, twisted in muscular postures, each more beautiful than any other, spread out in immense limbs which seemed ready to support the weight of the heavens. One after another of these trees were spaced along the riverbank, as though planted in the world's most beautiful garden. Great in knowledge of the stream that fed their roots, they reached over the water, knowing what portions of the river should be shaded and what should remain in sunlight. Satisfied with the accomplishment of their years of labor, they stared unselfconsciously into their own reflections, where the current was deep and slow. There were no disturbances in the surface of those waters; yet you could feel, simply by floating along, that they would not be turned aside.

These trees guarded a road that ran along on the other side of the bank, worn bare with the traffic of carts and coaches. At this hour of the day, when the sun went down into the shadows of the oaks, pedestrians were scattered along it. Women in white dress with parasols walked in groups, and gentlemen followed with canes and top-hats such as are seen in the streets of New Orleans. Beyond the road, where fields opened to the full light, sat a mansion like those along the Mississippi.

"The Eldress now, she has led us through a cut-off I didn't never know," said Prien, "to St Martinsville. Our business here it must be urgent."

Chapter Twenty-Seven

"The finest earth in this here bayou country, it sits beside Bayou Teche," said Prien. "It was settled by them French colonists now, soon as them lands along the Mississippi they were all taken. Them first Cajun exiles, too, they were welcome here, and now they found a land closer to paradise than their cove on them cold shores of ol' Canada. And it was not like their fore-fathers place in France neither; 'cause that now, that was the coast they called Brit'ney, them there was shores all beset by invaders all the time from the sea. But this now, this here was pastures no one in the world knew about. It was them Cajuns built that there Church of St Martin of Tours, for that saint whose spir'tual children filled up France and them British Isles, with all them names which them countries they are still known by!

"But now there was another band o' settlers, and this here was the one that gave this place its difference. They were them ones, them nobility that ran away from the Reign of Terror after that there French Revolution. The Elder now, he knew 'em." Prien explained that they, too, were welcomed to a land hidden in deep veils of swamp. They saw rich alluvial that cried out for cultivation, "and clearin's in the oak forest here that just sobbed for chateaus now, so it looked to them all. Them there streets that grew in this here bend of the bayou, they got to be known as 'Little Paris'".

He showed as evidence the Corinthian columns on a mansion that dreamed in the shade of an alley of oaks coming down to bayou. Around the bend, the town began at the Greek revival Courthouse with massive Ionic capitals supporting the pediment. In the lawn of the town square, between two towering magnolias, there sat in eternal marble the massive figure of a Roman emperor. I recognized it from drawings I had seen.

"Whom did they get to carve this exquisite copy of the statue of Hadrian?" I said.

"That there it's the original," said Prien.

"That's not possible," I said. "No one knows what happened to the original, which disappeared almost a hundred years ago. It was a priceless treasure from the second century."

"It was in that there palace of King Louis before that Revolution," Prien informed me. "Lafitte smuggled it now for them town fathers. That was one of his most famous adventures now."

The buildings surrounding the main square as well seemed to have been imported from a European village. The hotel, built out of bousillage bricks made from mud and moss, was fronted by two floors of covered wooden balconies. Similar single-storied buildings housed shops and offices. Splendid houses in fenced lawns he pointed out as town-homes of local planters.

At the edge of town, the gardens of the church began, like the entrance into another world. What flowers climbed the fenced churchyard and fell over in a riot of color, I cannot name. Azalea hedges and wisteria arbors I recognized, but these were only the

169

background for the rich explosions of tall red blossoms I had never seen, and yellow creeping flowers woven through the grass made a carpet of flames, sweeter than dew, on which to walk. There were bearded irises among the stained marble headstones of the graves, where the ancient priest was bent over, cultivating a plot of fresh earth.

"He looks just like the icon I was shown in the old abbess' room," said Mr. Matthews: "The icon she called 'The Joy of All Who Sorrow', with the Mother of God harvesting flowers from the graves of the righteous".

"Pere Jan he was sent here as a young man now, a Dutch missionary," said Prien; "But now you see, he is as much a part of this here land as them flowers he pulls."

We tied to the thick root that an ancient oak thrust into the stream, and used other giant roots for steps, as they seemed to offer themselves. Indeed, they appeared to be worn with such traffic.

The church, too, not of a kind that is seen within the borders of the states, made one think that he disembarked on another continent. Its stucco, a pale amber in the sun, but turning to suggestions of rose in the shadows, and showing a hint of Spanish influence in the soft outlines of its frontal facade, stood like an unmoving palette behind the vibrant painting of tall flowers shaking in the softest breeze.

It was an image of cultivated beauty comparable only to that of the convent, except that it was small enough that the eye could take in the whole picture at one view. And of course, there were no cloistered areas where visitors were not allowed.

Prien approached the elderly priest. "I don't know if you remember me now. I was just a boy when Lafitte adopted me as his cabin boy."

"Yes," said Pere Jan, with his great eyebrows bending over his large and penetrating eyes. "Yes, I remember you. And Lafitte told me more of you when I heard his confession."

"You heard his confession?" said Prien with a tone of amazement.

"I gave strict orders concerning his repentance, according to things that the Elder himself had said to him. Do you have his journal?"

"We do."

He straightened his old back, lifting his great eyes to the trees. "God be praised for His mercy! Do you know, I had never heard of this wonderful holy man or his nuns, before Lafitte told me of him. Lafitte was in the deepest despair when he confessed the murder to me. I brought him outside and showed him the stations of the cross which we have placed in the oaks that continue down the highway towards Catahoula. I showed him the people that mocked Christ. I showed the suffering face of divine patience, and His death, for their sake. I assured him that there is no sin which is beyond Christ's forgiveness. I promised him that if he carried out my directions and returned to me, I would give him absolution with my own hands, and I promised him that the Elder himself would be mystically present. He left deep in thought; but I never saw him again. Has the holy man's grave-site been found?"

"It has not," Prien replied.

"Perhaps that is for the best," said Pere Jan. "There are those who would try to destroy it, as they attempted to destroy the relics of our father St. Martin of Tours." He turned his face in reverence toward the church as he said this.

"Now, I was always told they succeeded in that there destruction," said Prien "when them revolutionaries they bombed the old Cathedral of Tours! The Elder hisself thought so – it was the reason he denounced them Masons."

"Everyone thought it was so," said the old priest. "Only the nuns knew the truth. They had been forewarned of the plan to blow up the cathedral. They hid the relics, telling no one where. When they fled from France themselves, they were not able to bring them. Somehow, they persuaded Lafitte to do this for them. It was his most perilous adventure by far, conducted in the greatest secrecy. His ship waited at Lyons, while his men brought the relics down the Soane River in the same cargo that brought the statue of Hadrian draped underneath a sail. They knew the right passwords to give at the revolutionaries' checkpoints. When these demanded to see the contraband, they were shown the statue and paid to let it through. The revolutionaries thought it was a great joke; but had they known what else was on board, the Masons would have tracked down Lafitte and killed him.

"Lafitte knew the power of holiness that resides in the relics of the saints. No one could have convinced him of this mystery had he not experienced it himself. He himself gave me the account of that voyage. It was a voyage of miracles that brought them here. It was because of the things that happened then that Lafitte came later to realize what his last and greatest crime had been.

"Here, on these blessed grounds, where the exiles of the French Revolution met the exiles of Acadia, Lafitte remembered the power of the relics of St Martin, and he wept for his crime against Fr. Honoratus. He wept like a man who had been needing for many years to be cleansed by tears. He wept to remember his own earliest childhood in France, son of noble parents, before the Inquisition caused him to hate the Church, when it persecuted his relatives that lived in Spain. I admitted to him that the Inquisition was the most hateful institution to have disguised itself in sheep's clothing! Nevertheless I made clear to Lafitte that every man is given a certain trial by God, never one beyond a man's own strength. He laughed at that. I told him, though, that how a man meets his own trial determines the growth of his character."

"The nuns have sent us to find the place of his burial," Prien said then.

"They always told me that someone would come," said Pere Jan. "The Elder was buried in an oak grove, with six trees. Lafitte told me that himself. 'I buried him where I could have access to his grave', he said to me. 'I was never acquitted of my sins, but I confessed all my thoughts at his grave-site, where no one else could see me. The presence of his resting place was oracular to me, even though I was the one who killed him.' All this I related to the nuns. I visited them with these details soon after he left; but they seemed to know it already. I, however, was forever changed by that visit to the nuns!"

"What else can you remember now?" said Prien. "Anything else that Lafitte said about the place?".

"There are many things I can not tell you, of course," said the priest. "He spoke to me in the confidence of a private confession."

"Them nuns are waiting by an empty reliquary you see," said Prien.

"In time, in time. The Elder himself will lead you," he answered. "There is nothing else on this matter that it would be helpful or appropriate for me to say. But tell me

171

about yourself. Have you been in contact with the nuns since Lafitte's disappearance?"

"Dionysia was my spir'tual mother," said Prien, humbly bowing his head.

"Excellent news, that is!" he answered, as a fire came into the aged eyes. "Then I don't have to ask you through what grace and suffering you were released from the marks that life left in you?"

Prien merely stood like a humble fisherman while the fire in those ancient eyes roared out as though to search into his heart. Neither man said anything. Then, seeming satisfied, Pere Jan spoke: "I myself have been under the guidance of the nuns since the time that I discovered them, as have so many in this part of the country. They have taught us to live according to the example of St. Martin himself, struggling to attain the perfection of prayer in his monastery in a ravine near Tours, from which Saint Ninian of Whithorn and all the apostles to the British Isles were sent! Like the other priests who accept their counsel, however, I have not adopted the Eastern Rite, as the nuns did; but this is as much for the sake of my people, as it is for my own love of the honorable dignity and antiquity of Latin chant."

"We believe that there is need for hurry in our search you see," Prien insisted. "Dionysia now, she appeared to us deep in them swamps, and led us through an unknown cut-off almost to your door."

At this news, the old priest sighed, as though a burden were lifted from his heart.

He stared at the earth, a gentle smile came over his face, and a tear fell to the ground.

"My days are soon at an end," he said. "It is time for my soul to be cultivated. I believe I remember that there is one person who probably knows where this grove lies. More of that later. I will show you what the Eldress Dionysia was leading you toward.

Come with me."

We followed him to the church door, where he stopped and turned.

"I am sorry," he said. "There are certain holy things that may only be beheld by those who have been baptized according to the apostolic canons. You will have to wait outside while I take Messieur Prien into the church, to show him the things that are hidden within the altar."

"How can we be baptized in to that tradition?" William responded immediately.

"Very good." replied the priest. "You are aware that you are being prepared for that. The nuns will see to it in time. Why don't you wait by that tree over there?"

He and Prien went into the church, and the door was closed behind them.

৵৶৵৶৵৶

The hundred-year-old live oaks bowed over Bayou Teche as though to usher us down its slow, pleasantly shaded turns. Like graceful aristocrats they turned their branches in every dignified pose, conducting us onward. The oldest, however, bending almost to the water as we passed under, seemed ready to whisper mysteries forgotten for more than a lifetime. I had begun to think they wished to lead us to a land sheltered by waters on every side from the agnosticism that rules the world.

"That there Bayou des Allemands is still pretty far off – almost to the Mississippi now," Prien mused. "I was hoping we would not have to cross the Atchafalaya during this here trip. I would rather take this here boat out on them Gulf waves now, than across that river. But now that is where we have got to go to find that there man Pere Jan told me about."

"How can this one man know what no one else knows?" I said. "How can he know where the priest is buried?"

"Lafitte hisself he showed him the spot," answered Prien. "It happened like this, said Pere Jan. A third man he come down that Mississippi from Natchez to New Orleans, asking all about Lafitte. His questions now were of a sort that Pierre and Alexander, them were Jean Lafitte's two brothers, they were called for. They had by that time no idea where Jean had gone and hid hisself. Pierre and Alexander now they had got to be respectable in that there New Orleans society. But at the same time now, they knew that them Masons they'd been lookin' about everywhere for Jean Lafitte and that there chest which the priest he had brought from Jerusalem.

"This stranger here, Pere Jan told me, he had seen what was in that chest when it was up in Natchez.

"Pierre and Alexander now, soon as they heard this, they hurried that there man out of town and hid him in a cabin, out on Bayou St. John. You see they knew that not only was his life in danger, but their own as well now. Well then they sent for the only man they could trust. He had once been one them high Masons, one them few you see they called them knights o' Solomon's Temple, in Jerusalem now. He was someone had knowed Elder Honoratus. He argued with him when he came back from that there Mt. Sinai; and the Elder he convinced him to renounce them Masons.

"This here fellow now, he quickly took the Natchez stranger off the hands o' them Lafitte brothers – which was all that they wanted. Like all the rest of them now, he was also looking for that there burial site. He believed, by the way this stranger's mind it had been changed, and he was right, that what he had seen was the remains of the Elder. So these two now, they put their heads together and to see if they could figure out where Lafitte had gone to. Maybe Lafitte would have nothing to hide from this man; maybe he would show him the grave. Then he was sent off alone; and Lafitte he showed him the place sure 'nough.

"All this was part of that there confession that Pere Jan he heard from Lafitte hisself."

◌◌

William, Gerald and I were studying each other's faces during this narrative. Mr. Matthews was staring only into himself, with an increasing frown. William and I were trying to find, each in the other's eyes, some word from which to start an explanation; but Gerald spoke freely: "I knew we would run into him again, somewhere on this journey!"

"If he knew what we were looking for," I said, "why didn't he just tell us from the beginning?"

"Because finding it would have been one thing," answered William, "but understanding its value would have remained impossible."

"You know who this here man is?" said Prien. "This fellow Pere Jan sent us to find?"

"He is the one who gave us this book of explanations for all the passages in the Bible," William answered.

173

"I find myself in the company of men and angels!" Prien exclaimed. "You will recognize him when you see him, then! I was told now that the settlers on Bayou des Allemands they will know where to find him. This is a village of Germans now, settled even before them French they had come out into the bayous. Some of them now, they have been converted by some them there Greeks and their priest, that have got a little church in New Orleans. They are the ones now we have got to find. Tell me now, this other man, that there Natchez stranger – I dare guess you know him too?"

"He has been dead for many years," William replied. "He was the grandfather of a nurse, who raised the girl I am to marry."

"Dead, you say – maybe that is not quite the word now. I find myself in strange company – making way against fallen men and fallen angels!"

"This would seem to confirm that the Natchez Treasure was never anything more than a shriveled corpse." I said. "The gold we have tossed aside to find this out! What could there be in the coffin of a priest that causes this kind of excitement?"

"What were the relics of St. Martin of Tours like?" said William.

"I can't tell you that," Prien replied. "I don't know if I was in heaven or on earth now."

"I felt that way myself," William answered, "standing by that tree outside while we were waiting for you. Underneath it was the first of the stations of the cross: Christ in Gethsemene..."

"My guess is that the wood-carver was an immigrant Frenchman," I said. "No one in the New World has inherited that degree of skill."

"My attention was focused on the painting of St. Martin around the side of the trunk," said William.

"Is that so?" I said without much interest. "I didn't see any painting."

"You didn't see that? Dionysia was shown with Fr. Honoratus among the crowds of his disciples," William said. "I recognized her face from the one we saw in the swamps; and I saw that her name was written above her, as it was for all those that were shown. St. Martin himself was shown in the company of monks whose teachings he inherited. I read the names of St. Anthony the Great, St. John Cassian, and St. Honoratus of Lerins. I wondered, though, why neither Dionysia nor the priest wore haloes."

"That now is because they have not yet been named as saints by that there Church," said Prien quietly.

"They were depicted climbing a ladder, were they not?" said Mr. Matthews.

"That's not what I saw!" said William. "They were in front of a church that stood near a ravine. St. Martin held a scroll which read: 'Blessed are the pure in heart, for they shall see God.'"

"It was on the side of the tree that faced toward the church, right?" said Mr. Matthews. "There was only one picture. I saw them following St. Martin and those same other saints up a ladder into the heavens."

"What did you see?" I said to Gerald. I felt that I could rely on his judgment, whatever might be happening to the others.

"I wasn't looking," he shrugged. "I was thinking; thinking of things that I could hardly believe I would dare to think – that's how he likes to say it." He nodded toward Prien.

"Yep, sir, that's right," Prien said. "I know how that is. What was them there thoughts now?"

"It was occurring to me what it is we are searching for, and what kind of a real treasure that might be. I can't explain it, because I really don't know what exists in the grave of a man who had that much effect on Lafitte and so many others. But it was occurring to me what kind of power might reside in such a place. At least, that is how it seems from what has been said.

"And then it was occurring to me that Prien, right at that same moment, was seeing an example of what that is, inside the church. I can't explain it – it was as though something was being revealed to me. And then I began slowly to comprehend the way we are being led by miracles and wonders toward gifts of understanding, impossible to put into words!"

"Yep sir, that's exactly right now!" Prien answered. "That St. Martin now, he was revealin' his mind to me in exactly that there same manner. It's not like I heard anybody speakin' in my head, but my understandin' now, it was a-growing while I was lookin' at him lying there peaceful."

"What are you saying?" I interrupted. "Martin of Tours lived more than a thousand years ago! If there was a single bone that has not turned to dust in that time, I would be amazed; but you speak as though there was flesh on the skeleton still, and a face to look at!"

"Wasn't you been payin' attention now to them there things?" Prien said. "That there St. Catherine now, she was before St. Martin; but the Elder he saw her body on Mt. Sinai, and her face it was still lovely as it was the day she breathed."

"What is this?" I challenged. "Did the early Christians learn this from the Egyptians? Are they still preserving mummies?"

The old man laughed, loud and long.

"What's funny?" I said, offended.

"Them there Masons now, that's just like what they would say. And them nuns now, they'd get so mad at hearin' it, they'd go chasing 'em with whatever shovel or broom was nearest at hand. I tell you now, you hain't lived 'till you seen that!" He paused while his expression burst in merriment again.

"And sometimes you see," he continued, "them Masons they come to me then, and they'd say to me, what was that now? Well I had more patience with 'em, having grown up around Lafitte. I'd tell 'em, nope sir, these hain't no wonders of science, nor no magical contortions neither. This here's the power of God Hisself, and them nuns they carry it sometimes in the end o' their shovels too."

Again he was interrupted by his own laughter.

"But what happened when you were in there with St. Martin?" Gerald persisted.

"Well then," he replied, "this was how I was thinkin' there. That holy Father Honoratus of Lerins, in old France, he was St. Martin's spir'tual father. Now I don't even know how I knowed that, unless mebbe them nuns told it me once, but just then I sure knowed it. And there was a monastery at that there Lerins, on an island in that sea now, and it was built like them monasteries in them there deserts o' Egypt. That's how St. Martin learned that there way o' life. Now this here new Father Honoratus he comes from Sinai, a-bringin with him that same life. And he taught that life through them nuns to that same people that they belong to him now, them exiles from St. Martin's own land. And the life of exile now, that there has always been the real life of the desert. And so there I was, a-starin' at his face, and I could see that there power o' grace in it. And seemed like he almost held my hand now, and wanted me to pluck out a few threads from the cross in his robe, to guide me to the relics of the new Father Honoratus. And so I did."

Chapter Twenty-Eight

Through landscapes of the Old World we floated: noble chateaux removed from the revolutions of Europe, and transplanted within the paradisiacal framework of ancient live oaks. Between those lovely banks of Bayou Teche, we continued to Spanish New Iberia, where the trees grow even larger. After that, the bayou turns east, and the banks begin to drown in swamp.

This was the first hint of a tremendous geographical change to come.

Between the European land grants of Bayou Teche, endowed by monarchies that the grand Masonic plans for a new world order had since destroyed, and the more Americanized plantations of Bayou LaFourche to the east, there is a river to cross which is like no other. If not as wide as the Mississippi, it is deeper and more turbulent. No man knows how deep it is. It is said there may be whirlpools all the way to hell. It is impossible to cross by those unfamiliar with its currents, and, surrounded on either side by lakes, swamps and bayous to such a distance that it creates a country of its own, it is known as the nearly inaccessible divide of the Atchafalaya.

There was no longer any real shore. Signs of human habitation became rare. Here and there were small islands with isolated fields of corn, but the only houses were built on boats. "When that there Mississippi comes floodin' in the spring, everything you see here it is under water, lots o' water," Prien explained. "Them folks who live in these here parts, they don't know nothing 'bout civilizin', and civilizin' don't know 'bout them neither. These here folks they're not trusted by them that don't know them now. I think they're some in these here swamps that no one has ever seen. Even Lafitte he was b'wary of 'em. Some you see they are not Christian. Their folks they don't know their own fore-fathers. You would have to go west as far as them Sabine swamps at the border o' Texas to find folks as wild. Except now I must say that these here folks, they might be lawless, but at least they hain't them all-out crim'nals now like them Texas border bandits."

Quietness reigned after that; and its rule increased. Each man entered that quiet in a different way. It seemed each personality was being revealed more instead of less in that silence. Reading the others' faces, it would appear that they profited by it, that the silence was making them better. To me, its rule was oppressive. I alone was miserable. I thought of Denise, I thought of Catherine, of Claudette, of my lost daughter and my lost life. I wanted speech, because this quiet was too unbearably honest. But I had become afraid of what that hot silence was welding into the other men, and I no longer dared to interrupt it.

At some point during the endless summer afternoon, the quiet bayou ran into a secondary channel of the braided course of the Atchafalaya. The waters no longer had the same appearance. Their surface was not explosive like that of shallow rapids, but instead, pockmarked with dimples that appeared and disappeared as quickly, constantly moving, it suggested that the channel was deep and far more violent beneath the surface.

Prien briefly warned that this was only a suggestion of what was to come, and he began to instruct us how to hold and move the oars, not for propulsion, which the current itself provided, but only for balance and guidance. We moved at alarming speed around a wide bend, where we saw the main body of the river. Prien roared commands to every man's oar as we rushed out into the main river and spun like a helpless leaf into currents in tremendous battle, with whirlpools opening to the depths and closing like mouths around us. Every terrible moment was consumed in fighting our way around these. Every movement of the oar, every movement of the arm and leaning of the body was performed in strict obedience to Prien's endless stream of commands. With one unadvised move we could have leaned too far into the edge of any whirlpool, capsized, and never come up. No man dared look up even to measure the distance to the shores that raced by until, by some miracle, the peaceful bayou managed to separate itself in the opposite bank. We found ourselves safely within its waters again, following its meandering path softly on its way to the Gulf.

"This little bayou intersects the Atchafalaya, and then just keeps on going?" I said this without being able to believe what my eyes showed me.

"Bayou Teche is one of our major rivers now," smiled Prien. "I hain't never heard nobody complain it was too little."

"How can a simple bayou maintain its own identity in the face of a river like that?" I responded.

"How is something I can't say I know," said Prien.

"The bayou is obviously the older watercourse, then," said William. "This channel must have been here before the overflow from the Mississippi increased the volume of the Atchafalaya. Probably, this ancient bayou was itself once the main course of the Mississippi."

"Well some folks now they say this here bayou on the east side of that there river it's got a different name though," said Prien, "and I think that's right. 'Cause that there Teche now, it's got a river-current, always toward the sea. But on this side here, see, there ain't no steady flow like that. Sometimes the tide goes this way and, sometimes that way; and sometimes, the water just sits here and doesn't go nowhere at all. And that's what's meant proper by that there word 'bayou' now."

"We'll bring a geology student down from Harvard and tell him he can earn his doctorate in this study," I suggested, "if he can survive that river!"

⌈

As soon as it crosses the Atchafalaya, the bayou country leaves its shadows behind. We emerged from their shelter into the blistering days of late July. The sun had grown in size by the magnification of humidity, and the air was so wet it could hardly be distinguished from the water. Prien tried again to set up the sail over our heads for some shade, but it became so heavy with moisture that it collapsed on our heads and clung to our shoulders and arms. We nearly capsized in the confusion. Gerald fell over the back of the boat into the water; and finding relief there, he called us in. We swam for an hour, and then, noticing that the sun had so many more hours of sailing through its wake of steam, we set up the sail as a tent on shore and abandoned the journey. We slept until sundown, and then set out on the peaceful stream under brilliant stars.

We proceeded through a brief but most pleasant night's journey under a Gulf breeze, navigating the dark, quiet bayou by the lighthouses of heaven, the constellations of the summer triangle. We measured the bayou's turns by the sweeping flight of the Swan, the Virgin's lamp, and the burning strings of the celestial Lyre, while Prien related the importance of their stories to their positions in the stellar latitudes. Night faded behind the rising dog star, Sirius, as his constellation came up upon the heels of the hunter Orion, whom he follows across the centuries. Prien pointed out his dawn rising, for which the infamous "dog days" of the late summer are named.

By sunrise we reached the sweeping turn where that streamlet heads south through plains of marsh to the sea. Instead of following that course, as peaceful and pretty as any ribbon of water that passes through the earth, we turned north into Lake Palourde. This wide, quiet body of water appeared to be the remnant of some season of floods when the bayou moved with more virile authority, changing its course at the turn as major rivers do when defining their history. We crossed the lake before the heat became too intense, and then camped where a smaller bayou from the north fed the lake. We slept and dreamed through the long afternoon in which July yields its days to August, then eagerly launched into another night of stars that led at the other end into Lake Verret.

This we crossed in two hours while the sun rose hot into a black thundercloud. Prien became anxious. He ordered us to cover the boat and tie it to a tree on the shore, then set up our tent in a thicket of myrtles. William suggested the stronger shelter of an oak grove nearby, but Prien ignored him, yelling at him to bring blankets from the boat. A strong blast of cold air nearly ripped the tent from our hands as we struggled to stake it down. We shivered together into the blankets in amazement while hail bombarded the tent around us, and lightning tore apart the black sky. Then we fell asleep to a gentle rain, cool and musical. We woke late in the afternoon to find the boat safe under its protecting canvas – and the oak grove destroyed by lightning.

∞

The east shore of Lake Verret had been connected by the Attakapas Canal – dug almost a hundred years before by the Spanish – to Bayou LaFourche at Napoleonville. We entered this canal on the second day of August before the dawn, in the hour of the morning star. (I know this only because I later read it in William's journal.) It was there that we began to notice an increase in flatboat traffic. These were sometimes empty, more often heavily loaded, and occasionally fitted with small, low houses. They were poled by wild-bearded, frowning Americans, some solitary, some in silent groups, that had the same appearance as the mining frontiersmen I had known in California. That is, they looked like men hunting for their own fortunes. Prien never took the trouble to greet them as they passed. I remarked that I found this out of keeping with his character.

"Even to talk to them is trouble now," he said. "They've gone and made themselves needed for trade in these here parts; but my people they keep clear of them. It was after they came around that them Americans came and started buying up the land; and then everythin' it changed.

"Lafitte's men now, they were the ones supplyin' all that there ferryin' of things at good prices. No one cared that them things they was smuggled, 'til these men came with all their lawyers. Lafitte he made his agreements with 'em at first; but he found out he could not to trust 'em, not at all. They look out just for themselves now; they're the next thing to robbers, not just with them prices they demand, but the way they demand now! The first ones that came to the bayous you see, they vanished without a trace. The folks they winked at Lafitte, and then blamed them Injuns for their disappearance. Now you see, they are everywhere 'round here. Them planters employ 'em when they can't get what they need off them there steamboats; but we'll be better off now if they just ignore us."

By the time we turned into Bayou LaFourche, the steam that was rising off the water was warm enough to suffocate a man, but we saw hard labor. Black men in the sun, their shining muscles clothed by rivers of sweat, were cutting cypresses out of the swamps, hewing them into logs and piling them onto wagons. These were then hauled over the higher ground on paths between the crops to be stacked by the brick sugar house. Prien explained that the wood was needed to fire the steam engine for the mill, as well as for the boiler and kettles to extract sugar from the crushed canes.

The growing canes were already taller than a man, and the fields gave the impression of solid fences along the water. They were divided at intervals by roads with ditches full of water on either side, giving an opening to a long row of sky. Sometimes the fields were separated by corn patches or leafy potato fields. There were also fields of stubble and smaller second-year canes sprouted from unremoved roots of the previous crop; but these were buried in blossoming peas which, besides giving food for men and cattle, Prien explained, sent fertilizing nitrogen from their roots into the ground.

He confided with pride that the chief worker on every plantation, the sugar maker, was always Cajun. Long before the planters came, he said, the Cajuns had learned the secret of how to boil the clarified cane juice to extract the maximum amount of crystallized sugar.

In every turn of Bayou LaFourche, there was a clearing for a lawn and plantation house with its docks. "After these here modern ways of refinin' sugar made it big cash," said Prien "these here planters they became Lafitte's best customers. That there was the big jump in trade. They'd never have got big profits going without his smugglin' though. I still know most of these here folks.

"Do you know the Pothier place?" said Mr. Matthews.

"Sure do," said Prien. "It's right down that there bayou, on the other side now."

"They are related to my wife," said Mr. Matthews. "I'd like to find out if they know anything of the child."

"What child is that now?" said Prien.

Mr. Matthews looked at me as though waiting for me to give the explanation, but my lips did not seem to want to move. He sighed, and said, "Denise – Dionysia, I mean – gave birth to a child before she came to the convent in Lake Charles."

"I didn't realize that she had ever been married!" said Prien.

"She never was," said her father.

I stood abruptly, and the boat jerked and swayed beneath my feet as I stared into

John Matthews' clear eyes.

"Easy there now!" Prien began; but when he saw my face, his own lost its expression.

"I loved your daughter like I never loved any woman, damn it, and you always knew that!" They could probably hear my voice around the bend of the bayou. "I apologize that I was young and stupid. That's a fact. I did not know that she loved me; she was as mysterious and unknown to me as my own mother. I did not know about the child."

"That's true," said Mr. Matthews calmly. "I am the one who made a mistake worse than yours. I could have prevented a great deal of unhappiness, not only for myself and my own estranged wife and daughter, but also for you."

His eyes, more eloquent than his words as he spoke, then fell. I sat angrily, turning away. Every man had to react quickly, leaning in counterbalance, to keep the boat from sitting up and going over. I retreated to my corner in the rear.

"But instead," he said, "we find ourselves in a strange journey."

"Did them nuns say anything about this child now?" asked Prien.

"Only that it was a girl, given for adoption when Denise was still with the Sisters of Charity in New Orleans," answered Mr. Matthews. "They promised they would write to find out more about her welfare."

"Then that will ha' been done already," said Prien, "by that there time we get back."

"Besides that," Mr. Matthews said, "I recently discovered that my wife knew something of the legends of Contraband Bayou, having grown up on the Sallier place..."

Prien looked stunned. "Hilary Sallier? You married Hilary Sallier? Are you telling me that she was Dionysia's mother now?"

Mr. Matthews was quiet for some moments before he replied. "I suppose, of course, I should not be surprised that you would have known her."

"Knowed her!" gasped Prien. "Everyone knowed her, of course! That there Elder Honoratus hisself knowed her. She, now, she is your wife?"

Mr. Matthews was no longer able to speak. William did so for him, saying simply, "She is no longer alive."

"She rests with them saints!" said Prien.

"She died of grief," I said cruelly.

"What, now!" said Prien. "Why's that?"

"After I had disowned our daughter," said Mr. Matthews quietly.

"Disowned her!" said Prien.

"That's why I lost contact with my daughter," Mr. Matthews confessed. "When she was with child out of wedlock. My wife's family placed her in the convent without my knowledge."

"Hilary's grief now, that would have been for you, not for her girl," said Prien. "She knowed what that convent was! Dionysia was the daughter? It was them there Sallier folks that gave the land for the convent hospital! Before that you see, them nuns lived in huts in that there forest; and Hilary she used to go visit with them there!"

Mr. Matthews was silent.

"Charles Sallier he was one of them first settlers on the lake!" Prien went on. "Lake Charles it was named for him. He married into them there LeBleu folks, which had settled a few years before, when there was only Choktaws and Coushettas on the lake, and a few o' them Cherokees exiled from out the east. Arsene he came from them folks – he was Hilary's uncle now! Catherine LeBleu, she was Hilary's mother. I'd think that them there folks might know more about them legends of Contraband Bayou than anyone a-livin'."

Mr. Matthews sighed. "Yes, well, I will ask them about that, if I can get that far in conversation with them."

"You will now, you will," said Prien. "Them there's folks you don't know now, if you think they'd keep any o' that there resentment."

"I never knew them well, but I believe you may be right," said Mr. Matthews, staring down the sun-drenched bayou.

"Well now, if that hain't another o' them wonders we gonna see here," said Prien, "that we gonna see you reconciled with your own folks. Think about it now. Them nuns, they would ha' foreseen it!"

"There were many things the old nun said to me," said Mr. Matthews, "which I did not comprehend."

☙

We approached the Pothier house. It seemed strangely empty, even from a distance. There were no servants in the lawn or gardens, and no movements behind the large, shaded windows, though the main doors were opened. There was only one man at the dock, sitting on a nearly empty flatboat and smoking a pipe. As we neared, a younger man, unshaven and in sweat-stained clothes, came out of the door pushing a couch on a wheeled cart toward the dock. We saw that chairs and a polished table were already on the boat. As we drifted near the dock, the sitting figure quietly turned and stared at us from under his hat.

"Howdy," said Mr. Matthews.

"You got business here?" was the reply.

Prien coughed. No one knew what to say.

"This is the Pothier place?" said Mr. Matthews at last.

"What if it is?"

"These are relations of mine," John Matthews answered with irritation.

"That so?" said the flatboatman. "How come you don't know the place, then?"

The younger man, seeing us, had stopped with his cart halfway across the lawn.

"How come I don't know if you're a robber?" said Mr. Matthews.

The flatboatman reached quickly under his seat, but a clap and explosion and a whistle ripped the air and made him freeze. Prien had been faster, firing with one hand even before he held his own smoking rifle under the chin; and now he lowered its barrel at the man.

"Now, old man, you sure your sight is steady?" said the flatboatman.

"I spent ten years with Lafitte now," said Prien. "Some things there are you don't forget."

"You spent ten years with Lafitte, and you'd call me a robber?" said the man, sitting up. "I was reaching for my papers, signed by Pothier himself. Right under my feet is the bill of sale for the new furniture from New Orleans, which we just finished unloading;

182

and then there's his order, written to me, to remove the old stuff."

"I see your gun down there, too," said Prien.

"And my strongbox is right next to it, if you've got eyes like that," said the flatboatman. "And if you tried to get anything but the papers I just told you about, you'd find out how fast my trigger-finger is, too."

By now, the slaves had run out of the backwoods to see about the gunshot. They ran onto the lawn and stopped, huddled in a crowd. They held scythes, plowshares and pitchforks in their muscular hands. The younger man cried out, abandoning his cart, but he didn't know where to run. He collapsed on the ground, covering his head.

"Tell them to go back to the woods," said the flatboatman with obvious fear.

"You tell them," said Prien, his gun still fixed on the stranger. "They don't know me."

The crowd of slaves began cautiously inching toward us in one mass.

"Hell, I don't know anything about talking to the slaves," the flatboatman said with panic.

Prien shouted a string of Cajun phrases, heavily weighted with strange words that might have been African or Jamaican. The largest of the slaves stepped forward and answered. There followed a quick dialogue, after which the tremendous slave marched down to the dock and walked fearlessly up to the flatboatman. Towering over him, he frowned down. In an unexpected movement he lifted him off his feet and deposited him in the rear of his own boat. Then picked up the flatboatman's rifle and, frowning at the cowering stranger, tossed it into the water. Next he lifted the strongbox from its place and carried it to Prien, who set it down and shot the lock off. He lifted out the papers and translated them for the slave. The latter nodded, brought the strongbox for Prien to place them back inside, then carried it again to the flatboatman. With that the giant slave turned, and a sweep of his hand ushered the crowd back to its work.

"Where is the family?" asked John Matthews.

"It's August," replied the flatboatman. "If you knew the planters in these parts, you'd know that they've gone to the coast. The planting and cultivating is finished, and there's nothing to do but gather wood for the sugar houses and watch the cane grow. The slaves can take care of that, so the planters go to the Gulf islands to escape the heat. Pretty soon there'll be hardly a planter on the bayou. A good time for robbers, as you say. How come you say you're related, and don't know any of this?"

"We're from Natchez," Mr. Matthews answered, "where, as I'm sure you know, cotton's the crop. There's no vacations during the growing season there. These are my late wife's cousins. How long have they been gone?"

"Left just this morning," was the answer.

"They went by steamboat, I assume," said Mr. Matthews, "so there's no way to catch up without going all the way to the Gulf."

"I don't know about that," said the flatboatman. "Hey!" he yelled at his helper. "Pick your butt up off the ground and get me loaded!" To Mr. Matthews, he said, "The steamboat will be picking up passengers at every dock down the river. I suppose you could catch them, if you had a mind to."

"Can you take me?" said Mr. Matthews.

"Are you crazy?" said Prien.

"I don't know how long this might take me," answered Mr. Matthews, "but I would want to talk to them if I can. They might lead me to my granddaughter."

"Then we'll take you," said Prien.

"No," said Mr. Matthews. "You've been sent on another search." To the flatboatman he said, "I'll pay you to take me to them, and I'll purchase a better rifle for you."

"You got a deal, there," said the flatboatman.

"I'll go with you," I said.

"That's not a good idea at all," he answered.

"Why is it a better idea for you to go alone with someone you don't even know?" I said.

"My wife's family is not likely to be so thrilled to see me," he said, "but what about you? Shall I introduce you as the father?"

"I see," was all I said.

"Why not camp here in the shade for the heat of the day?" said Mr. Matthews. "If I'm not back by morning, I'll meet you at Des Allemands; or, if not there, I'll wait here for your return."

Chapter Twenty-Nine

The steam that floated along the bayou had settled with the glowing evening, and the water shone like a golden mirror, reflecting the face of the west. The forest beyond the fields on the opposite shore had fallen into the muted green that follows sunset, a soft and magical color that no painter has been able to translate onto canvas. The sky still held light enough to make one think it could cast shadows, but this was the illusion of a summer evening. The only shadows were in the clouds. Thunderheads to the south towered orange and white, still climbing into the sunlight, while their bases, gliding over the chilled atmosphere beneath, were blacker than a moonless night in winter. Lightning crawled out of their sides, spread in alarming webs, and as immediately disappeared; but the clouds were too far distant for the thunder to reach us through the tremendous song of crickets and frogs. We sat outside our tent on one of the most pleasant lawns on the bank of any water, but our thoughts were uneasy.

"I don' know that we should ha' let him go with no flatboatman," said Prien.

"We could have taken him ourselves," suggested Gerald. "I think we might have moved faster than any flatboat."

"He seemed desperate to get away from us," I said.

"It was reasonable for him to want privacy with his wife's family, don't you think?" said William.

"And he couldn't know now," Prien recalled, "how long that there little trip might take."

"He didn't want us to go with him at all," I said. "He's up to something. What do you think it is?"

"He knows that you don't trust him," said Gerald.

"You could say that," I answered.

"Have you already forgotten how important it is," Gerald replied, "for him to get information on your daughter?"

Not wanting to admit that fact at the moment, I said nothing.

"Maybe I never understood you," Gerald said indignantly, "even all the time I thought I did. I won't say that locating the girl is the most important thing about this journey. There are things happening which I think are beyond my understanding, far beyond it. But this at least as important as anything else!"

"You always felt that there mistrust 'bout Dionysius' father now?" Prien wondered.

"Not at all," I admitted. "At one time, I trusted him more than any man. I never knew until recently how angry he was with me... but there's more than that. He knows too much about the Masons, far more than I realized when we started out on this trip. That is what has begun to make me nervous. And there are too many other things about his behavior that don't add up to any sense. At first, he wanted nothing to do with finding the treasure. He only wanted to find the child. He warned us of danger we didn't know, remember? Then, he became the one goading us to find the vault of the mysteries, as

185

he called it! He sent a message to the Donaldson Brothers, something with Masonic symbols, and then assured us they would no longer follow us, which, indeed they did not. But then, you recall, he was eager to get away as far as possible, urging us into the swamps where we could not be found! His impulses betray a conflict that I don't understand – do you? Even in the deepest part of the bayous, he kept watch like he was worried we were followed. Now, he takes the first opportunity to get away from us, putting himself at the mercy of a rather suspicious stranger. Am I the only one to see how bizarre his behavior has been? I doubt we'll see him for a while; and I'm not sure we'll want to see him then."

"Well," said Gerald, "it's true that your relationship with John Matthews has had a strange and stormy history. But his behavior has made more sense to me than your own, and you are the only one who does not see that."

"Them nuns they had no misgivings 'bout him," said Prien.

"Yes," I said defiantly. "They gave him a private interview, didn't they? I doubt he has shared most of those secrets with us as well."

"Nor should he now," said Prien. "There's things they might tell you in private too – none of that there would I want to hear!"

The big slave walked out of the dusk and stood over Prien, who gestured for him to sit. The slave then turned toward the darkness and spoke, and an ancient negro silently emerged. Prien greeted him with surprised recognition and laughter. They began a long conversation, none of which I could follow. William, picking up words and phrases, told us that one was the grandfather of the other. He and Prien shared memories of Lafitte, according to William, and were discussing the route to Des Allemands as I fell into sleep.

໖

At sunrise, the flatboatman returned with only his own younger companion and an empty barge. Silently he docked and handed Prien a note. Prien unfolded it quickly, glanced at the contents and, before reading, said to the boatman, "Why, now, has this here note been already opened?"

"It never was sealed," was the answer.

"Where's your cargo?" said Prien. "You was supposed to take it to New Orleans! Did Pothier change his mind?"

"We unloaded for quicker travel," said the flatboatman.

"Unloaded? Where?"

"Why is that your business?" said the flatboatman.

"Why don't I trust you now?" said Prien.

The youthful companion whipped out his rifle for an answer. "Here's the gun he bought me," said the flatboatman, "to prove we fulfilled our transaction."

"Fine," said Prien. They stared at one another for several minutes. Then the flatboatman retrieved his companion's pole and worked the boat out from the dock himself. The other kept his gun trained on Prien.

As they neared the bend upstream, the older flatboatman pulled his pole from the water and swung it into his companion, hitting him across the chest. The gun went off into the trees, scaring up crows and pelicans. He threw the pole down for the other to pick up, and then bent down to reload the rifle.

"A pretty breed now, them river rats!" said Prien.

"What does the note say?" said William.

"Here, read it," said Prien.

William did:

I am on my way by steamboat to New Orleans, with a letter from my wife's family for the Sisters of Charity. It authorizes them to give the full details on my granddaughter's condition and upbringing. The child was given into a certain home, according to the advice of the nuns, and with Denise's full knowledge. They also provided me with astonishing information: that the particular tract of land that was given for the hospital on Contraband Bayou was donated at Lafitte's repeated insistence. Lafitte also gave the money to add to the family's donation for the hospital's construction! I will meet you at Des Allemands on Monday. Look for me at the train stop. They tell me that the Opelousas-New Orleans crosses Bayou Des Allemands, just at the side of the old village.

"That is his handwriting?" Prien asked me. I nodded.

"That now is reassuring," said Prien. "It means he got on board that there steamboat alive, and with them Pothier folks lookin' on. What worries me though," he said, pointing to the letter's broken seal, "is that there flatboatman, whatever else he may be up to, he knows as much as we do. Now why did he unload for faster travel? Do you suspect he's a-tryin' to get to New Orleans just as that there steamboat shows up?"

I said nothing. There was no need. My suspicions had been heard; they were not mentioned again.

☙

No waterways connect Bayou LaFourche to the east until one comes to its spreading delta in the Gulf marshes. Though the bayou spins through swamplands almost from its origin on the flank of the Mississippi, its vigorous current, fortified by yearly floods, builds its own substantial levees against the watery lands it passes through. One needs only to walk less than a mile away from the bayou's edge, though, to encounter the extensive swamps that empty at last into the Barataria basin. With the help of the slaves, we lifted our boat onto a cart and hitched it to mules, accompanied it along a field road toward the back lands, and dragged it off again into the swamps. From there, we found the remnants of an ancient waterway leading into the wide expanse of Lac Des Allemands. Then we poled down the currentless bayou of the same name, wide enough to have once been a segment of the Mississippi, which, at the point that it left the lake, was only a few miles northeast.

William had resumed reading out loud from Lafitte's journal, and had come to its final pages. There were no longer any mention of the treasures he had hidden. The lengthy and painful reflections on the nature and progress of his own crimes likewise had vanished as mysteriously as the swamp fogs. Even the language of his deeply philosophical speculations had ceased. Instead, these pages were filled with memoirs of the Elder's teachings. It was as if Lafitte's own voice had been silenced, replaced by that of Father Honoratus. The old priest was here remembered at a time when he was himself entirely absorbed in memories of the life of the monks on Mt. Sinai. This life was de-

187

scribed as a rhythm of prayer, unbroken since the first centuries.

He described a procession up the mountain one feast day, with the simple but unending prayer that the monks continually whispered even in their sleep. They climbed to the twisted and timeworn, but still flowering, bush in which God's consuming fire had rested without destruction to the branches and leaves. They turned aside into the chapel and stood singing while St. Catherine's incorrupt body was brought out, the still sweet and beautiful face of the divine young philosopher shining. The ring was slipped from her warm and limber finger and passed among the monks, then replaced. After that, they processed singing to the summit. More than one monk that day saw the fire column moving before them. When the song was concluded, they stood in utter silence, as though surrounded by the roaring wind of centuries, but untouched by it:

When Moses came down from the mountain, God warned Moses that He would not go among the people, or He would consume them. How was it, then, that we stood in the middle of that very fire on the peak of Sinai that day? How was I not consumed? I was licked up into it, beyond recognition of myself into the love of God, brighter and brighter. He spoke to me in words I could not comprehend, though my heart, which was all flame, understood.

I saw the ladder of fire climbing upward from the top of that sacred mountain, and I saw the faces of all the saints of every century ascending. I recognized their faces wrapped in fire, and I saw their names written in it. And I saw the book opened, and I saw other things...

"And that," said William, closing the book, "is how Lafitte's journal ends."

❧❧❧❧❧❧

We came in sight of the railroad trestle that spans the bayou, just before it widens into a second lake. It had been many miles since any man had spoken.

We disembarked at the village and walked in silence toward the simple wooden church. It was in a state of reconstruction. The youthful black-robed priest was within, giving orders to workmen in alternate phrases of Greek, German, and Cajun French.

The church interior was utterly strange. It had no pews at all. Paintings of Greek saints, on wood panels with gold-leaf backgrounds, covered the walls. The altar was concealed behind a paneled wall completely painted in such manner. Prien, greeting this young priest in the name of the nuns, was answered with a Greek blessing and gesture which affected him in a way I could not interpret; and he stood awkwardly, for once seeming to not know what to say.

The priest put him at ease with apologies in strangely accented French, a language which was clearly new to him. After a few more orders to the workmen, he called one of these to accompany him outside with us. We sat at a table in the shade of three oaks, while Prien conversed with the workman. At the beginning, we sat only as observers, as did the priest also. Before long, though, there were conversations in every language: William and I in bad Greek with the priest, William and the priest in bad Cajun with Prien and the workman, and Gerald ignored for long stretches where no one noticed his bewildered silence.

It would be impossible to reconstruct the order of those conversations, overlapping as they were in three languages. The order in which they occurred would have been hopelessly shuffled anyway, according to whichever person was understanding them in his own mind at any one time. I will only give certain portions as they recur to my own thought:

☙

"We don't know the name of the person we are seeking. We know very little about him, except that he was once a leader in the Order of the Knights of the Temple in Jerusalem, and that he was converted to your Orthodox Faith by Father Honoratus himself."

"It was Pere Jan that sent you to us? Pere Jan himself? Yes, we know him very well, of course!"

"He told us that this person was responsible for this village's recent conversion to the Orthodox Faith."

"No, that is not true. Pere Jan himself was responsible for that. Of course, in his humility, he would not admit that. It happened in this way:

"We have been Lutherans since the time our German forefathers founded this community. That was more than a century and a half ago, with the permission of King Louis, at about the time that the first French colonists were exploring the Louisiana territory. Luther, as you may know, was the first Protestant to question the authenticity of the sacraments. We have always lived in peace with our French neighbors, have even adopted much of their language and customs. However, their unusual reverence for the Church of St. Martin of Tours aroused our indignation. We organized a raid upon the church and fell upon it at night, attempting to enter the altar and steal the bread that had been consecrated. We were unsuccessful. Something, we did not know what, kept us from entering the altar. I myself was a member of that raid. We came back from it with our consciences strangely bruised. We spent several days thinking it over, and came to the conclusion that our actions, however justified in our own eyes, had been wrong. We returned to apologize to Pere Jan and his people. They not only forgave us, but they freely gave us a portion of the bread we had attempted to steal. We ate, and were changed. Not one of us can explain to you how it happened any better than that. We are simple fishermen, not theologians. Pere Jan refused to baptize us himself. Instead, he sent for an elderly gentleman from New Orleans, who perhaps is the person you seek. He is the one who suggested that since we have no immediate ties with the French hierarchy or with that of Rome, there was no reason that we should not join ourselves directly to the faith of the monastic Elder of Mt. Sinai who had influenced the renewal of faith throughout the bayou country. This caused us some concern, of course. We did not know what it meant. We asked Pere Jan's advice, and he suggested that we write to the nuns. They advised us to follow this gentleman's suggestion, which we have not since regretted. But he is not here. Perhaps Father Nicodemus here knows where to find him."

"It will be easier to find the oasis of St. Paul the First Hermit in the depths of the Sahara, than to find him in the streets of New Orleans! All we know is that he has a house hidden somewhere in that city!"

℃ℬ

Prien himself appeared somewhat confounded by the unfolding of these conversations, and did not seem to know what else to ask. About that time, however, we heard the train whistle. We politely excused ourselves and made our way down the dusty street.

"That there priest, he dresses like Fr. Honoratus did," said Prien thoughtfully; "and he acts that same way too, even so young he is now!" Right then the train pulled up, screaming at its brakes.

"Do you think John Matthews will really be on this train?" I wondered out loud. I was in error, though. He jumped out before the train had properly stopped. He was pale and disheveled, and it appeared he might be lacking for sleep.

"I've made a terrible mistake, allowing myself to be seen in New Orleans," he began before we could greet him. "The city is crawling with Masons that are looking for us; the whole country is infested with them!"

"You didn't think of this?" I replied.

"I had no idea there were that many in the South. I don't know how I got away; but they'll be on the next train through, count on it. By tomorrow they will be swarming out into the bayous, and it will be best if we have disappeared from this place without anyone knowing what happened to us. It will be better for these villagers as well. I have to get to St. Martinsville before they do. Because of me, Pere Jan's life is in danger! I will go the fastest way, by train to Breaux Bridge, then down Bayou Teche. I'll have to get a boat. But you can't leave yours here, or they'll find it, with the journal. There's not time to unload it; as soon as they refuel the train will be on its way, and I must go with it. You will have to take the boat and disappear into the swamps. Meeting at St. Martinsville may not be easy, but we will have to do it. Then, somehow, we will have to get back to the convent without being found."

"That there ex-Templar we were told to find," Prien interrupted, "is not here."

"No, I knew he would not be," said Mr. Matthews. "He has been handling my letters to the Wells Plantation, and forwarding the replies to Lake Charles. That's the reason I went to New Orleans, when I realized that the Masons might begin to track him and intercept them. I thought I might warn him, and get the letters before they fell into their hands. I succeeded in getting the letters. There is much news to tell you. But he would have handled things better if I had not come. He had re-routed all our correspondence through the swamps, avoiding the Post Offices, arranging for fishermen to carry them through St. Martinsville and Abbeville and directly to the convent. As soon as I came out of the swamps, they discovered what route we had been following, and now they will track down our letters before we can get them. Their network of spies was even greater than I feared. They have already figured out that our ex-Templar and the priest in St. Martinsville are the only two who know where the casket is buried. Pere Jan sent us to the ex-Templar, thinking he could more safely lead us to the place. But we were supposed to wait for him to meet us here. Now, he has been forced to flee the country right away – not for his own safety, but for that of the nuns.

"Fr. Honoratus's casket is buried on the convent grounds. The nuns themselves do not know it. We will have to get details of its location from Pere Jan – if we can rescue

190

him before the Masons get to him!"

"I do not see now why Pere Jan did not tell us this thing!" said Prien.

"He and our ex-Templar have long planned the uncovering of the relics," said Mr. Matthews, "in a manner that would be safest for the nuns. It was out of consideration for their safety that he never told the nuns that the relics were beneath their own feet. In this way, Fr. Honoratus' presence has remained with them, guiding them without their knowledge.

"The Masons continue to believe that what is in that casket is for themselves alone. But I should not speak of them as if they were united in their objectives. There are many who have been influenced by this ex-Templar who want nothing other than the discovery of the relics. There is discord among them like I have never seen."

"What is the news from Natchez?" asked William.

"Catherine and Lady Wells have continued their research in the library under the ex-Templar's guidance. Catherine has found letters from her nurse Sarah's grandfather, describing the grave. I have copies of those descriptions, but I doubt they can be of much help now. Things will appear far different from what they were at that time. Lady Wells has uncovered more Masonic papers, but I don't have those letters. I am afraid they might have been intercepted already. She knows as much as we do now. The Masons have tried to fabricate reasons to invade the mansion. They almost succeeded in starting a slave revolt."

"We need to get back there, then!" said William anxiously.

"There is no way that we could get past the Masons now," Mr. Matthews replied. "If we did, we would only put them in more danger. They're getting ready to fire up the train; get yourselves lost!"

"Wait," I said. "What about the child? Were you able to find out anything, or was that just your pretence for leaving?"

"Oh," said Mr. Matthews. He sighed heavily. "The Sisters of Charity did indeed have that information, but they would not give it to me. They told me they would need the permission of the foster-home first. They said they would try to have an answer by letter, arriving at the convent by the time we returned there, if they could; but they could not promise it. And do you know why?"

He sighed again; and when he spoke, his voice was broken.

"The Sisters told me that their courier to the mansion, where the child was raised, had been forced to flee the country that morning!"

The shock of this news removed from sight the faces of the four men who stared at me. The entire journey collapsed into that one moment. My heart cracked. Earth and sky, when they returned to my eyes, were stunned by the size of tears they had never seen.

"You remember," he said to William and Gerald, "how upset Lady Wells was when she discovered that Denise had a child that was given to adoption in New Orleans, and that James was the father of that child? We thought she was upset because of simple outrage towards James, though her actions were strange. It turns out there was more in her outburst than we understood..."

Here, John Matthews, overcome with emotion, could say no more.

"Are you so surprised?" Gerald said gently. And William added, "The resemblance has been obvious to me all along; but I never dared to say it. Now I can. Catherine is your daughter."

Chapter Thirty

The peril of that journey of return awakened all the faculties Prien had developed during his years of smuggling with Lafitte. We disappeared into the swamps, avoiding open bayous. We crossed Bayou LaFourche at night, before the rising of the moon. Even in utter darkness, Prien knew every mile. We then made straight for the vast Atchafalaya swamps where no man would find us. We spent most of that week in the utter solitude and beauty of those forested and heavily flowering wetlands, with no shortage of food from their waters. We emerged south of Breaux Bridge and drifted silently down the few miles of Bayou Teche in the earliest hours, arriving at St. Martinsville immediately before dawn. Its glory unfolded around us as we made our landing at the Church of St. Martin of Tours, just in time to witness Pere Jan's funeral.

John Matthews had arrived too late to warn him. A flatboat crew had surrounded him at dusk in the garden and taken him into the church for questioning. There they had tortured him to death, but he revealed none of his sacred secrets. A parishioner, entering the church for confession, discovered them. Escaping, he sent up the alarm, and the flatboatmen had barely escaped with their lives. This was the scene John Matthews stumbled upon as he came into town.

No flatboats were seen on the bayou for the rest of that day, or for many following. Mr. Matthews also had noticed that no one unknown to the local population, other than himself, had been seen in the streets since that day. He surmised that the Masons, having failed to get the information they sought, would not dare to come near as long as the memory of Pere Jan lived. But the intensity of grief which Mr. Matthews himself experienced had made the townsfolk take kindly to him. Their own grief was tempered by awe, convinced as they were that their priest had died a martyr and a saint. The funeral ended with solemn ceremonies in his memory that quickly transformed into the music, dance and feasting that accompany any festival in that country.

Quickly leaving St. Martinsville, we labored with our oars up the Teche as far as Prien felt it safe to go, before again disappearing into the swamps. We made another night crossing at the Vermilion River and retraced our journey through the marshes surrounding the coastal lakes, except that we avoided settlements. From Lake Arthur, though, we turned north on the Mermentau River. Tracing its tributary bayous, we emerged from the swamps into rivers that drain Louisiana's southern prairie. We wound through splendid forests of oak and then entered the extensive pine woods that cover most of the state. We continued north through the final days of August, following rivers to their sources in the hills then turning back near Alexandria. Prien's plan was to approach Lake Charles from the northwest, which would be the direction from which we would be least expected.

Following this course, we found the mysterious source of the Mermentau River by way of its longest tributary, Bayou Cocodrie. This spills out of Lake Cocodrie, a large and deep natural reservoir that makes a mirror for its surrounding hills. According to

Choctaw legend, the village that now rests at its bottom sank beneath the flood while the braves were away in battle. We camped on its shore under a crescent moon and built a fire. I suggested fishing the lake. Prien answered that the Choktaws forbade it out of reverence for the legend. In silence, we sat by its murmuring waves and watched the moon expand and sink toward its trembling reflection. It became flame-colored as it touched a stand of pines on the opposite shore. As it sank into them, larger by the second, it seemed that the trees had been set on fire.

"You never noticed the resemblance?" said William.

"She is beautiful beyond anything I have ever seen," I answered. "There are hints in her face, and in the way she walks, that always reminded me of Denise. Her height and her hair, though, and of course her personality, veiled the similarity. She has neither my reddish hair, nor Denise's black waves. Her hair is as thick as mine, that's true, but it has not my color: which, now that I think of it, is that of my mother's hair – like curls of the crepe myrtles – but the way she thinks..."

"As alike to you as the moon to its reflection," said William. "Her eyes are yours; and not only the shape, but the way thought moves in them."

"The thoughts themselves are foreign to mine," I sighed.

"It never seemed that way to me," said William. "Look at the moon. You see the shadow of every crater in that narrow arc of light. Those perfect features are erased by the waves in its reflection. The parent is the image, and the child is the copy; but in the world of the soul the metaphor is reversed. In Catherine, you see the purity of every thought burning brilliantly. In you, the same thought has a different hue. It smolders under the weight of time and tragedy. But I have never doubted that the inspiration of your thoughts was the same. I have seen the two of you together, how your conversation climbs in strange harmonies. As unique and different as the two of you are, I have actually marveled how it could be that you were not father and daughter. She intuitively sensed that it was so, if you remember! "

The moment that the tip of the brilliant horn of the moon was doused in dark water, the sight was taken from my eyes by the volume of tears that filled them. It was no secret to my companions that I had not stopped crying since we left Des Allemands. They could not tell it from my voice, since I had rarely spoken, and they could not see it in my face, because I rarely showed it to them, but I was certain that they knew it. At Pere Jan's funeral I cried louder than any man or woman, and everyone there could see that my tears were not just for him. Now I allowed my voice to be broken with what had to be spoken:

"How is it possible for the purity of the image to be restored?"

"I can speak from experience on that now," said Prien gently. "First now, that there blessin' of a triple immersion, in that there Holy Trinity; and then, with some right hard work, it is possible now to live immersed in that there Father, Son, and that Holy Spirit too."

"With all this water," I said, "what prevents me?"

"Only your heart now," said Prien. "But you now, you'll be baptized in the presence of that there Father Honoratus I think."

"What if we don't make it back?" I said. "The Masons will do everything in their power to intercept us."

"Calm them fears now, and think," said Prien, looking up at the stars. "Father Honoratus he intends us for to uncover that there casket.

"If them Masons want the same thing now," he went on, "they will jus' have to cooperate. And Father Honoratus now, he was hisself once a Mason; he knows what he's doing."

"There were only two men who knew where that casket is," I objected, "and one of them is dead."

"Dead may not be the right word there," he replied, "and he assured us that there Elder would show us. Some folks there are who thought old Pere Jan he had a bit of the Elder's prophetic gift."

Mr. Matthews sighed. "This has been a journey of discovery," he said, "such as I would never have imagined."

Only then did it occur to me how long it had been since he had spoken; and in the same moment I realized the overwhelming feelings he was carrying in his own heart.

"Now that I have discovered my own daughter," I said to him, "I think can understand how it must be to lose one."

"It's not as bad as that at all," he smiled. "It's my own granddaughter that you have found, and a lovely girl she is, brought up in good hands. And my own daughter has found both you and I."

ᑕᔑ

Beyond that lake's opposite shore, we found at dawn the brooks that feed lesser tributaries of the Red River. Battling its currents by night we slipped past Alexandria and then found entry to the streams that led to the upper Calcasieu. By the time we crossed into the watershed of its western fork, the Sam Houston River, the approaching Autumn Equinox was snuffing out the length of days, and the first chill was bearing down behind us in the form of a black bank of rolling clouds out of the northwest. Prien welcomed the sudden rage of that terrible front, hoping that the storm would veil our entry into the lake and Contraband Bayou.

The rain was hard and cold, drilling us to the bone with a thousand bullets and sharp needles, and the wind, ripping at our clothes, felt as though it were tearing off our skin. Not one man in the boat could see another. Prien's voice could be heard shouting orders as though he still knew where we were, but I couldn't see how. I took advantage of the moment to reach into the bottom of my luggage for my talisman. It was given to me by George Fisher on his deathbed. It was not a Christian cross, or, at least, it was not a cross blessed by the Church, but it was what I had, and I slipped it around my neck. Prien read my movements by the feel of the boat and yelled for me to take my oar. But we were surrounded already. Shadows of men came out of the rain curtain on every side, some standing precariously for balance on their wave-tossed boats, some kneeling, more than half with guns. At least three boats were bumping against ours, and there appeared to be more. For every man on our boat, there were six guns pointed at his face. Night was dropping early with the storm, and there were lanterns, curses, threats: "Don't let them throw anything overboard! We'll search the boat as soon as we get them out." But we were too weary and cold to fight, and were glad to have that weird

195

armada escort us to shore and shelter.

༄ ༄ ༄ ༄ ༄ ༄

Morning dawned clear in a cold blue sky that quickly filled with light and revealed the town in freshly washed detail. We were led from the jail to the newly constructed Masonic Hall at the end of Goss Street, where, as Sheriff Ryan explained apologetically, we would need to answer some questions.

Lake Charles had extended its streets in a construction boom through the summer that we were gone. The Masonic Hall was not the only newly framed and freshly painted storefront, and there were exquisite new homes, not as imposing as river mansions, but large enough, displaying delightful and unusual details of architecture. Sheriff Ryan with pride pointed out several of these jewels of what he called the "charpentier" district, designed by the French carpenters for which the district was named.

The Masonic Hall itself, faced with marble columns like a miniature Roman temple, was grander than the courthouse. We ascended the stone steps and passed under the high pediment. The lofty hall within was not filled to its capacity, but I could see in one glance that the number of men in attendance had been carefully chosen from the most influential persons in all the Southern States.

The sheriff from Natchez greeted me just inside the door with a grin: "James, you scoundrel, you've really done it this time!"

I shrugged. "This hall is not as grand as ours, is it?" I said.

He laughed. "You'll have a joke ready for death himself, when you meet him! Don't worry about our timbered hall in Natchez. It has been fully repaired since the night of your speech. As for this one, I expect it will be sheathed in gold. I hear you've come upon some treasure."

We were seated in front, before the oak-carved podium, facing the somber audience seated formally against the other three walls. Sheriff Ryan ascended the podium to speak, when the door was opened to a blast of north wind and sunlight. The man who came in with it, quickly removing his overcoat and hat, needed no introduction. It was Grossetete, the most acclaimed lawyer in Louisiana, from New Orleans.

"I am here to represent Mr. James Thompson," he said.

"What do you think this is," said Sheriff Ryan. "A trial?"

"Yes," said Grossetete, "I certainly do. I was summoned at the expense of certain Masters of the New Orleans Lodge, of which I am a prominent member, if you did not know."

"No," said Sheriff Ryan, shuffling through his papers and quickly frowning at something in the lower margins of several of them, "I did not."

"I will be conducting the questioning of Mr. Thompson and other witnesses," said Grossetete.

Sheriff Ryan shot an alarmed look to one side of the room. "Is this acceptable?" he said.

"Mr. Ryan," said Grossetete, dramatically reaching up to place a thick file of papers on Jacob Ryan's podium, "the Masters of the New Orleans Lodge are the leaders of the Scottish Rite in America."

"I – I didn't know," said Sheriff Ryan, staring down at the documents.

"No, I would expect not," said Grossetete. "You have not been a member of our Order for very long."

Grossetete took advantage of that moment of embarrassed murmurings to whisper to me, "Listen, this may not go well for you. If it appears that you have betrayed the Brotherhood... well. You'd best cooperate with me." Then he turned to the podium and lined his words with fire: "Please proceed!"

☙

The room was utterly silent. Jacob Ryan cleared his throat.

"This is a most important meeting of the Southern Masonic Lodges: one that well may determine the course of the Masonic Order, and, ultimately, the course of our nation. On behalf of the descendents of the founding families of Lake Charles, LeBleu, Pujo, and Bilbo, I as Master of our newly formed Lake Charles Masonic Lodge, just finished with the generous help of the leading members of the Natchez Lodge, and especially the open-handed bankers of that respected town – (here I noticed the Donaldson Brothers smiling along the rear wall) – I welcome honorable Masters of the neighboring Lodges of Louisiana, Mississippi, Texas, and Georgia. I also want to welcome some of our highest initiates from California. These men were present at the death of our former Grand Master, George Fisher. They have assured me – and this brief from Mr. Grossetete confirms it – that the new Grand Master of the Masonic Brotherhood in America will himself be present before these proceedings have concluded."

This brought a prolonged gasp from his audience. Sheriff Ryan himself seemed to tremble as the words left his lips.

"I must also introduce high-ranking state and federal officials present today..."

This brought groans and barks of protest from the audience, rising toward a dangerous crescendo.

"Almost all these officials are loyal to our Southern cause, however," he shouted over those voices, which began to calm. "Our Louisiana Lieutenant Governor, our own United States Senator, and the United States Attorney General..." At this point, the protests erupted with more vigor, but Jacob Ryan shouted louder, "who is here to protect the interests of the government as represented also by the officers of our United States military establishment at the Cantonment Atkinson on the shores of our lake..." but now his voice was drowned in hisses. The army captain and his lieutenants glanced nervously at each other. Like men fearing a lynching, they measured the distance to the door. Like the soldiers they were, they took mental notes of strategic points around it, where a few men could make a stand against many.

"We are gathered," shouted Sheriff Ryan angrily, "as I said, to discuss matters of great importance for the future of our nation!" This brought all voices to a hush. "Let me make this clear to my Masonic Brothers: it is not up to us to decide the fate of our future, but rather to allow it to be revealed. We believe that our destiny has been planned long before our time by enlightened forefathers. We believe that the key to the divine mysteries of our nation has been hidden in a sacred vault, intended by the great illuminati of the European revolutions to be transported to the New World during the flight of Napoleon, stolen by Lafitte, and hidden again in the swamps of Louisiana. We have long planned the meticulous search which these gentlemen before us have conducted under our watchful eye. The search is at an end. We know where it lies."

Grossetete himself began the applause that followed. "Well said!" he shouted; and the hall was filled with acclaim.

Sheriff Ryan, however, had spread his papers across the podium, and seemed to glance from one to the other in confusion. "I have before me, however, so many conflicting claims to this mysterious treasure that I hardly know where to begin. Descendents of Arsene LeBleu, the most influential family in the founding of this new Lake Charles Lodge, and – forgive me if I do not understand this correctly – equally as influential in bringing the attention of the Natchez and New Orleans Lodges to the great value of this treasure, claim it for their own. The Natchez and New Orleans Lodges, meanwhile, have provided me with their own agendas for this meeting, each of which claims precedence. Each of these claims, as compelling as they appear to be, have shadows on their titles, cast by claims to the treasure made by Holy Cross Convent, where the treasure lies, and by the United States Government.

"Mr. Grossetete, if you have wisdom to untangle these claims so that the divine purpose of our Masonic Order is kept intact, please enlighten us."

"Thank you," said Grossetete. "May I present the evidence that has been uncovered. Here is Lafitte's journal, and the map that corresponds to it. It was drawn under Lafitte's direction by Mr. Prien, sitting at my left here. He is the one who, along with Arsene LeBleu, buried the treasure in its present location, am I correct? Unfortunately, Lafitte had the two gentlemen blindfolded at the time of that burial. Here are the maps drafted by Arsene LeBleu. Here is the Biblical commentary that was kept in the vaults of the Knights of the Holy Temple in Jerusalem. These are among the documents that so far have come into our possession. Let me now call upon our witnesses. First, I would ask for Mr. John Matthews to stand and swear an oath upon the Holy Scriptures."

"Then, as the Holy Scriptures teach," said John Matthews, standing, "let my answer be simply yea or nay."

"You will not swear on the Bible?" said Sheriff Ryan.

"I have answered you already," said Mr. Matthews.

"Mr. Donaldson," said Grossetete, "you may approach the podium and begin your questioning."

The elder Donaldson came forward. "Is it true," he said to John Matthews, "that you have renounced the Masonic Brotherhood?"

Mr. Matthews shrugged. "I thought everyone knew that."

"I expected some such vague answer," said Donaldson. "It seems strange then that you have communicated so freely with us during this adventure."

I jerked around in my seat and stared at him in disbelief.

"I have done what was prudent," he answered.

"Are you familiar with the name of Sir Martin of Sicily?" Donaldson asked.

"No," said Mr. Matthews.

"Sir Martin of Sicily, of the sacred Order of the Knights Templar, the most powerful secret Brotherhood in history? The anointed knights that stand at the summit of the hierarchy of Masonic Rites? Sir Martin of Sicily, second in command and next to be appointed Grand Master of the Knights Templar?"

Mr. Matthews said nothing.

"Sir Martin of Sicily, who rebelled against his own Grand Master and began to spread rumors of the Order's dissolution?"

"If you are referring to the ex-Templar whose correspondence to me you have stolen," said Mr. Matthews, "he gave his name as Ananias."

"Ananias! A Greek name to disguise his own," said Donaldson indignantly. "What is its meaning, do you suppose?"

"At his baptism by the hands of Father Honoratus," Mr. Matthews replied, "he was given the name of Ananias of Damascus, who opened the eyes of Paul, when the apostle came to him blinded by the vision of Christ and begging for baptism for himself. What his name and history were before that, I do not know; but I can assure you that since that time he has been worthy of his new name!"

"You knew, however," said Donaldson, "that he was formerly a guardian knight of Solomon's Temple; and, as a former member yourself of the Masons, you knew what that must mean. The Great Work, symbolized by Solomon's Temple – the guardians of that secret – and here was a man who defamed it. What I find interesting is that in the discussions that you and I shared before you departed Natchez for this search, planning our lines of communication and alternative back-ups, you never mentioned to me that you that you were also in communication with someone who had been a Templar and had turned against that Holy Order!"

"He was right under your own nose," said John Matthews. "His appearance was no secret; he came right into the Lodge and told his story in front of everyone. If I cared so much about your knowing of my correspondence with him, it would never have fallen into your hands."

"I see. And is this your letter to the Lake Charles Masonic Lodge," asked Donaldson, "mailed from Alexandria, advising us of your arrival from the north?"

I jumped from my seat. "What! How did you sneak into Alexandria?"

"While you were sleeping," John Matthews said to me. Grossetete advised me to return to my seat.

"You didn't learn anything from your mistake of sneaking into New Orleans!" I said angrily.

"It was a plea for reconciliation with the relatives of my late wife, the Salliers," answered Mr. Matthews. "I would never have thought that they would turn it over to the Lodge."

"Come on now, John," said Donaldson. "You know enough about that situation! Your wife was a Sallier. Yes, of course they have always been fiercely antagonistic to Masonic influence, ardent supporters of the Catholic Church and, in particular, supporters of the foundation of Holy Cross Convent. But you know just as well that Charles Sallier married Catherine LeBleu, sister of Arsene LeBleu, who was a Mason and an ardent disciple of Lafitte up to the time that that great and enlightened son of New World destiny began to go mad. You know quite well that the sons of Arsene LeBleu were influential in bringing the attention of Southern Lodges to intensify the search for Lafitte's lost treasure!"

Mr. Matthews sighed. "I was never aware of the conflicts that may have existed in my wife's family," he answered.

"Well, I suppose you did not think things through very well, or it would have certainly occurred to you how strong the LeBleu influence would be in Lake Charles at a time when you knew this lodge was being organized. It would have occurred to you, since you knew that we were intercepting your letters..."

"I was aware of the letters that you had in your possession," answered Mr. Matthews. "While in New Orleans, I made myself available to the advice of certain of your Masters in that city."

"Whether or not it was your intention, then, that these letters would come into our hand," said Donaldson, holding them up, "you knew that we were aware of the progress of your journey."

"I knew that the Bishop of New Orleans could not keep secret the tremendous amount of gold that was discovered in the graveyard vault in Lafayette," said Mr. Matthews.

This brought the U. S. Attorney General from his seat: "You handed Lafitte's gold over to the Church? What did you give it to the Church for? They don't need it! Damn! We can't even get taxes out of it that way!"

He was answered with laughter and applause.

"And the doctor, too, that was paid so generously for the surgery for that crippled boy from Pecan Island" said Mr. Matthews. "I know New Orleans well enough. I know what kind of secrets are not safe in that city."

"Wait a minute," said the younger Donaldson Brother, rising from his seat. "What have you done with the treasures you found? You're not expecting us to believe that you gave them all away!"

"No, I don't expect you to believe it," said Mr. Matthews. "Nevertheless it is a fact."

The younger brother frowned. "We will have to pursue these questions more vigorously, at another time perhaps."

"It was never up to me to decide what to do with any of Lafitte's treasures," said Mr. Matthews.

"No," said the older brother, "and you have honored your promise to us that you would keep us informed of your search, however questionable your intentions may have seemed. You communicated with us even while we followed you along the river, with a note in a bottle, didn't you? I suppose we lost trust in you for a while, especially after that message appeared to be your last communication. But we were able to find you again, with much needed help from your clumsy attempts to show yourself, or to hide yourself, whichever the case may have been. I suppose we should not question the manner in which these letters fell into our hands:

My most beloved William, and James, my most cherished friend and teacher; weeks and now months have passed since we have heard from you, and we begin to fear for the worst...

"These are some hot letters. You can tell which man she wants more..."

William and I lunged at the same moment, and Mr. Matthews was right behind us. I grabbed his arms and stared furiously into his eyes while John Matthews and William each got in one good blow to each jaw before they were pulled off. Just one blow each

– but they were well placed and well timed. The jaw cracked like a nut in a vise. I held him up, for the first time feeling pity for the man.

"Mr. Donaldson," said Sheriff Ryan, "I do not think that was necessary. Was there some point you were trying to make?"

I let go. Donaldson held his bleeding jaw helplessly in his hands.

"I have some questions, though," said Mr. Matthews as the younger came forward to help his older brother toward his seat.

"Yes?" said Grossetete.

"You know the progress of our search. You know the clues we followed. You know that Lafitte's most precious chest is buried somewhere on the grounds of Holy Cross Convent. You know as well that there are only three men, besides Lafitte, who ever saw the exact spot. One died more than a decade ago. Of the other two, one, who like myself was once a Mason but renounced the Order, has fled. The other was cruelly murdered in an attempt to wrestle that information from him."

"And your question?" said Grossetete.

"Who is responsible for his death?" said Mr. Matthews. "I was assured that no one would be harmed if I cooperated!"

"It will be investigated," said Grossetete.

"Investigated by whom? By the Masons who ordered him interrogated?"

"If the Masons ever knew or heard of this priest in St. Martinsville," said Grossetete, "they would not have cared about him. Many who call themselves Masons were looking for this treasure, but they are only robbers. Lafitte himself is believed by some to have been one such 'Mason'. If you had not so carelessly appeared in New Orleans at that time, the flatboatmen would not have known to follow your route to him."

"And with that easy denial of guilt," said John Matthews angrily, "your investigation comes to a close?"

"Not at all," said Grossetete. "I think there will have to be some questions about that before we leave here today. I believe the gentlemen from California would like to ask James Thompson to answer a few questions, is that right?"

They came to the front of the room and asked me to rise.

"We were with you at the hour of death of our Grand Master, George Fisher," said one of these.

"Yes," I said.

"You were given a mission to fulfill."

"I have followed it with all my energy," I said.

"You submitted certain speculations about Lafitte's activities to the public in the form of a novel, in order to attract information and hidden clues. Were the Masons of the Natchez Lodge made aware of this mission?"

"Not until this moment," I replied.

"Were you acting without their knowledge and approval?"

"I was," I replied.

"And why is that?"

"Because George Fisher warned me to do so," I said.

This brought waves of surprised exclamations through the room.

"When you first met George Fisher in San Francisco, you were in hiding from the Masons, is that right?"

"That is correct," I said.

"Can you tell us why?"

"I was in fear for my life. I had only just received initiation into the Order. That very night I heard for the first time the story of the Natchez Treasure from a Mississippi boatman, who was then found murdered the next day."

"Can you tell us anything about this boatman?"

"Very little" I said. "He wanted to find the treasure. He was searching up and down the river, asking questions about it. He showed us the warehouse where it had been kept at one time. And he knew, as soon as he saw me, that I had just received the Masonic initiation."

"What kind of boatman was this?"

"A river flatboatman," I said.

"Similar to the kind responsible for the murder of the priest in St. Martinsville?"

"He was different, thoughtful, even seemed wise to me at the time. His motivation to find the treasure was not one of self-seeking and greed. It has occurred to me, though, that there may be some connection," I admitted.

"Do you know why the Grand Master suspected the Natchez Lodge?"

"Its members had their own plans for claiming what they called 'The Natchez Treasure'," I replied.

"Perhaps Grossetete can shed some light on that?"

೮೪

He returned to his seat. Grossetete stood and said, "Will the Master of the Natchez Lodge come forward?"

There was no movement in the hall.

"Does anyone know who is in charge of the Natchez Lodge?" said my lawyer.

The Natchez sheriff cleared his throat and stood. "Mr. Donaldson has been rendered speechless, I'm afraid," he said.

"Are the Donaldson brothers in charge of the Lodge?"

The younger brother stared at his elder and refused to speak.

"Well," said the Natchez sheriff, "I – I don't know."

"Who knows, then?"

"There have been rivalries within the Lodge for so long…" the sheriff replied.

"How long?"

"Since before I joined it," said the sheriff. "I was made to swear allegiance to one faction and repudiate the other. I guess Mr. Matthews might be the only one who remembers what it was like before my time."

"Mr. John Matthews? Will you please rise and speak to this?"

"The trouble began in 1829," said Mr. Matthews. "It was the same year that I left the Lodge. I would describe the disruption in the Natchez Lodge at that time as a political coup. Newcomers from New Orleans came in and took power. My wife's uncle, Arsene LeBleu, as I recall now, was among them. There were some murders down at the docks and warehouses below the bluff."

202

"Were you of the party that was taken from power?"

"Yes," said Mr. Matthews. "I was Master of the Lodge until that time."

"Was this the reason you renounced the Lodge at that time?"

"Partially, yes," Mr. Matthews admitted. "My wife for years had been insisting that I leave it. But I was greatly disturbed by other things which I saw taking place within the Masonic Brotherhood."

"Would you care to say what things those were?"

"I am aware of the grave penalty of speaking about the Masonic rituals of the higher degrees," he answered. "But the crimes that I saw committed in the name of spiritual awakening so outraged me that I became outspoken against them."

A hostile murmur began to grow in the hall.

"Every man in Mississippi has heard what I had to say," said Mr. Mathews. "If anyone has not, it is because he stopped his ears against my sermons!"

Grossetete held up his hand to silence the hall. "Why were you allowed to see those particular rituals, Mr. Matthews?"

"I was being considered for the post of Grand Master of the Scottish Rite in America," he answered.

"Were the men who conducted you through those rites the same who took over the Natchez Lodge?"

"They were," said Mr. Matthews. "But they did not take the Lodge without a struggle. I resisted their influence."

"And were these same New Orleans Masons the ones whom you contacted while you were in New Orleans in August of this year?"

"No," said Mr. Matthews. "I thought I had become quite skilled in avoiding them."

"How would you describe the men whom you contacted in New Orleans?"

"Like myself," said Mr. Matthews, "they have renounced the Order."

"How did you come to know these men?"

"My late wife led me to them," he answered.

"And how did she know of them?"

"My late wife was familiar with the nuns of Holy Cross Convent," said Mr. Matthews. "Her family donated land for the convent. These men had also been Masons until the nuns persuaded them to embrace the Church instead."

"This is a disturbing picture of the Masonic Order that you have presented to us: men of the highest moral character renounce the Order, while more desperate and undisciplined men, who practice questionable rites, come to power. Tell me this: were you aware of the history of the Natchez Treasure before you embarked on your journey with James Thompson?"

"It was a legend, as far as I knew," answered Mr. Matthews. "I never heard of it until after I had left the Masonic Order."

"Thank you, you may sit down. May I ask the captain of the Cantonment Atkinson to come forward?"

"No," he said from his seat. "You won't get any information from me at this mockery of a trial!"

Men began to stand around him, uttering threats.

"Lynch me, hang me!" he said, turning to them. "You'll see how a soldier dies! I answer only to military judges."

"Don't be an idiot," said the U. S. Attorney General. "There are men in this room who can arrange that, too."

The captain stood. "Yes, sir," he said uncomfortably, walking to the front of the room.

"It may seem odd that a military establishment would have been necessary on the shores of Lake Charles," said Grossetete.

"It may," replied the captain.

"Especially since the Choktaws and Cherokees never presented any threat. May I ask the date of the fort's establishment?"

"1829," was the answer.

"1829," repeated my lawyer. "The same year that the disturbance in the Natchez Lodge took place. The government, perhaps, was interested in Lafitte's treasure?"

"Contraband was forbidden by law," answered the captain. "Since France had taken no steps to stop it during the years of its colonial occupation, the United States was forced to do so."

"As everyone knows, the American colonies would not have survived without contraband," replied Grossetete. "England and Spain prohibited trade with any but the mother country. These forced embargoes, along with the issue of taxation without representation, were the principal elements in the struggle for independence!"

"Once independence was gained," said the captain, "the new nation had new responsibilities to international law."

"Yes, of course," said Grossetete, "especially since Lafitte so vigorously raped the commerce of Spain."

"That is correct," said the captain. "The United States had signed treaties with Spain."

"And so," said my lawyer, "this fort was established at the very mouth of Contraband Bayou, and in the same year, as it may turn out, that the treasure was moved to Natchez. May I ask what the government conceives was buried by Lafitte? After all, you have claimed legal right to this treasure."

"I cannot answer that," said the captain.

"Answer the question," said the Attorney General.

"With all due respect, sir, I cannot be responsible for revealing the nature of my mission. You must answer the question yourself, if you would have it be known."

The Attorney General sighed. "The government has been in short supply of money since its beginning. It's as simple as that."

"Then I suppose Lafitte did not want the government to have it," said Grossetete, "if we can surmise that he smuggled the chest away and hid it in Natchez when he saw the fort being built. Is it possible that the government was concerned about the Masonic prophecies that have been connected to the lore of this treasure? Is it possible that the government was interested in the divine edicts concerning the establishment of America? Or is it possible that the government feared such an edict, feared that it may threaten its own faulty institutions and power, feared further revolutions within its borders?"

The captain's face held such a shocked expression that it was clear he could not be expected to answer such a question. Grossetete turned sharply. "Mr. Attorney General?"

The Attorney General remained seated. He spat on the floor between his feet. "Don't be an ass," he said.

"Why not? I'm a lawyer. It's my job."

The hall erupted in laughter, but the Attorney General was not amused. "If you wanted to bring the Federal Government to trial, you would find that not even the Masonic Brotherhood has that kind of power. If it did, though, the trial would not be worth the effort."

"No, of course not," said Grossetete. "The government is a shadow of power. The opinions of Republicans and Democrats, what is that among us but a joke? What I would question, if I could, is the will of the York Rite and its plans to suppress the second American Revolution!"

This brought every man in the room to his feet in an uproar. The captain stood and reached for his weapon, but it had been removed at the door. Grossetete moved into the middle of the hall and yelled for quiet, then turned to face the Attorney General.

"You know as well as I," said the Attorney General, "that if it comes to war, the federal soldiers will be evicted, if not murdered. Until then, you must put up with our presence."

"And I assume they will stay until then," said Grossetete, " since it is now known that the treasure has been returned to the convent grounds. How do you propose to take it away from the nuns? I doubt they will allow you to dig up their graveyard!"

"I don't know," said the Attorney General. "How would you do it?"

"Thank you," laughed my lawyer. "Your captain may go, if he wishes, or he may stay to observe our proceedings."

The captain returned to his seat.

"Mr. James Thompson," said Grossetete, "has pursued his mission with tremendous courage, I find. Not, however, without help. George Fisher's widow, Lady Wells, and John Matthews, both of whom know the secret workings of the Masons better than we might realize, have been enlisted to aid him. In particular, Mr. Matthews has been able to guide him clear of countless crises. However, there are things even they have not known.

"I would like to review the history of this treasure as it has been revealed for us.

ᭉᭉᭉᭉᭉᭉ

"We begin with Lafitte himself, a man well acquainted with the Masonic legends and prophecies, a man ardent about the destiny of the new republic. He was a man disgusted with the abuse of power among kings, though he was himself of noble birth, as evidenced by his learning, refinements, and ability to handle men. The War of 1812 would not have been won without his assistance. If the English had taken New Orleans and the Mississippi River, they could surely have been counted on to ignore the

205

peace that was signed just previous to the Battle of New Orleans. The sovereignty of the young nation, allowing a place for the Masonic plans of a new form of government to take root, would not have been assured without Lafitte's help. He was, however, immediately betrayed by the young nation he had saved. His property was unlawfully confiscated and he was considered an outlaw, despite the outcome of numerous trials on his behalf. As with so many great men of history, he was misunderstood and made into a fugitive by the very ones he had helped. Neither the United States nor the governments of Europe had any idea what he was searching for on the high seas. However discouraged he became, he never wholly abandoned his ideals. In retirement he studied the stars, and when he saw that it was time for the Masonic prophecies of the New World to come to fulfillment, he rushed to the aid of the fleeing Napoleon.

"What do we know of the treasures that Napoleon smuggled out of Europe? Only Lafitte has seen them. We know also that his ship contained a priest returning from the Holy Land, with a chest that contained, along with treasures that we do not know, documents from the hidden archives of the Knights Templar of Jerusalem. Among these was the volume of Scriptures upon the table before us. What else there may have been will only be known when the chest is recovered.

"At this point, our historical narrative turns to Napoleon's priest. Father Honoratus was well known in France to Churchmen and to leading Masons, as well as to the King and every ruler that took the King's place after him. He supported the idea of the French Revolution until it turned into a feast of blood. He was especially grieved at the destruction of the churches. He left France and made a pilgrimage to the Holy Land. In the Lord's own sepulcher, he argued with the monk from Mt. Sinai who was eventually responsible for his conversion to Greek Orthodoxy. That's when he began to make trouble for the Masons. He argued vehemently with the Knights Templar themselves. Now, the Knights Templar are no strangers to opposition and controversy. Whether by their swords or by their superior intelligence, they have had a history of remarkable success against their enemies. Father Honoratus, however, swayed the judgment of no less than Sir Martin of Sicily, who then began to circulate rumors of the conversion of a small number of the Knights Templar to Greek Orthodoxy.

"Father Honoratus was returning to France as Napoleon fled from his defeat at Waterloo. He had with him a chest which, he claimed, was given to him by the monks on Mt. Sinai. I must say a word now about the chest itself.

"The most precious artifact in Solomon's Temple was the chest known as the Ark of the Covenant. According to Biblical legend, it contained the tables of stone on which God Himself had written the Ten Commandments. It contained a piece of the miraculous manna by which the people in the wilderness were fed, as well as Aaron's rod which, in Moses' hand, parted the Red Sea; and other artifacts as well that are listed in the Scriptures. The power of this chest was awe-inspiring beyond imagination.

"The fate of this chest is a mystery. Masonic legends say that the emperor Constantine had a copy made from the Biblical descriptions to house certain relics of what Christians call the "New Covenant". In this new chest were kept the garment in which the Mother of God had been buried, which was left behind after her Assumption into heaven. There was also a fragment of the stone that had covered the Savior's tomb, along with a piece of the rock into which Moses had been placed when the glory of God passed before him on Mt. Sinai.

"Father Honoratus caused a tremendous stir when he returned from Mt. Sinai to the headquarters of the Knights Templar in Jerusalem, carrying a chest which matched the description of this very copy. He showed them its contents. They added to it certain documents of their own, intending that it should be brought to America. What these items were, I repeat, we do not know. This ancient copy of the Scriptures, with its marginal commentaries, was, as I have said, among them. Soon after this took place, Father Honoratus quarreled with the Knights and departed, taking with him the chest.

"The meeting of his ship at sea with that of the fleeing Napoleon may have been pure chance; but Lafitte believed he had foreseen it in the stars. Lafitte came upon them just after the priest and his trunk had been transferred to Napoleon's ship. Their meeting in the midst of a storm was made more chaotic by the appearance, just as the winds began to subside, of the English fleet. Lafitte shrewdly betrayed Napoleon for the price of his bounty, then made off with Napoleon's treasure and his priest.

"Lafitte by this time had transferred his smuggling operations to Galveston, Texas, but he brought these things to his hidden hide-outs along the Calcasieu River. As soon as Father Honoratus was brought here, the latter was found by followers.

"Certain French nuns, who had always considered him a spiritual father, had remained in correspondence during his pilgrimage to the Holy Land. Having fled France during the Reign of Terror, they had joined themselves to a convent in New Orleans. Lafitte was then surprised with their arrival on Contraband Bayou. He witnessed the priest's teachings to these nuns as he familiarized them with the intricacies of Orthodox theology. These seemed to impress Lafitte as well, as is evident in his journal. However, he did not take too kindly to the priest's challenges to Lafitte to repent of his own crimes. Lafitte was likewise enraged at the priest's fervent denouncing of Masonic doctrine. He therefore had the priest hanged, just as he had hanged so many who questioned his power and ideals. He hid the body and the chest. As it turns out, he did the unthinkable by burying them together.

"This was the time that the government, having learned of Lafitte's confiscation of Napoleon's treasures, began to pursue him. I have handed the government documents to Sheriff Jacob Ryan, so that everyone here may see my sources of information and understand the government's interests. The military fort, Cantonment Atkinson, was built on the lake. The chest was then smuggled away up the river and hidden in a Natchez warehouse. A few Masons, stumbling upon it there, began a furor in the Order. Arsene LeBleu organized support in the New Orleans Lodge to take control of the Natchez Lodge.

"Shortly thereafter, Lafitte removed the treasure from Natchez and hid it again in the last place that anyone suspected. He returned it to Contraband Bayou, under the very nose of the military fort. At that time, the nuns lived in huts in the forest, following the way of life that had been taught to them by Father Honoratus just before his death. Lafitte was instrumental in securing that land and more for them, and they built a hospital near the site of burial.

"Lafitte began to enter his senility. He dug up Napoleon's treasure and buried it

207

in other places. He authorized strange, symbolic maps, drawn by the hand of Arsene LeBleu. There was one, however, that he intended to contain the truth. I show it here. It gives the location of the burial of all his treasures, and it confirms, though in a hidden way, that the priest's chest is indeed buried on Contraband Bayou.

"The symbolism of these maps has been deciphered by James Thompson and his companions. It shows a deliberate method to his madness. Every treasure gives a clue, as it were, to the location of the final and most valuable treasure. It is to be found in the midst of a grove of oaks.

৵৵৵৵৵৵৵

"These, then, are the facts that Mr. James Thompson has uncovered in his unrelenting diligence" Grossetete concluded. "Have I omitted anything?"

"There should have been twenty-two treasures recovered," said the younger Donaldson brother. "That's what it shows on the map."

"And?" said Grossetete with a touch of ice in his voice.

"Only two vaults of gold have been mentioned," said the younger brother. "Where are the rest?"

"Some now, it was all washed away," answered Prien. "Others, them was treasure that was different from any gold. Did you count that there statue of Hadrian now, and them relics of St. Martin? They was on that map, if you interpret it right."

"Statues and relics!" said Donaldson. "Is this what you think Lafitte had in mind when he buried his treasures?"

Grossetete replied with a laugh of open derision.

"It is true that treasures are listed and mapped which we did not make an effort to uncover," said Mr. Matthews. "By the time we found the ones that we did, our search seemed to be leading in a different direction."

"There is still gold to be found, then," said Donaldson.

"You insist on gold?" said Grossetete.

"Or something else," Donaldson shrugged. "Until it is found, no one will know what it is."

"Has this any bearing upon the matter at hand?" Grossetete replied testily.

"I don't know," Donaldson admitted; "but if that map was intended to lead to a goal, either it was not taken seriously, or there were things that happened in this journey that have not been told."

Grossetete sighed and turned to me. "William Stuart kept a complete journal of all proceedings, discussions and reflections," he said. "It shows all your evidence for the symbolic interpretation of Lafitte's maps. By the time you found real treasure, you were more interested in their more symbolic meaning, following your three-fold interpretation of Lafitte's journal. Is it possible you misinterpreted this meaning?

"What are you suggesting?" I said.

"The number of twenty-two treasures seems significant," said Grossetete.

"You think that there is a Kabalistic interpretation?" John Matthews answered.

"That occurred to me also," I admitted. "That number corresponds to the twenty-two mystical paths mapped out upon the Kabalistic Tree of Life. I spent many nights in thought on that idea earlier in our journey; but I abandoned it."

"Why is that?" Grossetete pursued.

"Because it seemed to be leading nowhere, even after I exhausted every possibility I could think of. I examined the positions of the twenty-two treasures on the map, and I imagined interposing the chart of the Kabalistic Tree upon it. I considered what this might mean, sketched upon that area of the map that shows the places of Lafitte's crimes. These are mapped in black ink, as you see. The six treasure sites along the lower Calcasieu River are in blue; and there are three churches shown in gold. I compared these to the journal and to all the forged maps. No diagram emerges that I could make any sense of. Then, because other things in our journey seemed more important, and this no longer so, I forgot about it."

"Of course that study would lead nowhere," said Mr. Matthews, "except to illustrate that Kabala has no foundation in reality and is not the key to the interpretation of the Hebrew Scriptures!"

A murmur crept through the room.

"If there is mystical meaning within the Hebrew words and letters," he went on, "it is because that alphabet represents the handwriting of God. But your Gnostic interpretations, imported from Greek and Arabic mysticism, are foreign to the original Judaic revelation. Lafitte himself came to realize this, as we see in his journal, when he studied the two commentaries that were in the chest from Jerusalem."

"We have been tolerant enough of these sermons as you preached in your church, Mr. Matthews," our Natchez sheriff answered sharply; "but I doubt you will be safe doing so in this hall."

⁀

John Matthews began to walk silently back and forth in front of Sheriff Ryan's podium. He stared into all the faces that watched him. A terrible transformation walked over his face. The lion was awakened. The wrinkles around his eyes and mouth increased and deepened, his features glowed with power, his white hair fell around them like the oracular warnings of a man of wisdom. His pace was that of a lion. His eyes showed deep explosions. The hall was utterly silent. At last he opened his mouth – and the lion roared.

"You know nothing of the Tree of Life! When God revealed that tree again on the earth, it showed itself as a cross! But you, corrupters of things most beautiful and divine, enemies of God and His salvation, you believe and teach that crucifixion represents the curse of incarnation, the imprisoning of the spirit. You have an allegory of removing the rose from the cross, that terrible secret doctrine that spits upon the blood of the cross! By the three nails, you say, the spirit is fixed to the body; find them and remove them, and the soul is freed from the flesh and from any future reincarnation."

Sheriff Ryan laughed. "Where did you dig up these ideas? I never heard such ridiculous things. We do not teach them here!"

"These are the mysteries reserved for your higher initiations," said John Matthews. "You do not believe me? Your superiors are ready to sentence me to death right now, for divulging such secrets before you were made ready to receive them!"

His eyes swept the hall with fire. Some men were standing; their fists were clenched. He met their stares; then he turned again to Sheriff Ryan.

"If you continue in this brotherhood," he said, "they will convince you of the evils of incarnation and of the world's creation, and other lies. Whatever they say, the soul will never be sundered from the body. God will not allow it; the two were created one person. Even death is no more than a temporary separation; no living soul will escape the final resurrection of the body!"

Grossetete, for whatever strange reason, was smiling as though he were actually enjoying this evangelical oration.

"You sound just like that fiery philosopher who has been preaching against the Greek Freemasons," said Grossetete.

"And they've contrived to put Apostolos Makrakis in prison," said John Matthews, "and they would kill him if they didn't fear his popularity."

"Yes, well, I can't remember those Greek names, you know," said Grossetete. "It sounds like you have been corresponding with him."

"Ananias showed me his writings," said Mr. Matthews.

"I see. Well, let me ask you this. Do you think that Lafitte included twenty-two treasures on his map simply to deceive Masons who might find it?"

"That is what I think," Mr. Matthews answered.

"Such a theory would presume," said Grossetete, "that the Masonic brotherhood was never meant to discover the secret Lafitte buried!"

"I think you should consider that possibility," said Mr. Matthews.

A murmur in the hall grew to a roar. Grossetete was forced to shout again for silence.

"Or perhaps," Grossetete replied, "we should dismiss the possibility of your theory. We shall see! Is there anything else?" he said to the room in general.

I stood. "Only one thing that I can think of.

"I was also sent by the Grand Master to Natchez, as you know, to investigate the leadership of the Natchez Lodge. I have discovered, however, that the disorganization of leadership in the Masonic Lodges is far more severe than even the Grand Master of America realized. The extreme confusion in Masonic leadership is not limited to the Natchez Lodge. Nor is it limited to the antagonism of the American Lodges of the South against those of the North, or even to the international intrigues of the Scottish Rite against those of the York Rite. It is even deeper than that. Strife and confusion infects the entire Brotherhood, beginning at the very top."

There was immediate uproar in the hall. Some began to utter threats against my life, not caring who heard them say so. Grossetete again strode into the middle of the hall and held out his hand, turning to every side of the room.

"Please, gentlemen!" he shouted. "Mr. James Thompson is on trial for the things he has done and for the things he is about to say, that's for certain! Be so kind as to let us complete the investigation!"

The hall slowly returned to a semblance of quiet. Grossetete turned to me. "Is there anything more you would like to say about this?"

"Yes," I said, "there is.

"When I first heard the account of Sir Martin of Sicily, now known as Ananias, I myself was incredulous. When I saw for myself the Biblical commentary that the Knights Templar had kept hidden from the world, with its explanation of the truths of the Holy Writings so different from our own, I began to read with extreme skepticism. I read that entire great work from cover to cover, with every marginal note, and I was overcome by a depth of understanding far more profound than anything I had known to exist. But believe me, brothers, to see truth written on paper is impressive enough; but to see it written in the eyes and actions of men, women, and children, is a miracle as impossible to deny as a flame ignited on a candle-stand, where everyone can see it!

"Men and brothers of the Masonic Order, we have gone deep into the bayou country, thinking to follow the trail of Lafitte's treasures. The treasure we discovered is of another kind. We have completed a pilgrimage of a sort that is no longer accessible to modern man, and yet the possibility to enter that world exists today and has been opened before us.

"We did indeed locate some of Lafitte's treasure, following the details of his own writings. These we gave away, hardly realizing the way in which we were following the commandments of life which Lafitte himself discovered in his final days, when he entered a profound repentance of his deeds. The truth of his life, which you can read for yourselves in his own journal, is stranger than any fiction that I have written. In giving away his treasures, our own hearts tasted purification; we entered the sublime understanding in which he died like the thief on the cross. The vistas of another world began to open for us. We have seen things we dare not speak of. But it is clear in the pages of his own journal that this is the treasure Lafitte intended for us."

Some of the Masons had begun to laugh.

"Lafitte's priest himself is the treasure," I went on. "What he brought from the Holy Land was the renunciation of the Masonic Doctrine in favor of the tradition of the Ancient and True Church."

The laughter at this point had begun to turn to scorn.

"I understand too well the light in which you see this," I said. "The night-moth is made to fly beneath the moon. Guided by the moon, it is free and healthy, seeking its food and finding it. Blinded by an oil lantern, though, it burns up in a false light. This is how the Masonic Brotherhood has been misled in its understanding of the Sacred Writings. But we have seen the true light. We desire to return to it and live."

What surprised me was not the intensity of anger that moved through the room, bringing men to their feet with hard faces, but rather how many seemed to be listening and inclined to agree. My lawyer, however, had stepped forward and advised me to keep silence for my own good, responding with brevity to the questions put to me. He and Sheriff Ryan succeeded in calling for calm as several of the New Orleans Masons came forward to stand by the ones from California.

"Are there other questions?" said Sheriff Ryan.

"Yes," said Grossetete. "We would like to call your deputy who searched these men in the jail last night."

The sheriff nodded. A boy of no more than sixteen, scared and embarrassed, moved

211

from the door and walked to the front of the room.

"You searched these men?" he was asked. He nodded silently.

"What did you find when you searched this man?"

"I didn't find anything," said the youth, his voice cracking. "His pockets were empty."

"You found nothing anywhere on his person?"

"Well, uh, he had that medal on a ribbon around his neck, but I gave that to you when you asked for it."

The California Mason reached into his breast and pulled out a ribbon which hung from his hand. The medallion was concealed by his palm.

"This was given to you by George Fisher, in my presence," said the Mason to me, letting it drop from his palm and hang on its ribbon in the sight of all. To the deputy, he said, "Did you know what this was when you removed it from this man?"

"Well, no," said the young deputy. "I never saw anything like it."

The room was utterly silent. A few men dropped to their knees. This gesture was followed by everyone in one movement as they recognized the Great Seal of the United States. John Matthews did not kneel, but he looked like he had been hit in the face. Sheriff Ryan himself fell to his knees with fear, saying, "My God! We arrested the Grand Master!"

The California Master dropped the ribbon over my neck and then began to kneel himself, but I caught him by the elbow and said, "Arise, all."

Chapter Thirty-One

"Men and brothers," I said now:

"Since before Columbus sailed for the New World, looking for the Blessed Isles; since before Ponce de Leon came looking for the Fountain of Youth, and Cortez for El Dorado, it has been believed the land beyond the west would be not a new discovery, but something more profound than anything new or old: it would reveal the secrets of eternity.

"I did not invent the Masonic prophecies of the vault of the mysteries that would be uncovered in the New World. This is simply how it has turned out. I am the Grand Master whom Lafitte intended to find the casket he buried. You must allow me to go and find it."

⚘

The Donaldson brothers by this time had come out of shock, and the younger had remembered that he could talk. "This is incredible," he said. "Everyone knows that James Thompson, that famous author, was as famous for his immoral life in San Francisco! How could he have been made Grand Master? George Fisher's illness must have affected his judgment!"

"Many men have been harmed by bad influence at some time in their lives," answered the California Mason. "Not all finally succumb to evil. A young man fleeing from the dangers of the Natchez Lodge would have been understandably demoralized! After he was restored to the Masonic Order by George Fisher, however..."

Here I gave the gesture for silence. "I must admit the frailty of my character. I have learned a great deal about this in recent weeks."

"It's about time for that," sneered the younger Donaldson. "How do we know this medal was not planted on your person?"

"Be sensible, " said the California Mason. "There is only one person in the world who carries this emblem. If the Grand Master hid his own medal on Mr. James Thompson's person, as you seem to believe, what right would you have to object?"

"And what if he stole it off George Fisher's corpse? It's not beyond him to do such a thing!"

"Have you not yet realized that it is not he who is on trial today, but yourselves?"

"You might be a grave-robber as well, for all we know," snapped Donaldson.

"Sheriff Ryan," interrupted Grossetete, "I suggest that your deputy place these men from the Natchez Lodge under arrest at once."

"He just now denounced the ideals of the Masonic Doctrine before us all!" Donaldson shouted angrily. "I would be inclined to think this medal was planted on his person by someone who wanted the Masons destroyed. The only reason I would dare to think such a thing is because of a rumor I heard: that the office of the Grand Master of America died with George Fisher!"

Men were standing on all sides of the room, staring at each other as though each

213

thought he were the one who might have to take an uncertain situation into his own hands. I feared a repeat of the riot in the Natchez Masonic hall.

"Mr. Donaldson," said Sheriff Ryan, "as confounded as I am by all these proceedings, this disturbs me more than anything I have heard. You led us to believe that the Natchez Masons were the ruling and favored party in the Scottish Rite. That presumption has been seriously cast into doubt today. You had us believing that the new power in the Natchez Lodge had come from the influence of the descendents of Arsene LeBleu, and that the purpose of the Natchez Lodge was to found a greater lodge here in Lake Charles, where Lafitte's treasure was to be found. It appears instead that your only desire has been to claim this treasure for yourself. But to have truly believed that there is no Grand Master! This only shows that there was absolutely nothing to your credibility from the beginning."

"One thing he is right about, though," I said. "There are many who will simply not accept me as Grand Master. Not one person of the York Rite will accept me, and many of the Scottish Rite will resist me also, especially in the light of what I have said today. As in the Order of the Knights Templar, there will be those who wish to cling to the old factions. They will appoint their own Grand Master. I have thought about this for a long time. And so," I said solemnly, removing the medal and handing it to Grossetete, "I renounce the title. Choose whom you will."

☙

The hall was quieter than it had been when the Great Seal had been placed upon me. In that silence, there was a noise like growing wind outside; but when the young deputy opened the door and ran in, the uproar of voices in the street became known.

"Sheriff!" said the deputy. "There's a mob! Every Catholic in the parish is out there!"

The men in the hall looked at one another with fear. Before anyone could make any suggestion of escape, the voice of Claudette, shrill with command, was heard at the door. In walked the elderly abbess of the convent with one of her nuns, and Claudette was right behind.

The nun who supported the abbess was the one who spoke English. "These gentlemen are to come with us," she said.

"How dare these women to enter the sacred hall of the Masons?" said the Natchez sheriff, and many around him took up the murmur of his chant.

The old abbess did not wait for these words to be translated. She stared fiercely from man to man, exchanging French and Greek phrases. The other nun acted as translator for those who could not understand:

"You dare to use the word 'sacred'? I am here to put a stop to this illegal business!"

"How did she know what we were saying?" said some men; and others replied, "How can she know what we are doing?"

The Attorney General came forward and offered her a stiff bow. "Madam," he said, "we will seal the decisions of this council by whatever legal trials are necessary to confirm them. You would be wise to leave."

The nun translated for her abbess, who then smiled at the Attorney General and spoke so kindly that amazement spread over his face even before he heard the meaning of her answer.

"Sir, I understand that. I know your desire. I know how you can accomplish it, if you dare to follow the course laid out before you. I remind you that our Elder Honoratus was himself a Mason at one time, before he abandoned the false brotherhood for the true. Lafitte also knew this. When he discovered the truth, he killed and buried it. Now it shall rise again. But in order for that to happen, you have no choice but to allow these men to come with us."

"Mr. Attorney General," said Sheriff Jacob Ryan, "these nuns have been awfully influential in our settlement since long before you came into office. You will have to abide by my decision to allow them to do as they please."

"Stand aside!" shouted Claudette, oblivious to the fact that few understood her imperative Greek. "Will you take my hand?" she said to me, starting for the door.

"I will," I replied. "It will be a far greater honor than the one I just renounced."

೮೩

The commotion in the streets was nowhere as intense as the Masons had imagined. People crowded around the nuns, surprised and delighted to have come across them outside the convent gates, but no one seemed to take any interest in the Masonic Hall itself. Claudette led us to an open wagon, filled with supplies and pulled by two mules.

"We couldn't bring the carriage," explained Claudette; "it wouldn't hold the eight of us. Since we had to bring the wagon instead, we stopped at the store for our supplies before coming for you. You'll have to make yourselves comfortable. We were just in time, weren't we?"

John Matthews, especially, had the eyes of a man rescued from the guillotine. He stared at me, white-faced. "The Grand Pooh-Bah himself, hey?"

"I was as surprised as you to find out about that," I said.

"Wait a minute!" he said. "Are you telling me you didn't know? Did that lawyer make it up?"

"No, even he wouldn't have dared to do that," I said.

"What, then? Were you the Grand Master, or not?"

"I guess I was," I admitted. I noticed that my hands were shaking. "Nobody ever told me anything. I guess they assumed I knew it. Fisher was dying. He couldn't speak. He placed it around my neck in a moment of such solemnity that I dared do nothing but look into his eyes and accept it. I knew that the other men who were present at his death-bed were Masons of very high degree, but other than that..."

I might have fainted. The next thing I remember, I was sitting on the wagon-driver's bench. Claudette had the reins, and the abbess had my hand between both of hers. Her ancient, sky-piercing eyes were focused in mine with such love that I thought I saw my own mother.

"That was a brave thing you did," said Claudette, "denouncing those Masons right in front of their most celebrated members! I'm proud of you. I'm glad you listened to me, that night I was reading Father Chrysostom to you in my house."

"Brave!" I gasped. "Me? That's not what I've discovered about myself during this journey. Look at the ones who traveled with me. Each one is a better man than I am. Look at yourselves, heroic strugglers for virtue in solitude! How can I ever have been so prideful? I'm no more than a shadow of what I should have been!"

The smile in the old abbess' eyes grew slowly as I spoke. Now she and little Claudette looked at one another and nodded.

"We have already sent for the priest in Des Allemands," said the abbess to Claudette. "He will arrive by the New Orleans train. There will be baptisms tonight."

଼

There was a chapel in the hospital, but we were led to the font in the nun's own chapel. Next to Father Honoratus' reliquary, which, though empty, did not really seem so that evening, William, John Matthews, Gerald and myself were submerged in the triple immersion while the nuns chanted hymns of power out of the fiery source of language and inspiration. As we climbed from those waters to be wrapped in robes of white linen and in a new mind, Grossetete and another of the New Orleans Masons were led in to be brought through the baptismal font after us.

We were served a celebratory feast in the guest quarters of the hospital. The nuns were not with us, having retired to rest before the night's vigil. Grossetete opened his briefcase and handed out the letters from Natchez, a stack of them for every man. While we read them, he amazed us by humming through the eight Byzantine tones in a sol-la-fe nonsensical language of musical quarter-tones and eighth-tones.

During this musical interlude, John Matthews read the response of his letters to the Salliers. They gave him their archives of letters between his own late wife and the nuns. There he read the history of the convent and its relationship to the Sallier family, and also letters in which his wife's frustration with himself was evident.

I had letters from Catherine, from Emily Stuart, and from Lady Wells. The latter had discovered that there were many in the American Episcopal Church who were becoming interested in Russian Orthodoxy in San Francisco and New York. She also informed me that my own father, who had always been zealous for the Methodist cause, had discovered the correspondence between the Methodist founder John Wesley and an Eastern bishop. This bishop had counseled Wesley that the proper way to protest the abuses of Rome was not to organize a new Protestant church, but rather to join the ancient Orthodox Church where he could find spiritual fathers who could show him the truth of the Christian life. My own father was outraged to learn these things – and to learn that Wesley had preferred his own advice to that bishop's!

When we were done reading, Grossetete entertained us by describing the confusion in the Masonic Hall after our departure from it. "I don't know what they are going to do, but we can expect to be confronted by the Masons again," he said. "They want this treasure too badly to let it slip from their grasp, especially at the moment they expect it to be found."

"What do they think it is?" I said.

"You know what they think," said Grossetete. "Some really do believe the Masonic legends. Most think it is something of inestimable value. Every man has something different in his imagination, I would guess."

"And how," I said, "do they expect it will be found?"

"You will follow the clues you have been given, and find it," he laughed. "Do you doubt your abilities? No one else does!"

216

"My own abilities have accomplished nothing in this search so far," I said. "I have done nothing but follow the lead of others. Do you really think I have any idea where on these grounds to look?"

"James, there's nothing to fret about," said Grossetete. "Ananias himself could show you where to locate it. He assured me, however, that you would find it long before it is safe for him to return."

"And how can he know that?"

"I didn't question him about it. It was he who hired me to defend you."

"Let me ask you something," said Mr. Matthews to Grossetete. "Did you ever have any doubt as to the outcome of the trial?"

"Never," said Grossetete. "I had all the facts that no one else had."

"Did you know, then," said Mr. Matthews, "that James did not realize he had been appointed Grand Master?"

Grossetete laughed heartily. "He told you that, did he? James Thompson, you schemer..." He saw my face and abruptly fell silent. "By the holy... but I suppose it is no longer right for me to swear, but did you really not know? How could you not have known?"

I shrugged. "That's what everybody assumed, I suppose. Fisher was too weak to tell me anything. I always wore it when I thought I might get in trouble with the Masons. I knew instinctively they would respect the token that the Grand Master gave me on his death-bed, but it never crossed my mind..."

Grossetete whistled. "The way you handled yourself, no one could have known it! So when you said, at the conclusion of the trial, that you had long contemplated renouncing your title..."

"Ten minutes was long enough," I said, "for me to hold that office."

I'm afraid that our laughter may have awakened some of the patients. There was a knock on the wall, and we made an effort to quiet ourselves.

Gerald had been laughing louder than any, and so uncontrollably that he was almost sobbing. "You sure had me fooled," he said.

"That's for certain!" said William. "The Grand Master! It's too legendary for real life."

"No, not that," said Gerald. "I knew it all along. What I mean is, it never occurred to me that you didn't know it."

"What!" I shouted. William put his hand on my arm and frowned, so I continued in an imperative whisper: "You knew? How could that be? You knew, and I didn't?"

"Lady Wells and Ananias both warned me about it before we began," he said.

"You mean to tell me," William interrupted, "that during this entire journey you were aware of being in the presence of the Grand Master of the Masonic Order in America, and you continued to act normal?"

"I don't know anything about acting," said Gerald. "And as far as I am able to understand that high office, it never surprised me that James would be the one to fill it."

"I can't remember that you ever spoke with sarcasm," I said.

"That's because I never did," he replied.

"Then how can you say such a thing?" I wondered. "If anybody knows the depth of my faults, you do."

"I won't deny that," he said. "They have always bothered me, too, seeing as I can your abilities for excellence."

"That is as it should now be for all of us," Prien interrupted, grinning, "having just come out of them waters of purifyin'!"

"Nothing else really matters," William agreed.

"Not even what the Masons might still be planning to do to us," said Grossetete.

"As long as we stay here, I really do think we will be safe," said Mr. Matthews.

"What, then," said William, "are we staying here forever?"

"That might be all right with me now," said Prien.

ଔ

It seemed that way to me, too, as we were led back into the chapel for the night hours of prayer. Here we were in an enclosed paradise beyond the world, in the powerful embrace of its Creator. The moon rose outside the window, whispered past her trees and emerged in the full beauty of a sky filled with her light, while one divine chant merged into another. The sense of well-being, like nothing I had experienced ever in my life, completely overwhelmed me. This, after months of hard travel, a cold night in jail and the anxiety and catharsis of the trial... and I was sound asleep in a corner of the chapel.

ଔ

In the magical beauty of moonlight, the glowing oaks of the convent grounds stood silent with their maturing secrets. Their groves held arches of shadow away from the lawns that were bathed in the brilliance of the Louisiana harvest moon. It was toward one of these shadows that she led me.

How many weeks, how many years had it been since I had seen her face? The love it inspired had only grown deeper, far too deep to see; but now that I saw her eyes, her soft eyebrows and illumined cheeks, the perfect curve of her lips and mouth, I immediately understood what had kept me going in the long journey to find her.

"I always understood that you would come for me," she said as though reading my thoughts.

Underneath the oaks was a marble shrine and fountain. That altar was in shadow, and its writing was in shadow, but the fountain next to it leapt into the moonlight and threw droplets like quiet falling stars in every direction. I understood that she wanted to tell me something in the shadows near that shrine. Her eyes on me, she moved toward it, nodding.

Flowers, out of season, hung in the moonlight. Brilliant constellations covered the heavens like thick clusters of moonlit white wisteria.

A gate led into the shadows of the grove. Above it was a sign, in Greek and Latin: The Rose Garden .

"See?" she said. "I have found what you were looking for: the enclosed courtyard of the ancient wisdom, where Solomon walked with the Queen of Sheba."

As she said this, she walked into the deep and perfect shadows of the grove. Her face, form, and hair were as they were when she was young, when I first began to love her. I followed her toward the shrine, approaching nearer to the hidden Christ than even the

218

rose-encumbered cross of the secret Brotherhood, the Christ I had never known; and it seemed natural to be led by a woman who had been allowed into this garden and who knew these things. She stepped again into the moonlight, smiled and reached out for me. As my hand touched and enclosed hers, a tremendous power of love moved out of the stars and through my heart and arms, and the trees shook in a gentle breeze as I advanced to embrace her. The shadows of the oaks were moved, and the writing on the marble shrine was illumined out of the trembling veils of moonlight:

GERONDISA
DIONYSIA
Kyrie eleison

Only her wrinkled face was visible now, wrapped in the black monastic habit. The graceful posture gone from her stooped body, she frowned at me; but her eyes held more clustered light than had all the stars been gathered into one constellation.

She said some things that I was not able to comprehend. "Dig here," she commanded finally, "if you want to know my embrace!"

"Here," I sobbed, "how can I? This is your grave!"

She was nowhere to be seen. What I saw, though, were the Roman numerals Lafitte had carved into the six oaks around me, glowing in the moonlight. And in the tree over her grave, the tree carved with the numerals "VI", concealed in thick, intertwining vines of wisteria that had been growing for decades, I saw the frayed remnants of the hanged-man's noose where Father Honoratus had died, burning with an illumination different from that of the moon's.

෧෧෧෧෧෧

My first thoughts, as I stirred in the corner of the dark and empty chapel, were those of the deepest grief. I was still overcome with feeling, having just reached to embrace her. My heart was sick at her sudden vanishing.

"Denise!" I whispered. The echo of my own whisper answered throughout the chapel. "Where am I going, and why? I have no desire, and I don't want any. I want an empty road, with no destination. I can't face any struggle, other than the nameless one in my own heart."

As I gave voice to these words, I remembered that they were the same I had spoken on the road to California, when I first left Natchez twenty years ago.

Now, as I slowly became aware of where I was in the empty chapel, I added a few more: "Wipe out the calendar, cancel the year, and leave me alone!"

But the power of my despair was failing me. The memory of recent months and days was flooding back into my awakening consciousness, and Denise was inaudibly answering.

ෆ

"Prien! Get up!" I shook him again. The old man was snoring far too deeply and regularly for a mere sound and movement to rouse him. I turned his cot over.

"What's got into you now?" he coughed and sat up on the floor. "It's not even sunrise! Oh, you got a good night's sleep in the chapel, I guess, but me, I stayed awake for the vigil."

"Prien! Where is the gardener's shack? No, come on, you know where it is, you used to help with grounds-keeping. I need a shovel! No, right now! I've got to get started before the nuns wake up."

"Fine," said Prien. "I'll help when I wake up."

"I know where the casket is buried!" I said.

That was enough to wake him.

The skies were beginning to turn toward the light, and already the chapel was filled with the tiny fires of candles and oil lamps. Its windows celebrated with lively glimmerings, as though within them were all the brightest stars that gather in the fresh wind over the east, like singing virgins lighting their lamps from the fire of the sun as their bridegroom approaches. That same breeze came down on our heads, fresh and pure as we stood over Denise's grave with shovels; but it crawled into our skins like the touch of approaching winter.

"You're not serious now," said Prien. "You're asking me to help you dig up my spir'tual mother?"

"I don't care what you do," I said as my shovel took its first bite of earth.

"They'll be done with mornin' hours," said Prien, "by the time you get down through one foot of this here clay."

"Then you can sit on that tombstone over there," I suggested, "and think of what you will say to them when they come out. That should keep you occupied." My shovel, sinking its tooth deeper than the first bite, ripped up the sod with desire. "Engage them in conversation while I get down five feet more. I don't care what you say, as long as you keep them away until I'm done. Tell them graveyard jokes if you want to."

"Good idea," said Prien, "while you're tossin' up the bones of their revered abbess!"

William, Gerald and John Matthews came upon our conversation at that point.

"You're digging up my daughter!" shouted Mr. Matthews. "What the hell, have you lost your mind?"

"There's the riddle, old man," I said to Prien. "What's the answer?"

Mr. Matthews' voice had brought one of the nuns out the church. She immediately screamed, covered her face and ran back into the chapel. This brought an outpouring of black robes through those doors, but they kept their distance as though from a man possessed. Many were crying, some of them uncontrollably, begging me to stop. I, however, had measured the strength of that hard clay and mastered it. By the power of my burning will I overturned it, piling it around me as I sank.

Claudette tiptoed up to me and knelt down. "James, what are you doing?" she said gently.

I leaned on my shovel and took a breath before answering. "Denise appeared to me in my dream and told me to dig here," I said.

She shook her head. "Dreams and nocturnal fantasies," she said, "can be deceptive. Don't be angry with me for saying so, but I'm telling you what they have taught me. Did she perhaps say anything more to you?"

Her words in the dream came back to me. Things that had been incomprehensible were suddenly understood. "She said this: 'To enter my embrace, you must be dead to the world. I forgave you long ago. Do not concern yourself for my life of mourning. It was blessed to be so. This is not to ease your conscience. On the contrary, let it fill your whole soul with weeping. This is a gift from God that human nature cannot understand.'"

"Ah!" She leapt up turning and ran to the abbess with this information. The abbess nodded serenely, and as Claudette spread the report to the nuns they became calm. Slowly, they inched closer; but as my shovel crunched against the corner of her coffin they jumped back.

"Here's the answer to your joke now," said Prien, careful to say it to me in English: "This here's Louisiana. You don't got to go six feet down, unless you're a-looking to dig a well. Them caskets they are right under the surface o' that there clay."

The nuns watched, amazed as I carefully dug away from Denise's casket, watering its earth with my tears, and kept digging down underneath it. The ground collapsed from around the end of her coffin into my tunnel, revealing it to be a vault of flawless marble. The cross, which was attached to its lid and came up through the surface of the ground, where Dionysia's name had been carved, was of one piece of stone with the rest.

Prien leapt to the edge of my crater. "That there's the vault!" He shouted. "That there's the one I buried with Lafitte now!" He turned to the aged abbess. "The Elder's chest it was inside that now!"

"It was empty when we placed our mother Abbess within it," the old nun replied.

"Then what happened to Father Honoratus now?" said Prien. "I reckon no one uncovered it since that there time we buried it right here!"

"This vault was sitting here, opened and empty, when we were given the land," said the abbess to him. "The lid was there, the vault was here. Dionysia instructed us, before she died, that we must bury her in it at this spot."

"Is that so now?" he said. "Well now. It must ha' been when Lafitte showed that there chest to Ananias, when that there other fella who came down from Natchez. Where's that chest that was in it now?"

I had not stopped digging during this conversation, because I knew the answer. My mind was illumined by thoughts as they spoke. There was a light and warmth in my legs, back, and arms as I dug. The clay became wet and sticky with moisture, and the labor of scraping and moving it brought perspiration streaming out of my limbs, but it could have been sand against the increase in my determination. My muscles moved with a power beyond myself, and it seemed to me that the smell of clay released the fragrance of an exotic garden. I didn't see that the nuns had gathered almost to my elbows until I heard them commenting in French and Greek upon the fragrance that they, too, were noticing, comparing it to different aromatics of incense.

Suddenly the fragrance was overpowering, filling my mind entirely with light and guiding my shovel. I scraped against the second casket underneath the first as gently as though I swept sand away with an archaeologist's brush, revealing the Greek lettering embossed on a metal rim. The old abbess gasped, and several of the nuns began to weep with joy.

ଔ

"Great job!" It was a man's voice, startling everyone as all turned to stare beyond the fence.

It was the younger Donaldson brother who had spoken, since the older still had his jaw tied to his face with a napkin. The Natchez sheriff stood with them. All three had their guns pointed at me.

"Keep digging," said Donaldson.

"I don't know," I said. "It's kind of hard to work with a gun at your head."

"You'll have to get used to it," was the answer.

"Well, I don't know," I said, dropping the shovel and taking a step up out of the pit. "Maybe you want to finish the job."

"I don't think so. Grave-digging is a bit beneath my dignity. But you're doing fine at it."

"Shoot me," I said. "Then you dig. That's easy. What are you waiting for? Pull the trigger! All your miserable life you've waited for this advantage over me. I know you're not afraid of me now. What, then? Are you afraid of the shovel? Or what it might find?"

The shadows of emotion that crossed his face while I spoke showed me that I was right. "You can live to see what the treasure is, or not," he said. "There's your choice."

"Either way," I said, "is just fine. Last night I was baptized here. Today I have found what I was looking for. I'm ready to die, right in this trench."

Grossetete stepped out from the trees. "You're not in a position of much advantage in that," he said to me. "They've got the Masons locked up in the hall. As soon as we see what Lafitte buried for us here, there will likely be a regrettable and accidental fire in the Masonic Hall, in which all will lose their lives, including you, I'm afraid."

"You led them here?" I said to Grossetete.

"That's the kind of man I am," he said, grinning. "I always play for the winner."

"You," said the Natchez sheriff to Grossetete, "go over there with them."

"Now, wait..." Grossetete began.

"You snake, I don't know if you're with us or not," said the sheriff. "You led us here because we put a gun to your temple, too. Maybe I'll just blow your head off right now."

John Matthews took a step toward them. "I told you, it was not Sir Martin of Sicily and the New Orleans Masons who hired Grossetete, even if that's what they thought. I was the one who hired him, to throw the others off the track, so that we could have the treasure for ourselves. All this we discussed. You have no reason to distrust me."

"So what are you telling me, then?" laughed Donaldson. "Are you saying Grossetete gets a cut?"

"That's the deal," said John Matthews. "The cards have been played, and it's time to see what hand fate has dealt. You keep the gold, the jewels, any artifact of monetary value. Papers, documents, instructions, blueprints – anything of strictly intellectual or spiritual value, Grossetete and I decide what becomes of that. Lafitte's journal and the records of the trial are ours as well."

"We knew when we started this scheme," sneered Donaldson, "that the Masonic organization was dead. I can't see what you want with that stuff. I was thinking maybe we could start the fatal fire with your papers."

"Your understanding was never part of the deal," said John Matthews. "I was the one who kept you informed of the progress of our discoveries. I was the one who showed you the interpretation of the map; I told you James would be digging in this grove today, right here."

"It seems to me," said Donaldson, "that we are the ones with the guns. I don't really see why we have to abide by your agreements."

"Am I standing in your daughter's grave and hearing you say these things?" I said to Mr. Matthews.

"I'm sorry, James," he said. "I know this isn't what you expected from me."

"How could you know where I would be digging?"

"I looked at that map again last night," he said. "Most of it I had figured out a month ago, while you were still trying to make sense of it. There is a hidden diagram there, just as you suspected.

"In the black-ink section,' he said, "using the twenty-two treasure sites as a guide, one can find an inverted Kabalistic Tree of Life. In blue, with an axis along the river, one could superimpose a three-armed Byzantine cross, like those reported to have been on the chest that was brought from Jerusalem. There, you see such a cross right there on the chest itself. Gold shows the outline of a wide triangle across the two figures, just touching the top of each. From the center of the triangle to the center of each cross shows another invisible triangle. The two triangles float on the map in such a manner that, if one were the foreshortened shadow of the other, one could find a point of focus – right here on the convent grounds. And this is confirmed by the other information we have gathered. One simply has to find a grove of six ancient oaks on these grounds, and then find the Roman numerals cut into the trunks. But I see you have already done that."

"I always had my doubts about you; but my worst suspicions never ran this deep!" I said. "I will die free, washed of my worst errors, and they were plenty. But you have denied your own baptism!"

Donaldson laughed: "That's right, Matthews! I can pull this trigger and send you straight to hell. Even in killing you, I won't be in danger of judgment like that!"

"You have to understand," said John Matthews to me, "that this is a treasure like none in the world. Since the first explorers came to the New World, it has not been found. My only purpose, since the time that I became Master of the Natchez Lodge, was to have it brought to my town and have it kept hidden there. I arranged to get it from Lafitte. Even he did not suspect my plans at first. But when he did, then he found a way to get it back from me. I am the only man here who has seen it and knows what it is. I suggest that you live at least long enough to see what it is; and then maybe you will understand why I have acted in this way."

I stared at him long enough to see the tears he was fighting back, and then I looked over at William and Gerald. "Give me a hand with this," I said to them.

They responded immediately, jumping into the pit, clearing the earth from the Jerusalem chest and helping me to pull it onto the surface of the ground. The weird scene of the dialogue that had just taken place could have occurred in another year and place, so far was it to my mind at that moment. Indeed, it seemed that time itself had been ruptured. It was a bright morning, and we were in the presence of sacred things beyond time, unveiling mysteries in the sight of holy men and women. In another century, pirates were digging up treasure with murder on their minds, preparing the death of all witnesses to the crime.

Whatever lock that once secured the chest had long succumbed to rust in the moist clay. I put my hands to the latch.

Chapter Thirty-Two

The latch gave easily to my touch, as I knew it would.

In the myths of El Dorado, in the strange mixtures of Spanish and Indian folklore that I heard in California, there was a box in the altar of the sun temple in which the daylight was kept safely entrusted. Every morning, a priest entered the altar and, while looking away and closing his eyes, opened the lid only a crack to let the morning out. If he looked at the box while opening it, he would die; if he opened it all the way, the world would be consumed.

The light that leaked from the edges of the casket's lid was brighter even than the sun, but it did not blind me. Instead, it inflamed my desire to see more. My hands obeyed with a consent of their own; as they lifted the lid, my hands were immersed in streaming light, and my heart also was lifted in an indescribable manner. When I threw open the lid, though, it might have been then that I did indeed cross beyond the boundary of life and death, because of what I saw there.

The form of a man lay in the light that filled and overflowed from the chest as though its walls were constructed from fire. It was, however, a fire whiter than the sun's, like the fire that perhaps rested on the tabernacle and drove the priests out from its glory. In the middle of that light, a man's face glowed like an ember.

His wrinkled face was one of indescribable beauty. Some of his features I could describe, but they would not tell what was truly revealed in that face. I could say that the forehead had been nobly formed by deep furrows of thought, that the cheeks were great sunken valleys of the wisdom of humility, that the beard was perfect in its whiteness down to the breast. Perhaps I could come closest to its hidden beauty in the eyes that were closed in tremendous peace. Even my dreams of Denise, even the divine visitations experienced in waking and shared by others, had not prepared me for the living presence of a man so sanctified that in death he was clearly not dead. This was what was written in those closed eyelids.

His hands were like white gold, and in them was a scroll. There was also a sheet of parchment placed underneath the cross that lay on his breast.

As my eyes adjusted to the strange glory of that light, I began to see the priceless treasures that had been buried with him.

Crowded all around him in the chest were richly woven folded vestments in gold, green, purple and white. There were also other expensive linens and brocades woven with crosses in silver and gold thread. There were gold jeweled crosses and a large Gospel embossed with silver icons and bound with rubies. There were stacks of wooden icons and silver-cased reliquaries. There were as well gold and brass dishes and implements which must have been of use in the altar – I had never seen anything like them.

The old abbess was kneeling next to me and thrusting her hands into the light, lifting out these objects to kiss them and then replace them in order. Her tears fell abundantly into the chest and joined themselves to that light, and as I turned to look up at her, I saw it exploding in her own face and weaving itself into the frayed threads of her robe.

"This is the fulfillment of his promise to us," she wept. "He assured us that he had brought with him everything necessary to plant the Orthodox Tradition in the New World. He said that if the seed were only planted, it would grow at the proper season."

The other nuns crowded around her, beside themselves with weeping, speaking to the elder as if he were alive and thanking him.

"What, then," came Donaldson's voice from the distance. "Is it really Father Rosencreutz?"

"You lose the bet!" said Grossetete from the trees.

"The vault of the mysteries," said John Matthews, who had slowly and fearfully backed up near the opposite oak by the church door. "Just like the legends."

"That whole story was true?" said the Natchez sheriff.

"He brought the fire of God from Mt. Sinai," chanted the old abbess.

"Everything necessary to plant the Orthodox Tradition in the New World," sang the nuns.

"You could never have dreamed what terrible trouble you were getting yourselves into!" said Grossetete from the trees. "The Knights Templar themselves will mercilessly hunt you down until they see this for themselves!"

"He's right," said Donaldson.

"Of course he's right," snapped the Natchez sheriff. "For this they would ransom their entire fortune!"

"But you see," said Grossetete, slowly advancing toward them from the trees, "this is not Father Rosencreutz. Only those who understand the Orthodox Tradition would understand the value of what you see here."

"Well, then," said Donaldson, turning to point his gun at Grossetete, "I suppose there are things here that would fetch a right fair sum in the markets of Istanbul."

"To hell with that idea!" said the sheriff. "You could offer these things to the Russian Tsar for half of his empire!"

"You are so accustomed to robbing men of their possessions," said John Matthews, slowly walking toward them from the opposite direction. The sheriff turned his gun on him. "But if you think you can rob men of their spiritual traditions," said Mr. Matthews, "you will find that you are wrong."

"He brought the undying prayer from the lips of the apostles," said the old abbess.

"Everything necessary to plant the Orthodox Tradition in the New World," the nuns agreed.

"Where's Prien?" said Donaldson suddenly.

"I'm right behind you," said the old man. I myself had not noticed when he slipped away. The older Donaldson turned his gun on him. "I was ten years with Lafitte," said Prien, slowly walking toward them from the third direction. "There's some things now you don't forget how to do."

"You've only got three guns, but you're surrounded from four directions," said William, standing next to me. "And any one of us is ready to die for what we have found. You won't be taking the casket from this place."

"He brought the sacred silence from the ancient monasteries," whispered the old abbess.

"Everything necessary to plant the Orthodox Tradition in the New World," chanted the nuns.

The sheriff kept his gun on John Matthews. "Just now we struck a deal, and you were on our side," he said to him.

"Maybe we could be a little more generous with your cut," said Donaldson to Grossetete.

"I never did make deals with the devil," said John Matthews. "If I had, I would have been Grand Master. But I renounced the Masonic doctrine before you joined the Natchez Lodge, and have had nothing to do with it since."

"We had to have a plan ready for your arrival here today," Grossetete said. "We knew you were coming. You have always been an awfully predictable bunch."

"You've spun some clever lies for us," Donaldson growled.

"You would have gunned me down in the streets of Natchez had I not," said John Matthews. "Even now, you can't see the truth. You can't even see the same thing that we see in this chest. You don't see that radiance, do you? If you did, you would be blinded by it!"

"He brought the light of the Transfiguration from Mt. Tabor," sang the abbess.

"Everything necessary to plant the Orthodox Tradition in the New World," chanted the nuns.

"I have a theory of my own," said the sheriff. "Napoleon's treasure, I think, is what might be still in that marble vault. I think we should have a look."

☙

Up to this point, I had been a silent witness to the strange dialogues that had unfolded around me like a slow operatic ritual. My mind was stunned by the depth of John Matthews' character, who only a moment before had revealed himself as our betrayer, and now, even more incredibly, showed that he had taken that indignant disguise, not just to save us, but to preserve the nuns and their incomparable treasure. I was lost in thought, thinking that there must still have been things that had passed between himself and the aged abbess that only the two of them understood.

Now, however, I found that I had something to say:

"That tomb is not going to be opened, now or ever."

"I also think," said the sheriff, "that if James does not open it right now, he might survive this day, but he will watch his three friends die!"

One of the nuns stepped out toward him.

"This one understands English!" said the sheriff. To her, he said, "You'd better step back."

She continued to walk toward him.

He turned and fired his gun into her breast.

At that, every man jumped from his place, falling upon the Donaldson brothers and the Natchez sheriff from every direction. Before we could get to them, however, all three had turned and emptied their guns into the nun.

It was two on top of every one, pinning them to the ground, but they didn't seem to

227

be paying any attention to us. They were staring at the nun.

"Die, damn you!" screamed Donaldson.

I didn't see her face until just at the moment that she vanished. It was Denise.

They went limp with terror, making it easy to secure them with our leather belts.

William, Gerald and John Matthews agreed to go with Grossetete, to escort them to Sheriff Ryan and the others locked in the hall. I was excused from having to return to that building; and Prien, too, decided to stay with me. As the others were leaving on their errand, I pulled Mr. Matthews aside.

"Did you really see those diagrams on the map?" I demanded.

"Like I told you," he said, "Grossetete and I had to have a plan ready; we knew what the Donaldson brothers would probably do. Don't you think I showed some imagination?"

"Are those hidden diagrams there or not?"

"I highly doubt that!"

I must have been staring at him like an idiot. Who was this complex personality, the father of Denise?

"I really don't think Lafitte was interested in those things anymore," he said. "Are you disappointed?"

ख

At some point during the previous confrontation, the light that had rested on the elder had faded, but the nuns seemed unconcerned. Perhaps they still could see it; for all I knew, the entire universe in their eyes may have been always bathed in that fire!

"That there sheet o' writin' on the elder's breast," said Prien. "I recognize that writin'. It's Lafitte's."

He said the same, I assume, in French to the abbess. She nodded to him.

Prien knelt down to kiss the elder's cross, his hand, and his forehead. Then he tenderly removed the parchment. The nuns crowded around to hear him read it in classical French. Claudette translated into Greek for me:

I have had a vision tonight, and it has brought me some peace.

I have been shown the other who will come looking for this treasure, not knowing what he seeks. My blessed father has consented that he will be found by this one and no one else, for the sake of his repentance; and he shall also know mine.

After I killed the holy man, I repented of all my deeds. Pere Jan heard my confession and instructed me to record my crimes in a journal that would illustrate the progress of my crimes and the manner in which I was painfully freed from them through a ruthless self-examination. This record is meant also as a guide to the one who finds it.

The bitterness of my final days was rewarded by the hope which this vision has brought me. There is indeed great treasure in heaven for those who turn from the desires of the world which so snared me. As small as the amount of the reward that has been measured out for me, a morsel is enough.

Following is the complete list of all the crimes over which I have mourned, as I have submitted it to my blessed father's hand. Jean Lafitte.

"Now, see here," said Prien, holding up the parchment for all to see. "There 'hain't

228

nothing wrote down after this."

"His crimes have been erased by the heavenly Judge," said the abbess, as Claudette translated, "through the prayers of our holy Father Honoratus. No one is to know of this."

Then she pointed to the scroll in the elder's hand, and looked at me.

I knelt, kissing the cross, the hand and the forehead as Prien had done. As I did so, I was aware of the power of Father Honoratus' blessing. Like a new man, I stood and unrolled the scroll.

Chapter Thirty-Three

Ominous signs of a change in the weather, deeper than could be attributed simply to a change in seasons, were displaying themselves in the bird migrations and the clouds, in the sudden blush of the sweet-gum leaves and in the manner in which the pecans disrobed themselves, dropping all their leaves overnight in a chill north breeze. Prien read the same signs in the increased activity of insects and in the thicker winter fur of all woodland creatures, and he advised us against traveling on the Gulf.

"These letters from Natchez demand our immediate return," protested William, having read that the preparations for his wedding to Catherine were now in order. "If we can't go by ship, I'll have to write concerning our delay..."

"There's other ways to travel now," replied Prien as he escorted us into town, "why not take that there stagecoach that'd be carryin' your letter? It's faster than a ship anyway!"

At Jacob Ryan's general store and post office, he managed to secure new coats for us on Lady Wells' credit, since we had not come prepared to stay for the onset of winter. George Ryan was there to send us off with a supply of jokes, to keep us laughing all the way.

With the exception of a winter when I had to climb the Sierra Nevada foothills by horseback from Sonora to Twain Hart, that journey by stage was the most miserable I ever spent. Through mud and driving rain by day and night we sped from post to post. The only time spent by the fire in any inn was for taking quick meals and for changing horses where that was possible. Two horses did not survive that journey. We crossed the Mississippi at Natchez on a wind-tossed ferry, during a solid pelting of sleet.

The Natchez stage post was at Gerald's store. His boy screamed with delight as we came in with a blast of wind. He leaped into his father's arms, who held him only a moment to his drenched and shivering breast before throwing open the iron door on the pot-bellied stove and stoking the coals. We gathered around it like chicks to a nesting mother.

Gerald's son could not wait for stories of our adventures. His father would only open the possibility of narrative before he was peppered with questions. Finally the boy was sent home with news of our arrival.

Within the hour a carriage arrived from the plantation. Catherine burst through the door weeping, and gathered William and myself into one embrace. Though thoroughly winded with excitement, she was not lost for words. Immediately she engaged William in details of the wedding, who, for his part, said little; but his face was beginning to catch fire. Suddenly she stopped, staring from Mr. Matthews to myself.

"Something is the matter," she said fearfully.

I took her hand in mine. "Nothing is wrong, my dear. Nothing at all. There is, however, a great deal to tell you of which we have learned."

She leaned her head on my shoulder as naturally as if she had already learned the news which I was bringing her. But I knew she did not. "And if you want to understand what we have learned," I said to her, "you will have to stop talking for a moment, and listen!"

Laughing, we parted ways with Gerald. William and John Matthews and I, with Catherine and Lady Wells, climbed through a fierce wind into the carriage toward the plantation, in what was to be, for all purposes, the first, though informal, stage of a wedding procession.

છ

After exchanging our clothes for some that were dry, I took Catherine by the hand and led her up the stairs toward the attic library, with William and John Matthews following. Lady Wells had decided that she would not be present for this interview. Catherine ascended the stairs lightly, gazing from myself ahead to William behind, her face glowing with love.

We sat by the fireplace under the rafters of the eave, pulling the upholstered chairs over the thick rugs away from the stacked books and close to the fire, while rain hammered the roof and the freezing wind cried at the corners of the narrow windows.

She sat wordlessly while her soul came to the surface of her eyes, and, mixed with reflected firelight, drank the details of our journey as we took turns to tell them. If she wept at the discovery of Denise's tomb, if she sat in wonder of the wisdom of Prien as he sat in council with the Choktaw elders, if she laughed at our meeting with the lively Claudette and then sat silent on the banks of Bayou Teche, none of these things prepared her for the unveiling of her identity at Bayou des Allemands. She cried in my arms until the furious increase of hard rain all at once fell off, subsiding into uncanny silence, and the world outside the windows went white with snow. It was the sweetest moment of my life.

At some point withdrawing from her father's embrace, she met the eyes of her grandfather and their deeper wisdom, and then she sat by his chair and wept on his knees with his hand on her head. Then she wiped her eyes, replaced herself in her own chair with William's hands in her own, and demanded to hear the rest of the story.

I let her grandfather John Matthews tell the story of the trial in the Masonic Hall in Lake Charles. Her eyes became like sails released before a full wind, wide as the sky, stretched larger than the whole ship, as she stared first at me and then at her grandfather, answering such questions in front of the most important men in the country. And so it was that such a soul was prepared to hear the conclusion of the tale.

Now I stood in front of the fire and, unrolling my own handwritten copy of the scroll that I had taken from the elder's hand, I read:

> *A pearl of great price, so said our Lord Jesus Christ, was found in a field by a merchant, who then went and sold everything he had to buy that field.*
>
> *Our holy fathers interpret the meaning of that parable: the merchant's possessions included the whole world, which he gave away; the field which he purchased is the sacred tradition. The pearl of great price within it is the Resurrected and indwelling God.*
>
> *But how can the merchant understand the value of the treasures of heaven, for the purchase of which he must renounce all the world, if he does not understand the value of those possessions which he must sell?*

231

A man holds his greatest treasure in his own hand, and does not know it. So great is the providence of God, who always gives what we need; so great is the weakness of our understanding, that we never seem to realize this.

Honoratus of Marseilles, archpriest and confessor of the hermits of the Holy Sepulchre, with the blessing of my Lord; and confessed son of France, Jean Lafitte, who gave his treasures to the Convent of the Holy Cross and disappeared from the world, as I had done; to James my brother, named for the very brother of the Lord, I record this prophecy on the night that his mother died, on the eve of the Day of the Holy Spirit, the day following the Feast of Pentecost, when he was yet a young child and all these things are still to come to pass:

"What do you seek so far from home? First you must return and measure the value of your Natchez treasure. Her name is that of the great-martyr Catherine, by whose ring I was presented to the wedding-feast of the Lord.

Then, when you have measured the value of your treasure, I give you the same counsel of the Lord that I have always given: you must give your treasure to the poor in order to receive a hundred-fold.

Therefore, obey my command to you. When the time is right, and she will know when that is, bring your treasure to me. Bring my precious daughter Catherine to me and to my disciple Dionysia."

Epilogue

It was at my own daughter's wedding that I proposed to Emily Stuart. That unique blush, running from the corners of her eyes and spreading in ribbons of fire across her face, was most satisfying to see. She was too surprised to speak, but she did give an unhesitating nod.

Lady Wells' grand plans for an academy were transferred to Holy Cross Convent, where she became the principal donor. William was given the inheritance of some of the Sallier lands on Lake Charles, which he managed while Catherine continued her education as a fellow-scholar to Claudette in the convent. William's apprenticeship in the business of planting was taken seriously, since he was to inherit both the Stuart and the more sizable Wells plantations in Natchez. Meanwhile, I took over the management of his estates along the Mississippi River in name only, since Emily and Lady Wells were both more than sufficient to that task. They left me to my studies in Greek theology, which burned in me with a fire that would not be put out.

All these preparations for a peaceful and brilliant future, like those of so many hundreds of thousands of sons of the hard-working pioneer families, were destroyed to the foundations by the war.

ೞ

The signs of winter that Prien had read in the earth and sky were too ominous to have been brought by weather. Emily worked hard with the tailor until William, Gerald and I, and even John Matthews wore the gray uniform of the South. There was no question of refusing the Confederate draft, when that came. Those detachments assigned to hunt down draft evaders and deserters, the so-called "Homeland Patrol", were at times more vicious than any that saw action on the battle fronts. That was not an issue until much later, when things were going badly. In the beginning, all that mattered was defense of our homelands.

The Natchez regiment was immediately dispatched against the invading wind that blew down from the north. At first, we saw success in counter-invasion under the brilliance of Robert E. Lee. At Gettysburg, we thought the season might be favorable to the southlands. When the winter gale turned against us, though, we survived longer than most. In the worst fighting, we realized the value of what Prien had taught us. William died valiantly at Shiloh, and Gerald starved to death in the siege of Vicksburg; but they died better than others. John Matthews was captured and pardoned by President Lincoln, and by the following week he was wearing a new Confederate officer's uniform and leading a guerilla band fighting from New Orleans south and west through the Louisiana swamps. By then, the cause was desperate, and I, like a thousand others, fled into the forests, surviving like an outlaw Cherokee until the white men killed each other off...

There is no reason, though, to repeat those grim details. Every citizen has studied the chronology of battlefields, and has seen the photographs. Newspaper reporters like carrion bees swarmed over the battlefields, after the living had retreated, astonished by the magnitude of death. Their curtained, zinc-plate cameras were the latest invention, along with steam-powered printing presses that mass-produced the new magazines. What they could not capture with their cameras in the thickly piled, open-eyed corpses, with blood at the corner of the grinning mouths and crows excavating their hearts, was the even more unbelievable manner in which those slaughters were carried out. I will go to my grave in the conviction that the American Civil War was the pinnacle of insanity.

I suppose there is no reason to wonder whether the emancipation of the slaves could in time have taken place without the violence of war. Nevertheless, it is something I have often pondered, since, after the destruction of the plantations and the redistributing of land to the northern carpet-baggers, the one remaining slave shack behind Emily's burned house became our mansion. We have lived a hard life here, scratching a new future out of the soil, but one that I do not regret. I have been able to show her the life I learned from the Cajun farmers. One treasure she was able to keep in her possession through all the destruction: her son William's journal. Without its help, I would never have been able to record so complete a memoir as this.

The nuns took advantage of the disruption of communications brought about by invasion, to slip away from their bishop with their holy Father Honoratus' relics. Following the advice of Lady Wells, they found another spot within the boundaries of America and yet beyond the boundaries of the world, joining themselves to a Russian Orthodox convent in San Francisco. Holy Cross Convent in Lake Charles was subsequently given over to the Sisters Marionites.

Lady Wells, retiring to England after the burning of her incomparable library and the seizing of her lands, was in correspondence with the Russian bishop in America until she died. Catherine writes regularly from San Francisco. She was tonsured a year after William's death, and though she still grieves for him, she has found the nuns' way of life and instruction to her liking.

Dedicatory Notes

The people of Natchez, Mississippi, and of Lake Charles, Louisiana, will not have read far into this story before realizing that I have taken some of the most romantic scenes in the history of the Deep South and made them more romantic. In other words, I have romanticized them beyond the reach of facts. This has been for many years now my approach to historical fiction – to take history by the throat and force it to yield its more hidden secrets.

I do humbly dedicate this story to the heirs of George Fisher, among whom was my own father's step-father. George Fisher's life was so wildly romantic that one could not do much to embellish it more. As far as I know, he was never the Grand Master of the American Masons. The rest of his story as I give it is not too far from the facts.

Though it is surely, as Gerald protested, only the wildest speculation that could place Masonic intrigue behind the American Civil War (although this has become a theme in much popular fiction), their role in the European revolutions and in the founding of America is not a new theory. That the Masons were in the center of controversy, which included anti-Masonic hysteria, in the first half of the nineteenth century is a fact. Masonic doctrine was denounced in many pulpits. Afterwards, they appeared to become little more than gentlemen's clubs until A. E. Waite, W. B. Yeats, Madame Blavatsky and Manly P. Hall began to hint at access to their ancient occult secrets at the turn of the century. I will not deny that I was at one time swept up into the power of their influence.

Here I must also acknowledge my debt to the historical enlightenment found in the life and writings of Father Seraphim Rose, who was converted to the Orthodox Faith under the influence of an exiled Russian saint, Bishop John Maximovitch, in San Francisco in the 1960's. I especially thank the Fr. Seraphim Rose Foundation for allowing me to read his historical lectures on the progress of western philosophy, before their publication. The publication of those valuable texts, I hope, will not be long in coming.

I make no apology for my use of the legend of Jean Lafitte. He made his own legend and disappeared from the world. Until that disappearance, much of what I have given of his life is based on fact. The journal of his last days in St. Louis, which has such a fascinating history of its own and which has now been published in English, if it be accepted as authentic – and I see no compelling reason why it should not – differs radically from the one which I have fabricated. I find it alarming that in his old age Lafitte should have embraced the ideology of Karl Marx to the point of financing him! I should say this, however, to anyone who enjoys a story: in *The Memoirs of Jean Lafitte*, translated by Gene Marshall, will be found scenes of the highest adventure, made all the more exciting by the possibility that these things may actually have been written out of the vivid memory of that man.

To the Sisters Marionites of Holy Cross Convent and the founders of St. Patrick's Hospital, to the descendents of the Sallier, LeBleu, Pujo, Bilbo, and Ryan families, to the Lake Charles American Press historical archives, and to the friends of my youth whose portraits I distorted in the creation of my characters, I beg forgiveness for the facts which I have altered, hoping that they know that my imaginative fiction is merely a tribute to the far more substantial work of having built the town in which I was raised.

Finally, I dedicate this story to my own rich California treasure, my daughter Rachel.

Clifton Edward (Christopher) Lewis